# BEYOND THE VEIL OF STARS

**Other books by Robert Reed**

*The Remarkables*
*Down the Bright Way*
*Black Milk*
*The Hormone Jungle*
*The Leeshore*

# BEYOND THE VEIL OF STARS

ROBERT REED

A TOM DOHERTY ASSOCIATES BOOK
NEW YORK

This is a work of fiction. All the characters and events portrayed in this book are fictitious, and any resemblance to real people or events is purely coincidental.

BEYOND THE VEIL OF STARS



This book is printed on acid-free paper.

A Tor Book
Published by Tom Doherty Associates, Inc.
175 Fifth Avenue
New York, N.Y. 10010



Design by Lynn Newmark

Library of Congress Cataloging-in-Publication Data

Reed, Robert.
Beyond the veil of stars / Robert Reed.
p. cm.
"A Tom Doherty Associates Book."
ISBN 0-312-85730-6
I. Title.
PS3568.E3696B45 1994
813'.54—dc20 94-2352
CIP

Printed in the United States of America

0 9 8 7 6 5 4 3 2

To my brother, Charles Q.

# BEYOND THE VEIL OF STARS

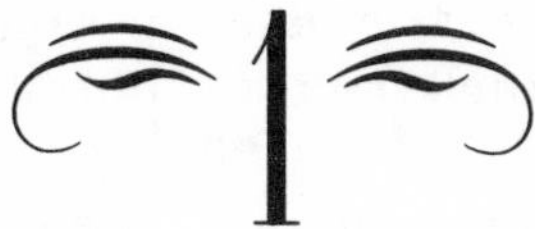

**What Cornell loved best was the driving, that smooth** act of motion, with him looking out through the smudged glass as the countryside flowed around them. They typically traveled on little highways and white graveled roads, past fields and long shelterbelts, muddy ponds and the occasional farmstead—a slumping barn, perhaps, and shiny aluminum silos, garages for giant tractors and someone's house in the middle of it all. Most of the farmhouses were modern, suburban and unimpressive; but the old ones possessed a palpable dignity, tall windows and tall turrets, with vast porches wrapped around their waists. Dad, who believed in ghosts when it suited him, claimed that a lot of the oldest homes were filled with spirits. People had died inside them in olden times. Babies died at birth, and their mothers died bearing them. Machinery and horses had mangled the grown men. Extinct illnesses wiped out entire families. Even a simple scratched finger could become infected, killing an inch at a time. "Someday I'll study ghosts and their hauntings," Dad would claim. "What are they? Residual energies? Intrusions from another dimension? Or authentic souls in their afterlife?" A pause and a little smile, then he added, "Whatever they are, don't they make a lovely mystery?"

And Pete would say, "They're not lovely to me."

Pete was driving, today and always. Dad had troubles behind the wheel, too cautious and perpetually flustered; and that's why he sat in the front passenger seat, a map opened on his lap, his title being Navigator. Yet he had a poor sense of direction, at best. Even simple maps seemed to confuse him. Besides, Pete was a wonderful driver, steady and rock-calm, and he needed nobody's help. He could find any address in any of four or five states, never a wrong move in all these years; and Cornell respected him almost as much as he loved his father.

"Ghosts don't appeal to me," Pete said, as always. A grumpy growl, a little smile of his own. Then he added, "Not in the least little bit."

"But what if they're related to our work?" Dad responded. "What if they're different manifestations of the same grand puzzle?"

"Who cares?" Pete picked up his coffee cup and took a last cold sip, then bit the white foam, nibbling off pieces and spitting them out again. His habit was to gnaw each cup down as far as possible, filling it with itself, then dumping the remains into the little trash sack hung on the dash. "If you're planning to chase spooks," he warned, "you're on your own. I mean it."

"Now, Pete."

"I mean it."

"Well . . ."

This was an ancient conversation, much practiced and done with an emotional flatness. Sometimes it made Cornell angry: why couldn't they use new words, at least? Then other days it was a comfortable collection of familiar sounds, reliable and lightly humorous. Like today, Pete claiming, "The dead can keep their secrets, I think. I think. I think we'll get our answers soon enough, and why rush?"

"You're not curious?" Dad teased.

"No, I'm not."

"Scared then?"

"Damn well terrified." And Pete seemed like a man incapable of fear. He was powerfully built, particularly through the chest and arms, dark whiskers on a square face and dark eyes staring straight ahead. Even the way he held the steering wheel seemed fearless. That's what Cornell was thinking. This was the day of the Change, though he didn't know it; he was sitting in the backseat, feeling happy, watching the cornfields and beanfields and the planted trees between them, everything bending under a hot dry wind. This was flat country for now, a river somewhere on their left and not more than a couple of farmsteads visible at once. They came here last year, Cornell recalled, visiting a different farm and an old woman who'd seen odd lights. Living with the old woman was an ancient, humpbacked creature—her grandmother, Cornell had learned—and she was more than a century old, toothless and almost blind. Yet her memories were intact. With Cornell sitting near her, she spoke at length about being a little girl, even younger than him, and riding in a wagon across the prairie, seeing sunflowers beside the dirt road and the occasional white skull of a buffalo. Cornell had been enormously impressed. They had come here chasing alien spaceships, him and Dad and Pete, but there sat someone from the realm of horses and wagons. That humpbacked woman had lived through an entire century, and that was strange and unsettling, and lovely in its own way. For days and days, afterward, he had thought of little else.

Most of their trips weren't that interesting. Most involved lights in the sky, and the witnesses were ordinary people, and Dad would ask the same old questions, in interviews of only a few minutes. Then the witnesses had their own changeless questions: How did you start doing this work? Have you seen flying saucers yourself? And what do you think *they* are? Dad was patient, answering each question at length, and Cornell always grew bored. Not that he complained, of course. Boredom, he assumed, was part of the job and a consequence of being with adults. Being grown up, he sensed, meant doing the same stuff every day. And besides, there was the remote chance that they might see a spaceship for themselves, or better, that on one of these trips they would make contact with the alien pilots. . . .

Someday, he thought. Maybe so.

The ghost talk was taking its traditional pause. Cornell listened to the dual hums of the engine and the road, knowing what would be said next. He watched the back of Dad's long neck, imagining the smiling and pale thin face; and sure enough, Dad cleared his throat, announcing with a determined voice, "Well, if I hunt ghosts, I guess I'll drive myself."

Pete laughed, sort of. Leaning back in his seat, thick hands high on the steering wheel, he said, "Right. You can't find the Quik Shop four blocks from your house. How are you getting to these spook houses?"

That was Cornell's cue. He leaned between the front seats, saying, "I'll drive you, Dad. Three years, and I get my learner's permit."

More than three, but that wasn't the point. Dad turned and looked at him, smiling with his little mouth and vague bright eyes. "That's what I was hoping to hear, son. Thank you. Thanks."

Cornell settled back into his seat, feeling fine, looking outside and imagining himself driving some toothless, humpbacked version of his father along this road. Cornell was Pete's age, and the landscape was cut into green squares with strange crops growing in perfect rows. It wasn't a car that he was driving, but some kind of floating vehicle. Yet the pavement was the same—straight highways had a kind of noble authority—and they were going somewhere important. It didn't matter exactly where. And riding in the backseat was a third person. Cornell could see her, unchanged by time. And in his daydream she leaned forward, telling him, "You drive beautifully, Corny. Perfectly." Which made him smile, shutting his eyes, wishing hard that it could come true.

They left the highway, then the river bottom. A graveled road lifted into loess bluffs, and Pete slowed and downshifted and took a gentle right turn into a tree-lined lane. Farm dogs waited in ambush. Despite the heat, or maybe because of it, they howled and ran beside the car as it approached the house. They were big dogs led by a grizzled German shepherd, and Cornell didn't want to step outside. Dad was worried, too, sitting taller than before. Motionless. Pete gave both of them a smiling sideways glance. The dogs became quieter, probably anticipating their feast. But Pete didn't hesitate, opening his door and standing, allowing the hot air to blow into the car while dogs danced around him, snapping and yelping.

"GET DOWN!"

The voice was sudden and booming, causing dogs to scatter. Cornell dipped his head, seeing the farmer standing on his front porch. It was an old-style farmhouse, originally painted white and covered with big grimy windows. Weathering gave it character, and weathering did the same for the farmer. He was a beefy man, red from the sun and wind, wearing clean, mostly new jeans and a dark denim workshirt, his seed cap set at an angle, the forehead broad and bright.

The farmer stepped down among his dogs, half-kicking them while asking, "Are you Novak?"

"No. I'm Pete Forrest."

Dad opened his door reluctantly, rose and introduced himself. "I'm Nathan Novak. Glad to meet you."

"Glad you made it," the farmer said, then kicked again.

Dad bent and said, "Come on, son." His face was pale, but he smelled work. Anticipation made him brave.

Cornell imagined how it would feel to be gnawed on. Farm dogs were, he knew, half-wild, untrusting and untrustworthy. Yet once he was out among them, they seemed merely curious, sniffing at his feet and crotch, then wagging their tails. Probably to fool him, he thought. They were waiting to get him alone.

"This is my boy. Cornell."

The farmer nodded, his attention divided. "It's out back, not far."

"We've got equipment," Dad began.

"Sure."

"We'll be a minute."

Pete opened the back end of the station wagon. Every dog had to sniff at the various boxes and whatnot. There were cameras, still and video, and electronic devices with dials and shiny sensors that came from mail-order houses and garage sales and the dumpsters behind the local computer plant. What hadn't come finished, Dad finished himself. He built each machine along lines known only to himself. If he actually understood them, that is. Sometimes Cornell had to wonder.

The toolbox was Cornell's responsibility. It was heavy and loud, cool at first touch and then fiercely hot once in the sunshine.

The ritual was for Dad to lead, then tire and drop behind Pete before they reached the site. The farmer carried nothing, acting patient but in a put-out fashion. He'd called Dad, probably having seen him on the news. It was his idea to invite an expert, but he'd done it a couple of days ago. A person's interests had ways of fading. Events receded into memory, losing their shock and intrigue. Yet the farmer had invited Dad, and he would take them to the place. He had better things to do, said his face, but maybe these strangers would hurry.

Thinking of ghosts, Cornell avoided looking at the house. Past it and a deep backyard was the cornfield. The corn wasn't tall or green like the stuff in the river bottom. The four of them walked between rows with the dogs sniffing at their heels. Cornell spotted the clearing as Dad reached it—Dad was behind Pete now—and he felt excitement, sudden and fun, his stomach moving and his heart quickening.

"Beautiful," said Dad, his voice soft and respectful.

A circle of corn was dead, and the black earth beneath it had been transformed into a smooth blackish glass, thick and almost slick. It was the same as all the other circles they had visited this year. They weren't to be confused with English crop circles, what with the glassy ground and the way they could appear anywhere. In corn, or in forests. Or on people's front yards, for instance.

This place had an eeriness, a wrongness. Cornell stepped out on the glass. The heat had dried the dead stalks and wind had pushed them to the north edge. Corn leaves brushed together with a living sound, and the motions of the living corn made the glass circle seem all the more inanimate. Yet the dogs, supposedly sensitive to things odd, acted indifferent, chasing each other now, running in and out of cover.

Cornell set the toolbox near the center, then opened the warming lid and removed a long metal tape measure.

Pete met him, taking the tape's dispenser and walking to the circle's edge as Cornell did the same. They measured its diameter several times, always reading 33 feet, one-half inch, and Pete recorded the data in a small battered notebook.

Dad spoke with the farmer while he assembled their electromagnetic sensor. Dad was a tall man, but slight, with a handsome smooth face and silver hair and those bright odd eyes. He had a way of smiling whenever he listened to a witness, relishing the experience. Delicate long hands fiddled with a connection, and he asked about the dogs. "Did they make a fuss that night?"

"After midnight sometime," the farmer replied.

"You heard them?"

"I was sleeping. No, my wife did."

Dad liked to tell Cornell that he was an impartial investigator, even though he wasn't. He did nothing overt, but there were times when he could lead the witnesses. Like now. "Did your wife see anything unusual? Lights on the ground? In the sky, maybe?"

"We get planes, sometimes."

"Did she see a plane?"

The farmer moved as if uncomfortable, arms crossing on his chest and the hands slipping into wet armpits.

"What kind of plane?"

"I didn't say she saw one."

"Was it over this spot?"

Uncrossing his arms, the farmer shook his hands dry.

"And your dogs were howling," Dad persisted. "Right?"

"Which isn't exactly strange. I mean, something's usually pissing them off."

As if to prove its bad humor, the German shepherd began to snarl at the healthy corn, the hair lifting off its neck. There was a long moment when nobody moved, some little part of everyone wondering if the circle's makers had returned. Then the bristly tail was wagging, brushing against Cornell's leg, and a wire-thin boy stepped into view. He was the same age as Cornell. Judging by his complexion and plain face, he was the farmer's son.

"Everything okay?" asked the farmer.

"Yes, sir."

"Need work? Because I can give you some."

"Can I watch? For a minute?" The boy stuck his tongue out one side of his mouth, eyes alert and excited. "Can I watch them?"

"Keep out of their way, or else."

"Yes, sir."

"Unless you'd rather be alone," the farmer told Dad. "I've got my work to do now."

"No, the boy's welcome." Dad loved audiences, believing that much of his work was to educate an ignorant public. "He can help, if he wants."

The farmer didn't respond, thinking hard about something. Then he said, "Listen. Mostly I called you because I want to know this thing is safe. These tests you're doing—"

"We check for radiation, and I'll run a chemical analysis, too."

"That stuff, yeah." He nodded. "And on the phone . . . you said you'd keep this place secret, right . . . ?"

Witnesses who wanted to remain anonymous were sincere, Dad claimed. The liars were the ones who wanted their faces on the news. Dad hated almost nothing, but liars were an exception. He had nothing but scorn for someone who would twist the truth for his own gain. Nothing in the universe was so evil as the man who debased what was real.

Dad told the farmer that yes, this place and his name would be kept secret.

"Good enough," said the farmer, satisfied enough to leave.

Then came a sound—a tiny buzz in the hot blue sky—and everyone glanced at the plane, thinking the same thing. What could be more obvious than a black circle set in the middle of a big green field?

"If it's any consolation," Dad offered, "there are lots of these structures about. All around the world, and more every night."

The farmer blinked and gave the glass a little kick.

"I wish I could tell you why," said Dad. "Maybe someday soon."

Another kick, harder this time. Then the ruddy face was saying, "I don't care who or why, just so long as they leave me alone."

The boy was the friendliest part of the farm. He sat with his legs crossed, right on the warm glass, eyes huge and unblinking, watching Cornell take a hammer and chisel to it. They needed samples from the edges and the center. Every sharp piece went into its own Ziploc bag; every bag was numbered and dated, then put away for later analysis. The boy was enormously impressed that Cornell was helping. He asked if the three of them went out on a lot of calls.

"A bunch," said Cornell.

"Particularly now," Pete added.

What did they know about the circles? The boy had seen them on the news, sometimes every night.

"They're a puzzle," was Dad's nonanswer. "So far, that's all they are. One lovely puzzle."

Did saucers make them? The boy had seen shows about saucers and the circles. A lot of saucers were being seen, although maybe more people were watching the sky. Like him, he confessed. He'd stayed up late some nights, trying to see anything odd.

"That's a good fellow," said Dad. "Glad to hear it."

This year had been busy, Cornell thought. Pete was using his summer break to drive Dad to and from. To and from. It was a good thing he was a teacher and had this free time. Of course he believed in aliens, and of course Dad paid him for his troubles. Cornell didn't know how much money, but it was enough that Pete would say, "This is too much," when he was paid.

Dad was looking at the boy, eyes smiling. And when their eyes met, he asked, "Did you see anything that night, son?"

"No." The boy squirmed and put on a sour face. "I fell asleep early and heard nothing."

"Too bad," Cornell offered.

Then the boy looked at him. "You ever see an alien ship?"

Cornell was able to say, "Yes," with a quiet, unprideful voice.

"How many times?"

"Three."

It was fun, this taste of celebrity.

"Did you see the aliens? How'd they look?"

No, no aliens. He wished he could have, sure—how many had been in his dreams?—but their ships were the best he could claim. Once it was a golden light in the distance, swift and eerily silent. Another time was just last year, a house-sized something crossing the highway ahead of them. Pete had stopped and shaken Dad awake, and the three of them had watched it slide away at treetop level, vanishing behind some hill. The whole sighting took maybe thirty seconds, and it had been infuriating because it was so real and quick and matter-of-fact, nothing particularly mysterious and not one useful photograph of the thing.

The boy nodded soberly, understanding unfairness. He hadn't even heard the dogs barking the other night, and it was his father who'd found the circle. He'd come in before breakfast, scared enough to shake. Never before had he seen his old man acting scared, and he sounded pleased to admit it now.

Cornell looked at the glass circle, black and shiny, and at his own father. Dad was taking photographs while Pete worked the videocamera, panning back and forth.

"What about the third time?"

Cornell wasn't listening.

"You said three times. What's the third?"

The men paused. Or they didn't pause, but merely slowed for a moment. Sound had a way of traveling on these circles, reflecting off the glass and always feeling close. Dad gave Cornell a glance, more curious than concerned. "I saw one up close," Cornell allowed, "but that was long ago. I was little—"

"How close?"

"Twenty feet, maybe."

"Goddamn." The boy shivered and grinned to himself.

The men set their cameras down and began working with sensors, writing numbers into the notebooks.

"So," said the boy, "do you always help?"

"If I'm not in school." Cornell put another glass shard into a Ziploc, then asked, "Do you help your dad?"

"Walking the beans. Crap like that, sure."

He couldn't imagine living on a farm. It could sound fun, except most farmers seemed to be in bad moods. There wasn't enough rain, and they were in debt. They'd tell strangers about equipment troubles and weed troubles and generally make it seem like a stupid way to live.

"So what do the aliens want?" asked the boy. "To study us?"

"They've got to be," Cornell replied.

"I'd like to meet them. You know?"

What remained to be done? Nothing, except to hunt for anything odd about this circle. Cornell started walking, his head down, feet sliding across the glass. He could see himself in it, his image too tall and the sky beyond colored a brilliant gray.

"So what's your mom think about this stuff?"

An invisible hand closed on his chest, then his throat.

"Does she help, too?" The boy asked his questions, then sensed something was wrong. He glanced at the men—Dad over the Geiger counter and Pete placing a sensor at the circle's center—and then curiosity made him ask, "Where's your mom? Back home?"

Cornell said, "No," with care.

The boy blinked and asked, "Where then?"

"She's dead."

That shut him up, his mouth down to a dot.

"She died long ago," Cornell lied; he was thinking how Dad said lies were permissible when they protected someone. "In an accident, long ago. In a car crash." He was talking faster, unable to stop himself. "It's just me and Dad now. Which is fine. We do okay by ourselves."

A brief pause, then he added:

"She's in a better place."

He spoke loudly, for emphasis, and the words echoed off the glassy ground, rising into the sky.

**There was guilt, reliable and deep, whenever Cornell** thought of his mother. She wasn't a vivid part of his life, and he felt it was his fault that he didn't think of her often enough or with suitable intensity. He was some color of traitor, selfish and shallow. Some nights he cried about it in secret. Sometimes he feared Dad would see inside his head, identifying his considerable failures. Guilt, then shame. That was the normal course. And from there he'd drift into practiced memories of Mom. His apology to her was to make her live in his mind, and years of practice served to make Pamela Novak feel genuine, if only now and again. If only for as long as he concentrated with all of his ability.

She had been pretty, and probably still was. Cornell could recall bits and pieces of her by himself. She was in their little kitchen, in the master bedroom, or watching TV with a little pillow pulled to her chest. Once—he couldn't recall the circumstance—Dad was driving them somewhere, unlikely as that seemed; and Mom turned and looked into the back, asking, "What are you doing, Corny?" Corny. Only she called him that. "What trouble is finding you, Corny?"

In memory she had a sly knowing smile, cutting through a four-year-old's tiny capacity to mislead.

"Put it down," she had warned him. "Don't play with that."

She seemed perpetually tired in his memories, particularly in the eyes. A small woman, nonetheless he remembered her as being gigantic. Her voice was strong and certain; light brown hair was kept long; and her skin was tanned, even in winter.

"That's your mother," Dad would laugh. "Tanning beds and the creams, even when I lectured her about the effects of ultraviolet. But you know your mom. She'd act as if biology didn't apply to her."

Except he didn't know Mom. Not in any substantial way. There were photographs in several half-filled albums, plus some holiday videos. There had been more videos, but Dad had wiped them clean by accident. "Besides," he would add, "she avoided cameras. Not that she was shy, of course. I think she was vain, and she hated every picture of herself."

Vain. Only recently had Cornell understood that comment. In the photographs she stood with hands on hips, the face daring the lens to focus on her. Vanity? Pretty women can be critical self-judges, he was learning; but once trapped, Mom had done her best to shine. Indeed, she dominated every shot, even if she was on the periphery. Even Pete, stocky and strong, looked insubstantial beside Pamela Novak, his hands behind his back and his perpetual four-day beard almost black—Cornell remembered the picture—and she not quite smiling, staring up at Cornell with an amused quality in those tired unshy eyes.

Dad loved her. He said so every day, if only with some distant watery look. He fell in love with her when they met, and Cornell knew the story by heart, perhaps better than he knew much of his own past. It was back in the 1980s, long before circles and the upswing in sightings, and some rancher in the west reported odd lights and a landing site. This was before Pete, and somehow Dad had driven that far on his own, finding the right ranch amid miles of grass. But the rancher proved unreliable, as a witness and as a person. He smelled of bourbon and made obvious lies whenever Dad's attentions wavered. He hadn't just seen the ship. He'd seen the pilots, too. Little men, he said. Dressed in silver, naturally. He and the pilots had waved at one another, like neighbors . . . the rancher showing Dad what he meant, his drunken red face grinning the whole time and the story one big joke, nothing more.

The landing site looked like someone had burned diesel fuel and grass, the ground stinking of fuel. All very sloppy, Dad conceded, and he would have left at once except for the girl. There was a daughter, seventeen and bright and pretty, and she took an interest in the work. She'd read about Dad in the paper, and she won his undying confidence by admitting that her father might be stretching the truth more than a little bit.

Years later, Dad admitted to being shy in the girl's presence, and that left to his own capacities, he would have done nothing. He would have left the ranch and forgotten her. But Pam befriended him, then helped collect samples of the burned grass and the unburned tractor juice. "Some memories don't fade," he liked to say. "Years make them more real, as if they've got threads connected to you, and distance and time just make the threads tighten. You can't stop feeling their tug. Which is how I feel about your mother. I'll be doing something, or nothing, and suddenly I'll see that ranch and your mother, a red bandanna tied around her hair and the black ashes sticking to her hands, to her cheeks, and I can see where she knelt, helping me dig at the burned earth. She calls me *sir,* making me feel old. And she tells me about her father and living here and how when she's done with high school she's going places. 'The ends of the world,' she says. 'No more schools.' She tells me how she doesn't do well with book learning. And I'm thinking: No, but you're smart. Which she is. Some people's brains work so well, son, that you can hear them working. You feel asleep and stupid beside them, and that's how your mother is."

At the end of the day, done with work, Dad prepared to say good-bye. But the rancher, thank God, invented some fresh lies, grinning as he reported, "I've done more than wave at them. You're a good fellow, I can tell you . . . I talked to the little shits. What's the word? Telepathy. Yeah, we telepathied, and I learned plenty. Want to hear?"

Dad stayed for dinner, listening to the impossible stories,

taking indifferent notes and eating most of an entire frozen dinner. Pam had cooked it. "She was never a chef in the making, let me tell you." Laughter, then he turned serious. "Her father fell asleep before eight, just after we met the Venusian princess, and I was embarrassed as well as thankful. It was easy to leave, I thought. I told Pam that I wanted to drive partway home that night. And she looked at me. Staring, you know?" A pause. "Sometimes I'm not very bright. Particularly about everything that's obvious."

Dad had excused himself, using the bathroom before embarking. When he came into the living room he found the rancher sleeping, a blanket thrown over him and the bottle set outside bumping range. He called out, "Thank you," and stepped outside, into the darkness. There wasn't any moon, just country stars glittering overhead, and he nearly kicked Pam, who was sitting on her packed suitcase, waiting at his car. It took him an age to realize what she wanted. And not even Cornell had heard the entire story, Dad alluding to troubles between her and her father. Beatings, and maybe worse things. "Take me to the interstate?" she asked Dad. "I can hitch from there." All she wanted was a ride, he had believed; and for the first twenty miles she kept saying, "I'm taking charge of my life. Now I'm my own person, and I always will be."

Dad fell in love during that ride. In the empty country, nothing around them but darkness and belching steers, he heard something magical in that voice. They were married several weeks later. Her father threatened to have Dad thrown in jail; then, learning that there was money at home, he began asking for loans. The miserable man died a couple years later, just after Cornell was born. The banks took what remained of the ranch. Sometimes when he told the story, Dad would gaze off into the distance, eyes becoming simple and wet. Once, for no clear reason, he told Cornell, "Go anywhere people live, and you see order. Regularity. You see streets and houses and fields, everything laid out just so, and do you know why? It's because everyone owns a special hurt, chaotic at its heart, and that's why we dress up the world like we do. We struggle to make it predictable and sensible. And fair. To diminish the hurt, if only a little bit."

How that fit into the story, Cornell didn't know. They were talking about Mom, not humanity; but maybe he would understand someday, when he was older, having acquired his own special hurt, just as his father promised.

They celebrated Mom's birthdays and the wedding anniversaries, and every holiday dinner included a place set for her. Pete frowned on that business, claiming it went overboard. But to Cornell it seemed natural, even lovely. Who could say when Mom would come home? If it happened to be Christmas Eve, then they'd be ready, their loyalty proven, that scene imagined and reimagined by Cornell for most of his conscious life.

Mom had a house key. At least she'd had it when she was abducted. Recruited. Whatever the term. That's one reason Dad wouldn't think of moving away. Pam needed a landmark, a familiar place that would cushion her homecoming.

"She'll need help," Cornell had heard many times. "Help and a lot of understanding."

Riding home that day, Cornell imagined Christmas Eve, coloring it with a boy's unflinching sentimentality. He and Dad were sitting at the dining room table, the little turkey steaming as they began to cut . . . and suddenly there was a sound at the front door. *Click-click-click.* They raced through the living room, finding Mom pushing her way inside. In the daydream, she smiled weakly, but happily. She said, "Oh, thank God," and then, "Hello, darlings." Excited, but composed, too. "Corny, look at you!" She engulfed him, kissing his head and eyes, then weeping . . . and this despite Dad's assertion that she wasn't a crying sort of person. Yet tears seemed mandatory from everyone. The three of them hugged and wept, then Mom took her place at the table, accepting the cooling turkey and the canned corn, rolls and instant potatoes, eating the indifferent food in fast gulps while telling them again and again how wonderful it felt to be home.

Sometimes Cornell pictured her in the clothes she wore in the old photos, nothing changed. Other times, letting his imagination expand, he saw her wearing odd one-piece jumpsuits made from glossy, otherworldly fabrics, deep pockets crammed full of gifts from around the galaxy. And she looked older, didn't she? Tanned by alien suns, and most definitely wiser.

He saw her sitting in their living room, on the old sofa with the photo of Jupiter above her and a pillow in her lap, and she was telling them what had happened during these last years. Dad liked to warn him that abducted people had few recollections of their adventures, at least outside hypnosis; aliens had skills besides star drives and radar evasion. But in his daydream she had perfect recall. Cornell asked what she saw. And she was grinning, pausing for a moment before beginning her enormous story.

Cornell's mind couldn't produce more than a faltering narrative. Much of his imagery was borrowed from Dad's speculations and from science fiction. Starships streaked across moon-rich skies; humanoids moved in tight, disciplined lines; the sounds of strange music and machinery punctuated an orange-lit landscape. Yet none of it felt real. Even as his imaginary mother spoke at length, describing rivers running upstream or a ringed world with five suns . . . even then it was as if some barrier existed between those places and him. She spoke of miracles, and what could he rightly comprehend? All he knew was that his mother was home, finally and forever; and she'd witnessed things too great for the likes of him. She had walked with gods, very nearly; how could anyone appreciate such wonders?

He couldn't. And maybe he shouldn't. Maybe comprehension would have too great of a cost, requiring him to lose his humanity . . . yet Mom hadn't lost hers, in his daydream, home again and crying again, mopping her big eyes with the frilly edges of the old pillow.

Pete and his wife—Cornell called her Mrs. Pete—moved in next door not long after Mom arrived. They were in most of the family pictures, Mom pregnant and then Cornell as a baby, then as a toddler. Pete was thin back then, at least through the waist. And Mrs. Pete, as if following some cosmic sense of balance, had been chubby twelve years ago, losing weight as her husband gained. They lived in a chubby four-bedroom house. They'd planned to have children, except later they learned that children were impossible. "It's not Elaine's fault, or anyone's," Pete had told Dad. "You can't blame anyone." Which made Cornell think it was Mrs. Pete's fault. Pete would take the blame if it was his.

Pete had known Mom pretty well, and he spoke of her if Cornell asked, though he wasn't as willing as Dad. And no, he wasn't present when she vanished. When she was abducted. Pete didn't help with the work until afterward. But sure, he remembered Pam. A lovely young lady, obviously intelligent. Anyone who met her knew she was the smarter Novak; and Dad always took that barb well, shrugging and admitting, "She was, she is," or sometimes, "They knew quality, didn't they?"

*They*. Whoever *they* were, thought Cornell. Dad spoke of the aliens in concrete terms, making assumptions and reasoning from those starting points. It was his basic assumption that *they* were compassionate and wise; lifeforms, he argued, had to evolve just as an individual life evolves. Humans were children, incapable of making complex decisions for themselves. So why hadn't we destroyed our world? Because the aliens had protected us from ourselves in subtle ways. The aliens, he maintained, were free of disease and age and every color of misery. Hundreds and thousands of species were scattered through the galaxy, members of a great fraternity of civilized states; they were watching us, studying our lives, busily making ready for the day of First Contact.

"It'll happen in your lifetime." Dad spoke with ominous certainty. "Why do you think the world is at peace now? Not everywhere, but mostly. Because we're maturing, Cornell. More and more democratic states in the U.N. And why? Because democracy is the highest political state. And soon the galactic community will make an overture, initiating its first careful contacts, and you'll witness it. I'm absolutely convinced."

Yet part of Cornell couldn't believe in the nourishing aliens. He had no mother because aliens had taken her. If terrorists had kidnapped her, wouldn't anger be reasonable? There was a gaping, unfair void in his life. It wasn't right that he had to wait for someone who might never return. Abductions weren't suppose to last more than a day or two; Dad's own books claimed as much. Why would compassionate entities steal someone for years? But Dad seemed to anticipate these doubts, telling him, "She's being trained. Probably for some great purpose, I should think. Or maybe they've got her in suspended animation, not stealing a minute of her life."

But he wasn't thinking of Mom's life. Cornell was concerned for himself. Riding home from the farm, watching the smooth motion of the countryside, he felt pleasantly selfish. He had lied to that boy, telling him that his mother was dead. And he was tired of lying. What if he went to the president, telling the truth until she took an interest. She could call important subordinates on her cherry-colored phone. Appeals could be broadcast to the stars. Or maybe the Air Force could give back the dead aliens they were storing in New Mexico. Whatever it took to retrieve Pamela Novak, that was his feeling.

Cornell shut his eyes and thought of the farm boy. "I saw a bright ship," he should have said, "and it took her away. She was there, then she wasn't."

There, then gone.

He was four years old, and the three of them had gone into the country to watch the sky. It was unusual, Mom going with them. But there they were, near a little town where odd lights had been seen all summer, and Mom had packed food and drinks, bug-spray and blankets. Dad had his long white telescope set on its tripod. Cornell remembered seeing Jupiter in the tiny eyepiece, bright and silvery. He could remember the softness of a blanket and the biting insects. A shooting star had streaked halfway across the sky, throwing sparks before it vanished, and Dad had said, "An old Soviet satellite, I bet. One of their dead eyes in the sky."

The alien spacecraft had appeared over a hilltop. At first it was dull yellow and slow, but as it moved it gained speed and brightness. There was no distinct shape behind the lights. He remembered a throbbing sound, felt as well as heard. Dad had tried to take pictures; Mom had held on to Corny. He could still feel the warmth of her small hands and how they shook, yet he couldn't recall his own fear. Why be afraid of *them?* He felt himself floating, leaving the ground. Then he was back on the soft blanket, the ship gone, the warm air still and still smelling of Mom's perfume. But where was she? "Mommy?" He thought he had been sleeping. Dreaming. He rose and saw Dad sitting in the grass, his back to Cornell and his voice making a low sound, strange and tired.

"Where's Mommy? Where'd she go?"

Dad turned and gazed at him, tears on his face.

"What happened, Daddy?"

And Dad responded with a question. "What do you remember?"

Cornell told him. Lights, and floating . . . and coming awake again. . . .

"We saw a spaceship," said Dad. "Don't you remember?"

But where was Mommy? Maybe at the car, he thought, and he started to run downhill, shouting for her and crying, wiping at his eyes with the backs of his hands.

Then Dad caught him and held on tight; and after a crushing hug, he said, "Listen," and said nothing. He was pushing at the tears on his son's face. Then he breathed and said, "It was a spaceship, Corny. A spaceship, and it stole her away."

It was the only time Dad called him by that name.

Cornell felt as if he were sliding down a long slick slope, gaining speed and out of control. "Why would they? Why?"

But his father had no response, rising to his feet and turning away, crying eyes toward the sky—moonless, in memory, and perfectly dark, sprinkled with the blazing cold fires of faraway suns.

THEIR HOUSE WAS SMALL AND UNTIDY, THE UNSIGHTLY COMPONENT in an otherwise attractive cul-de-sac. Dad had no love for lawnwork or shoveling snow. He spoke of wasting resources and distorting nature's balance, though Cornell sensed there were other reasons. The old man didn't like pushing mowers and snowblowers. That's why if things got bad—and they inevitably would—Pete would offer his services, probably after prodding from the other neighbors on the little dead-end street.

There were four other houses on the cul-de-sac. Pete's house was largest, two stories tall with a mammoth yard kept trimmed and green even in the depths of summer. (Mrs. Pete worked in the yard every day, fighting lazy flowers and the weeds creeping over from the Novaks'.) The Underhills' house was nearly as large, but it seemed small for their needs. They had three kids, including two boys around Cornell's age. Their house was on one side of the Petes', and Cornell's was on the other side. A bachelor named Mr. Lynn had the little house on the far side of the cul-de-sac. And on the other side of Cornell's house, at the cul-de-sac's mouth, were surly old people named Tucker.

The houses had been built during the last boom. The cul-de-sac straddled a long ridge, and behind it, to the west, the ground sloped down into a creek bottom. Another developer had prepared the ground for houses. When Cornell was six, he had watched the construction crews destroying pastures and an alfalfa field to lay down concrete streets and storm sewers, power lines and sidewalks. Then came the Four-Year Recession, banks dying and people going broke. Or worse. The developer went to jail for some vague crime, and the land was abandoned, weeds of a hundred flavors growing up thick and green, bugs singing from them every summer night.

It was like living on the brink of civilization. That was the game Cornell would play. Some nights, he sat with the bedroom window open, lights off, watching the little jungle and the darkness stretching west to the Rockies.

His room had always been his room. He could remember when it felt huge, an empire of his own, and he was small enough to climb under his bed, hugging the dusty carpeting and watching Mom's feet. The bed had always been his bed, left behind by Mom's father. He had a fancy clock/radio that projected the time as glowing, dancing letters suspended in the air. The longest wall had a map of Mars, complete with Rover pictures in the corners, his favorite one showing a view from the top of Vallis Marineris. Over his bed was one of Dad's favorite pictures—a color snapshot of a silvery being floating in front of a cringing leopard, the being's hand extended as if in peace. It was a fake, Cornell knew. But Dad approved of the idea behind the picture, saying, "That sense of communion is never wrong." And Cornell liked the leopard, powerful and lovely and wonderfully dangerous.

Sometimes he would wonder how it would be to live elsewhere, in another city or country. Cornell tried to imagine a different bedroom with new pictures and maps . . . and it made him uneasy, possibilities crowding in on him. There were times, particularly after their long trips, when he was glad to be here and ready to stay home the rest of his life. The musty smells of unmade bedding and old books meant *home.* He knew the red faces of Mars better than he knew his own face, it seemed. And he felt a powerful loyalty, to his room and the entire house, and even to the cul-de-sac itself. This was his realm. He couldn't imagine outgrowing it; not like he'd outgrown the dusty shelter beneath his bed.

They ate dinner at a Hardees, Dad paying and Pete making his usual protests. The sun was low when they finally pulled into the driveway. Cornell changed into shorts, wanting to feel cool. Todd Underhill was outside, shouting at his brother, calling him Lame instead of Lane. They were riding bikes around the island at the cul-de-sac's center. Racing, like always. And Todd winning every race.

Cornell's bike was nothing special. It had old-fashioned gears and tires worn smooth and not all the padding that new bikes had to wear. It clicked when he pedaled hard, never quite in gear. "Let me adjust it," Pete would say. "Anytime." Except he liked the clicking. He was accustomed to it and used it as a measure of his speed. He considered himself a smart racer, knowing how to position himself and get ahead, and how to guard a lead; Todd always let Cornell slip ahead, always too confident in his own legs and his fancy bike.

Making low motor sounds, Cornell rolled onto the circular street, hollering when he joined the race. The Underhills were blond, round-faced and a little heavy, looking as if they were carved from warm butter. Dusk was beginning, streetlamps and stars ready to come out. Todd screamed, "A new entry in tonight's field!" and Lane said, "Killer Cornell!" They circled the island, the brothers working against each other and Cornell closing the gap. He kept close to the island's curb, knowing from hard experience that too close meant catching a pedal and crashing, limbs and twisted spokes everywhere. But shortening your orbit was critical, and after a lot of hard work, he found himself nearly touching Lane's back wheel.

Todd screamed, "A three-man race."

Voices filled with engine sounds and cheering crowds. "The challenger makes his move," Cornell shouted, swinging outside and back again. Lane went outside, trying to block him. Then it was too late, and he was passed, ten years old and unable to hold the pace.

Todd sensed the change, pumping harder and calling out, "One more lap."

The finish line was always the concrete seam aligned with the cul-de-sac's mouth. That was an ancient rule. Cornell felt time slowing as he struggled with his bike and inertia. His breathing was labored, full of toxins and excitement, but he managed to close on target with half a lap to go. And Todd, like always, kept too far outside and wobbled, allowing his opponent to draw even with him before one last burst to the finish line. The world watched, and he won in the end. By the width of a tire, if that. But Cornell knew he'd won and Todd was just a poor sport, like always, saying, "You didn't, you didn't. You're goddamn blind, Novak."

It was better to agree, Cornell knew.

It was better to coast to a stop while Todd took his victory laps. "Okay. You won." It wasn't lying, since he was giving something up. He wasn't profiting. And besides, he knew what was true. True was true despite what anyone said or wished.

"I won," Todd cried out.

It was almost dark. A clear, starry night, Cornell saw, and he sat on the curb and carefully ignored his friend, watching the sky and thinking about a million things.

The island had evergreen bushes at its center, thin grass and a few tired flowers at the edges—courtesy of Mrs. Pete—and there were places worn bare by the boys, places where they sat and talked and watched the cul-de-sac. Mr. Lynn, the bachelor, arrived home in his old Corvette—a '91—and a blond woman got out with him. "He'll screw her," said Todd, a matter-of-factness edging into disgust. Cornell couldn't talk that way, but he felt a surge of interest. More than once, they'd dared each other to sneak around back and spy, using weeds as cover. One time, for half an instant, they'd seen one woman's bare chest as the curtains parted, no warning given and no memory more clear. She'd had little breasts, and the breasts had intoxicated him. The blond had large ones, and what effect would they have? Chewing on a stalk of grass, Todd remarked, "I bet they're doing it now." He sounded worldly and unimpressed. "Right on the floor, I bet. What do you think?"

Cornell thought he was thirsty and tired, and for a moment he considered going inside. But the urge passed. He turned the other way, studying the Tuckers' house. The flickering colored light of a television looked like a campfire. Just like Dad said. He said that TV's purpose and its pleasure was the same as a campfire's, stories told around it, and gossip, and sometimes important teaching. Dad had to like TV. His own father, long dead, had made a heap of money from a local station, and it was Grandpa Novak's trust fund that let Dad do nothing but research the aliens. Dad wasn't rich, no. But he liked to tell Cornell they were comfortable and fortunate by any reasonable measure.

"Where'd you go today?" asked Lane.

Cornell told the brothers everything, in brief.

"So," said the worldly, disinterested Todd, "see any aliens?"

They weren't true friends. Lane was halfway interested in Dad's work, but Todd didn't care about aliens. They had an unspoken agreement not to discuss them, and Todd was being intentionally rude now.

"What? No purple people? No talking blobs?"

He was angry about being beaten. Cornell realized it, then his thoughts shifted to the farmer's son. That kid was interested in the work. It was too bad he didn't live nearby. Cornell had felt at ease with him.

"Hey," Todd pestered. "Aliens nab your tongue?"

Cornell glanced at Mr. Lynn's house. "Look. Tits."

"Where—?"

Both boys were gawking, and Cornell smiled to himself.

"You didn't see anything," Todd complained.

"Maybe. Maybe not."

That confused his companions, making them fidget and break dead sticks. One of the brothers always stared at the house, his head full of images. Then Todd said, "We can sneak out back. Want to?"

Mr. Lynn was nice. More than other neighbors, he would ask Cornell about Dad's work and the famous glass circles. That made Cornell feel bad about spying in the past. Every time he did it, he felt as if he was breaking some promise to himself. A vow. Besides, he reasoned, on a hot night like tonight, the windows would be shut tight, curtains closed and motionless.

"Well," Todd announced, "I'm going."

Lane broke a stick. *Crack.*

"You coming?" asked his brother.

"Are you?" Lane asked Cornell.

"Later." He glanced at the sky.

"You can watch for spaceships anywhere," Todd reminded him.

Lane stood beside Todd, ready to leave.

"Let's go, Novak."

And it occurred to Cornell that the brazen kid wasn't. That it was an act. When he said, "Later," the cocky face dipped, eyes narrowing and losing some of their confidence.

"Are we going?" asked Lane.

Todd said, "Sure."

Cornell was surprised how much he missed them when they left. Even when he was pissed at someone, there always was that moment when it felt like part of him was leaving, too.

It worried him.

He couldn't say why, but it did.

Sightings had been growing for years, no place was spared the odd lights, and this had been the best summer ever. Plus there were the glass circles, too. In June, without warning, a big circle had appeared in New York's Central Park. No one saw or heard anything odd. One morning it was there, and about a hundred thousand people came to see it, chipping off bits of glass as souvenirs. The whole thing was gone in about two days, if that.

Dad had his own collection of glass. The shards weren't radioactive, and they didn't make noise, and they didn't seem to prevent cancers or make radish seeds grow faster.

But Dad kept studying them, sitting down in the basement, in his workshop, working on the puzzle practically every night.

"This is an area without experts," he liked to say. Scientists looked as lost as anyone, it was true. Circles had been found in the middle of deserts, deep in the Amazon, and at least once inside an office building. Some days Dad claimed they were communication devices; other days they were launching pads. "The data prove nothing yet." The data. As if this was real science. Cornell liked to read about scientists, and sometimes he could see where Dad wasn't much of one. Real scientists didn't lead witnesses. They didn't have equipment that was bought secondhand and originally built for other jobs. The best scientists made graceful leaps from places well-mapped, everything managed along rigorous scientific lines.

"It boils down to this," said one Nobel prize winner. He was talking on CNN, telling the world, "Odd things *seem* to be happening, yes. But blaming aliens is no explanation. Aliens are the end product of a series of guesses. Can other worlds make life? How common are these living worlds? Is interstellar travel possible? And why treat our world in exactly this way?" A smiling pause. "Do you see my point? Guess wrong just once, and your rationale collapses. Sad as it seems, science *must* focus on natural phenomena to create explanations. Unseen aliens aren't natural phenomena, thus they are useless to us. Outside bar talk, of course, and lame fantasies."

"But they exist!" Dad had moaned at the TV screen. "Nonetheless, they exist!"

Cornell thought of his mother living among the aliens. Dad liked to say that extraterrestrials would differ from us in countless ways, and he had only scorn for crazy people who claimed to have fathered children with big-brained ladies from Sirius. Yet despite knowing better, Cornell would picture Mom living with an alien man, in his fancy house, figuring that if she was abducted she might as well be happily abducted, particularly in some golden world without hunger, without want.

Was she thinking of him now? Was she ever sad?

If she couldn't feel sad, he decided, then that was wrong.

The golden world would seem tainted then. Sometimes Dad's speeches about Edenlike societies and deep wisdom became suffocating; mandated joy, he could see, would be a terrible burden for its citizens. How would anyone know when and how he had done something wrong?

Cornell blinked, looking at his worn shoes, at his right toe which stuck through the double hole of his sock and mesh top.

Anger surged. It was directed at the aliens, but not for abducting his mother. Not this time. Now he was angry at their subtlety, at their collective shyness. Nobody would make fun of him if the critters would just step forward and say, "Hi!" Just once. Just so they became *natural phenomena.*

"Mr. Novak," said someone.

Not a friendly voice, or unfriendly. It was Mrs. Pete. The woman walked past him, her arms working, her little headphones playing loudly enough that he could make out the thin insecty buzz of taped music.

"Hello," he offered, waving too late.

Mrs. Pete continued walking, periodically glancing at her watch. She wasn't a pretty woman, or unpretty. In the old photographs she'd been attractive in a round-faced way, but then her weight went into Pete's gut and her dark hair showed early gray. She walked every evening, usually at dusk. This was late for her. Circling the island with weights strapped to her ankles and held in both hands, she did a reliable twenty minutes; then she finished with more weights and the stationary bike in one of the almost-empty bedrooms.

Mrs. Pete didn't look strong like an athlete, but the lean face had a hardness, a sense of endurance. Sometimes she was nice, and sometimes Cornell like her. She and Pete were a little like parents, giving him Christmas gifts and birthday money while watching over him. Maybe they watched over him too much, scolding and praising as they felt necessary.

The odd thing was, Mrs. Pete didn't believe in aliens. Not at all. Not even this summer had changed her mind.

It wasn't something she said aloud. Cornell knew it from

the way she rolled her eyes when Pete and Dad were talking. And it was the way Pete spoke of her, calling her, "Milady," and then admitting, "Milady doesn't approve of humanity's greatest step."

"Doesn't approve?" Dad would respond. "She doesn't want us to make contact?"

"She thinks it's hysteria, these things people see."

Dad seemed to grow weak when he heard about complete doubters. "What does she think about the thousands of circles?"

"Government experiments," Pete would claim.

"Oh, good lord, how?"

"The military has some new weapon." Pete would laugh at his wife's paranoia, clucking his tongue and shaking his head. "From orbit, she says. The space station is zapping us."

Even Cornell knew that was a stupid idea. There weren't any big armies anymore, and nobody had more than a few hundred nukes. Why would any government play with death beams? Watching Mrs. Pete walk past him again, he considered shouting out questions. But he didn't. He couldn't. Instead, he watched the warm August air making her sweat, her T-shirt dark on its front and back, and how she wiped her face with her wristband, with a practiced motion, her lean face intense, almost distant.

Only she and Pete knew about Mom. Everyone else thought she died in a car crash. It wasn't a hard secret to keep. People didn't like asking, "How did your mom die?" Even Todd accepted the story without complaint, doubting everything else in the world. But not that.

One time—only once—Cornell asked Pete, "What does Mrs. Pete say about Mom? That the government stole her away?"

He expected laughter, but instead there was silence, Pete dropping his head and glancing at Dad. And Dad, his face stony and simple, merely admitted, "I don't know what she believes, son."

There was a long, uncomfortable silence.

Then Dad added, "And I don't care, either. Not at all. Not for the slenderest little instant."

* * *

She had to be nearly done walking.

It was after ten o'clock, maybe near ten-fifteen. The Tuckers were watching the weather report, no doubt, and Mrs. Pete was sweating hard, breathing fast and hard, picking up her pace at the tail end of the workout. Cornell wondered what Todd and Lane were seeing. Should he sneak around back and find them? Then their mother appeared, as if on a signal, screaming their names a couple of times. She had a big voice, sharp and scary. Which was funny, because she was smaller than almost any grown woman Cornell had ever known.

He heard the front door shut again, no more screaming.

He happened to glance at the sky.

Mrs. Pete's watch beeped, and she stopped in front of him. He heard a couple of gasps, then a sniff. "Any saucers tonight?" She giggled, hands on her hips and her head tilting backward. Cornell glanced at her—a stupid, doubting woman—then he started to play a game that he'd mostly outgrown. Which star was Mom's? He looked at them and looked at them, expecting nothing, his butt on the concrete curb and his bare elbows digging at the half-dead grass. Bright, bright stars glittered overhead, only a little thinned by city lights, and there was no warning, no sensation, not even a slight tremor when the Change took place. By chance, Cornell was gazing upward, not a thought in his head; and the sky became a different sky, in an instant, with no more effort than the blink of a single eye.

**He began to scream.**

Cornell heard himself without realizing who it was, the scream far off and thin—something born deep inside his chest—and he scrambled backward into the evergreen bushes, panic seizing him. Needles cut at his face and bare arms. He turned and saw Mrs. Pete again. She stood in the street with her legs apart and hands half-raised and the mouth open, eyes unblinking. She could see it, too. He wasn't insane, was he? Everything was suffused with a hyper-clarity—Mrs. Pete's sweaty clothes; the backdrop of houses; that endless, tireless scream—and now he realized that he was the one screaming. He put a hand into his mouth to stop it. He bit at the hand, going silent; then he climbed to his feet and stepped onto the pavement, breathing deeply before looking at the sky again.

A bluish haze was in the west and straight overhead, with swirls and streaks of white, the vista familiar enough to frustrate Cornell when he couldn't think of its identity, too much happening too quickly for him to make the mental leap.

Then Mrs. Pete said, "What is it?" She grabbed him by an arm and shook him. Her hand-weights were on the pavement, dropped and forgotten. Her face was numbed, eyes vague and empty. "What . . . ?" Then she couldn't speak, couldn't even breathe, taking a backward step and looking up, catching the curb with her heel. Losing her balance, she fell backward, her thin butt absorbing the impact, the rest of her oblivious. Mrs. Pete just kept gazing at the sky, and it was her turn to scream. She was louder than Cornell, using all of herself, and the warm air started to tear into shreds as she said: "Ah! AH! *AHHH!*"

Cornell realized what he was seeing. Or at least he knew what it resembled, senseless as that seemed. This was a new sky, but what he saw was ordinary, sort of, and it had to be some kind of elaborate illusion. Rare and temporary, no doubt. Yet every time he looked, there it was above him, bathing the cul-de-sac in its soft blue and white light.

People began to come outdoors, singly and in groups.

The Tuckers must have heard the screams. They wore bathrobes, watching in stern amazement while Mrs. Pete walked circles with her head reared back. Cautious but curious, they came out from under their porch roof, gazing up; and Mr. Tucker shouted, "I don't see anything," followed by his wife's near-breathless admonition, "Well, then, go find your glasses!"

Mrs. Underhill assumed the screams involved her boys, and she came out ready to punish. She was halfway to the island, building steam, when she noticed the upturned faces and looked for herself. Her legs nearly collapsed beneath her. A moan, a graceless turn, and she was running for her house, shouting at her husband, "Honey, you won't believe it. Get out here."

Cornell glanced at his house, thinking of Dad. He was working in the basement, most likely, music playing and no idea what was happening.

Mr. Lynn emerged from his house wearing trousers, nothing else, bare feet slapping on the concrete walk. The blond woman followed, a fancy bathrobe pulled around her and her hair looking as if it had been hit by a strong wind. She pulled on the robe's belt, cinching it tighter. Mr. Lynn ignored her, gawking at the sky, stepping onto his lawn and lifting his hands as high as possible, trying to touch what he saw.

Again Cornell thought of Dad, but he couldn't make himself move.

"What is it?" Mrs. Pete muttered. She came close and grabbed an arm, squeezing him. "Do you know what's happening?"

It was an illusion, he thought. What else was possible?

Todd and Lane appeared, running out from between houses, and their father saw them. "What've you boys been doing?" Assuming they were at the heart of some trouble, he asked, "Can't I trust you for a second?"

Nobody paid attention to him.

Lane said, "Did you see it?" He shot past his parents, straight to Cornell and happy enough to fly. "Did you see it? I did. I was looking up. . . when it happened—!"

"So was I," Todd claimed.

"You were not," his brother countered.

"Was."

"You were watching windows, you shit."

Todd glanced uneasily at the blonde. "Was not."

"You were."

"Liar."

"You're the liar."

Cornell stepped away from them and everyone else, trying to sort out what he could see. He remembered the big inflated globe in their living room, the shapes of the continents and islands, then he thought to look north. Sure enough, there was a white splash bigger than the moon, and he knew, just knew, that he was looking at the North Pole, Arctic ice reflecting summer sun.

A door shut somewhere, hard.

Pete was marching across his front yard, saying with a loud voice, "On the news . . . there's bulletins . . . " Then he thought to stop and look overhead, starting to tremble, arms at his side and his big body looking insubstantial. Weak. A sudden breeze could have rolled him over, he was that astonished.

"What is it, Pete?"

Mrs. Pete asked the question, joining him and reaching with both hands, sinking them into his meaty sides.

"Just like they said," Pete began. "Christ!"

"What are they saying?" she asked.

"The sky's changed—"

"I know," she squealed. "But into what? And how?"

Pete saw Cornell and gave him a half-wink, and he hugged Mrs. Pete—Cornell had never seen them hug—then took her head with both hands and lifted her gaze. "Don't you recognize it? Tell me what it is."

Cornell had recognized it.

"Tell me."

Then Cornell muttered, "It's us."

"What's us?" said Mrs. Pete.

There was silence, people converging on Cornell. He swallowed, his throat dry and sore; then he said, "It's the earth."

"The earth?" she echoed.

And Pete said, "As if it's been turned inside out." He nodded and let go of his wife, suddenly laughing. "An illusion? I don't know. But it is the earth, isn't it? Cornell?"

Turned inside out like a sock, yes. Bizarre as that seemed.

The world had changed—*poof*—and nobody felt a thing.

Mrs. Tucker mentioned Dad, and Mr. Underhill solemnly said, "He should see this." There were nods, soft agreement, the tone almost respectful and almost as surprising as the sky. Even Mrs. Underhill, who called Dad odd or crazy on any other day, remarked with a loud voice, "He might understand this. Maybe. Maybe someone should ask him to come look."

Pete touched Cornell, smiling with relish. "Go on," he suggested, "and hurry. Hurry."

Cornell ran, as much for himself as Dad. He was full of pent-up energy. He didn't want to be inside an instant longer than necessary, through the front doors and the living room, pausing while in motion. On the fly, he heard music flowing from the basement. *The Planets,* he would later realize. A coincidence, meaningless and not even a large one, knowing Dad's tastes. He shot through the kitchen, turning and starting downstairs, wood slats creaking beneath him, and he saw the bright fluorescent light in the basement's far corner, shelves and worktables illuminated, Dad sitting exactly where Cornell expected to see him, perched on a high stool and wearing fancy jeweler's glasses, examining one of the day's bits of black glass.

Suddenly Cornell couldn't speak. He had crossed the slick concrete floor and stopped, the air full of potentials, and he found himself wrestling for the best words. This moment demanded perfection; anything else would diminish the impact. But all he could manage was a quiet moan, and the music paused, and Dad turned to him, the peaceful face wearing those stupid distorting glasses. Giant blue eyes gazed at him, curious and then alarmed. Dad set the sample on the tabletop and asked, "What?" Then when Cornell couldn't respond, he climbed off the stool, asking, "What's going on? What is it?"

He thinks Mom is home, Cornell guessed. The face seemed pale under the blue lights, and simple, and of course he thought this was about Mom.

"What's happened, son?"

"The sky," the boy blurted. "It's changed!"

Dad seemed puzzled, but not much. Cornell might have said, "The dishwasher is broken," for all the reaction he saw. Dad was wearing comfortable old trousers, standing with his rumpled legs apart, and he removed the jeweler's glasses with a rock-steady hand, the other hand turning off the stereo as the music began to swell again. There was no other sound now but the slow inhalation of his breath, his mouth opening wider, and nothing to say.

"I saw it," Cornell told him. "I saw the sky change."

"When?" Dad whispered.

"Now. Just now."

The man turned, putting the glasses down and setting the sample into the appropriate bag, the hint of a tremor showing in the long fingers.

And Cornell said, "The world's been turned inside out."

Inside out? The question seemed to float before Dad's face, like a cartoon thought. At last he looked genuinely startled. He looked old. It was the first time Cornell noticed the wrinkles as more than an accent, spreading out from the eyes, and the hair a weak gray made thin by the light. Dad tilted his head, his mouth open and silent. There was some comprehensive failure of will or his intellect. Or youth, maybe. It was a shock for Cornell. He couldn't move for a long moment; and finally Dad managed to say:

"I should take a look, then, shouldn't I?"

Cornell nodded and took a couple steps, then looked back at him.

Dad remained at the worktable, feeble in a hundred ways. He kept turning his head from side to side, acting as if he was lost inside his own basement.

"Come on," Cornell snapped. "*They* just changed the sky."

*They?*

"Will you come on?" And now Cornell turned and charged the stairs, unable to wait, mounting them two at a time, and was gone.

People were scattered about the island and the street, necks craned back and arms pointing. They were looking for landmarks. Some said, "It's just amazing." "How did it happen?" they kept asking; but nobody dared give answers. There was something childlike about everyone. Even the Tuckers seemed eight years old, shaking their heads and asking, "How? How? How?"

Mr. Lynn had gone inside, reemerging with a shirt on and a boombox in one hand. He found the all-news AM station, everyone hearing the thin, almost weak voice of a reporter in Washington, D.C. Hundreds of people were gathering in front of the Capitol building, everyone staring skyward. They were excited, said the reporter. And puzzled. But surprisingly calm. Yet her voice sounded anything but calm, her voice breaking, nothing in her experience able to help her now.

Car horns sounded in the distance, the summery buzz of insects louder and nearer. The crickets weren't very impressed, thought Cornell. Had they stopped chirping when the sky changed?

He looked up. And it occurred to him that even if the world had been turned inside out, it wasn't as bright or clearly defined as he would have guessed. The North Pole should be brighter, shouldn't it? He could tell which half of the earth was in daylight—the Pacific and eastern Asia—but the total light felt weak. Overhead, straight above, was the Indian Ocean and the winter hemisphere, cold and blue. Australia was a distinctive brown smear. And reversed, as if seen in a mirror. As if looking up was the same as looking down, the earth's rock and steel made transparent. On the continent's left was the line marking dawn, ocean blue bleeding into darkness. Dawn implied the sun, but Cornell couldn't see it. Which made zero sense. As if anything else was reasonable. . . .

"Here he comes," Mrs. Tucker announced, sounding relieved.

"Need help?" asked her husband. "Anything?"

It was Dad. He was carrying the white telescope in both hands, taking the porch steps one at a time. "Thank you, no," he said, eyes down. Then he said, "Pete? Get the tripod, will you? You know where."

Pete broke into a shuffling run. "Got it."

Dad hadn't looked up. Even on the sidewalk, on flat easy ground, he wouldn't let his gaze rise, taking no chances and perhaps holding to the suspense a little longer. To his doubting neighbors, he looked cool and objective. A professional. All the decades of preaching, claiming that aliens were everywhere; and for this moment, he simply refused to join in with the astonishment, doing his job as if it were merely work.

Approaching Cornell, he said, "Help me?" He looked at the boy's face, saying, "Let's put it on the grass, right here."

They set the telescope on the island, waiting for the tripod.

Dad grinned at everyone, and only then did he tilt his head back, squinting through the glare of streetlamps. Everyone was silent. Nathan Novak was the center of attention, and they waited to see how he'd respond to this impossibility. Would he jump up and down? Scream? What? Yet Dad refused to do anything, just a hint of a smile showing around his mouth. Finally, very softly, he cleared his throat and said, "I knew they'd give us a sign, when they wanted to be noticed. But I never imagined this." A brief breathless laugh, then he added, "Isn't it amazing?"

People who thought him crazy an hour ago were nodding.

"Notice," Dad said, "our horizon. It hasn't changed, has it?"

What did he mean? Mr. Underhill, tall as his wife was tiny, got up on the island and looked in every direction, trying to see what Dad saw.

"Of course, the air and city lights might obscure things," said Dad. "But if there was an upswing, if the earth were physically turned inside out . . . wouldn't we see Denver over there? And Chicago over there?"

The voice was calm, but the hands trembled and the face looked damp, tears mixing with his sweat. Dad took a breath, then told his audience, "It could be an illusion. Something's bending light, photons . . . perhaps . . . ?"

"Who's doing it?" asked Mrs. Tucker.

Mr. Lynn's date—dressed again, minus shoes and socks—offered, "Aliens, maybe?"

"Do you think so?" the old woman pressed.

"Who else could?" asked Mr. Underhill.

And Dad said, "Maybe yes, maybe no." He was the voice of reason, of skepticism. "Perhaps there is some natural phenomena at work."

People listened to the radio again. A reporter in New York City was interviewing people in Central Park, and one woman claimed to have seen the change. She had just come out of the Madame Bovary musical—two hundred dollars for lousy seats—and she'd looked upward, commenting that at least it was a nice evening. And then the sky was different, all at once.

"That's how it was," Cornell reported.

"What did you see, son? Exactly."

He looked at Dad, trying to recall details. Suddenly the day seemed filled with premonitions. The glass circle; the conversation about his mother; and playing that game about which is Mom's star.

"I felt nothing," Mrs. Pete reported. "It just happened."

"I saw it, too," said Lane.

Todd said, "So did I."

"Liar. You were looking for tits, liar."

Their father glared at them, but only for a moment.

Dad was nodding, calm and silent.

Then Pete arrived with the tripod, excusing the delay. "You put it in a different place, sorry."

Dad said, "We don't need the motor. I don't think." Then both men set to work, motions practiced to a slippery informality. Cornell watched the audience watching them, and he realized they were impressed. He'd seen this show for years, had grown up seeing it, and he remembered people making fun of Dad, and to a lesser degree, Pete. Suddenly those people looked like fools. Rocking back on his feet, he allowed himself a quiet laugh at their expense. Then Dad said, "Okay. Volunteers?"

There was silence, then a surge of bodies.

But Dad said, "Cornell? You saw it change. Take first crack."

The telescope was pointed at the dawn line as it moved across Asia. The little sparkles were cities. Russian cities, he decided. Were they seeing the same new sky?

"I saw it change," said Lane.

"And you're after Mrs. Forrest," said Dad. "I promise."

Even Todd waited in line, wanting his turn. Maybe it wasn't respect they were showing Dad, but at least it was a kind of numbed, cattlelike amiability. Dad readjusted the telescope between each person, allowing himself peeks and long looks. Then he'd wipe at his eyes, using the back of a hand. Pete would nod at him and smile. Wasn't it something? The Tuckers were last—a small revenge for all their bitching about weeds—and then the little Underhill girl could be heard crying inside her house, probably scared to be alone.

"Get her," snapped her mother. Then in a softer voice, "Please?"

But first Mr. Underhill asked, "What does it mean, do you suppose?"

Dad pursed his lips, looking at Australia. "It's a signpost, I guess."

The girl screamed louder.

"A signpost?" asked the harried man.

"Or many signposts," Dad added. Nodding with satisfaction, he remarked, "Something this large could mean a multitude of things, and all at once. Of course."

Cornell had never felt so proud of his father, watching him hold court over his snippy, small-minded neighbors. Pete and Mr. Lynn dragged Pete's big TV out onto the porch, turning up the volume. It was Dad who made the point about the communication satellites. They were working, weren't they? Which meant they were in position, right? Odd, odd, odd. People down the street heard about the telescope, and several dozen of them gathered around the island. CNN talked about the satellites, following Dad's lead. The Weather Channel showed fresh pictures from high orbit, and nothing seemed out of place. "Interesting," was Dad's response. Then the Tuckers got dressed and made buckets of coffee. Mr. Lynn brought out lawn furniture, and the Underhills found blankets. Their four-year-old daughter was still angry about being abandoned, and she was too young to care about the sky. CNN showed views from everywhere. An amateur astronomer called from Samoa, reporting normalcy. The sun seemed to be the same sun as always.

"Huh," Dad would say. "Isn't that interesting?"

CNN spliced into the mirror field in Utah. It had just been finished, hundreds of telescopes married by computer. Its images were impressive and ordinary, all that fancy gadgetry looking across a few thousand miles instead of the universe. It was like flying low over Australia, the geography reversed, billions of dollars focused on a single farmer plowing his field, dust rising and falling again and him wholly unaware of the Change.

And now, with a careful informality, Dad began to lecture about aliens. It was stuff that Cornell had heard every day, in various guises, but it wasn't at all old or stale. Dad had a spark, and every adult listened, and Cornell had never seen a more earnest, enthralled audience in his life.

"The universe is full of worlds," Dad began. "The Utah Project has seen some of them. Enough that we can estimate millions of life-bearing worlds just in our galaxy. If just a handful give rise to intelligent species, then it would take no time for intelligence to spread everywhere. Assuming even a sluggish star drive, an alien species could cross the Milky Way in just a few million years." A smiling pause. "Do you see where I'm going?"

Not entirely, no. People shook their heads, then a man from down the street inquired, "But what if we're the first smarties?"

Smarties?

Dad said, "Unlikely," with easy authority. "Even if our neighbors evolved just yesterday—a few hundred thousand years ago—they'd be here now. And why? Because life has certain common tendencies. One tendency is to grow and build on success, just like people do. How many people are there today? Eight billion? Eventually we'll fill up our little world, then spill off and need new homes elsewhere."

Nods. Silence.

"Which leaves one substantial, essential question," said Dad. *"Where in the heck are the aliens?"*

There was a long, uncertain pause.

Then he told them what Cornell knew by heart. "They're everywhere, of course." He gestured at the sky. "Everywhere and advanced, and maybe that's what they're telling us tonight. That they can do the most amazing things, and do them easily."

People grew uneasy; there was too much to digest too fast.

Then someone from the back asked, "So where are they? Standing here with us?"

Laughter. Sharp, edgy.

And Dad helped keep people anxious, shaking his head and saying, "I won't discount anything at this point."

Nobody looked at anyone else, eyes forward.

"Where are they?" Dad laughed and said, "Close and watching us, I'm sure. Influencing us and probably protecting us, waiting for us to mature to where they can step forward and welcome us into the galactic community." A pause, then he said, "That's what I believe more than anything."

Nods. Sighs. Little smiles.

"And I'm sure," he concluded, "they will make contact with us soon." He gave the sky one last dramatic look, then promised, "But that's enough of my noise. I'm going to sit. This isn't my show, and I'm sorry to have gone on this way."

He sat on a creaking lawn chair.

Some people applauded, Pete doing it loudest and smiling at Cornell. Others filed over to the telescope or to Pete's TV. Calm, dry voices made conjectures about everything. A few neighbors spoke about strange lights they'd seen, last week or twenty years ago. Some even approached Cornell, knowing he was the expert's son. "Do you think they'll come soon?"

Cornell nodded, glad to be optimistic.

"What will they look like? Like people?"

Humanoids were normal, yes. Big heads, small bodies. Otherwise, the saucer pilots looked human. Basically.

"Can they talk like us?"

"They can do anything they want," Cornell assured them.

"This is wondrous," said one woman.

Mr. Lynn said, "Isn't it?"

His date brushed up against Cornell, telling him, "You're so lucky. You saw it change. You'll look back on tonight as something special."

He felt her breasts against him, and he tried to commit them to memory.

Then Mr. Tucker, grouchy as ever, gave a wet snort and said, "I don't know. I like stars better than this."

Nobody paid attention to him.

"A helluva lot better."

The group seemed to take a silent vote, and they turned away from him, continuing their celebration, watching the sky and speculating about all things while drinking beer as well as the strong, cooling coffee.

There was a news conference after one in the morning. Members of the government and NASA filed into a Washington conference room, faces showing the strain of the last few hours. The press corps nearly charged them, demanding answers. The president's science advisor rose and took the podium, promising to take questions after he read a brief assessment of "recent events." There was a hush, inside the conference room and across the world; the man visibly shivered, unfolding notes while he gathered himself, this moment the culmination of his entire professional life.

"First of all," he read, "there are many questions without answers. For instance, we don't know what has caused this visible change. We have no idea what agency or natural phenomena is responsible. The United States of America has made no contact with alien beings. And contrary to certain rumors, no government or any researcher can make more than rash speculations at this time. I emphasize that word—*rash*—reminding everyone that facts are scarce, and every fact is puzzling. That said, here are the facts as we see them now—"

The Change—he said the words with force—had been witnessed by a variety of astronomers and other qualified observers, both in day and night, and from every part of the globe. No unusual tremors were detected at the instant of the Change. There were no mysterious astronomical events, either. From earth's perspective, the stars had vanished. A small portion of the planet's own light was falling back on itself. This was what people were seeing now. Cosmic radiations and starlight continued to fall, but they were being funneled through a diffuse region corresponding to the center of the inside-out earth. Four thousand miles overhead, in effect. And with that the advisor attempted to smile. "Our weather," he said, "seems normal. Absolutely normal. And the fundamental principles of the universe, gravity and the other forces, appear perfectly healthy. Perfectly fine."

He paused, and hands rose. A forest of limbs obscured him.

No, no. He refused questions, doggedly continuing with his briefing. He mentioned the space station and its thirty-person crew. Their view of the planet was essentially unchanged. A slightly diminished albedo, but that was consistent with the earthshine being registered down here. Satellites in low and high orbits showed the same blue-white ball. Dimmer, but quite familiar. That was why there was no interruption in worldwide communications, and that's why many experts were hoping this was an elaborate, temporary illusion.

"Whatever it is," he reported, "every specialist is working on the problem. Science is focusing, and answers, I'm sure, will be forthcoming soon. We already have run one intriguing experiment."

The hyperplane Exodus had just returned from orbit, and its first reports said that the inside-out illusion began fifty miles overhead. From a coat pocket, the advisor brought out a large serving spoon—an unexpected visual aid straight from the White House kitchen—and he described how Exodus had purposefully dipped in and out of the illusion. Like a reflection in the spoon, the planet's shape seemed to change according to your position. Above fifty miles, and it was normal. Below, and most of the planet was above you. Save for what was directly beneath you . . . that part of the visible disk appearing perfectly ordinary. . . .

The advisor paused, a wet hand mopping the wet forehead.

Again the forest of arms came up.

"Yes? You—"

"Could foreign powers be responsible?"

The advisor blinked, disgust surfacing. Then he snorted and said, "No. Next?"

A second reporter said, "There's a report that the sun's neutrino emissions have quit. Do have any comment?"

"What's a neutrino?" people muttered around Cornell. And he knew. He tried to describe the tiny particles born in the hearts of stars, then he heard the advisor saying some of the same words, adding, "Not at all. Like cosmic radiation, the neutrinos still are with us."

"What about the aliens?" someone shouted. "Are you making overtures to speak with them?"

A frustrated sigh, and he said, "Give me their phone number. I'll call right now."

The room laughed. Nervous, but relieved to find any humor.

Then another reporter mentioned seeing the president in the Oval Office with a strange figure, perhaps alien. "Any comment on that?"

The advisor had to smile, on a roll now. "The president was watching television with her husband. Does that explain things?"

It was a ruthless stroke. The First Husband was a tall and homely man, and that he would be confused for an alien delegate was the perfect touch. Laughter continued for a full minute. The advisor had a chance to step back and take a drink of water. Then he asked for more questions, and a determined man stepped forward, both hands in the air.

"What's a neutrino?" he asked with a shrill voice. "And how can we protect ourselves from them?"

The press conference ground along for an hour; the cul-de-sac grew bored with repeated questions and the lack of concrete answers. They migrated back to Dad, and he showed them the starlight coming from straight overhead, the tripod straddling the curb and nothing to see but a ghostly white fog. The universe funneled through a little cloud, Cornell was thinking. Then Dad sat in his creaking lawn chair and began spinning explanations and speculations, smiling all the while, happier than Cornell had ever seen him.

"I think there's a galactic union," he allowed. "Advanced and quite peaceful. Wise and talented. Possessing enormous powers, but very much aware of its responsibilities. And perhaps we're about to join the union, if only in some limited, novice role."

It was the reliable galactic-union speech, reconfigured for the audience and the moment.

Dad spoke of starships and hidden bases and humanity living on a microscopic slide, and those wonders suddenly seemed ordinary, perhaps even out of date. Yet the speculations were too much for some. Heads shook; people grew tired of astonishment; the audience changed members as the morning wore along.

Cornell returned to the big TV. The press conference was finished, CNN turning to a West Coast studio to interview a Nobel laureate. A brilliant balding man with radioactive eyes, he began to voice some of Dad's opinions about aliens and intelligence, then moving on to wilder ideas of his own design. It was a sweet vindication. The cul-de-sac saw this certified genius speaking Nathan Novak's words, and faces glanced at one another, again and again, wondering what kind of genius they'd been living near for all these years.

"I'm guessing," confessed the physicist, "but I'll bet you any sum that contact is imminent. Perhaps it's already underway—"

"The government denies that," a reporter interrupted.

"Governments deny. It's their nature, son. How long have you been on your beat?" The eyes filled with satisfaction. Just like Dad, he spoke of the new sky being a signpost, and the Change had to be a prelude to some wonderful event. Then he laughed for what seemed like hours, making himself gasp for breath. "It's funny. I always thought First Contact would be some meek signal on the waterhole band. Not this. Don't I look like the idiot right now?"

The reporter didn't answer. Instead he asked, "Do you believe our government is talking to the aliens?"

"Well, yes. . . . I mean, no. Now that you mention it, that's an awfully ordinary answer, isn't it?" A wise shrug, then a harsh growl. "As big as these critters think? Eight billion of them could show up at our doors. Shake everyone's hand. You know? Neighbor to neighbor?"

LATER, AFTER THREE IN THE MORNING, CLOUDS BEGAN RIDING IN from the west, high and thin but ample enough to obscure the sky. Pete took his TV back inside. Dad and Cornell retrieved the telescope. Then it was four, and a burst of rain sent the last of the people home. Sleeping children were carried unaware. Televisions skipped between channels, politicians and scientists and at least one top-dollar actress gushing speculations. But what Cornell would recall, years later, was the view from the East Coast, from Maine, the CNN camera showing the sun as it rose on schedule, the sky becoming an almost ordinary blue—save for a splash of white, very faint, that was Greenland—and the impossibility of it seemed only half as incredible as before.

He was growing accustomed to everything, or he was tired. Probably a little of both, he realized. Or maybe a lot of both.

The Petes came to their house. Mrs. Pete never visited, at least since Mom vanished; but this was a special occasion, and she was too excited to even comment on the disorder, the grime. She made fresh coffee, and Cornell asked for a cup's worth. Dad's rules needed amending. "Have some," Dad told him, distracted. Happy to tears. "You don't want to miss anything."

If it was just Dad and him, he'd ask about Mom. Was her arrival imminent? Or if just Pete was here, maybe he'd ask anyway. But not with Mrs. Pete. That's something Cornell understood, tired or not.

Dad sat in his lumpy lounge chair, leaning forward.

Cornell finished the coffee and felt better, not alert but confident enough to lie on the floor with his head on little pillows. It was nearly dawn, a steady rain falling. And now the president came on every network, telling the nation and world that her government was continuing its day-to-day business, no need to declare an emergency, no need to involve Congress or the military. She spoke about American resilience, particularly resilience in the face of change, and she trusted people to live up to their reputation. Finally, with a kind of solemn fire, she promised her people that this phenomenon—natural or artificial—would be studied in full, no expense spared. Teams already were outlining a new agency whose only focus would be the Great Change.

"What do you think it means, darling?" Pete was watching his wife, smiling slyly. "You're the skeptic. Are you at least impressed?"

Mrs. Pete nodded, grinned. "A little bit."

"Just a little?"

"I'm like the scientists. No final opinions, please."

Then Cornell thought, What if Mom came home now? Wouldn't that be perfect? He could practically see her, dressed in a shiny waterproof suit and smiling at them . . . and his eyes closed of their own volition, the caffeine no match for a long day and a longer night. He was dreaming, asleep in an instant and seeing his mother in the dreams. He was running toward her, pressing between the astonished Petes; and she knelt and kissed him, wet lips smiling and saying, "Here I am! I'm home, and with a message. Welcome to the neighborhood." She said it again and again. "Welcome, welcome. We're glad to have you as neighbors, and a thousand times *welcome.*"

Cornell slept and woke, then slept again, hearing slivers of conversation. Voices from the TV mixed with the adults behind him, their identities a jumble. Dad sounded like a mathematician talking about a new geometry, the earth and space all tucked together into some kind of bizarre hypersphere. Then came a biologist who sounded like Pete, the deep voice mixed with thunder; and he told how life should riddle the cosmos, born on earthlike worlds and strange worlds and perhaps inside the giant warm clouds of interstellar gas and dust. It was astonishing to him that life was hard to find—the universe should be one endless jungle—

—and now Cornell dreamt of jungles with strange wet skies, swirling clouds of stars giving way to twin suns. There was a sudden heat, intense and suffocating. He woke with a start, the TV playing but nobody in the room. Sunshine poured through the windows; he was baking in a bright rectangle. Where was everyone? For a sleepy instant, Cornell wondered if the aliens had come and abducted everyone but him. What if they had? He rose and searched the empty house, through the bedrooms and back into the kitchen, pausing at the basement door and hearing just the quiet burning of the water heater. Then he noticed figures in the front yard. Dad? He peered through streaked glass, seeing his father and the Petes. And a fourth person, too, her back to him; and of course it was Mom. Twelve-year-olds spend an inordinate energy looking for what is fair, and this was fair. Fair was Pam Novak returning home, unharmed and happy. That's why Cornell ran. He flung open the front door and hit the screen door hard enough to break its latch. Everyone turned to look, startled but still smiling; and for an instant, for no better reason than wanting, Cornell saw his mother standing there.

Then he realized it wasn't her. It was Mrs. Underhill standing on the shaggy lawn, looking tired like everyone else, and joyous. And Dad, barely noticing the damaged door, called out, "The sun's up, Cornell!"

The boy felt foolish, starting to blush.

"If you didn't know better," Dad continued, "you'd think the world was back to normal. You almost could."

No aliens arrived on the world's doorstep, inviting themselves inside for coffee. Nor did any radio messages fall from the new sky. One persistent rumor was that everyone in Tulsa, Oklahoma, had received the same eerie phone call, an otherworldly voice saying, "Your rent is due." That led to some nervous moments—what kind of rent do *they* need?—then the discovery of teenage boys with speed-dial machines. And for weeks and weeks, pundits joked that if Tulsa was the first place *they* contacted, then *they* weren't particularly smart, were they?

Scientists worked without sleep, slurries of coffee and pills helping them invent tests and then wrestle with the results. No, they determined, the universe hadn't truly vanished. Its starlight and X-rays and gravity waves were just more difficult to see, mashed together at the center of the everted earth, their cold gray glow resembling a god's night-light. An amorphous glow scrubbed of information, it turned out. Yet from orbit, from the space station and elsewhere, everything seemed ordinary. Planets and stars moved according to old-fashioned plans. The only change was the earth's albedo, its brightness diminished by a few percentage points. Measurements on top of measurements proved that this missing light matched what people saw overhead, almost to the photon; and the jittery, overdosed scientists could at least find a crazy sensibility to the circumstance. That implied rules; and like twelve-year-old boys, scientists took enormous stock in things like rules and fair play.

Then came a wizard, a twenty-five-year-old Russian already notorious in the small world of mathematics. He guaranteed himself everlasting fame and the Nobel prize with a string of hurried calculations. He began with an assumption: *Life is common.* Not just now, he argued, but always. He pictured a universe where intelligence and self-awareness bubbled up everywhere. How would life act, surrounded by stars and black holes, dust clouds and quasars? How could it remake its surroundings? Not in a year or ten million years, but in billions of persistent years . . . how might life redecorate its quarters . . . ?

Cold baryonic matter can be sculpted, he decided. With elegant symbols and guile, he proved that space-time could be bent, normally invisible dimensions coming into play, and the result was a universe filled with delicate, closely packed structures. Where did they get the baryonic matter? From planets and dust, at first. But later whole suns could be dismantled, cooled and transformed into useful elements. And perhaps dark matter would be rebuilt as well. Instead of vacuum punctuated with little wild suns, the universe would be orderly and crowded, each new world existing somewhere among all the structure. There were all sorts of potentials, wrote the Russian. Meters and miles no longer applied. The human mind was, at best, badly equipped to picture the geometry. Which was sad. "Evolution hasn't made us ready for this new order," he confessed, "and the beauty escapes us. I'm the best, and all I can see is the fringe of it. All I smell is an intoxicating hint of what is."

So what did these fringes and hints show him?

The earth was many things, he wrote. It was a sphere in space, like always, and an everted sphere in a different space. Plus it had other shapes, each more complicated than the last. When the sky was darkness and stars, the earth "saw" a carefully structured rain of photons and charged particles. But remember, nobody has ever actually seen a star. People saw a few photons, a representative sample supplied at little cost. There might be very few stars, the Russian argued. Or more likely, artificial ones meant to give light and life to myriad worlds at the same time. It would be an efficient system, and safe. Only the cold bodies were real—planets and asteroids, moons and dust motes—all of them stacked into fancy hyperdimensional walls.

"But why the sudden change?" people asked. "Why change the sky now?"

The Russian didn't know the trigger, not knowing the exact machinery. It could be anything, though he liked the idea of watchful aliens. They must have decided mankind was ready for the challenge. And it wasn't as if the stars were lost, he added, giving a big smile. People still could travel into space, above the fifty-mile transition, and see the old universe. The projected universe. "Think of that sky being like a photograph in your living room. A photograph of a forest, say. A lovely wild place that doesn't exist any longer, but you keep it as a reminder. That's what our old sky was. A picture on the wall. A view of the wilderness."

But a few years later, accepting his Nobel, the Russian proposed one possible trigger for the Change. What if it was a human mind? What if a single earthly brain had reached the point where it could understand and appreciate this new order, and that mind was the trigger? His mind, in other words. What if the aliens saw *him* as being worthy, and the whole Change was for his education and his glory?

Despite the ego, people admired him.

And the ego blossomed, even long after the man's talent was gone. Even years after his last published paper, after three ugly public marriages and a squandered fortune . . . that old Russian was convinced that he was solely responsible for the Change, and he told it to anyone who would listen. He told it to barflies down in Key West, and one particularly beefy barfly said, "That's bullshit, and shut up." But the Russian wouldn't quiet himself. The two men ended up trading blows, and that special perfect precious brain struck the floor, blood vessels breaking and the Nobel laureate never regaining consciousness.

It was an important funeral, but friendless. The networks sent cameras and reporters, and colleagues gave terse eulogies. "Think of it," said one old physicist. "A few days of jotting down symbols and relationships, and the poor man spent the rest of his life being proud. He described a universe full of life, some of it more gifted than any of us, and he was proud. We're like children who discover the color blue or the joy of love, and by what right do we feel pride?" A long pause, then with a pained voice, he said, "And think of this. Maybe he was our finest mind, yet he lacked the wit and wisdom to live his own life well. Given everything, he won nothing. How sad. How apt. How wickedly true."

Reporters from the local stations interviewed Dad during the first week. He was the UFO expert, and his views seemed appropriate. One reporter thought it would be interesting to interview his neighbors, asking most of them what they thought about having a visionary in their midst.

"Oh, he's brilliant," chirped Mrs. Underhill. "A deep thinker, that's Nathan."

Mr. Tucker was less effusive. "Yeah, he knows stuff. But look at that lawn. You think maybe he could cut the grass once in a blue moon?"

Mr. Lynn called Dad, "Perceptive. Even mystical."

His blond girlfriend, soon to be his fiancée, squinted at the camera lens and said, "He's cute, sort of. I think."

"I've known Nathan for years," said Pete, "and he's a sincere, curious individual. I admire him more than I can tell you. I don't always follow what he's saying, but I sure admire him."

Mrs. Pete merely said, "He means well," with something disapproving about the narrowed eyes.

Cornell was last. The reporter pushed her microphone into his face, asking, "What can you tell me about your dad?" What could he say? Summing him up in a phrase seemed ridiculous, even stupid. But he tried, clearing his throat and hearing himself saying:

"He's the best father ever."

Pete's testimony led the piece, then Dad spoke about the goodness of the unseen aliens. Cornell's blurb was tacked on at the end. Nobody else made the cut, which caused grumbling. Then the piece went across CNN, one of hundreds of stories done in those crazy weeks.

And Cornell found himself feeling guilty. *The best father ever?* How could he make such a claim? Who could ever actually measure such a thing?

He couldn't, obviously.

No one had that kind of power.

There was a nightly party for the first weeks, informal and quickly routine. People would gather at the island after dinner, the sun dropping behind distant farmland and the new sky emerging in its glory. What had been astonishing was now merely interesting. Merely natural. Yet people pestered Dad with questions, devouring his speculations about aliens and their unseen worlds. The old man loved it. He talked himself hoarse, recounting every famous sighting; and Cornell found himself growing bored, a little bit. One evening, getting ready for bed, he asked, "Why don't you tell them about Mom? Tomorrow night, could you?"

The man took a breath and held it, then said, "Oh, I think not."

Why not?

"First, we don't know when she'll come home. Why involve them in our wait? And secondly, I think what you really want is pity. Don't you?"

He hadn't considered it, but yes, maybe somewhat. Their neighbors' pity would be nice, he thought. But later, lying awake in bed, Cornell discovered another reason. He considered all the happiness in the world, and he felt left out. He felt cheated. Turning on his side, staring at the round red faces of Mars, he experienced a sudden bilious anger verging on rage. It frightened him, and it made him feel alive; and for half the night he couldn't relax enough to even pretend sleep.

Rumors mentioned secret talks in Maryland and the Yucatan, and the pope had been seen strolling through the Vatican with angelic creatures. Every kind of story made the rounds. Euphoria was infectious. And Cornell felt a surge of anticipation with each story, then despair when it turned out to be pure fantasy.

It sickened him, all these changes of mood.

He finally found the courage to ask Dad, "Where is she?" They were in the basement, Dad fiddling with a piece of machinery. Cornell had practiced this moment for some time, his questions clear and his resolve cool. "Why don't they let her go now? What good does it do, keeping her?"

Dad set down a tiny screwdriver, acting as if it were fragile.

"Why don't they?"

"I don't know," the old man allowed, almost nodding and the pink tip of his tongue licking his dry lips. "But I'm assuming . . . we have to assume . . . they have splendid reasons, even if we can't appreciate them."

Cornell didn't want to talk about things he didn't understand. "So why don't they explain why? Can't they?"

Dad shrugged, saying, "I guess not. I'm sorry."

"That Russian? He says the universe is full of worlds, and the aliens are practically next door."

"I know the theory," Dad assured him.

"Maybe it's simple to go between worlds."

"What's your point, son?"

What was it? He paused, trying to calm himself. Then he explained, "She might be close. She's always been close, not light-years away."

"And why doesn't she walk home?"

"Why not?"

Dad had a way of thinking with his entire body, with his face and posture and even the thoughtful curl of his fingers. Finally, with a pained tone, he replied, "She might not be allowed to come here."

"Why not?" Anger made Cornell tremble. "The aliens are assholes, I think . . . !"

The old man didn't approve of the language or its intent. Yet he wouldn't let his own anger blossom, no, shaking his head and with the mildest of voices saying, "Now, now. You don't mean that. . . ."

Cornell hated that patience. He hated running up against it, bouncing off and nothing to show for the collision.

"You mustn't hate *them,*" said Dad, almost whispering.

"I do."

The thin face shook no, the mouth fused into a pale pink line.

"Maybe she doesn't want to come back," Cornell offered. "She likes it better there. Wherever it is."

Dad sat back on his stool, appearing weak. Bloodless. Then he recovered enough poise to say, "I guess that's possible. It isn't hard to believe. A better place, and we have to respect her wishes, of course. Of course."

Crazy talk. The old man muttered too softly to be understood, and Cornell retreated, defeated and angry because of it. He thought about nothing else for days, as if acid were eating his guts. The man was crazy . . . he saw it more and more . . . all that talk about beautiful places, places where he'd never been . . .

. . . places better than this ugly dump. . . .

*Easily.*

They returned to the farm where they'd been on Change Day, as people called it now. This was late September. There weren't any new disks to investigate, and sightings were down, despite huge interest and millions of night-watching eyes. That's why Dad wanted to visit the farm and other old sites. Touch bases again, and all that.

"Did you call and warn them?" asked Pete. He was wearing a flannel shirt with the sleeves rolled to his elbows, the perpetual whiskers longer and darker than in summer. "I bet they don't know we're coming, do they?"

"We'll just drop by," Dad confessed.

Cornell felt embarrassed and a little disgusted.

"We won't bother anyone," Dad added. A backward glance at Cornell. A wink and smile. "I'm sure it'll be fine."

But the woman at the front door didn't like surprises. Three strangers were on her porch, and her eyes were round against a round farmwife face. Cornell smelled cleansers. "Yes," she said, "can I help you?" Dad explained their purpose while Cornell hung behind him and Pete. The dogs sniffed at his heels and butt. The German shepherd wagged its bristly tail, letting the fur on its neck rise. "I remember," said the woman. "You came here a few months ago."

Last month, thought Cornell.

"My husband's in town," she continued. "I'll need to ask him, if you can wait."

"The circle's still there?" Dad asked the question in a polite but worried fashion. "Nothing's happened to it, has it?"

"Oh, it's there," she allowed. "Nobody's taken it."

She made them wait on the porch while she made a phone call. Through the screen door, Cornell saw oak trim and dingy wallpaper and wooden stairs slumping after decades of hard use. Where was the boy? he wondered. Then the woman returned, telling them, "Okay, but be careful. The corn's had a hard year."

"We will be, ma'am."

"Really, we haven't seen anything unusual. Except for the sky, that is." Then she gave a sly wink, laughing and shutting the old oak door with a solid *thunk.*

Like last time, the dogs shadowed them, trying to understand their equipment with their noses. Again Cornell carried the warming toolbox. Again Pete helped him measure the circle. Ragged yellow corn stalks stood around them, making dry dead sounds in the breeze. The circle had changed, cracking at its edges and slumping near its center. Maybe it had been built by aliens—creatures of supreme intelligence—but Cornell decided it looked unremarkable, even ugly. It wasn't even good glass, dusty and hot, and what was he doing here? He wanted to be . . . where? No place came to mind. Then he thought: Wouldn't it be something if this was nothing? If the circles were nothing but some alien's shit?

"What's funny?" Pete asked.

Cornell said, "Nothing," with a mind-your-business tone.

Pete approached, not smiling, something about his face cool and impassive. "Feeling moody, are you?"

What could he say to that?

"Your mom always was. Moody. More and more, you're like her."

The words had a sense of foreboding, of doom, rattling off the glass and through him.

"You've got her fire, all right. A real temper." The big man shook his head, amusement mixed with caution. "Oh, she could explode. Get on her wrong side, and heaven help you."

Cornell looked at his feet, at his own dusty reflection.

"Much as you look like her, I guess you should get her temper, too."

Mom had a temper? It seemed unlikely, nothing in Cornell's memories hinting at such a thing. But if he couldn't recall something so important—something so obvious—then what else was lost to him? It made him suddenly uneasy.

"Can someone help me?" Dad interrupted, standing at the far end of the circle. "I can't get the magnetometer to calibrate."

Pete went to help, thank God.

Cornell finished his work and walked back to the car, the German shepherd trotting beside him. The boy was in the front yard, tossing a worn leather football into the sky. A boombox on the porch was blaring, some local college game going well; but what was different? Cornell paused and stared. The boy looked older, and not just because he was taller. Something had changed in his eyes and his stance, in the way he glanced at Cornell, and in the tone of his voice. "Catch them aliens yet?"

It was a harsh, belittling tone.

Cornell felt anger surging, then he swallowed it. It was like stuffing a wild animal into a tiny cage. That's how it felt.

"Touchdown, touchdown," screamed the radio announcer.

The boy asked, "Think we'll win everything this year?"

In football, he meant. Cornell said, "I don't know." Football was a silly, violent game. Dad said so, and he'd always believed him.

"Figure out the circles yet?"

"No." Cornell shook his head. "Not yet, no."

"Thought not." Another toss. A solid catch. "My dad says you're just a bunch of nickel and dimers—"

And again his temper engaged, sudden and involving a lot more than this boy. Weeks of frustration made him detonate. No warning. He was aware of motion, screams and kicks. Then Pete was pulling him off the boy, the mother saying, "He's cut, bleeding . . . look what your son did. . . . "

"Easy," said Pete, holding him with both hands. "Easy, easy."

And Dad, flustered and pale, kept saying, "I'm sorry," to the mother, "Are you all right?" to the boy, and "What's happened to you?'' to Cornell. All the way home, mile after mile, he kept asking, ''What's going on with you, son? What is the matter?''

He didn't know, couldn't say. Couldn't find words worth speaking, and so he sat in the backseat, perfectly silent, watching the countryside flow past.

The first cool nights cut down on the cul-de-sac's parties. Neighbors from down the street kept to themselves, content with their own vantage points. Then the Tuckers quit coming outdoors, blaming fatigue and their dinner schedule. People stopped expecting aliens. Even the rumors of contact fell off to a trickle. There was a new governmental agency—large and well-funded, devoted to understanding this new world—but its offices weren't half-completed, and it would take years for the lunar observatories and other facilities to come on-line.

Life was dropping back into old patterns.

Some nights, even in November and early December, Dad would dress in warm clothes, set up the telescope, and watch New Zealand or the wilds of Mongolia. For Cornell, peering through the curtains, the old man was an embarrassment standing in plain view. What was he doing? There was nothing to see but the earth itself, and what a stupid, shivering waste of time!

''Maybe he thinks the sky'll change again,'' said Todd, teasing his friend. ''Pretty weird, huh?''

A twinge of anger, then Cornell agreed. ''Really weird.''

''My folks say he needs lithium.''

Lithium? Cornell would have to read about it, learn what it did. Maybe he could slip some into Dad's morning cereal.

Then later, in mid-December, the nightly rituals changed again. A new cable network began showing nothing but magnified views of the earth's far reaches, using big telescopes left useless by the Change; and Dad would sit in his lumpy chair, wearing ugly sweaters and the same old sweatpants, drinking cocoa while the views switched again and again. The scenes weren't as crisp as real life, since only a fraction of the light was reflected. But the network was popular, letting people see things that in the past could be seen only by astronauts. Rainforests, cut and standing. Sprawling cities and orderly croplands. Endless reaches of blue ocean. Mountains and rivers and glaciers and deserts. And sometimes, now and again, neighborhoods like this one—tiny homes on tiny lots set along curling little roads.

Ten o'clock meant the news. Dad would make Cornell watch. Why, he couldn't tell. But he'd come out of his room, sit on the floor, pretending to pay attention. News was boring. Dad was boring, talking about everything and nothing at the same time. Wasn't it sad? All the excitement that people had felt was now past. Lost. The wonder had been washed out of their faces, Dad claimed, and he wished he could bring it back again. One night, a couple days before Christmas, the lead story was about a double murder; and while Cornell watched images of bloody pavement and body bags, his father spoke about Antarctica. "It's visible in the morning, before the sun gets too high." Oblivious to the carnage, the old man said, "All that pure white ice . . . it's beautiful. . . . "

What did he want?

"Come look at it with me. Will you?"

"No," said Cornell. Then, "No, thank you."

Dad nodded, not looking sad or happy. Or surprised. Maybe he hadn't heard his son, swallowing before remarking, "Maybe *they* just wanted us to be more aware of one another. Do you suppose? The Great Change . . . it's their way of building us a mirror for ourselves . . . what do you think . . . ?"

Cornell wanted to be alone. Nothing but alone, now and forever.

Please.

THE RUMOR BEGAN NOWHERE AND EVERYWHERE, POSSESSING ITS own vigorous life, and everyone wanted to believe it. It was almost a year since the Change, and supposedly a shuttle full of diplomats had gone up to space station Freedom. They were meeting a delegation of aliens, and there would be an announcement coming. Soon. People spoke of a zero-gee dinner and a great silver spaceship docked with Freedom; and after dinner, the diplomats—human and not—had gone on board the mother ship for dessert and final negotiations. A new union of worlds would come on the first anniversary. The rumor was specific in its details, including promises of new technologies and other aid. Tabloids wrote of little else, and even CNN dropped spicy tidbits—confidential shuttle flights, and so on. Of course the president made public denials. No government had heard so much as a peep from extraterrestrials. The silver object near Freedom was part of ongoing research—an elongated balloon housing delicate instruments—and the leaked photographs had been misinterpreted. Like everyone, the president hungered to meet with whoever was responsible for the new sky. But patience was the watchword, and she begged for the public's indulgence and continued support.

Regardless of her noise, the anniversary had a celebratory air. That August day saw people taking vacation time and sick leave. Groups clustered near TVs, counting down to the fateful moment—10:11 P.M. CDT—when *something* was bound to happen.

"Where are you going?" asked Dad, dinner finished and the dishes waiting to be stacked in the washer. "Cornell—?"

"Bike riding," he replied, not quite snapping.

The old man seemed unsure how to respond. The business of chores was something new, something imposed when Cornell complained about the general mess. But tonight his father decided to say nothing, ignoring the revolt. Which made Cornell a little angry. At least the old man could growl, making him feel as if he was worming out of something important.

"Ride safe—"

"Bye." Cornell trotted outside. Todd and Lane were waiting on the island, as promised. "Where to?" asked Cornell.

"The lots," said Todd.

They rolled out of the cul-de-sac, down the hill and right on the through street, over the ridge and onto the unbuilt area. Weeds stood tall and brown behind the curbs. Millions of bugs buzzed in unison. Rain had washed fill earth over the pavement, leaving sloppy deltas where little weeds struggled to make do. Cornell looked at their houses from behind. He paused, foot on a curb, wondering what Dad was doing. He'd been acting odd lately, even odder than normal: moody and distant, often muttering to himself in a voice too soft to understand. In secret ways, Cornell worried about him. He thought it was the aliens and the time of year. Maybe the old man was scared that the aliens wouldn't come. Which had to seem pretty shitty, what with them showing everyone the new sky and all. . . .

"Race me?" said Todd.

"Sure."

They decided on a course. Men with surveying equipment had come through last week, leaving the landscape dotted with little flags, aggressively red and snapping in the hot wind. From the hill's crest they could see where the curling street ended in a cul-de-sac; their finish line was the cul-de-sac's mouth, it was decided. Lane started them, raising an arm—"GO!"—and the race beginning with a sloppy spray of gravel.

There was a pleasant sense of danger. Cornell knew the street, but not perfectly. Had the last rains spread more gravel? More earth? Tires skidded; Todd pulled ahead. Cornell had left his helmet at home, but he decided to press the pace anyway, pumping his legs and cutting Todd off at the next curve.

He was almost at the finish line when he lost control.

Cutting across a new delta, he went airborne, and when he hit the ground he was pitched forward, his front tire kissing the curb and the weeds reaching for him as he tumbled into a limp, breathless heap. For a long while he lay stunned, his body taking an accounting of itself. Then someone asked, "Are you hurt?" and it wasn't Todd. A face appeared above him. An adult; a stranger. A woman, Cornell realized, her hair cut short and the mouth and eyes all smiling. "You should be careful," she coached, "and wear a helmet, too."

"I know."

Todd and Lane stood nearby, watching the woman touch him.

"Anything broken? No?"

He felt embarrassed, more than anything.

"Can you stand?"

The woman wasn't of any particular age, pretty but for no particular reason, and she seemed amused by everything, starting to laugh to herself. She wore jeans and a light shirt, no bra visible, and when Cornell stared at her, he felt a sudden infatuation, powerful and startling.

"What are you doing here?" snapped Todd.

The woman extended a finger, touching Cornell on the nose, on its tip, and said, "I'm walking through, just wandering." Sure enough, behind her was a backpack propped against sunflowers. "Is this your property? Am I trespassing?"

She was asking Cornell.

He tried to speak, no breath in him.

She turned and pointed. "What do the little flags mean?"

Todd said, "They're going to build houses soon."

But she must have known that, Cornell realized. She was playing a game, letting them sound smart. Another poke at his nose, then a bright laugh. "Know any places to camp?" Then she lifted her pack and adjusted the straps, her shirt pressed against her chest. The boys could see nothing else. "Ride carefully," she advised Cornell; he watched her leave them, watched her walk and thinking that she was a magical person. Enchanted. *Perfect.*

She vanished among the sunflowers. Cornell picked up his bike and checked it over, making sure the brakes worked and the wheels turned.

"Let's follow her," said Todd.

Lane squirmed and said, "Why?"

"Why not?"

But she's gone, Cornell thought. She was magical and could vanish at will. Which was why he said, "All right." They couldn't bother what wasn't there anymore.

Yet the woman hadn't vanished. She had cut over to the next empty street, walking alone, face down and her rump moving. Cornell felt a little weak and strange. He couldn't stop staring. And as he rolled past her, glancing sideways, he saw the silhouettes of her breasts and a knowing smile and wink, and he fell again. His bike slammed straight into a curb, and he was down, bleeding and in love, feeling nothing but a floating sensation and her kneeling over him again, asking him:

"Should you be riding these things? Because you don't seem very good at it."

The woman walked away for the last time, and the boys wandered home when it was dusk, Cornell washing his bloody elbow in the Underhills' bathroom sink. Then it was night, and everyone was outside, gathered around the island. Mr. Lynn was with his wife, and she was enormous, due any day, carrying twins. The Tuckers sat side by side, Mr. Tucker suffering from some vague ailment that left his head shaking and his senses dulled. Mrs. Pete played with Todd's little sister, tickling her and both of them giggling. Dad's expression was tight and hard to read. It was Pete who was reminiscing about last year, about how they'd spent the day investigating one of the mysterious glass disks. He wasn't a natural storyteller, and the narrative jerked along, sometimes halting altogether. Cornell became frustrated. More and more he wondered how the world could hold together every day, when the adults were so obviously bad at doing almost everything.

Most of them, at least.

Big TVs had been brought into the front yards. CNN was keeping vigil. Smiling, nervous announcers counted down the seconds as if it was New Year's Eve, and billions of eyes turned skyward.

And nothing happened.

Groans. Uneasy laughter. A few soft murmurs of, "Oh, well."

The adults drank and returned to their party. The boys played basketball on the Underhills' driveway. CNN ran features about the world one year after the Change. The economic upswing; the renewed eco-movement; and the surge of interest in science. The new Cosmic Event Agency was funding every kind of project. Hyperplanes were studying the zone of transition. A lunar city was being built, telescopes trained on the stars and earth. Biologists were watching bird migrations, pleased to find that the flocks could still navigate. There was even a branch of the CEA which investigated UFO sightings. A small branch. Despite rumors and the expectations, not many people were reporting lights that couldn't be explained away with ease.

The basketball game was ended. CNN broke away for commercials, hemorrhoids and Hyundais; Dad began to talk, his voice sudden and dark. "What I think," he told everyone, "I think we were given our chance. A great, grand opportunity. *They* showed us the Change, and they watched us react, and we didn't. Not like they hoped, we didn't. Which is why we haven't heard from them."

There was silence and a tangible confusion.

When did you decide this? Cornell wondered. He watched the narrow face become focused. Determined.

"Sure, we throw a few dollars at the problem. But the aliens . . . they were hoping for much more—"

"What are you saying?" growled Pete.

Dad swallowed, then said, "People are stupid."

Neighbors glanced at each other.

"Oh, sure," said Dad, "we were fascinated for a day or two. But then the novelty wore thin. Nothing of substance has changed."

Cornell was close enough to smell liquor on his father's breath.

"The greatest event in history, and it's old news now."

The man never drank. Cornell found himself scrambling for a cause. The anniversary? Because Mom hadn't come home? Maybe Dad had expected her, even when he told Cornell to be patient. They never talked about Mom anymore. Why not? Was disappointment eating at him—?

"We aren't worthy," said the old man.

And Pete told him, "You don't mean it."

"I sure as hell do."

People began to move, picking up chairs and other belongings. Mr. Lynn asked for help with the dolly and his TV. Everyone avoided Dad's black gaze. Cornell felt embarrassment, and he was outraged, wished he could vanish with the blink of his eyes.

"People are fools," Dad muttered.

"No," Pete replied. "But I'm wondering about you."

A pressure built inside Cornell, steam mixed with acids.

Pete told Dad, "You've had too many, I think."

Now everyone knew he was drunk. Shame washed over Cornell.

"What we need to do," said Pete, "is get back on the road. How long has it been?"

Almost a month. Cornell hadn't gone on that trip, staying with the Underhills for three days. And had a fine time, too. They were normal people, and happy.

"A long trip," Pete promised.

"But *they* aren't here anymore," Dad responded, wiping his hands on his trousers and then lifting them, looking at his palms as if to see answers written on them. "They've abandoned us. I'm sure of it."

It was incredible to hear. Even if Dad was drunk and disappointed, it was awful. And despite his embarrassment and shame, Cornell found himself sorry for the man, some part of him trying to think of a phrase or deed that would help make everything better.

"We're ignorant, stupid creatures, and we deserve to be ignored."

Cornell had the basketball. He retreated to the island's other side, bouncing the ball, filling the air with its ringing rubbery sound. Nobody was left with Dad, save Pete. Pete got to his feet, offering to take Dad home. The two men began to wrestle, the drunken one weak and ineffectual; and Cornell bounced the ball harder, his friends standing near him, watching him and pretending nothing was more fascinating than the ball's violent rise and fall.

"He misses the old days," Pete told Cornell.

Cornell avoided the man's gaze.

"You have to understand." Pete came closer, making sure he was seen. "Everything's changed for him. I think that's the problem." Didn't he *know?* "I can't do everything for him. I don't have time or the power."

"So?" said Cornell, almost whispering.

Pete scratched his chin, whiskers making a dry sound under his fingers. "Pretty tough being your age, isn't it? Full of yourself, growing an inch an hour . . . and no time for fathers. . . . "

No time? That wasn't true. Dad was always with him; privacy was impossible in their little house. Other parents had normal jobs, and they worked almost every day—

"Just try to talk with him, can you?"

It was late September, and they were in Pete's backyard. Past his chain-link fence, big new houses were springing from the raw earth, castlelike turrets and fancy weather vanes beneath the faint white glare of Antarctica. Only a fraction of the lots were sold, but already this didn't feel like their neighborhood. The new homes were intruders; they brought a kind of claustrophobia.

"We'll both talk to him," said Pete, "and help him. Whatever it is, we can get him to talk it through. We owe him that much."

And Cornell snapped, "Why do you care?"

The question had an impact, surprising both of them. Pete set his jaw and seemed to ponder. Then he asked his own question. "Why do I help your dad with his work?"

"He pays you."

"A fair wage, but not a fortune." He paused. "What's the main reason?"

"To find aliens." Only was that the main reason? Cornell heard his words and realized he wasn't sure—

"Actually," said Pete, "it's because your mom vanished. That's why."

And Cornell said, "Yeah?"

The dark face blinked, and he said, "I was fond of her. And when she vanished, I was the one to help put your dad back together again. But you don't remember that, do you?"

Not at all.

"He came to our house and told us . . . well, about the abduction. And he cried. I've never seen any grown person, man or woman, cry as hard as he did that day."

"So?"

Pete blinked and said, "So I started going with him, helping him travel. Helping him carry. And after a year or two, I realized what a wonderful person he could be. Generous and open. Childlike, really. We could all learn lessons from Nathan."

Cornell moved his feet, and he snorted.

"I know, he's difficult. At times more than difficult, I know. But that's because he looks at everything differently. You know that."

Too well, he thought.

"Do you remember Mrs. Pete taking care of you? While we were on the road?"

Sort of. A warm blur of half-memories came and left.

"For a little while, she got to play mother with you. And both of us have always, always looked at you as the closest thing to a son."

Cornell drummed his hands against his thighs, hard enough to sting. His temper surged—his mother's temper, he remembered—and he heard himself shouting, "Leave me alone. Get out of my business."

Pete blinked and said nothing.

"It's my business. Our business. You stay away."

"If you need to talk, any time—"

Cornell didn't hear the rest. He turned and ran to the fence between their yards, grasping the top pipe with both hands and neatly, almost gracefully, vaulting over into the long grass, his feet kicking up nameless little bugs that flew and settled and flew again.

He fought with Dad all winter.

The worst fight came on the heels of a long hard snow, neither one of them able to escape the tiny house. With nowhere to go, Cornell sat in the living room and watched TV, and Dad stayed in the basement, classical music making the floor shake. It was like being sick, only worse. Sickness insulated a person, diminishing capacities and compressing time. But here Cornell had to live every damned second, and worse, he discovered that Dad hadn't bought enough food. There was exactly one choice for dinner—pepperoni pizza in a colorful, frosted-over box—and he put it on a cookie sheet, then into the oven. From the kitchen's window the world was made of blowing snow and black skies, and he stood at the window until the timer went *bing*.

Dad heard it. He emerged from the basement, ruining the solitude, a faint whiff of bourbon clinging to him.

Cornell removed the pizza and put a slice on one old plate.

Dad blinked, then said, "Pizza," as if he'd just learned the word. He found his own plate and slice. The music from the basement quit with a flourish of notes. Then it was just them, the tiny kitchen warmed by the oven, and the wind making a steady far-off sound. The old man dabbed at his crumbs with a dampened fingertip and licked it clean. God, Cornell hated when he did that. Dad stopped, seemingly reading his thoughts, eyes frowning and then the smooth voice saying the most unlikely word.

"Love," he said.

Cornell blinked, a chill spreading through him.

Then Dad said, "Love," again, with force, nodding and dabbing, licking and continuing with his point. "The alien worlds, wherever they reside . . . they must be rich with love. They must have a wondrous sense of purpose and union. We can't imagine it. People, I think . . . we just sip at love, in tiny sweet doses—"

More crazy talk, thought Cornell.

"—and we can't even control when we'll sip, or for how long." A pause, then he said, "I used to argue that *they* were superior because of their intellects, their technology. But their greatness . . . now I can see that it comes from their emotions. First and always. And what emotion is larger than love?"

This was a mutated version of the old utopia speech, and Cornell was sick of it, almost physically sick, snapping at him, "You don't know anything about aliens. All these years, and you haven't learned anything."

Dad swallowed, eyes distant. Simple.

Cornell wanted a reaction. He grabbed the old man's plate, shattering it against the table, thick ceramic shards everywhere and both of them stunned.

Then Dad rose and tried shouting, his voice never quite loud. "What do you need? Please just tell me, what do you need?"

A fair question. Cornell groaned and said, "You embarrass me."

"I what?"

"Embarrass me."

"Since when?"

And Cornell couldn't think of an example. Not now, not this quickly. Instead he said, "You're crazy," and pulled his hands across his dampened face. "Everyone knows it. You're the flying saucer nut—"

"What have I done?" the man whispered. His eyes slipped

sideways, face sickly white, and Cornell felt victorious for all of ten seconds. Then, summoning a vague resolve, Dad declared, "They are my life's work. Or don't you understand that?"

Cornell looked at the floor.

Dad breathed, breathed again, then went downstairs, feet sounding on the wooden steps.

Then Cornell picked up the shards, throwing them away and putting the last of the pizza into an old margarine tub and it into the refrigerator. He felt worse by the moment, and sorry, but he couldn't think how to apologize. He didn't dare try. This temper was a living thing inside him, and he was afraid of what it might do next. Better to wait, he decided. I'll say something nice tomorrow, he promised himself. Then he sat at the table again, watching the snow falling, flakes melting against the warm glass and the tiny beads of new water coalescing into jerky little rivers.

The girl was in his homeroom class—not pretty as much as willing—and they used the last half-built house behind the cul-de-sac. The big room was either the master bedroom or a family room. The outside walls were finished, the inner ones just a skeleton of clean yellow pine. It didn't take Cornell long to do more than ever before. The girl used her hand, and she shuddered when he did the same to her, her moans loud and self-involved and a little frightening. He knew enough to hold her afterward, saying things like, "Thank you," and "Nice," and pretending he was comfortable on the springy plywood floor.

It was evening, in April, a few months before the second anniversary of the Change. People still spoke about the sky and aliens, in public and private, but opinions had hardened over time. The Change had nothing to do with humanity, said some; it was an act of God to humble man, said others; and there always were people who believed there had been contacts with aliens, but in secret. Who knew what was true? Cornell had made the rebellious stand of taking no opinion, at least none he'd admit to or make coherent. Let others make fools of themselves. "I won't say a word," he promised himself.

The girl stood and pulled up her pants, asking, "Which is yours?"

Which house, she meant. He joined her and pointed, noticing the light in the kitchen. Past it was Alaska, still in daylight and white with clouds and snow; and for an instant Cornell forgot not to be amazed with the scene, feeling that kick of the heart before he could breathe again.

The girl asked, "Are your folks together?"

He said, "No," and then added, "My mom's gone." He wouldn't say *died.* It was another recent promise to himself, to dilute the lies whenever possible. To be a little less dishonest.

But she asked, "Gone where?"

"I don't know."

She said, "Too bad."

Except she didn't sound sorry. Cornell looked at her face in the bad light, wishing she was prettier.

"My folks are together," she said, smiling to herself. "They're doctors. They make a ton." Then she glanced at him, saying, "Isn't your dad a scientist?"

"No," he growled.

"But isn't he some kind of researcher?"

"Not much anymore."

"I heard he works for the CEA."

Cornell laughed. "Who told you that?"

"I don't remember. Why?"

He didn't answer, didn't look at her.

She straightened, then said, "Sorry."

Coaxing her back to the floor, he got her to neck until she said, "So, do you miss your mom?"

"Sometimes."

"Think about her?"

All the time, in all the practiced ways, but he wouldn't let himself say it. And he wouldn't admit to anyone that he wished he was with her, even if she lived on some dead old moon. Life with her had to be better than life here. That's what he believed, at least when it suited him. But for now he simply shrugged and said, "I think about her, sure."

He felt better when he was unknown. He felt safe then.

The girl pushed closer, and a cool wind blew through the open windows, stirring up sawdust that smelled good in the back of his nose. She said, "Hold me," and he did, one hand under her shirt until she said, "No more of that." They were still and quiet, and Cornell was thinking about love, how people could only sip it and how they never knew where love would find them. When he fell in love, someday, he would tell the story of his mother. But this wasn't love and it could never be, nice as it seemed, and suddenly the girl asked him, "What are you thinking?"

"About stars," he lied.

"Yeah?"

Cornell nodded and said, "I miss them, sometimes." And he wiped at his eyes once, then again, not crying but needing to pull the moisture out of them. A third time, and a fourth.

"MR. NOVAK? HELP ME FOR A MINUTE?"

Cornell was climbing out of his car—a stubby Chinese model that he'd gotten last year, third-hand—and the voice seemed to fall from the bright, slightly smoky air. He saw Mrs. Pete standing on her perfect yard, her big-brimmed hat half-obscuring her face, one hand holding a spun-cellulose can of beer. Again she asked, "Help me?"

"Okay."

"There's a shelf I can't reach, back in the garage. I need my Dutch oven. I'm making a quick-and-dirty stew for tonight."

Another Change Day; another party for the cul-de-sac. Cornell said, "Sure," and remembered last year. The new people, the Guthries, had brought an enormous inedible ham. And the Lynns fought. Or was that the year before?

"Were you working?"

"Yeah." He'd done the early shift at the pool, lifeguarding for a herd of hyperactive kids. Todd got him the job, and he hated it. He hated the sun and noise and the responsibility of watching so many bodies. This was a boring summer, and he'd look forward to fall except that school was just a different flavor of boring.

"You've managed quite a tan, Mr. Novak. I'm jealous."

It was teasing, the way she said his name. They were inside

the big garage, her voice echoing and the air cool; she pointed to the oven, twice saying, "Thanks for your help."

He hadn't done anything yet.

"Pete hid the big ladder. There's just this shaky thing." A pause. "Can you manage?"

Cornell was tall, having long ago outgrown his father. He wore his hair in the modern style, three little pigtails ending with synthetic diamonds. He wanted a beard, but it was too soon. He had fought with Dad about topical hormone treatments, finally dropping the idea. It always was like that. Everything was a fight, and he never quite won. They'd have long stretches where a kind of stasis was reached—not peace, but at least a quietness—and then everything went sour, usually surprising both of them.

"Reach it?"

Cornell had the oven by its handles. It was designed for a sonicwave oven, a popular Christmas gift two or three years ago. It wasn't heavy, but it was clumsy to carry, what with his position and the shivering ladder. And Mrs. Pete wouldn't help, standing to one side while telling him, "You just saved my life."

Cornell managed to safely climb down.

"Drag it inside for me?"

He hadn't been inside the Petes' house for months, maybe since last New Year's. It might have been the longest absence in his life, which was strange to consider. The house's roominess and silence were unchanged, and it was astonishingly bright, big windows and skylights facing west. The air smelled of commercial scents until Mrs. Pete stepped close, sharing her beer breath.

Cornell pretended not to notice.

She confessed, "I don't belong on ladders."

"Glad to help."

A wistful smile, then she asked, "Want one?"

She took two beers from the refrigerator, and he said, "Okay." He didn't like the flavor, but he liked the wickedness. Mrs. Pete watched him sipping, and she talked, and he sat on a stool with the kitchen counter stabbing him in the back. When would Dad come home? he was wondering. Cornell was going out tonight with a girl from the pool. Had he told Dad? Probably not. "Where were they going?" Cornell had to ask. Halfway across the state, Mrs. Pete told him. Some idiot claimed to have seen aliens cavorting in his front yard. Just like old times, wasn't it?

Cornell shrugged his shoulders.

"I miss the old days," she claimed, almost laughing. "I didn't believe, but things were exciting . . . and Pete had a lot of fun. . . . "

"I suppose."

She paused, her breathing audible, wet and quick. With a deeper voice, she said, "I do like my house."

He didn't respond, unsure of her point.

"I use to hate it," she confessed. "All these rooms and nobody here but the two of us. But you know all that. About my complaints. My threats. Whatever Pete called them. . . . "

Never. Pete never mentioned anything so personal, and she had to know it. Pete was nothing if not intensely private, and what was she thinking?

"I should have collected dogs." Mrs. Pete spoke slowly, with drunken precision. "Except, frankly, I've never approved of women who keep beasts in lieu of children. Talking to them, dressing them in baby clothes . . . that's rather disgusting, I think. . . . "

Cornell said nothing.

And she breathed deeply, once and again, then stepped closer without touching him. One hand lifted as if she would touch him, but then it hung in space, its destination forgotten. She looked more worn than old, sunlight making wrinkles look deep and the thick hair shot full of white strands. And then she was crying, suddenly and without sound, and Cornell was angry with her for crying. He felt embarrassed, then repulsed, her hand finding the will to clasp hold of his shoulder and the deep, old-woman voice asking, "Can't you once call me Elaine?"

The free shoulder shrugged.

"I should have tried mothering you. At least more than I did."

"What do you mean?"

"You know," she said, "you're the loveliest little man."

Cornell felt distant. Unreachable.

"Not as pretty as your mother, but close."

Then he halfway pushed her, not meaning to be abrupt but adrenaline giving him speed. And he moaned, telling her, "Get away," with a voice harsher than intended.

She looked at him, eyes unblinking and red, her mouth set, and suddenly the crying was replaced with something worse. There was a resolve, clear and frightening, and she said, "She called you Corny, didn't she?"

He didn't answer, and she said:

"She thought it was funny, that name." A fire seemed to blaze up in the woman's eyes. "Oh, it's so awful about your mother, isn't it? Taken away by aliens. Kidnapped. Stolen."

"What do you mean?"

"And a beautiful girl. The sort of girl every woman fears, absolutely fears, because women know her at a glance. By instinct." A pause, an odd glance skyward. "Because women know her in some way men can't. Which makes her worse, of course. Not that I didn't like your mother. Don't misunderstand. Pam was a sweet creature, in her fashion—"

"What are you saying?"

A theatrical sigh. "What am I saying? That men went crazy around her. She had a way of enchanting them, making them fall in love. Like Pete did. And I was jealous, I suppose. He'd stare at her, and what could I do? I might as well have been jealous of his food, as much chance as he had to ignore her."

Pete had mentioned being fond of Mom. When had he—?

"You men are so simple. So sentimental. Do you know that, Corny?" She tilted her head, sipped a beer and said, "Like children, you are."

He said nothing.

She told him, "Your father wept buckets, telling us how the aliens had abducted Pam and how lost he felt. I think he believed it, in his fashion. Maybe even Pete believed him. Sometimes I think that's why he started helping Nathan, hoping to find Pam along the road somewhere." A long pause. "Who knows what he believes now? I don't. He's only my husband. Who knows what anyone thinks?"

"What are you saying?" Cornell muttered.

And her face said she was enjoying this business, extracting as much relish from it as possible. The grin broadened into a full smile, none of her bitterness extinguished. This involved more than Cornell, more than today. It was about jealousy and the years, he realized; and she leaned close enough to make him taste her beer breath, saying, "Oh, Corny. You still haven't figured out what must have happened."

"What must have—?"

"An abduction? By aliens?" She violently shook her head, asking him, "Does that sound real? Corny? Do those impossible things really sound true?"

It was almost dark, and the figure was backlit by the single streetlamp, standing in the doorway and aware of Cornell, perhaps even seeing him sitting on the floor against the far wall. The thin face tilted one way, then another. Cornell thought of a simple creature trying to make sense of something novel, unexpected. And he felt a remarkable surge of hatred, his heart kicking and his hands closing into fists.

"Is that you?" asked his father. Then, "Son?" Then, "Why are you sitting in the dark?"

Cornell said, "Thinking."

"Thinking?" The old man sounded puzzled but hopeful, stepping closer and again tilting his head, changing perspectives. "What about, son?"

Cornell bit his lower lip, tasting blood.

"The sighting," said Dad, "was nothing. Too bad. A shaky witness, I think addicted to one of the new drugs. I may start demanding urine tests with my interviews. . . ."

The boy felt an unexpected pity, and that was worse than hatred or scorn. Pity delayed what he wanted to do, making him stretch it out. "I was thinking about Mom," he allowed, taking an enormous breath and holding it for as long as possible.

"Were you . . . ?"

Exhaling, he asked, "How did she vanish? Tell me again."

Dad came closer, the features of his face resolving. A tentative smile became a questioning frown, and he told the old story with haste and authority, almost through it when he realized that his audience didn't believe him. Disbelief was a shock, and he paused as if physically struck. The mouth came open. "What is it, son?"

"She left you. That's what really happened."

The old man wouldn't speak or move.

Cornell was amazed to hear his own voice, level and dry, in complete control of itself. "There wasn't any abduction. Was there?"

Dad tilted his head and held it at an odd angle. His mouth moved, no sound coming from it.

"She saw other men. Before. Always."

"Who told you this?"

"I wasn't supposed to go with you two. But my babysitters were going out to dinner, and you had to take me—"

"Elaine told you? Is that it?"

He didn't care what the man knew. He said, "Yes," and then, "She's guessing. Mom didn't tell her anything. But Elaine . . . she told me how you and Mom would fight . . . how she found men when you were on the road . . . how she was—"

"Difficult," Dad moaned. "But she had a difficult childhood, you see. I knew I had to be patient—"

"—and you lied to me."

"No. Don't say that." The voice was too large, sudden and furious. "I didn't know what she was planning. I thought . . . thought we could have a nice evening, for a change . . . but she'd taken money from our accounts and arranged for a ride . . . from a younger man. . . . "

Cornell rose to his feet, his own anger huge and radiant. He felt as if the room should be lit up with the emotions.

"You fell asleep," said Dad. "You may have seen headlights, or you dreamed . . . I don't know . . . but when you woke and I told you she was gone, you were the one who said Mom was abducted. You were."

"And you let me believe it?"

The old man didn't answer him, shaking his head while saying, "A difficult person, but I kept thinking . . . I kept hoping she'd come to her senses, come home again." A long pause, then he said, "I had reasons for what I did and didn't do."

Cornell grabbed his pigtails and pulled, and a hard black moan slipped from his mouth, and he pulled harder, making pain.

Dad said, "Listen," and said nothing.

The linchpin of Cornell's life—his mother's abduction—was a fabrication. For these last hours, sitting alone, he had imagined his father denying Mrs. Pete's suspicions, if only to keep the lie up and moving, allowing him time to adapt. But Dad was doing nothing to deny the charges. Nothing. Cornell was an idiot. Anger wobbled and fell inward, slicing through him. He was pathetic. He hadn't agreed with Dad in years, not about anything, yet he'd never doubted the story about Mom. He had his memory, false and thoroughly practiced, and how could he not trust himself?

"I had good reasons," Dad kept whispering.

I want to die, thought Cornell.

"For everything, reasons."

Or I can kill him, he realized. A murderous instinct was building, and Cornell had to leave, had to save both of them. He started for the door and kicked shadows and the bulky old magnetometer. Then he cursed, kneeled and flung the machine through the front window, shattering glass bright with earthshine.

Dad said something too soft to understand.

Cornell was gone.

And the man spoke to the empty room, saying, "Reasons," once again, with the mildest voice, tilting his head at an odd angle and holding it motionless for a long moment.

Dinner was done. The party's mood was more happy than not. Several people said it was a lovely evening, almost perfect; then came the shouts and the breaking glass and the Novak boy running from his house. Neighbors paused and stared. Pete was standing among them. The boy climbed into his car, its tiny engine whining and smoke squirting from the tailpipe. He rolled fast out of the driveway, never glancing backward. The Lynns grabbed their girls, pulling them close. Todd called to Cornell, waving his arms and jumping up. Then Cornell accelerated, cranking the wheel and driving fast and close around the concrete island.

Pete and others jumped back. Lawn chairs were crushed. Tires screeched, the hot air smelling of exhaust. And the boy went once more around the island, finally straightening out and jumping the curb, crossing the Guthries' lawn and uprooting their mailbox before dropping hard onto the pavement again, gaining velocity, dropping out of sight.

Everyone listened for another crash, hearing none.

Then Pete heard giggling—close, peculiar—and he saw his wife laughing at the ground. She'd dropped their Dutch oven, uneaten stew everywhere. He knew she'd been drinking again. A premonition made him uneasy, suspicious . . . and he looked at Nathan's house, his friend standing on his little porch with arms raised overhead. His friend didn't look sad or angry, or anything. He merely looked insubstantial, as if any strong light would wash him away.

First things first, he told himself.

No truer rule existed in life.

"First things first," he whispered; and he walked toward his friend, poor Nathan gazing upward with fragile eyes, nothing to see but a tiny indifferent sky.

# A NEW WORLD

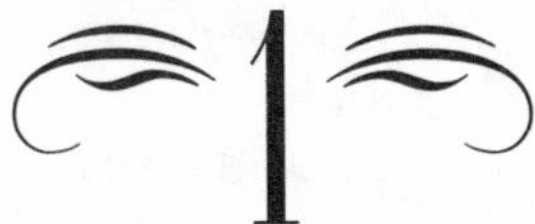

"THIS IS ALL QUITE PRELIMINARY, MR. NOVAK. WE'LL BE ASKING each other questions, trying to understand ourselves a little better. Clearing the air, so to speak."

"All right."

"Are you comfortable?"

"Mostly."

"Mostly." The woman repeated the word with an amused expression—a solid, no-nonsense face topped with thick gray hair—then she cocked her head as if examining Cornell from the slightly changed perspective, eyes pale and unblinking. On her desk was a simple name placard that read *F. Smith.* "Would you like anything to drink?" asked F. Smith.

"No, thank you."

"Coffee?"

"No."

"Tea? Hot or cold?"

Cornell shook his head.

"Or something carbonated?"

When he said, "Thanks, no," it occurred to him this was part of the test. She was pressing him for a purpose. How did they measure responses? The office was neat and officious, belonging to no one. No holos of a loving family; no decorative touches connected with F. Smith. Were sensors buried in his chair? Microcameras in the walls? He didn't feel nervous or even particularly curious. His curiosity had been exhausted by six days of tests, the last three days taxing and oftentimes incoherent.

"Perhaps bottled water?"

Cornell grinned. "If it makes you happy."

The woman blinked. "I'm just trying to make you comfortable, Mr. Novak. If you'd like anything—"

"Tell me what's going on."

The woman shut her eyes, and for an instant, Cornell wondered if she was alive. Robotics had made huge advances of late. Was some complex algorithm playing out inside some laser-light mind? But then she began to laugh, moderately amused, and he guessed that no machine could duplicate that sound.

"Perhaps if you tell me what you know," she said. "Perhaps then I might be able to explain this to your satisfaction."

Cornell licked his lips, suddenly thirsty.

"I saw your ads," he began. "Good money for testing pharmaceuticals on healthy subjects. Flu medicines, anticancer agents. Those sorts of things." He shrugged his shoulders. "Three days of tests, and for my time and body you squirted a fair amount of electronic money into my account. Then you asked if I'd like to stay a little longer, test out some antioxidants—"

"Slowing the aging process, yes."

"It had a kick, whatever you gave me. I haven't slept a normal night in three. Dreaming, waking up. Crazy dreams mixed in with your crazy little tests. Personality inventories and coordination studies and the rest of it, and someone always watching."

She softly laughed. "You sound paranoid."

"*Am* paranoid. Am."

"I'm sorry if the medicines are a bother—"

"They're not even medicines." He breathed and promised, "I'm not gullible. That's what I'm telling you. I'm not, and I doubt if you'd piggyback one study on top of another. That's not good science."

She leaned forward, elbows perched on her desk and the thick little hands meshed together, chin on top of them. "What else?"

"The size of this place." He glanced out the single window, sunshine golden and warm. "I've seen a square mile, but that's just a slice of it. Ground traffic moves east, and there's open country north and south. Untended country. Pretty good for a corporation that didn't exist twenty years ago."

"We've been fortunate," F. Smith allowed.

"Particularly when you consider you don't have big sales from any drug. Particularly when you know what this land has to cost. What do they say? 'They're not making any more land, and there's never been enough of California.' "

"Is that what they say?"

A shrug.

"But we've also got an electronics division, a gene-tailoring division, plus a general research staff."

"Oh, I'm sure."

Again she cocked her head. "You act suspicious," she remarked, sounding pleased. Appreciative. "What do the clues mean, Mr. Novak?"

"Mean? Tangent Incorp. appears out of nowhere, possessing unlimited cash and a bunch of semi-new products. Its corporate headquarters are built in a populated region, and it spends a fortune advertising for subjects. For secretaries. For lab techs and janitors. The average unemployment rate in California is seventeen percent, which constitutes a huge resource." He rose to his feet, thinking that he'd make them work to measure his galvanic responses. "The guards at the gates? And downstairs? They look military to me. And you've got state-of-the-art security systems, too." He paused, then asked, "What do you think I'm thinking?"

"You tell me," she challenged.

He looked out the window, oaks and green lawns stretching toward the glittery field-fence, shaped energies causing the sunshine to twist and fragment into countless wavering rainbows.

"What's it mean, Cornell?"

He said, "A government operation, naturally. Which isn't just my thinking. The big rumor among my fellow subjects is that the government is feeding Tangent money and business."

"Is that so?"

"That you're making biological weapons, in case of war with Brazil. Or maybe Japan."

The woman made no comment, her tongue pressed against her cheek.

"But that's too simple. Too ordinary. Shrewd people might plant that paranoid story in order to deflect suspicions."

"An interesting logic," she conceded. "Go on."

"The Pentagon doesn't have this kind of budget." He walked away from the window, saying, "But the CEA could pay for the show with its petty cash. This must be some kind of proving ground, I'm guessing. A testing facility. You want recruits, and you're looking for something specific."

"Yes?"

"My compadres? I've noticed similarities."

She placed both hands flat on the desktop, something in her eyes thoroughly satisfied.

"We don't have close families. Most of us change jobs too often, though we're a bright lot. Healthy. Younger than not. Free of drug habits and mental illness." A pause. A sigh. "Obviously you're hiring from a select pool. The personality tests? What you want is a specific flavor of person—"

"Flavor?" she said, intrigued by the word. "And what flavor are you, Mr. Novak?"

He sat in a different chair. "You gave us a test yesterday," he reported. "I was riding with six others in one of your automated vans, and the van broke down. No warning given. Some people were passive, willing to wait for help to come. But I was in a mood, I guess. I got this other fellow—Jordick Something—to help me pop the hood and the driver's housing. We didn't know shit, but it didn't take much to read the instructions. We bypassed the driver and drove in ourselves."

"Good for you," she offered.

"It was a pretty obvious game." He gave a big shrug. "I figured you wanted something from us. So I did something. That's all."

She watched him.

"How many cameras?"

"About twenty, I believe."

Better. A dose of honesty. "How'd I do? Okay?"

"Above average," she allowed.

And Cornell was pleased. He came close to smiling at the thought of success. But maybe this also was a test, and that's why he didn't let himself smile, staring at her while saying, "Good, then."

"But," said F. Smith, "you did exceptionally well with the virtual reality tests. You nearly matched the record, in fact."

"Which tests?"

Straight white teeth caught the light. "Your dreams? The ones that kept waking you? They were illusions produced by computers. They're the critical tests. Instead of sleeping, you were drugged and experiencing a wide range of novel sights and sensations—"

Cornell recalled pieces. Colored clouds filled with colored lightning; a tar-black river sliding past his feet; a floating sensation with great, slow fish drifting past, eyeing him.

"—and overall, you're in the top three percent of our candidates. Since we offer automatic contracts to anyone in the top twenty percent, you should feel proud. It's quite an accomplishment."

In one dream he had flown . . . he recalled flapping wings fixed to his back . . . and then he'd vomited, right? But in the morning he was back in bed, someone having taken the trouble to soap him off.

And he was in the top three percent?

"Do you have any more questions, Cornell?"

"Yeah." He blinked and settled back into the chair. "Can I have that water now?"

Reading from a screen built into the desk, F. Smith recapitulated much of Cornell's thirty-plus years. Her files were more thorough than any private company could have managed.

There were details that implied footwork, even interviews. Did they do this for each candidate? Or just the ones hired? They might not want too much attention. The image of gray-clad government workers scattering across the United States made him grin; he had never been so important. Then F. Smith asked, "How long since you last saw your father?"

Cornell blinked. "I don't know."

"Does sixteen years sound reasonable?"

He thought of jokes playing off the word *reasonable.* Then he said, "Something like that, I guess."

Pale eyes measured him. "And your mother? She and your father separated when you were four?"

He said nothing.

"You've never married." It wasn't a question. "Your longest relationship has been for a little more than a year."

"Has it?"

"Frequent job changes, oftentimes accepting lower pay." She listed a string of employers, including some that Cornell had forgotten. "Yet you've never been fired. Your work records are good to excellent. And back to your girlfriends . . . a couple of them asked about you. How you are, and that sort of thing."

He guessed which two, seeing faces.

F. Smith cleared her throat. "This is fascinating. I mean it. You grew up chasing flying saucers. Not a normal upbringing, was it? Perhaps this helps account for some of your personality traits. For your skills. You show a certain comfort with novelty."

He said nothing.

"So tell me," she went on, "what do you think we're doing here? You must have your guesses."

"It's about the Change, naturally."

"Naturally."

"And the Architects, I would think."

Her strong face nodded. "What do you think about the Architects?"

That was the newest name for the unseen aliens. They were responsible for twisting cold matter into these bizarre topological shapes, rebuilding the galaxy and presumably the universe. The exotic mathematics had been diluted and debased on a thousand PBS specials. Planets could exist in more than one state, and everyone knew it. Earth and its sisters in this solar system were connected by old-fashioned space. Perhaps other worlds were connected by different, less imaginable avenues.

"People assume you're talking to Architects. I mean the CEA is, the government is. There's a secret launchpad on Wake Island, or somewhere, and alien ships come and go every day or every year." A pause, then he added, "Maybe I'm a recruit, and I'm going into space."

The woman's face was impassive, inert.

"Except I don't think it's happened. You don't talk to them. You'd love the chance, particularly if it means wondrous new technologies. I mean, if someone has to be first—"

"Don't you have any faith in rumors?"

"Not when they smell wrong."

"Do they?"

"And I don't believe in Architects. And I particularly don't think they give a good goddamn about you and me."

"Why did our sky change?"

Cornell sipped his fancy bottled water, then smiled. "I think it just changed back to normal. This is how it's supposed to look."

The surprise seemed genuine. "Really?"

"Our sky was in the shop for repairs. What we saw before? The stars? They're the equivalent of a test pattern. We just happened to evolve while the test pattern was up and humming."

A sober nod, then she asked, "Why do the moon and Mars have stars? And space itself?"

"Dead places. A primitive, simple sky for the dead places." He enjoyed this bullshitting, laughing as he added, "The machinery probably is doing everything automatically, the Architects long dead—"

"And you believe that explanation?"

"As much as any."

"Which means?"

"Not particularly, no."

She read something on the screen, using a fingernail to underscore it.

"I'm not that interested," he continued. "I spent my childhood chasing saucers and fat-headed aliens, and I've thought up every incredible answer for myself. And believed each of them. And what I think now is that what is, is. My opinions don't matter, one way or the other."

She looked up at him, saying nothing.

"What's my job?"

"What do you want to do?"

"Pay me, and I'll try almost anything."

"Almost anything." She echoed the words, then laughed while shaking her head. "First of all, I'm required to give fair warning. If we continue from this point, I'll need signatures on several forms. You'll need to pledge that what you see and hear is private. According to the disclosure laws formulated in 2012, you can be tried and convicted for breaking any trust with your government. Are you listening, Mr. Novak? Anything you learn from this minute, no matter how trivial, is not your knowledge to share. And the agency does have means of knowing—"

"Sure. What's second?"

A grin. "That you shouldn't believe in things as prosaic as flying saucers and little green men. And don't pretend that you've imagined every possible answer when it comes to the Change, either."

He felt a stab of fear, watching that hard certain face.

F. Smith pulled forms from a drawer, a neat officious stack of them, handing them over along with an electronic pen. The pen would record his fingerprints while he wrote, squirting the data into someone's computer. "From now on, you'll stay in a different building, in an entirely different compound . . . and you'll undergo more tests. . . . "

"But I've got the job?"

She blinked and said, "Almost certainly."

He signed the forms, reading as he turned the pages. It was standard stuff written in a tortured legal tongue. The disclosure laws had been intended to stem the flow of technologies to foreign competitors, not to keep knowledge from the citizens. But he needed the money, and part of him was curious, handing back the stack and asking, "What's my salary? Assuming I make the grade."

She gave figures.

And it was more than he had guessed, or hoped. Satisfaction dissolved into worry. "It's a lot of money, Ms. Smith."

"Quite a lot." From her eyes, their tilt and light, he guessed that she made less. "But I'll warn you, and others will, too . . . there is an attrition rate among our participants. We have casualties. Physical and psychological losses—"

"You mean deaths, right?"

"A few. A very few, yes."

He waited for a moment, then asked, "What else?"

"Whatever happens," she promised, "you'll be cared for. We aren't monsters. We are caring, considerate people doing important, astonishing work. And we need trustworthy people with special talents."

Cornell felt his palms become wet.

"Am I clear, Mr. Novak? Cornell?" She tried a smile with those straight white teeth. "Trust is something that flows both ways. Always. But you know that already, don't you?"

NOW THE VIRTUAL REALITY TESTS WERE DONE OPENLY, THE ENtire business handled with a mixture of professionalism and nonchalance. Cornell's attendants dressed him in a sophisticated suit and facemask, glass wires plugged into a clean white wall, then came a long wait while some kind of technical problem was solved or skipped over. All at once, with minimal warning, he saw two distinct images of some desert. Maybe Arizona, but no . . . it only resembled an ordinary place. Double images—one for each eye—and a distant voice, professional and encouraging, was asking him, "How do you feel? Are you all right, Mr. Novak?"

Two images; two vantage points. He reached simultaneously with both hands, trying to grasp the trunk of a tree visible in just one eye. One gloved hand closed on air, the other on old wood polished slick by desert wind. The illusion seemed real enough, much improved over commercial virtual entertainment. A sense of touch was new. And odors, he realized, sniffing hard and a strange living stink inside just one nostril, the machinery able to synthesize smells he couldn't quite name.

"What color is the sky, Mr. Novak?"

Purple, he realized. Faded but definitely purple, and what color was it suppose to be?

"How do you feel, sir?"

Peculiar, that's all. It took him a few moments to realize what they were simulating. Cornell was split into two distinct bodies . . . or rather, his body-halves were detached in some way. He told the attendant his observation, and the response was another question:

"Can you see yourself?"

Clumsily turning both half-bodies, his right eye managed to see a dark figure standing beneath some stout desert tree. He lifted both hands and waved, and the figure waved, facing the wrong direction and just with its left arm. Cornell wrestled with his left side, thinking this was how a stroke victim must feel. He brought the other body around to face himself, and suddenly he could see the first body, his right-side one, standing in the open, on fine gray sand, cloudless purple skies overhead—

"Did you find yourself, sir?"

—and he looked upward, both faces rising.

"Sir?"

He saw a large cool sun. Not Sol, he sensed. This was somewhere else, and again the attendant asked if he could find himself. Cornell ignored the noise, making both bodies walk forward, converging on middle ground.

"How are you, Mr. Novak?"

Faces became apparent, dark and framed with dark fur, nostrils missing and big black eyes blinking. First the clear inner lids closed, then the fleshy outer lids. Each body was covered with fur, three-fingered hands still waving, and these weren't his faces, or human. Cornell paused all at once, feeling a weakness spreading from his legs . . . a momentary warning before he collapsed. . . .

"Here's the bucket," said one attendant. "In case."

"I won't need it," Cornell promised.

The attendant was young and suspicious. "Everyone loses it. That, or we did something wrong."

"What are you doing?"

"Testing." He swallowed, then said, "Observing your nervous system absorbing novel inputs."

Cornell was naked again. He breathed, then asked, "Where was I?"

The attendant said nothing. Others pressed buttons, examined readouts, following some rigorous, much-practiced protocol.

"Is that where I'm going?"

The young man said, "Don't you feel a little sick?"

"No."

A solemn nod—this meant trouble—and he picked up two stiff cards from a nearby table. "Here's your pass, and here's your room key. A van is waiting at the entrance."

Cornell shut his eyes, remembering little details. The feel of sand; the wrong sun; the odd, lingering smell.

"Are you dizzy? Everyone complains about dizziness—"

"Sorry, no." He rose and ignored the wobbling floor. "Where'd you put my clothes?"

"Outer room, on your right."

Cornell said, "Thanks," and walked a straight line, through swinging doors and out of sight. But he continued to pretend while dressing, hiding the occasional belch, the faltering sense of balance; then he made it to the van and sat near the front, alone inside it and rode through what seemed like miles of open country. Grass and little woods. Once an elk in the distance. Then he muttered, "Stop," and began to stand.

As if expecting trouble, the van braked and opened every door.

Cornell vomited on the new pavement, once and then again. Then he paused to gasp, looking at the green grass and the deep blue sky, puffy clouds slowly passing in front of a setting sun.

The facility resembled a luxury motel, built low and with different wings added over time. There was a lot of brick and warm brown paint. Three swimming pools stood empty; countless hot tubs bubbled away. A synthetic voice welcomed him by name and directed him to his room. It was large and decorated with a certain care, big potted plants amid solid dark furniture. Cornell found his clothes and other belongings cleaned and neatly arranged, everything where he might place it . . . which was unsettling. His bosses were showing their thoroughness, which he took as a warning, and he sighed and walked to his long window, watching a distant oak wood while the last daylight vanished. For a long while, he stood motionless, thinking about everything; then a voice said, "Hello there?" A woman's voice. "I'm looking for Cornell Novak."

She was speaking over the intercom.

"Is this critter working—?" The voice ended with a thud, as if someone was striking a microphone. *Whump.*

Cornell asked, "What is it?"

"Who are you?"

"Novak. What do you want—?"

"Food. I'm famished. Want to get a late dinner?"

He was more queasy than hungry, but he assumed this was an official visit. His tormentors had something else planned.

"Come down to the lobby," she told him.

"Now?"

"Sooner, if you can." She laughed and said, "I'm waiting," and the line went dead.

Cornell changed clothes, trying to imagine the person to match that deep strong teasing voice. But he didn't imagine a woman more than six feet tall, and he didn't picture her handsome smiling face. Thick brown hair was tied into a ponytail—enough hair for two normal women—and she took his hand, saying, "Porsche Neal." Why'd the name sound familiar? "What do you go by? Cornell?"

"Sure."

"Pretty fancy. Why not Novak? Okay, Novak?"

He didn't have time to respond.

"I'll warn you, I'm under orders. I'm your cordial hostess for this evening, ready to answer every question with a muddle. You're suppose to feel at ease but uninformed." A brief pause. "The bureaucrats are still making up their minds about you. But I'm a hundred and two percent sure how they'll decide—"

"Are you?"

"Absolutely." A light sudden laugh, everything humorous. "How about food? Ever eat at a world-class restaurant?"

His stomach twisted in fear.

"At least it seems world-class, if you're in the mood." Porsche led him out of the lobby, down a hallway into a deep hushed darkness. "Robot service, robot cooks. Actually, the food is average. Ruthlessly average." In the gloom, Cornell could make out booths, tall and padded, and sometimes a face or two, or more, no voice louder than a whisper. "Over here." He skipped out of the way of a rolling waiter, then caught up to Porsche. She had a certain walk. Strong, distinctive. A long gait, with bounce and an aggressiveness.

"Here," she offered; and he said:

"You played basketball, didn't you?"

"Tall girls do." A sideways glance and smile. "In my youth."

She couldn't be thirty-five. "There was a Porsche Neal in the women's league. Played for Cleveland—"

"For six years," she confessed, sliding deep into the booth.

Cornell sat and absorbed his surroundings. Half a dozen people were sharing the opposite booth, packed close and their plates covered with steaming food, every face round and buttery. They were steadily eating, speaking only in passing. Words were muted. Almost inaudible. "Negative noise," Porsche explained. "Isn't that what it's called? Each booth generates its own, for security's sake."

Too bad I can't read lips, he thought.

Their waiter arrived. Porsche said, "My standard last-nighter."

"What's that?" asked Cornell.

"Steak and taters, always."

Looking at the boxy machine, he said, "Soup . . . vegetable, with some crackers."

Porsche grinned and said, "They had you wired, didn't they? Those goofy virtual toys of theirs . . . ?"

He nodded, watching the waiter roll off.

"Well," she assured him, "that's not even close, what you saw."

He straightened his back, waiting.

"And we keep telling them it's not. But they insist in believing in tests, trying to decide who belongs where. You know why?" She was talking with a too-loud voice, no one able to hear it but him. "Our project heads are clever girls and boys. Ignorant, but clever. Which is a dangerous mix, if you ask me."

"So what is it like, if it's not what I've seen . . . ?"

A blink and smile, but all she said was, "Instinct is a better judge of who's suitable. The best. I see someone, and I can guess if they'll work out. More often than not, I can."

He almost asked, "What about me?"

But Porsche anticipated the question, telling him, "You've got promise, Novak. Which is more than most people have in anything, if you think about it. Promise, I mean. It's a rare commodity, don't you agree?"

Dinner arrived, and wine, and the allusions moved into ordinary conversation, Porsche telling basketball stories and grousing about the lousy pay for woman athletes. Cornell remembered her playing—he had watched the games on obscure sports channels—and she was the rare white girl who could drive the ball, coast-to-coast, putting on a final surge and doing an artful layup. Then he was thinking of basketball with Todd and Lane, memory lending his legs bounce and his hands touch . . . and he recalled a specific moment when he beat both of the Underhills with his graceless steam. Funny, wasn't it? The summit of his athletic career came on an oil-stained driveway, a blind charge followed by a circus throw while airborne, the worn orange ball catching nothing but hoop—

"You're not listening," snapped his companion.

"I am," he protested. "The coach kept coming on to you, right?"

"Shamelessly." A sip of wine, a bloody bite of steak. Her hands were big and pale, and Cornell thought to say:

"Wherever you've been, it's not outside. You don't have a tan."

She peered at her hands, smiling. "Think not?" A nod, then she asked, "How's the soup?"

"Salty." He had finished all but the last cold spoonfuls. Sipping wine, he considered his stomach and almost felt hungry again. Almost.

"Talk about yourself. Any fame claims?"

Cornell asked, "What do you want to know?"

"I saw your file. Your case officer let me take a peek—"

"F. Smith."

"She's mine, too. A good lady, just a titch stiff." A pause, a wink. "So you're a Midwestern boy, right?"

"Haven't been back in years."

Grinning, she said, "Here's my picture. A frame house. A nice green lawn and fence. Very middle-class, very suburban."

"Pretty much."

"How pretty?"

He described basketball with the Underhills, then the cul-de-sac, swimming through the endless details. It was as if he'd forgotten nothing. Then he slipped into his standard, much practiced account of watching the sky change. He didn't mention Dad or the glass disks. It was just Cornell, him and the sky, and he looked up at the perfect moment . . . and that usually impressed people, which was its only real worth. A badge of distinction; a fame claim, as she'd called it. But he couldn't read Porsche's expression, her gaze distant and thoughtful, dinner done and the last of the wine in their bellies.

The booth full of buttery people was still eating, and eating.

Porsche blinked, gave a wise little smile and said, "You're tired. And they'll call you early, so maybe we should head home."

He did feel drained. They rose and walked back to the lobby, then climbed stairs. It was a huge facility, and empty enough to make him nervous. But he didn't ask questions. He turned and she turned in the same direction, and she mentioned, "Our team has this wing. The room is yours for good.'' His door came first, and when they paused, Porsche gave him a long look that he misinterpreted.

''Want to come in?'' he asked.

''No. Thanks.''

But her staring didn't end. He felt like he was stepping out onto the court, being sized up. A certain hardness in her eyes and mouth was intimidating as well as welcoming. How did she manage it? He was looking at her face, smooth and attractive and untanned, and at all that rich brown hair, wondering how it would feel to run his fingers through it; then she told him, ''Some other time, maybe.''

He'd almost forgotten his invitation. ''Well,'' he said, ''maybe I'll see you tomorrow.''

''No. I'm leaving.''

And he asked, ''Going where?''

Eyes smiled. ''Do you know what the universe is, Novak?''

''No. What?''

''It's just like that neighborhood where you grew up. It's all these little properties with fences between them.''

She wasn't joking, he realized.

''Suppose you're playing, and your ball goes into your neighbor's yard. What are you doing?''

He thought for a moment, then guessed. ''Trespassing?''

''As good a word as any.''

And later, watching the late local news, Cornell found himself sorting through memories of the day, pretending they made sense. He pictured the desert and its odd sky and sun, and he heard Porsche Neal describing the universe as tract housing. Was that what this was about? Were they going to trespass on someone's property?

He had asked, but she wouldn't tell him.

Whose desert was it? he wondered. And what did they think about the wayward children in their midst?

''If asked,'' said F. Smith, ''you've been given a sales position with Tangent Incorp. Here are your IDs. A credit card. The home address is authentic, as are phone, fax and E-mail numbers. If anyone asks, tell them you're traveling for us. Company security keeps you from disclosing too much."

"I doubt if there'll be questions," he offered.

She seemed to agree. "You have three days to yourself. I recommend getting your affairs in order. Return here by Thursday morning, ten o'clock, for one week's training. Then you'll start your first shift—"

"Where?"

She moved in her chair and grimaced. "I can't give you specifics. Let's say it's a plum. Our current number one posting." She showed him a maternal smile, then said, "You're starting on a great adventure, Mr. Novak."

"On a desert world?"

No reaction. Cold eyes staring, and no hint of emotion.

He wasn't intimidated, he told himself. More than once.

Then she was saying, "You've given us a pledge. Forget the forms you signed. Forget laws and punishments. You made a promise, and everything we can see in your character tells us that you take promises seriously."

A stern talking-down, this was.

Then she abruptly changed gears, telling him, "Just one more bit of business. We offer a five-hundred-thousand-dollar insurance policy, paid in full should you be disabled while on duty."

Cornell decided to stand up.

"You see? We do what we can for our people."

He walked to the window, the distant security fence shimmering in the low morning light.

"Who should I name as your beneficiary?"

He said, "How about my mother?"

"Address?"

"I guess I thought you might know." He looked at the old woman, then said, "Your background checks didn't find her?"

"Apparently not." She squirmed a little bit, as if bothered by the gap. "Perhaps you'd rather leave the money to your father—"

"No."

"I see." She dipped her head.

And he said, "I don't care who gets it."

"All right." She jotted a note on a pad, then looked at him and promised, "We'll find your mother. If it comes to that." Then, "Which it won't, of course." Then, "Rest easy, and we'll see you Thursday."

CORNELL'S APARTMENT WAS ON THE GROUND FLOOR OF AN OLD building beside the Panhandle, in Haight-Ashbury. It was surrounded by newer buildings put up after the '06 quake, everything done in the standard Victorian style but with modern materials. Cornell's landlord still grieved that his building survived, nature's muscle inadequate and every municipal law intended to save it for all time. That's why his repairs were few, hoping rot would unburden him. That's why Cornell could afford the place, the air smelling of mold, the plaster cracked and the roaches scuttling through the cracks, their sounds dry and unpleasant. Now he could move to a better place, he realized. The thought struck him the instant he stepped inside, the cheap house computer saying, "Hello. Who are you?"

A blind computer; a dead flat voice.

He said his name twice, making sure he was recognized.

"I have eleven messages," the machine reported. "There were no attempted burglaries, but your coffee maker is inactive—"

"Fine." The messages were from bill collectors, he guessed. But of course now he had money and could erase his debts. Such a freedom, money was. Images of a sunny apartment and electronic toys made him laugh out loud. It wasn't until later, eating a microwave dinner, that Cornell stopped to wonder when he would be around long enough to enjoy any of it. Four weeks on duty, including his training. Then a mandatory three weeks off. Then three more on, or longer, depending on his abilities. More duty meant greater pay. He started to calculate the fortune he would make in two or three years of endless work, teasing himself with the zeros.

"All right," he said in a loud, clear voice. "Play the messages."

Strangers spoke. Just as he'd guessed, they wanted money. They were a tougher cadre of bill collectors than the last lot, Cornell decided. Then came a woman's voice, someone he had dated last year, and she was wondering how he was doing and could he give her a call? Then came another collection agency, moral outrage washing over him. Then a tone, and he heard a familiar voice. Older and thicker, but unmistakable.

"Cornell? This is Pete Forrest. Just calling to ask how you're doing, the usual. Just to be nosy. Why don't you call me back when you get the chance? Collect, if you want. Same number as always. We'd love hearing from you."

He sat motionless, elbows on the hard kitchen table. What time was it? Late enough that it was too late back home, and he rose and walked into the tiny living room, lights turning off and on in response to his motions. He punched on the old TV, then hit the phone function and the right numbers. Save for the last two digits, Pete's number was the same as Dad's. It was a coincidence, and it was dangerous. He punched with care, then a familiar face appeared, squinting and smiling. "Why look! Mr. Cornell."

Mrs. Pete sat in her living room, appearing amused.

"Hello," he managed. "How are you?"

Putting on weight, he saw. And gray again, tired of those impossibly dark dyes that she'd used for years.

She said, "I'm fine. And you?"

"Good enough."

"How's California? You look tired."

Which made him feel tired, hearing that assessment.

"Want to talk to Pete?"

"If he's up—"

"I'm up," cried a distant voice. "Send him upstairs."

"Well, good seeing you," she said, giving him a little wink as she punched the proper button—

—and Pete was staring at him, his face a little more worn but not with age. It was like old wood, dried and polished by the elements. Cornell smiled, and Pete smiled, pulling his robe tighter and sitting on the edge of the bed. He was sixty now, wasn't he? Which seemed impossible and unfair. "So what's going on?" said the old man. "You sure look tired."

"I must be," he allowed. "Anyway, I got your message."

"What's going on?" Pete said again.

Cornell shrugged, then said, "I got a new job."

"So we hear."

He said nothing.

"Your employers sent us a couple suits-and-ties. Yesterday. They looked like insurance salesmen, sounded like cops . . . going from house to house, asking about you."

"They're being careful." He swallowed. "It's an important job, and I'm lucky to get it." Then he launched into the cover story, the thing practiced enough that it didn't feel like a complete lie. But if Pete bought the story, he didn't show it. His face grew more skeptical as the fabrications increased, and finally, maybe two-thirds of the way through it, he interrupted, saying:

"By the way, I recognized one of the suits-and-ties."

That startled Cornell. He stopped, forgetting his place.

"You never saw him. But remember back . . . I don't know . . . a couple of years before the Change? A big saucer was suppose to have landed on the highway near Tweaksburg, leaving skid marks in the asphalt—"

"I didn't go."

"That's what I thought." He gave a nod and smiled to himself. "It wasn't a saucer. It was some crippled stealth ship, and we'd just gotten there when this jerk came over and told us to put our fucking cameras away. He told us to fuck off. A lot less polite than he was yesterday. Mr. Forrest this, Mr. Forrest that. Didn't remember me, but I sure remembered his face."

Once, years ago, Cornell had thought Pete wasn't the brightest fellow. Ever since he'd been learning how wrong he could be. Swallowing, he gathered himself. Then he said, "My job's got government connections, security clearances, that sort of thing."

"Sure, I understand." A sly smile. "Anyway, the two gentlemen talked to the neighbors. Then your dad. He watched them going door-to-door, and he called me every couple minutes, asking what I knew."

Cornell could think of nothing worth saying.

"Your dad's gotten kind of paranoid anyway. I guess. We don't spend as much time together anymore." A deep breath. "Not that I blame him for spooking, what with the government asking about his son. On your best day, that's hard to swallow."

Were his bosses that graceless with everyone? But then again, how many candidates got as far as he had? Suits-and-ties could invade a thousand neighborhoods, and the world at large wouldn't be the wiser.

Pete said, "They spent a couple of hours with your dad. He taped the whole thing, on the sly. Mostly they asked about you. About school, about friends. That kind of thing." He paused for a long moment, considering his audience. "It was smoke. Banal shit meant to get your dad to relax. Then they hit him with questions about when he saw you last, and why the two of you went to war. Always sounding polite, but nothing nice about it."

"Dad told you?"

"And I heard the tape." A calm, sober nod. "I don't know what they were hunting, but they sure rattled him."

Cornell said, "Sorry."

"Hey, I'm fine. Don't worry about me."

"So what did he tell them? Anything?"

" 'It's none of your goddamn business,' he said. True. He cursed at them, your mild-mannered dad did. It was something."

Cornell took deep breaths, then thought of something else. Years ago, more than once, he had borrowed money from the Petes; now he could say, "I'll pay you back. In a few weeks, maybe sooner."

The old man shrugged his shoulders. "Whenever. I'm not worried."

No, he never was a worrier, was he?

"Anyway, I just wanted to call, see how you're doing. Any messages for your dad?"

Cornell's mind went blank.

"Or nothing. Whatever." Pete adjusted the robe's belt, and Cornell wondered what it was that made old men wear ugly socks to bed. He could see the brown things reach halfway up his ivory shins.

"Thanks for everything," Cornell offered.

Pete said, "And take care of yourself. And congratulations on the big job. Elaine and I are proud of you. You know that."

"Thanks," he said. Then, "Bye," and he disconnected the line, sitting back and staring at the ceiling, its cracks longer than he remembered and the room smaller. His mind shifted into a useful paranoia. His house computer had said there weren't any burglaries, which seemed unlikely. Hadn't one of the Panhandle nobodies tried his windows at least once? In all this time? What if someone had come and left, editing the computer's memories? What if these next days were a test, Cornell given every chance to fail, his bosses waiting for him to tell what he knew before he knew too much?

Still staring at the ceiling, he whispered, "I hope I did all right." Then he shut his eyes, speaking louder, telling them, "Now, if you please, fuck off."

He had never learned which trees grew in San Francisco, which was unlike him. But then moving here had been a temporary adventure, expensive and foolish. A several year adventure, he realized. He came after he grew tired of Texas with its hard sun and guiltless wealth, and San Francisco had seemed like a natural antithesis. It was crowded and its climate was mild, verging on boring. Despite some good times, he'd always felt like a tourist here. That night, walking through the Panhandle, he felt more displaced than ever. He could have been a Midwesterner fresh from the bullet train, save for his indifference to the scenery and the old, unwashed clothes.

It was a foggy night, skyless and unnaturally quiet. Only electric cars were allowed this deep into the city, and even their hums seemed subdued by the hanging curtains of vapor.

Eventually Cornell found himself inside the park, surrounded by robot-tended flowers and shadowy couples, a few automated sentries drifting nearby, rotors whirring. What time was it? Nearly eleven. But he couldn't sleep, and he might never sleep again. That's how awake he felt.

He remembered the last time he talked to Dad.

It was stupid and Freudian, a conspiracy of the fingers. He'd been calling Pete, and suddenly he saw Dad staring at him, the white hair thin and the blue eyes hidden in shadow. Cornell's first thought was to wonder why Dad was sitting in Pete's house. Then he knew what had happened, and he considered disconnecting, not caring how it looked. Except those conspiring hands refused to move, grasping one another and the seconds stretching on.

It was Dad who found something to say.

"Remember the glass circle in the park, here in town?" he began. "Well, the parks people got tired of it, brought in heavy machinery and broke it up into chunks. Carted the whole thing away. Can you imagine?" No greeting, no sense of pleasure. The man acted as if Cornell hadn't been out of his sight for ten minutes, the bright eyes coming closer, that ageless voice telling him, "It's a tragedy. I think their brains must be damaged. Can you imagine doing such a criminal thing?"

Always the difficult man. It had been two years since their last conversation, and Dad had nothing but this one thin obsession. "I keep working on the circles, Cornell. Every day."

And Cornell muttered, "That so?"

"Working with the samples, the data. I'm pestering the physics department at the university, trying to get them to run tests.'' The face was composed and focused, and distant. The voice had a practiced quality, as if this was a lecture kept bottled up until needed. It practically bubbled out of Dad, words blurring together. ''I have a theory. I'm thinking that the circles are complex messages from *them.* Did you know that glass isn't a true solid? That it's not crystalline at all?''

How would a physicist deal with him? Cornell wondered. He imagined a man in a lab coat, his face wary, watching some dangerous loner shove sacks of black glass into his hands.

''It's an amorphous substance, I've been reading. Individual atoms frozen in random positions. But what if the positions aren't random? I'm thinking, what if they form a careful pattern? I've estimated the numbers of atoms in the typical circle, and how much potential information is there—''

Cornell imagined what the physicists might call his father. ''The glass man.'' ''The loon.'' Or the always poignant, ''Nutcase.''

''—and the potential is enormous. Almost endless. Just one of these samples of mine can hold more data than any encyclopedia—''

''What are you doing?'' Cornell snapped.

Dad paused, nothing showing on his face.

''I call, and what do you do? Ramble on about circles and glass. That's not much of a hello.''

Eyes dropped, the expression chastened now. ''I thought you'd be interested.''

''And where's your evidence?'' Cornell persisted. ''A theory isn't something thought up in the shower. It's the result of a lot of work, a lot of positive evidence, and saying 'theory' is going to set off a lot of alarms. Scientists will know you're a crank.''

''Sorry,'' the man responded. ''I forgot about your advanced degrees. How's MIT?''

''Don't do that.''

''What? What shouldn't I do?''

''I'm just saying—''

"I know." Dad wiped both hands on his trousers, then straightened and said, "The work is pointless. I forgot."

As if Cornell's defection was recent, he thought. As if this was the first time Dad had admitted there was a gulf.

"I thought you'd be interested, that's all."

Then came a stiff prolonged silence, both men considering things never mentioned aloud. Like Mom. And Cornell's disgust with his father's fathering. Not that he was angry anymore; that wasn't the point. This was tradition, their animosity. It was a kind of safety device. What if they did bring up old issues? They might enrage each other, severing their last ties. Perhaps that's what both of them sensed, sad as it seemed, instincts warning them this was the best they could manage for now.

"Anyway," Dad concluded, "it doesn't matter. Everyone's destroying the circles now. Who cares what they mean?"

"Too bad," Cornell offered.

A helpless shrug of the shoulders made Dad look feeble, and the blue eyes gazed at the floor, at his own feet. "I am keeping the samples you helped collect. Safe and sound."

"Well . . . good. . . . "

A sluggish nod, and he whispered, "Safe. And sound."

Sitting on the beach when the early morning light emerged, Cornell watched the steady cold surf, the first gulls searching for whatever the ocean had brought to them. Opening his wallet, he picked through pockets until he found the one photograph he allowed himself—an old snapshot of his mother—and he pulled it out and touched the slick paper. He wasn't sure about any of his memories about her. What was real, and what was wishful fancy? Shutting his eyes, he saw Mom and Mrs. Pete talking over the fence. He saw Mom and Dad in the kitchen, saying nothing in that conspicuous way of people who are at odds. Then he remembered Mom alone, sitting in the middle of the sofa with a pillow on her lap, watching TV. The image was banal, and it was true, and it meant nothing, giving him absolutely no insights.

He put the photograph away. The tide was rising, pulled

up by the unseen moon. Looking above, the everted earth was dissolving into sunshine—first the night face, then the brighter day face—and he was thinking about everything, and nothing. Then he noticed the stranger passing nearby, looking at him with an odd expression. Was she some agent keeping tabs on him? Then why the look of pity?

Touching his face, Cornell discovered he was crying. For how long? He began to wipe his eyes with both sleeves, and he sniffed and gave a little moan, accomplishing nothing, tears still coming but the wiping motions soothing, in a fashion.

JORDICK TILLER WAS A PECULIAR MAN AT FIRST GLANCE, AND AT second glance, too. He had raven-black hair kept long and dirty, yet everything else about him seemed precise, in its place. Cornell remembered him from the broken van. Yet Jordick didn't seem to recall him, glancing up at the sound of the door, the eyes showing no hint of recognition. The lounge was empty save for the two of them. Was this the right place? Cornell checked the number on the door. Yes, it was. Jordick dipped his head, a pen in his left hand, a little comppad covered with a precise drawing of the chair opposite him. Just like in the van, he was wearing pressed slacks and a brown too-heavy sweater. Cornell sat, but not close to him, waiting a moment and then asking, "How have you been?"

"We've got to wait," Jordick replied. His head remained down, the hand making more lines. "The woman said so."

"Then what?"

Jordick frowned at his drawing. "I don't know." Dark eyes betrayed nervousness, perhaps even fear. "I guess we take some kind of class, I don't know. . . . "

"Nice drawing," Cornell offered.

"Thank you."

They sat without speaking for several moments, then a woman entered the lounge through a second door. "Gentlemen?" She smiled and said, "Come this way, please," and the smile dropped away.

They were led into a long hallway lined with closed doors, and once in a while there were sounds. Cornell heard people talking and bits of music, emotional Romantic stuff dominating. The hallway was very white. A white floor and white walls and a long white ceiling. Cornell joked, "I'm having an out-of-body experience."

Then:

"I must have died."

His companions turned, almost glaring at him. Then the woman, crisp and officious, and perhaps bloodless, pointed to two doors set together. "Please remember your room numbers. Mr. Tiller? 115. Mr. Novak has 116." Again she remembered to smile. "You'll be tutored by interactive computers programmed for your specific needs. The restrooms are here. You're free to work at your own pace—"

"Learning what?" Jordick blurted. Then he coughed, surprised by his little outburst. "I'm just wondering—"

"No doubt," the woman replied.

Cornell touched his door, hearing a distinct *click* before it swung open. The room inside would make a deep closet, a large flat screen built into the far wall, a desk and chair and some kind of food dispenser set in front of the screen. A voice said, "Hello, Mr. Novak. Welcome." It was a woman's voice, young and charming.

The woman in the hallway said, "Good luck, gentlemen," and began to leave.

Jordick tugged at his long hair, glancing at Cornell and swallowing. When he opened his door, a stiff masculine voice said, "Come in, Mr. Tiller."

A different voice; a different attitude.

Interesting.

"Good luck," Cornell offered.

Jordick gave a weak, lost nod, then vanished. His door clicked shut after him, and nothing else could be heard in the still white air.

"What I saw," said the man, "was a hole right in front of me. Close. I mean so close that I jumped back to keep from falling, and the hole pulled away from me. A thousand feet, it felt like. Which is crazy. I know. It's just that distances and sizes got all confused. A step back was a thousand feet, but a big step forward got you nothing. Like you were inside some carnival's supermadhouse, you know?''

Cornell could see the man's face on the monitor, and he couldn't. Computers had scrubbed his features, leaving only his expressions and a generic identity. The man could be anyone. Everyone. That gave his narrative an unexpected force.

Someone offstage asked, ''What happened next?''

'' 'Go closer,' I heard. Then, 'Look inside it.' As if I was looking down a gopher hole. But I got down low—that seemed to help—and started crawling. And all of a sudden the hole turned huge and close, and I was on its lip, looking down.''

''Down at what?'' asked the invisible person.

''I don't know.'' He paused to drink water from a big glass. He seemed winded, colorless eyes beginning to squint. ''Like a whirlpool, sort of. At least at first. All black, except it seemed bright, too. I know, that doesn't make sense. But that's how it was. And there weren't any whirlpool motions, just a lot of back and forth twisting. And someone said, 'Go deeper.' So I did. I was laid out on my belly, getting stretched out—like a wire? That's how it seemed. And that's how I looked to the people watching me.'' The image jumped, time passing. What had been edited out? The man was saying, ''I kept getting thinner, and I got my head through the hole. To me, the hole looked miles across. To everyone else, it was fist-sized. But it all made sense by then. You know? The way dreams make sense, no matter how crazy they sound later?''

''What happened next?''

The man paused, breathing fast. Gathering himself. Cornell took a sip of coffee, hot and fresh; then the story continued:

''I felt like I was falling, falling down a thousand-mile hole, going faster all the time, and the hole kept swirling, then stopped and swirled the other way. And all of a sudden I felt odd. I mean, it was more than being pulled out of shape. It was me. I was changing. Things were looking different because my eyes were different. I know because I touched them, I thought something was in them . . . I brought my hand up from a million miles back . . . and I felt hard surfaces and no eyelids and it wasn't even a hand touching my eyes. I mean, I had this bug limb. Full of joints and hard parts. Like a roach's, only bigger. And I tried screaming—you don't know how scared I was!—only I didn't have a real voice anymore. I let out this crazy fucking screech, like metal tearing, and here's what's craziest. I understood myself. I mean, it was a bug's voice, and I knew the screech meant *shit* or something like that. My feet were back up on the earth, and normal, but the rest of me was turning into this monster, like in that old fly movie . . . ?"

"What else did you see?" And now Cornell recognized the voice, solid and steady. It was F. Smith, his case officer. "You were on the other side, somewhere else," she continued. "What else did you see?"

"It's hard, to make it make sense—"

"Try," said Ms. Smith.

"The sky was green, only it wasn't. And the clouds were white, only white meant something else on the other side. With my new eyes." A brief pause, then a gasp. "It was someone else's sky. On a different planet. I know that. I felt it. And I was this big bug, bigger than any man, and smart."

"You didn't stay there."

The man said nothing.

"Why did you come back so soon?"

His simple mannequin features held a generic fear, Cornell feeling his own pulse quickening.

"We're not angry. We just want to know why you came back."

"I was going to be eaten," said the man. "I mean, I just *knew* I was exposed there, in trouble."

"Eaten by what?"

"I'm not sure anymore. I don't think I ever knew." He swallowed audibly, then said, "I was this creature all done up in armor, and I was scared of being in the open. Think of it.

My eyes were built to point up, to watch that green sky, and the clouds, because something could come and get me."

"I see."

And he laughed in a thin, forced way. "I wasn't high on the food chain. You know?"

"Perhaps," said Ms. Smith, "you'd like to go back again?"

Nothing.

"It would be an enormous help—"

"No. No way." Defiance mixed with fear, one giving the other backbone. "Don't seriously ask me."

She said nothing.

"You go. Go and come back," he told Ms. Smith. Another thin laugh, then he said, "You can tell me all about it."

The screen went black, and Cornell thought about a bright blackness. How would that look?

"Any questions, sir?"

He sipped his coffee. Music began to play, soothing and soft. Bach, he realized. But performed by synthesizers. He put down his cup and said, "Okay. You found a way into other worlds. Right?"

"We call them quantum intrusions. In essence, they are holes. Very strange passageways, indeed."

"Quantum intrusions." He nodded and sat back.

"They involve complex physical principles. Principles only marginally understood."

"How'd you find them?"

"That's classified. I'm sorry." The voice almost sounded apologetic. "The technical aspects require the highest security clearances."

"Do you know how?"

"No, sir." It waited for a moment, then said, "I can tell you that it was unexpected, an example of extreme serendipity."

"Who was the man? The witness?"

"I can't tell you."

"But why him? Was he the first one?"

"He was a volunteer, and he seemed qualified." A pause. "It's taken some time for us to learn who is most qualified."

Years ago, accompanying his father, Cornell had listened

to rambling accounts from UFO witnesses. Something about their adventures mirrored this one. Not the events themselves, but in that kind of astonished inability to explain what was seen and felt.

"Yes, he was an early volunteer," the voice continued.

Cornell picked up the coffee cup, finishing the last dark drops. "So how many intrusions have you found?"

"That's classified."

"A few? A bunch?"

"Sir," the voice reprimanded.

The cup was spun cellulose, soft and foamy, and he bit off one of the white edges and spit it into the remaining cup. "If there's one intrusion, there's probably a lot of them."

Silence.

"Classified. I know." He grinned and remembered Porsche's tale. The universe was an enormous suburb, fences between the worlds and the geometry much more complicated than rectangles and curling streets. "Are the intrusions like gates? Gates in a fence?"

"I don't know, sir."

"Okay. How about this. You pass through an intrusion, and what? You're transformed—?"

"I can't pass through. Only living matter makes the journey, and then, it seems, only when the lifeform possesses minimal neurological functions. We don't know why. But large primates are capable, as are porpoises. And elephants, too."

Cornell laughed. He was playing with the image of stuffing an elephant down an otherworldly hole, then F. Smith trying to interview the bedazzled elephant on its return.

"Different intrusions allow different species," the computer volunteered. "We think it has to do with having an appropriate species on the other side, one which can be used as a template."

Another bite of the cup, another chunk spit back into what remained. "I bet you used Special Forces boys. Didn't you? Big tough disciplined souls, and they didn't work out. Am I right?"

Silence with a whiff of disapproval.

He smiled. "And machines can never go through?"

"To my knowledge, no."

"Maybe we need smarter machines."

"Perhaps," it allowed.

"How about clothes? Do they pass through?"

"No."

"Tools?"

"Never, no."

"Only the living organism?"

"Yes, sir."

"And what about coming back? I'm assuming people can come back, free and easy."

"Yes, the process is reversible. The intrusion's machinery—I use that term loosely—retains records of each organism that passes through it, then remakes them when they return. We carry out thorough physicals, and there's never been a discrepancy. Fingerprints and scars, weight and age remain the same. Always."

"So you're saying the only real thing that makes the trip is a person's soul. Is that what you mean?"

"I don't know if 'soul' is appropriate."

"What's a better word?"

That stumped the machine. "Self" was its best effort, but neither of them seemed happy with it.

"Soul," Cornell repeated. Another bite, and he leaned back, smiling at the ceiling while saying, "Huh," several times. "Huh, huh, huh."

He reached the point of saturation, in several ways. Rising, he announced, "I need to pee."

"To your right, then left."

"Thanks."

The restroom was clean enough for surgery, human wastes feeling like an insult. A tall black man gave him a weak smile, then left, and Cornell took his time, letting his mind wander. Intrusions; transformations; souls. No, he wouldn't try to make it sensible. Instead he thought about Porsche, how she was a tough person to do this stuff. To do it and be eager to do it. He wondered where she was now, and what she might be doing. Could it be described in human terms?

He flushed and washed his hands, and Jordick entered.

"Oh, hi," said the black-haired man. "How are you?"

"Fine. And you?"

"Fine. I'm fine."

"What are they showing you?"

"An interview." Except Jordick's interview was different. An entirely different world with its own character. "This girl became a fish," said Jordick, "and she was swimming in a warm ocean."

These lessons were matched to each person, probably. What did their bosses think? That Cornell would rise to a challenge, but Jordick needed to be eased into the insanity?

"She's gone over many times since. Sometimes for days."

Cornell nodded absently.

"Was yours the same?"

"Mostly," he lied. "Pretty much."

"I'm excited." If anything, Jordick looked more peculiar when he was excited, his pale skin and eyes almost glowing. "Are you eager to start?"

Cornell nodded again, saying, "Pretty much."

He left the man standing in the middle of that rampant cleanliness, staring at his reflection in the mirror. Practicing fish expressions, Cornell realized. Getting ready.

"Okay, help me. I pass through an intrusion, and magic is done. I come out with a different body, alien eyes, and I'm preprogrammed to understand the language. The basic rules. Is that it?"

"In essence, yes."

The process struck him as incredible, impossible . . . a thorough and instantaneous transformation of flesh and mind. But then again, someone or something had rebuilt the universe in the past. Remodeling the human self was a smaller job, wasn't it?

"But why turn into a bug? Why not become the bug's predator?"

Silence. Then the voice said, "On that particular world, at least one large insect is a good match for humans. Presumably the predators are either less intelligent or well beyond human capacities."

"Are people exploring the bug world now?"

"I can't answer that."

Cornell shrugged. "It's funny. I've always assumed that intelligence would be tied with tools and technology. Is that a bad assumption?"

"It is a simple one."

"Okay." Another shrug. "I go through, but I'm still Cornell Novak . . . right? I keep my identity?"

"Yes."

"With all my memories? And the same winning personality?"

"Yes, and yes."

"Thank you," he joked.

The computer made a soft sound, then said, "Within certain parameters, your basic profile is maintained. In fact, we have personnel on each world whose only task is testing and retesting themselves and others. Since there is no way to transfer modern medical equipment, the research is limited. Perhaps in some future time—"

"But what if no critter is our equal? What if we cross, only the world is uninhabited?"

"You cannot cross then. No intrusion will form."

"No?"

"The transformation is tuned to neurological activity."

Questions were forming, too many of them, and Cornell couldn't speak. All at once he felt tired. Sleepy. Looking at the chewed-up cup, he remembered how Pete would drive him and Dad across the country. That's where he learned this nervous habit, from watching Pete chew on his cups. And for a moment, without trying, Cornell heard his father's smooth soft voice talking about worlds and galaxies without number, life forming and spreading, growing wiser by the moment.

He groaned, then asked, "Where am I going?"

"Its designation is High Desert."

He thought of the virtual images.

"It's a fortunate posting," the computer promised. "For some, it is easy to adapt to the new circumstances."

"For others?"

"Our testing is much improved, and your scores are quite good. You should have no problem."

"High Desert . . . is it earthlike?"

"In some details, yes."

"Show me."

"I'd prefer to discuss our support facilities here. We have a dozen psychiatrists ready to help you readjust, should you need help. Plus we have several recreational facilities. The agency owns resorts in three states, including American Samoa. Off shift time is meant to be restful. You are precious to us."

"I want to see High Desert." The prospect of looking at an alien world made him excited, almost giddy. "Get permission, if you've got to. But that's what I want to see."

The screen lit up. There was a dusty gray landscape, raw and cold, stretching towards a high purplish sky. Bits of bristly vegetation grew in the low spots. The only clouds were thin. "Of course you won't perceive colors in this exact way. Your new eyes will be sensitive to different frequencies, all of your senses changed—"

"What?" Cornell interrupted. "Is the atmosphere thin?"

"Yes, and oxygen-poor. There's a scarcity of water, as you see, and the surface gravity is perhaps two-thirds of Earth's. It's not a small world, but it seems less dense. And there's a lack of metals, at least locally."

Cornell touched the screen. "It's not a photograph."

"No, it's a computer image based on testimony and artistic renderings." A pause. "I can generate other views, if you'd like."

"Go on." Then after a few minutes, he said, "It's almost pretty. Do you think? Stark, but handsome."

"I can't express an opinion, sir."

"It looks like Mars, before we found out what Mars really was." Purple skies. Desert scrub. Based on the testimony of dreamers, that's what the old Mars had been.

Silence.

"Okay," said Cornell. "Tell me about these resorts. Whatever's on the agenda, feel free."

Yet the last picture lingered for a few moments, as if the computer were studying it too. As if it was struggling to make some kind of judgment about the world's beauty. However slight; however bad. And Cornell was wondering if that's why machines couldn't pass through the intrusions. Maybe some were smart enough, but they were missing in other areas. Like appreciating beauty, for instance.

Maybe they just weren't a good enough audience.

CORNELL ATE DINNER BY HIMSELF, IN HIS ROOM. THE TV WAS ON but muted, full of professional and banal images. A cough syrup ad gave way to an automobile ad, then some cops-and-robbers show, automobiles flying across the wide screen and villains shot, cough syrup pouring from neat little wounds. A jarring voice startled Cornell. He blinked and straightened, realizing it was the intercom. "Are you there?" asked Jordick. "Could we talk?" he whimpered. Then he paused before asking, "Can you hear me?"

Cornell ate the last cold bites of food, wiped his face and remained seated. I'll talk to him tomorrow, he told himself. I don't feel like company. Sorry.

"I'll try later," Jordick promised. Or threatened.

Cornell changed channels, finding one of the sports networks. Tall women and small men played basketball in the Coed League, the cameras conspicuously ignoring the almost empty auditorium. The game itself was threadbare but honest, blessed with an amateurish charm. He moved to bed and lay there watching the game. This could be the last ordinary thing he ever did, and he wanted to make the most out of it.

Later, someone knocked on his door. The *boom-boom* jerked him out of a shallow sleep. The familiar voice asked, "Are you there?"

Not really, no.

The knocking continued, soft and nagging. Then came a very long pause before Jordick said, "I'll see you tomorrow, Cornell."

One of the basketball teams had won, running on the plastic floor with arms raised high. Good for them. Cornell fell back into sleep, waking in the early morning. The sports channel was off the air; he was getting a channel from China, apparently. Am I dreaming? he wondered. Chinese cops were chasing Chinese bad guys, the bad guys crashing into the Great Wall. Then came a commercial selling cough syrup, of all things. With a sleepy profundity, Cornell was thinking how this world was one place where once it had been countless places. One place; one identity; one soul.

He laughed to himself, rolling over and falling asleep again.

Jordick wasn't in the lounge this time. There was no woman, but the inner door automatically opened. Cornell walked to his cubicle, then paused and stepped in front of Jordick's cubicle. He knocked on the door. From inside he heard music, then a deep male voice. Nobody answered him. Tit-for-tat, probably. Which seemed only fair.

Sitting in his own cubicle, he exchanged greetings with his tutor. Coffee was delivered, and he blew on it, then said, "So tell me about where I'm going. Tell me everything."

High Desert had several parallels to Earth, he learned. Both were terrestrial worlds. On both water existed as a liquid, though it was scarce on one. And both worlds had evolved vertebrates. Both had reptiles, both had mammals. Or at least lines that mirrored each other in certain basic ways. Lizards. Rodents. And such.

"Okay," Cornell whispered.

"And though your senses will change, they won't change in fundamental ways." The female voice promised him, "You'll have a good sense of hearing, considering the thin atmosphere. And an improved sense of smell. And in some ways, you'll find your architecture quite ordinary—two legs and two arms and a face capable of rather human expressions—"

"I'll have two bodies, right?" He was recalling the virtual image.

But the tutor said, "No." A schematic appeared on the screen, white lines on a black background. "Vertebrates on HD reproduce asexually. It might be the harsh environment, or maybe the benefits of sexual reproduction aren't as great as we assumed."

"I dated a naturalist once," Cornell offered. "She studied whiptail lizards in the Southwest. The species has no males. Only females. And they reproduced parthenogenetically. No sperm needed, and the eggs develop into genetic duplicates of their mother. Clones, in essence."

"Perhaps for similar reasons." The tutor sounded less than interested. "We don't really know the reasons."

An egg formed on the black background, squiggly lines implying chromosomes. The egg split into eight identical eggs, each one growing while he watched. Seven were similar to any embryo, including gill slits and stubby limbs. But the last egg was radically different, its head swelling and absorbing most of the body. "These are based on studies of a local herbivore. Rock rats, they're called." A pause, then it said, "Rock rats possess up to ten mobile bodies, plus a mind that's left inside a deep and well-protected burrow."

The adults resembled pikas more than rats, round and furry, verging on cute. Except for the mind, that is. It was nearly ninety percent head, helpless in appearance, its limbs upturned and resembling handles more than legs.

"What? Is it a social organism?"

"Not at all."

Cornell thought for a long moment. "It's a single organism . . . built from all these pieces . . . ?"

"Essentially, yes." A pause. "Our staff biologists believe it's an adaptation to the environment. Natural selection has produced mammals capable of a kind of telepathy. It's a short-range phenomenon, but useful. Our physicists think it might be as simple as a personally generated radio signal, weak but sophisticated."

Cornell was breathing faster, trying to think.

"Multibodied lifeforms can range over large areas, in all directions at once. I'm sure you can see the usefulness of it." A pause. "Small bodies take the risks, and the mind is protected inside a deep, secure hole."

"How will I look?" he blurted.

The screen changed views. Gray streets were laid out straight with simple earthen buildings set along them. It could have been a miserable hamlet in North Africa, but the voice said, "This is our headquarters on High Desert. It's designation is HD Prime, but most call it New Reno."

Seven distinct dots appeared on a barren street. No, he realized, watching the dots grow larger. One of them was different, limbless and shaped something like a football or an enormous egg, wearing a heavy coat of fur and dust. Its longest hairs were in braids, making ropes or harnesses. And while he watched, amazed and numbed, six furred bipeds began to move, towing the hairy egg along the street, three-fingered hands holding the harnesses and their black eyes gazing at him through transparent lids.

"Shit," said Cornell. "This is crazy."

"Yet," his tutor replied, "you're doing fine. I've had worse panic from other recruits."

Six bodies per human? A detached, invalid mind? All joined together—?

"You'll be surprised," promised the female voice. "It's strange to imagine, but the transformation will be easy enough."

Cornell couldn't think of anything to say.

"Consider your body on earth as being one ensemble of clothes, and these bodies are another ensemble. That's all. When you travel from world to world, you dress accordingly."

"I suppose," he whispered.

"And the soul remains within, unchanged."

"That," said Cornell, "I really, truly doubt."

Entering the restaurant, he heard his name, turned and saw Jordick sitting in a booth with another man. It was the stranger who had called to him, waving now and smiling. "Our Mr. Novak. Good to meet you." A firm, dry handshake, then he said, "Join us. Can you?"

Cornell obeyed.

"I'm Hank Logan. Your field chief? Heard the name before?" He paused, then said, "Well, you will. Soon, soon." Another quick pause. "I'm back for a little R&R, starting about ninety minutes ago. So excuse me for being a little keyed up, which is perfectly normal, believe me."

The booth's leather felt warm, as if he was taking someone's seat. Nodding at Jordick, Cornell felt a pang of guilt about last night. He asked, "How's your training going?"

"Been changed," Logan called out. "Our boy here's being stationed on High Desert."

Jordick gave an odd smile. "Hank happened to see my files—"

"—and got him off the hook!" The man laughed, the sound of it puncturing the antinoise buffers. As other patrons turned to look, he said, "That's a joke. Our poor boy here was scheduled to join up with the Cold Seas project, which is just about the biggest fucking bore you can imagine."

Cornell nodded, saying nothing.

"Fish." Jordick said the word with precision, one thin hand picking at his nose. "That's all it is."

"Yeah," said Logan, "you end up with gills and this icy metabolism. You swim and swim. All the time, and all in slow motion. Oh yeah, I saved your ass. Or asses, depending on how you look at it."

Jordick seemed most thankful for the attention, nodding and laughing too easily.

"Hey, Novak. See the big folks over there? I was just telling your buddy about them."

It was a group like the one he'd seen earlier. Fat men and fat women were consuming huge dinners, round faces barely speaking, everyone possessed by the same compulsive agenda.

"We call them Mayflies," Logan continued. "Not officially. Officially they're part of the Jupiter 3 project. A huge world, just like our Jupiter, except it's closer to its sun. Believe it or not, Mayflies sprout wings when they pass through. They fly through storms and huge winds and past cloudlike critters, and it's lovely, but they can't stay for more than a couple hours. Tops."

"Why not?" Cornell asked.

"Think of mayflies on earth." Logan leaned back, leather squeaking under him. "Because they don't live long. They lack mouths and have nothing to eat but their body fat." He laughed and gestured at them. "See, what you are here seems to translate in the intrusions. Fat here, then fat there. Or on High Desert. But only 'fat' by local standards. They're not quite as buttery up in those clouds."

Cornell could guess as much from the day's lessons.

"Like you, Cornell. You're tall here, so you'll be tall everywhere. Relatively speaking. What are you? Six four?"

"Two plus, I guess."

"Man, I wish I was tall." Logan's dinner was half-eaten and cold, a raw burger showing bite marks and corn on the cob blanketed with margarine. "I bet you get along with the ladies, am I right?"

Cornell made a neutral motion.

"Thick is what matters, but no. No. Girls these days, they expect something they can tie in knots. Am I right?"

Jordick tried to move the conversation back to him. "I'll have black fur, won't I? On High Desert?"

Logan looked off into the distance. "Absolutely. Right down to that bald patch on the back of your mind."

Jordick touched his scalp.

Logan roared, fists hitting the table. "No, you won't. That doesn't translate, since the locals don't go bald."

Cornell glanced at the Mayflies again. "Why do they only live for a hours?"

"We've got a guess," Logan replied. "Maybe only their adults are smart as people. They come out of a larval stage, maybe from inside those living clouds, and their flying is a big mating ritual." A huge coarse laugh. "Horny bastards.

The translation gives them all these local sex hormones, and we've lost a couple of them to screwing. They starve to death, the poor sick bastards, and fall for a thousand miles."

Jordick touched Cornell on the shoulder. "We've visited something like three dozen worlds. Right now we're going to five or six of them on a regular basis."

"Ours is best," Logan promised. "You guys are lucky."

Jordick sighed and looked into the ceiling. "I can't wait to leave."

Their boss shouted, "That's the boy!"

Cornell looked at him. A large dynamic voice, and the face couldn't be more ordinary. He smelled of the military, and not in a reassuring way. He had a makeshift discipline wrapped tight around his nervousness, and there was a palpable strangeness underneath everything. Too much time on the front lines? But Porsche seemed like an old hand, and she wasn't this way. Logan was two notches too loud, and he was too willing to tell secrets. Cornell was glad to know more, but the man was flaunting his knowledge, using it to impress his buck privates.

"I can't wait to get back," Logan announced. He picked up the half-eaten burger, then he set it down again. "A few days, a little fun, then back to rat meat and greasewood nuts. God, I miss them already."

Cornell watched the ordinary face.

"Hey, and wait till you take your first shit over there." Logan shook his head and grinned. "Talk about wild times! You've got these hard little turds, not a drop of water in them, and they *stink.* We think they're supposed to mark our territories for us. Like dogs do? A turd here, a turd there. And stay the fuck out!"

Jordick took a bite of his hamburger. He had ordered the same meal, emulating his new hero. Cornell began thinking of a quiet meal in his room, free of turds.

"We're a close-knit bunch, I can tell you." Logan squeaked against the leather again. "Oh, I'm in charge. Don't forget it. But I run a loose shift. I've got to. That's a whole damned world, all wilderness, and I sure can't watch over everyone myself." A pause. "A huge world, particularly when you're eight inches tall."

Give or take, that was a single body's height.

Logan kept laughing until the others laughed with him, then he seemed happy.

Cornell asked, "Why is High Desert the best post?"

"Why?" A snort, and he said, "The scenery. The normalcy, if you like being humanoid." He shook his head. "And I shouldn't tell you this, not here, but we've got a good, good chance of making the first First Contact. With an honest to God worthwhile native, I mean."

"What's a worthwhile native?" Cornell wondered aloud.

"Tools. Technology. That kind of thing." Logan made shapes in the air above his plate. "We've found spearheads, and more. Bits of refined metal? Copper. Aluminum. And there's more than that. Something big and smart, which we can feel . . . don't ask me how . . . and just think if it happens. We make the first First Contact, the three of us do . . . and won't we be something special . . . ?"

Jordick said, "It sounds exciting."

"Is. It is." He took a deep breath, then said, "Right now, even while we're sitting here on our asses, the best of my best are getting closer to the answers." A pause. "That's what this whole operation is chasing. One intelligent, technological species, and you think people'll give a shit about those Mayflies over there? Who's going to matter then, do you think?"

A couple of round faces glanced at them, suspicion interrupting the meal.

Cornell was wondering how you could *feel* something big and smart. But instead of asking, he said, "I've met one of your people. Porsche Neal? I think she's over there now."

Logan's face tightened, then he gave a little cough. "Oh, sure. She's one of my best, probably." He spoke carefully, his voice flat and a little smile tacked on at the end. Meaning what?

Cornell had lost his appetite.

Logan broke into a laugh. "So, did you jump her?" Then he said, "Just kidding." He kept laughing, looking at Jordick until Jordick joined in. "Christ, Novak. Have a sense of humor, would you?"

I'm leaving, Cornell was thinking. Right now—

"Boys," said Logan, "I want to get back to it."

"I bet so," Jordick squeaked.

"Know something, gentlemen? Coming home gets harder and harder. For me it does."

Then it was Logan who left, standing and wiping his hands on the cloth napkin. He put one hand before his face, staring at it and giggling. "Five fingers. Believe me, one day you'll be surprised to find yourself sporting five on a hand."

The two men watched him, wondering what odd thing he would say next.

"You gentlemen take care," Logan told them. "Train hard, and good luck, and I'm sure you'll do fine."

Jordick seemed to take solace in those words, nodding and grinning as Logan left them. And Cornell was thinking how hearing those words—"Good luck"—always picked you up a little bit. Your worst enemy could wish you luck, and there was no defense against that pleasant surge. The words had an impact, and somewhere you had to smile.

His speech would become a series of whistling words, his bodies able to speak with one voice, or several. He might hold six different conversations with six other people, impossible as that seemed. Shaking his head, Cornell had to ask the computer, "Whose language will I be speaking?"

"We presume it's the native language."

"Have we made contact yet?"

"No."

"What's the point of making contact? What are we after?"

"Knowledge, of course. The betterment of the human condition."

He offered a little nod.

"Tomorrow," promised his tutor, "you'll begin classes with human teachers. Our staff will show you how to make stone tools and braid your fur into harnesses."

"With three fingers," Cornell muttered.

"Yes."

"Will I be right-handed?"

"Yes. On HD, handedness transfers over."

He shut his eyes, imagining the new hands and how it might feel to have twelve of them. Twelve hands, and twelve three-toed feet. Controlled by cat-quick reflexes. Seven hearts, including the mind's head, and seven sets of lungs. Except the lungs were more like gills, the thin cold air flowing through them, exhaled out the rear.

"More questions?"

"If I lose a body," he began, "what happens?"

"A surviving body becomes pregnant. It replicates itself in a very brief period—"

"Suppose I lose all of my bodies. Nothing's left but my mind."

"That wouldn't be good news," the voice warned.

"I guessed that."

"If you can be found in time, then brought back through the intrusion, you will survive. But minds cannot produce new bodies, to our knowledge. Without bodies, you cannot function on HD."

Cornell touched one of the cubicle's close walls. "If I die there, what happens to my soul?"

"I have no idea, sir."

He straightened and asked, "All right, what's next?"

"Geography," said the tutor. "Navigating on the open desert is a critical skill."

The screen showed him New Reno, then the view pulled back to where he looked down on the big gray world. Mountains stood in the north, rough and extensive. South of New Reno, in the extreme distance, was a series of arroyos leading into deeper canyons. Cornell noticed how the map varied in details. There were gaps and vague stretches. That southern area was called the Breaks, and one canyon system looked like a high-quality photograph. "Is this where the aliens live?"

The tutor said, "Perhaps."

"It's like dreaming, isn't it?"

"How do you mean, sir?"

"People go there, but they can only bring back memories. Isn't that like dreaming?"

"In that sense, I suppose it is. Yes."

Cornell couldn't speak, arms wrapped around himself and his eyes shutting, his throat making a steady low moan. He was thinking:

*I don't believe this.*

Then:

*Who in his right mind would believe it?*

And he knew who. Knew exactly who. He opened his eyes and relaxed his arms, thinking how sometimes this world seemed thick with coincidences and ironies. *Dad would swallow it all in an instant.*

The tutor said, "Sir?"

"Go on," said Cornell. "I'm listening."

# 6

**He awoke long before the alarm, watching sunrise from** his window and dressing in old clothes. His keys and wallet ended up tucked inside spare shoes at the back of the closet. Breakfast arrived early—scrambled eggs and chicken sausage—and Cornell barely sampled it. He had a clear premonition of death, which wasn't unusual. Premonitions had accompanied every trip he'd taken in years. One final check of his room, then he went down to the lobby.

Jordick was already sitting near the front door. He looked at Cornell as if he didn't remember him, then swallowed and made room for him on the firm sofa. Neither man spoke. A van arrived—not theirs, they realized—and several people disembarked, one young woman crying. Her companions clustered around her. Cornell's first assumption was they were giving comfort. But no, it was more protection than comfort. A shielding of bodies. The other people were alert, arms locked together. Cornell thought of musk oxen on the tundra, the strong ones guarding their weak citizens from the wolves.

"Just back," Cornell whispered. "I wonder from where."

With a stiff voice, Jordick said, "We can't ask. You know the rules."

"Know them? I believe them with all my hearts."

It was a joke, but his companion seemed offended. Their

van arrived, and they boarded it and waited, and waited. Its robot driver did nothing, and Cornell wondered if this was some final test. Should they dismantle the driver and take themselves to the proper place? But no, someone else was coming. Logan. He climbed onboard, somehow looking changed. More calm, even placid. He sat in the front, alone, smiling as the door closed, and only when they were moving did he turn and acknowledge his companions. "Morning, boys." The smile brightened. "Ready for fun?"

"Sure," said Cornell.

Jordick said nothing, staring out the window.

There were security fences, four sets of them, then a field full of giant tents and an unpaved lot with parked vans and other official vehicles. Uniformed guards met them, leading them into a small prefabricated hut. Logan joked with the guards, asking about their girlfriends and wives. "I'm not getting any where I'm going, you see." The guards were amiable, laughing because Logan was a superior. He slapped one of them on the back, saying, "Want to join us? Room for a fourth!"

"Thank you, no. Sir."

"Sure?"

"Maybe next time, sir."

A door opened at the back of the hut, and orange light poured over them. They stepped beneath an orange-colored tent, and Cornell saw the bare ground worn smooth by boots and bare feet. There were clicks, pops. Someone said, "Undress, sirs. If you will." The tent was enormous, not tall but covering several acres; and he spotted machinery standing at the tent's center. Again there were clicks and pops, then a constant deep hum.

"Know how we found the intrusions?" Logan asked the question, his voice soft, almost respectful.

Jordick asked, "How?"

They were naked, walking forward. Three nude men, orange-colored. It was silly and solemn in equal measure.

"How did you find them?" Jordick asked again.

"This was a weapons lab, a long time ago." The man's

voice picked up speed, sounding more like his old self. "They would try out all sorts of fancy toys here. Neutron beams and laser beams, that kind of fun. And they found places where the machines didn't work quite right. Where energy got lost, or maybe the sensors malfunctioned. The science types joked about the places being haunted, and they moved their equipment a few feet, which solved the problem."

They entered a forest of machinery, following a dirt path past bulky ceramic housings and humming transformers.

"One of the weapons boys went to work for the CEA. And what he did, he started playing games with the Russian's equations. The equations that say Earth is many shapes and space is full of twisted worlds? That boy figured out there were imperfections. Seams, I guess you'd call them. And he remembered this haunted ground here, and of course the CEA had the money to investigate, and look at it!"

They had come to open ground, or what seemed open at first glance. Sophisticated machines stood on every side of them, a strange liquid blackness in the middle. Then Cornell looked again, noticing distortions in everything. The edges of the machines were drawn out, seemingly pounded flat yet never quite reaching the black zone. The air smelled dry and perfectly clean. Already they were walking on a squishy half-real surface—this wasn't the earth's surface anymore—and nothing made easy sense. Cornell looked down as he stepped, everyone's feet miles away, pink and nervously wiggling. Here he was! And beyond, forming without a motion, a great swirling hole smaller than the point on a needle—

"Move," shouted someone. Logan.

And Cornell was walking, then jogging, the hole opening for him, as if it had been waiting for him for all the ages.

Everything was bizarre, and everything was ordinary. The insanity felt reasonable. Time was comfortably odd. Distances were what the mind wanted to perceive. From somewhere came a mammoth sound, a thousand jets roaring at take-off, yet Cornell felt no pain. Jordick appeared beside him, body lean and pale, flecked with big red pimples. Then Logan came up on the other side of him, muscles and a jiggling belt of fat riding his middle. Cornell was thinking this was some kind of supernatural locker room, and he laughed aloud, without sound—

—pressing ahead, always faster.

The twisting blackness had a bright throat some thousand miles across. He stared ahead, eyes focusing, finding a curtain of radiant dust. What was that? Then he remembered: An old-fashioned sky full of stars, perhaps hundreds of thousands of them. High Desert was deep inside a cluster or a galactic core, no one could guess where. . . .

If I can see stars, he reasoned, I must be halfway.

Lifting his right hand, he touched his face and felt six faces, new fingers thick and long and shockingly strong. No nose, just slits that could close in a dust storm. A thick luscious fur covered his scalp and neck and almost everywhere else. Six hands, then twelve, began groping and exploring, everything as promised and the transformation strangest for being ordinary. His training didn't help, or hurt. The magic seemed effortless, Cornell wearing new clothes and a new set of instincts taking charge. There was something he needed to do, to find. Every head was turning . . . and there was his mind, just where he knew it would be.

A blunt-nosed football, the mind had brown fur over bone, slick callus below and the vital organs tucked within. There was no trace of limbs or a true head. Evolution had sculpted a dense, armored creature with no senses but the dimmest sense of touch. Its mouth and nostrils were at the rear, hidden by articulating bony shields. Its fur was long, particularly at the front; he found himself picking up hairs, tying rough braids, everything frighteningly natural. It was as if he'd always possessed six bodies, always lived this way. He felt like a person waking from a dream where he'd had no limbs, relieved to discover that he could move at will.

Cornell felt whole. Complete.

Muscles and neurons knew how to work. The new hands were deft and rapid. There was an unconscious unity, each body taking hold of the new braids, then pulling—in one motion—and the mind sliding forward on its slick bottom.

Cornell picked up speed, toes gripping the rubbery surface.

The stars jumped closer, feeling more like a real sky. Just when he thought he should pop into the new world, his motions slowed, a dense transparent syrup making his every motion hard work. His bodies bent, pulled and pulled, and he glanced up long enough to see body-shapes and a mind in front of him.

Logan.

Where's Jordick? he wondered. A single head turned, his rightmost body searching. The eyes found a huddle of black-furred bodies in front of their mind. No braids; no progress. Cornell tried to shout, but all he heard was a thin whistle. He made his body drop the harness and move toward Jordick. "Come on, come on." His lips didn't work properly, but he understood what he heard. He nervously touched his mouth, feeling teeth and biting once, needlelike teeth piercing his skin, a supersalty blood flowing over a slender tongue.

Spitting, Cornell told Jordick, "Move. Go."

The man shook every head, then finally, grudgingly, made himself kneel and grab at his mind's fur, clumsily pulling at handfuls of the stuff.

Cornell's other bodies and mind were far ahead. He felt the distance in the same way someone feels their hand reaching toward a high shelf. And that body ran after the other pieces, catching them and helping again.

Now the sky was above him, a very slight incline to the rubbery black ground. He could see Logan waiting where the ground flattened, bodies with hands on hips, something both cocky and impatient in their stances. Without warning, Cornell's lead mouth took its first true breath, a bitter chill numbing it. The toes felt honest dry grit, and he heard the grit moving. Efficient lungs pulled oxygen free and left the cold alone, complicated heat exchangers keeping the night out of his blood. And he was exhaling, every lung together, cold dry bursts of air out of his asses and his mind.

It was a few hours before dawn, local time.

Days were longer than on earth, but not much. And it was the equivalent of summertime now.

Logan asked, "Where's your friend?"

The whistling voice had a sharp, accusing tone. Was he blaming Cornell for leaving him behind?

Then Logan said, "Nope, here he comes. Last. Just like I thought he'd be."

Whistled words; another language. Cornell tried an experiment, saying his own name softly. "Cornell, Cornell." It emerged as a mixture of the native tongue and English, its humanness recognizable beneath a vivid string of notes. He thought of a parakeet taught its master's name.

There were whistles behind him, and motion.

From what looked like ordinary ground—from the center of a ring of white flags and white stones—came bodies and a mind, each of them breathing hard and fast, their exhalations kicking up little clouds of dust behind them.

*Poof* and *poof* and *poof.*

It tasted like home, this air did.

Cornell looked everywhere at once, noticing details. Logan had five bodies, one of them bloated. Pregnant with a replacement. A manly creature, and it made Cornell laugh to himself. Did Logan get teased by colleagues? When he was on leave, did the other field chiefs slap his butt with towels, asking how his baby was coming along?

"I'll take you in, show you your quarters."

It was Logan's voice. Cornell knew it without hearing anything like the old voice. But the five faces had the same square-jawed ordinariness, as if makeup artists had slapped on pigment and phony fur on five identical Logans.

"Fiddle with the harnesses later, Jordick."

New Reno wasn't far. Cornell could see the Rumpled Mountains in the north, the first buildings due east. Then came the thin stink of smoke. Dung was being burned. Greasewood was the main native plant, with some thornbrush in the wettest places. But wood fires were outlawed, building materials at a premium. And besides, why burn anything for heat? Everyone was preadapted to this climate. Callused feet; layers of fat; heat-exchanging lungs. They were hardened by a life they had never lived, and all of these preadaptations would fall away once they stepped back onto the earth.

"Here," Logan announced. Bodies gestured, a row of tiny earthen hemispheres before them. "Find empties. Get some sleep. There's a morning assembly in the town square. We'll make your assignments then."

This was the oldest part of New Reno. Not three years old, but already worn out. The buildings were greasewood frames covered with dirt, hides serving as doors and barely enough room inside for one person's parts. It looked as if every building had collapsed at least once, some repaired and others cannibalized for lumber. Cornell sent a couple of bodies to investigate a likely structure, lifting its dusty doorway and smelling a stranger. A sharp whistle said, "Get out." His bodies retreated, moved next door and sniffing first. He smelled no one. The place was empty, dark and chill.

Jordick was telling Logan, "Thanks for your help."

Logan watched them with a couple of heads. There was something unnerving about his bodies' stance, in their bright black eyes and the odd smiles.

"Thanks for getting me this post," Jordick added.

Laughter, then one mouth snorted. "Glad to help, always. Always."

They watched Logan drag his mind down the street, turn and vanish. Then Jordick took the next building in the row and did a clumsy job of pulling his mind inside. Front first, or back first? Cornell recalled what a human teacher had told him. The man had spent time on High Desert, offering no reason why he wasn't there anymore. But he explained, "With most things, and particularly the simplest things . . . just pause and let your instincts take hold. If you don't know, do what *smells* right." Which meant back first, as soon as possible. His mind needed to be hidden. Pulling it down between splintery timbers felt right, and suddenly he was more at ease: secure, and safe.

The little home had no furniture, only rat hides pushed

against the far wall, and the only light was starlight falling through the ventilation holes overhead. But his eyes adapted. Details emerged. A slab of micalike rock had been hung on the greasewood studs, making a crude mirror. Every fur was infested with slow gray worms, legless and wiry. Some previous tenant had used a knife, carving his name into one stud—Marvin Eugene Hicks, Jr. The confused odors of dozens of visitors mingled, and Cornell's noses were able to distinguish each one of them. As a dog might, or maybe better.

He touched himself again, in private spots. His geography was exactly as promised, more sexless than female, dry and not particularly sensitive.

Then he put a face to the mirror, this whole business thrilling and frightening, and more than anything, funny. A nervous smile; sharp teeth and the sharp tongue; eyes rhythmically opening and closing their inner lids. Three-fingered hands, smooth and dry, stroked the new face. A scab had formed on his bitten lip. No residual pain. A human would feel a twinge, he knew, and he poked at his eyes and cheekbones and the wound, glossy blunt fingernails catching the starlight. Here was a tougher package, no doubt. Quick and tiny and tough. Stepping through someone's elaborate fence, he had acquired the genetics of a meaner world.

"Cornell," whistled the face, "you are lovely."

And he kissed his reflection, all of his bodies laughing out loud.

"Hello?"

It was Jordick, and Cornell's first instinct was to stay quiet, feigning sleep. But it wouldn't work, and it wouldn't be nice. He felt an obligation, one of his bodies stepping through the hanging doorway, saying, "How's your mansion?"

"Oh, okay. Yours?"

"Comfortable enough."

Jordick's body was smaller than Cornell's. Not frail, but with a frail man's posture. Toes curled in the dust. Hands held out a half-shredded sack made from woven greasewood bark. Jordick withdrew a chunk of leather. No, it was dried meat. Instinct made Cornell sniff. It was rat dried over a dung fire, and it smelled lovely. Gorgeous.

He suddenly was starving, and Jordick said, "Be my guest."

The body ate, sharp teeth slicing and no chewing required. The taste mixed alien and ordinary, lingering in the mouth. Smiling afterward, he said, "Thanks."

"I can't sleep," Jordick offered, his smile lopsided. "Want to walk?"

Cornell saw no harm.

"Keep the rest." Jordick handed him the sack. "I've had my share."

"Thank you."

Again he smelled smoke, stronger now. Familiar. Just the two bodies strolled through New Reno, the rest left behind, feeding themselves and their minds. Minds required no more calories than any hard-working body, despite being larger and packed with neural tissue. No limbs; few muscles. The ultimate invalids. And doing several things at once proved easy, astonishingly easy, making both men a little giddy as parts of them walked along the street.

Logan had come this way. Cornell knew the man's scent; when Jordick realized that they were following him, he said, "Maybe we shouldn't."

"Shush," Cornell warned.

There was a massive structure near the town square, sprawling and thick-walled, bleeding firelight from its tiny windows. In the first days, before the surrounding terrain was thoroughly explored, it had served as a fortification. Now it was the administrative headquarters. There still were rumors of gray bodies watching New Reno from a distance, still fears of attack; but there was no official paranoia anymore, no bodies standing guard in the night.

Again Jordick said, "Maybe we shouldn't."

And again Cornell said, "Shush."

Logan was nearby. First came a strong fresh scent, then the sound of his voice. Voices. Several mouths were speaking simultaneously. They were close enough that the sharp, berating tone shone through. Cornell edged up near a window, hearing, "—a few fucking days, and you make a mess of things. I leave orders, strict and clear, and what happens?"

Someone responded, a single mouth muttering some excuse.

"Shut up. Just shut up." A pause. "I don't believe it. You're claiming we aren't behind schedule? That delays aren't delays? That every last goal is being met, regardless of appearances?"

Cornell's body took a breath and held it inside.

"You think I was on vacation? Who here thinks I was sunning my ass by the fucking pool?"

Little whistles; silence.

"Meetings," said Logan. "And more meetings." Something was thrown, or it was dropped. *Thud.* "You don't know how they're pushing. They want results. Solid, bona fide results. 'Why do we keep flooding your world with volunteers?' they ask me. 'What makes you special?' And I tell them about the artifacts, again. I remind them that the goddamn fish worlds aren't exactly giving us new technologies. And I tell them how we keep feeling something. Something big living deep in the Breaks. Practically calling to us, I promise, and give us more time. Please, please."

Someone spoke, asking a question.

"Two came," said Logan. Then he groaned, adding, "More like one and a half, really. I pulled a recruit off the fish detail. He's warm, he's upright. Don't complain."

Cornell glanced at his companion, Jordick's eyes dropping, focusing on his new toes.

"Who's going to be famous?" Logan asked his audience. "Think. We're one team in a dozen, our necks on the cutting block. You tell me. Who matters in a thousand years? It's the team that makes First Contact. The team who can claim shaking paws with the first intelligent race. Second place is the same as last place. Keep that in mind. You ball-less wonders are going to do better, or I'll replace you. Understood? I'm not going to be cheated out of this prize. Not now, not ever. Do you comprehend?"

There were muttered, intimidated responses. Then silence.

Then someone opened a nearby doorway, without warning, the skin making a dry sound and a sputtering dung fire throwing a wedge of light across the open ground. Jordick broke into a run; Cornell trotted after him. It was like being twelve again, spying on Mr. Lynn and his girlfriends. Only this kind of excitement tasted different. A richer brew, every one of Cornell's bodies shivering.

Some kind of cage stood on the west edge of New Reno. Neither man remembered it from the computer images, which was strange, since the greasewood was old, bleached by wind and sun. It might be a jail, Cornell guessed. But Jordick pointed out, "It doesn't look used." He meant that in a positive light, adding, "They've never needed it." As if his fellow explorers were too decent, too honorable. But what if it was being saved for a different kind of prisoner? Cornell touched the wood. His companion said, "Look. Someone's moving out there."

People stood on the open desert, under starlight—

—and Cornell realized it was one person. Three bodies, but all the same shape and color. He remembered the rumored strangers, cautiously approaching. Then he saw the wooden tube and how one body would kneel, peering into an eyepiece; and he trotted forward, asking, "What do you see?"

"Pardon?" A woman's startled voice.

"That's a telescope," he stated, astonished to find one here.

She had built it herself, they learned. She was the entire astronomy division on High Desert; but no, she wasn't a true astronomer. She'd gotten only halfway through her graduate work, ending up teaching high school science. "Not that this work needs a Ph.D.," she joked. "I mean, look at it. Iffy lenses. Bad focus. Chromatic aberrations, and I've got to keep readjusting my direction."

Cornell touched the wooden tube with a fingertip.

"Galileo had better equipment," she told them.

Yet she sounded happy. Excited.

"May I?" Cornell asked.

"Please do."

It had been ages, and this was a different set of eyes. Yet it felt natural enough. He found himself gazing at countless stars, the brightest ones near enough to touch. Spectrums were twisted apart by the clumsy lenses, making little rainbows. And the colors were different from the ones at home, purples and blues less intense, oranges and reds full of subtle new shadings.

He stepped back, breathed hard and made a cloud of dust rise. Then he looked up, feeling the stars as much as seeing them. He had been here his entire life, he kept thinking. Some new part of him did nothing but assure him that this was the sky of his childhood.

"What kind of work are you doing?" Jordick asked.

"With parallaxes," she reported.

"What's that mean?"

Cornell explained, "It's the motion of stars against a fixed background. It's a way of estimating distances."

Jordick made a puzzled sound.

"Some aren't a tenth of a light-year away," said the woman.

"If this is a cluster," Cornell asked, "can you tell where it is?"

"Give me a radio telescope. Let me find some millisecond pulsars, then match them with the pulsars we see from the moon. And maybe. If this is within a few tens of thousands of light-years." A big laugh. "If that kind of measuring applies."

Jordick was squinting into the eyepiece.

"Where do you gentlemen work?" she asked. "Have I seen you?"

Cornell gave a sketch of himself. Jordick had to point out, "We could be anywhere in the universe. You'll never know just where this is."

There was a pause, then one of the woman's bodies spoke. Ignoring Jordick, she recounted school stories and her marriage and divorce, no children and nothing exceptional. "Who'd have guessed this?" She laughed. "Not bad for an old broad with varicose veins, huh?"

The sky began to brighten in the east, all but the closest

stars washed away by the ruddy glow. And Jordick had to say, "This entire sky could be a phony. Just like the earth's was."

Cornell blinked, the inner lids shutting and then the outer ones. Then he turned back to the astronomer, asking, "How long have you been coming here?"

"Two years," she reported. "Short shifts, long breaks."

"Yeah?"

"I don't have much aptitude being alien, honestly." Her smile seemed more human, the muscles of her face having more practice with the expression. "A few days on, then a couple of weeks off. Sometimes longer."

"What if you stay here longer?"

"I get strange." She lifted her hands and shook them as if nervous. "I sleep badly. My thoughts jumble. I start losing coordination among my bodies. I guess you'd say I just generally collapse."

First light struck the Rumpled Mountains, spreading down from the rough gray peaks. They resembled someone's titanic blanket kicked to the foot of the bed.

"We should go get our postings," said Jordick.

"Soon," Cornell allowed.

"I want the Breaks." With authority, Jordick said, "That's the best posting. That is."

Cornell watched the woman's faces, aware of her silence.

Then after a long pause, she was saying, "It's strange. Some people can stay here forever. And others, most of us . . . we're just missing something, it feels like. Not even practice helps us."

A pause.

She looked at Cornell with every face, telling him, "It's as if some of us belong here and everyone else doesn't. It's that simple. And after a while, it's easy to see who is who." Every head nodded, and she squinted into the fresh sunlight. "I see a recruit, and it's as if I can foretell his future. Which is about the worst part of being here. To me."

A LONG BODY STOOD IN THE STREET, DUST SWIRLING AROUND IT. Cornell squinted, sensing something was wrong. The body was too thin, fragile and moving as if painfully weakened. Cornell and Jordick were dragging their minds toward it, on the way to the town square; a single hand was extended, palm up, the vaguely human face capable of a feeble longing.

"It's begging," Jordick realized, astonished and then amused.

There wasn't any intelligence in the eyes. They were dull and slow to react, and it didn't speak save for a soft meaningless whistling.

"Its mind must have died," Jordick offered. "I bet so."

Died or left without it. Although he couldn't believe—

"Remember? They warned us about these fellows." Jordick laughed, one body kneeling, picking up a random stone. "Watch this."

Cornell felt uneasy.

His companion offered the stone to the begging hand, and the hand closed on it and lifted it to the mouth, a tentative bite followed by a vigorous sideways spit. Then the hand reached out again, nothing learned, the dead face staring at them, incapable of even the slightest anger.

Jordick laughed louder.

"Come on," said Cornell. "We've got to go."

* * *

A dozen people were scattered about the square—"scattered" had a whole new meaning here—long shadows overlapping and the thin air warming fast where there was sun. People spoke, laughed, and sang. Most of them were veterans between assignments, a palpable sense of familiarity hanging on them. Logan and a couple of subordinates were at one end of the square, and Cornell kept his distance, trying to watch everything. A dozen people—no, he counted fourteen minds—and he found he could keep them separate at a glance. Bodies had a characteristic shape and size, fur color and bearing; the minds had the same color cues and telltale variations, each one marked by personal touches. Decorative braids. Adornments of shiny stones and rat bones set in artful patterns. One person's mind was sprinkled with the dried yellowy husks of flightless bees. Strange, strange. And what's more, Cornell could *feel* the connections between bodies and minds. It was as if there were spiderwebs strung across the square, bizarre energies running through them and almost visible. He was so busy mastering this new sense that he didn't notice someone coming up behind him.

"Novak," he heard, "you look different."

He started to turn his heads—

"Change your hair, did you?"

—six tall bodies smiling at him, hands holding spears made of greasewood and sharpened bone. They were brown bodies, and a big brown mind shone in the morning light. "Porsche?"

"And you've lost a couple pounds, haven't you?"

This had to be Porsche. The bodies had her stance and height—on a relative scale—and they moved with her confidence, long legs well-muscled and every mouth giving a sharp toothy smile. Tied to her mind were an assortment of sacks made from skins, plus dried greasewood blossoms, thin and golden, lending her a strange femininity.

"Got your assignment yet?" she asked.

He shook several heads.

"Good. Let me talk."

A pair of Logan's bodies were talking to Jordick, one body writing on a crude piece of paper. Or parchment. "I'm taking a big group to the Breaks. That's our priority now."

Black-furred bodies nodded, eager to begin.

"Novak." Logan glanced at Porsche, then back at him. "Think you can help do some bridge building?"

"No, I get him," said Porsche. "I need him."

The bodies approached, one hand squeezing the charcoal pencil. "Need him where?"

"I found a grove of greasewood." She pointed with several spears, the bone tips drawing precise circles. "West and south. Nuts and wood and plenty of both."

"Take someone else," said Logan.

"No."

The voice was mild, but solid.

"Jordick'll go. Won't you, son?"

"I was promised Novak," she claimed.

"Who promised him?"

"His case officer," Porsche reported. And she was lying, her voice sounding just false enough that everyone listening would know it. "I need someone strong, and you need the wood. Am I right?"

Logan made a low sound, one head shaking. Cornell could see the paper, his name written in clumsy black letters.

"All right," said Logan. "Take him."

"Thanks," she sang.

Then Logan came closer with one body, the one not playing secretary, and it laid a hand on one of Cornell's crotches, whispering, "How's it feel, having a slit?"

Cornell backed away, fur lifting in anger.

"I'm teasing!" Logan laughed and snorted, then said, "Sure, Porsche. But you train him. Teach every trick, darling."

He left, and she said, "Idiot."

"Idiot squared."

"When I was on the other side, once or twice—?" She paused and grinned. "He made passes at me."

"And?"

"No *and.* Nothing happened." Shrugs, and she added, "One time here he tried fondling me. Just once."

Cornell looked at her bodies, tall and obviously strong. "How did he lose his body?"

"I don't know." She laughed. "The one I hit had broken ribs."

And he was laughing, too. He had missed this woman.

Logan's pregnant body was sitting in the sun, its belly already bigger than it was just hours ago. And Porsche was saying, "He lost it in the Breaks, I heard. Someone got pissed about something. Which is hard to imagine, I know."

"Thanks for helping me," Cornell told her.

She smiled, snaky tongues showing behind predatory teeth. "Wait till you work for me," she warned him. "A few days from now, and the Breaks might look awfully sweet."

Cornell wished Jordick good luck.

"See you soon," his companion promised, arms lifting his newly tied harnesses, fitting them over his shoulders and jerking his mind into motion.

Porsche led Cornell in another direction, to an abandoned hut where she had hidden equipment and food. They dug them up, and she made him ready for the open desert, lending him spears and sacks full of dried meat. She showed him how to secure the sacks to the mind. She gave him tips on how to position the harnesses, how to lean and pull and reduce chafing. She promised to teach him how to hunt, and he mentioned the classes . . . which caused her to say, "Knowing it wrong is worse than knowing nothing."

They were outside New Reno by midmorning, past the empty cage and soon out of sight of anything human, and it was like no march he could have imagined for himself. The alien day seemed to last forever, and they moved without pause, shadows turning short and the air almost warm, the clear cloudless sky a washed-out bluish purple. The novelty was exciting, then it would vanish. There were unexpected moments when he felt as if he'd always lived this way, dragging his mind across dusty wastelands. He mentioned it to

Porsche, who replied, "We've all had brain-dragging days." And she laughed, enjoying everything. Nothing seemed to bother the woman.

Cornell grew tired and thirsty, and confessed to both.

"You're not thirsty," she warned him. "That's habit talking. You were hydrated when you came across, so you've got plenty of water stored in your fat, camel-style. Believe me, a couple of sips a day are too much."

He tried to ignore the dry mouths.

She used three bodies to pull her mind. "Practice helps," she promised. "But a lot of what we do is by guess and by golly."

He asked, "Why not build wagons?"

"Wheels in this dust? With wood scarce?" She told him, "It doesn't work. I know because I tried it. Several times."

"Yeah?"

"Did I tell you? I was part of the first team across." A pause. A wave of spears. "This is easiest. This is what nature wants us to do."

Sure enough, he improved. Three bodies could put the harnesses over their shoulders, pulling the slick-bottomed mind over dust and rock and up the mild slopes. Momentum was critical. Don't stop, or you have to jerk hard to win back your momentum. But with three bodies free, he could help Porsche's bodies scout ahead, and he learned how to hunt ground that had been hunted a hundred times in the last years: which holes and crevices had promise; which low places might hold buried seeds and eggs. All they found were a pair of flightless bees—small ones, said Porsche, and half-starved—yet it took Cornell a little while to eat his share. The raw wet insides had a sharp flavor that was not unpleasant but certainly was new.

"Be thankful," she told him. "We've got a ten-legged spider that tastes like gasoline."

He asked about the others from that first team.

There had been twenty of them, she reported, including Logan. More than half had quit, usually through psych discharges. "A few serious breakdowns. They're still under care,

I've heard." She paused, then admitted that several had died, and several more had vanished and were presumed dead. "Although you hear rumors they went native. They decided there was no point going home again, and they crossed to the other side of the Rumpleds. Or wherever."

Cornell watched her bodies in motion, wondering if his lust was his human nature. Captive rock rats had never engaged in sex, yet there seemed to be a reshuffling of genetic traits. A rat's mind gave birth to a new mind, and its bodies to new bodies, yet the child wasn't identical to its parent. Were viral agents carrying DNA from nearby rats? Or were offspring intentionally mutating? Nobody could say. There weren't any proper tools, and biology wasn't the priority. Science here had a distinctly Dark Age feel about it.

"What do you see?"

Cornell blinked, most of his eyes fixed on Porsche's rump and sexless broad chests. "It's beautiful country."

"Think so?"

He made a show of looking everywhere, absorbing his surroundings. "This is where the Coyote chases the Road Runner."

She enjoyed that inspiration.

Minus the roads, he thought. And with the players all mortal.

Eventually they passed through what was left of a greasewood grove, nothing but tidy stumps and a few chips. Greasewood was like bristlecone pines, ancient and stout, existing on the brink of a habitable zone. One body stepped onto a stump, noticing the fine, closely spaced rings; and he asked, "Are they annual rings?"

"Probably."

"Then they're centuries old," he realized.

Sober nods, and she said, "Some were thousands of years old."

Cornell looked at himself and Porsche, again feeling that sense of belonging here. "How do the natives live? Any ideas?"

She said, "Not like us," with certainty.

"Have you seen them?"

"Twice, I think." She paused, looking toward the horizons. "The first time was that first year. Logan had us out on a hunt for them. I was supposed to drive the natives toward him, and I found tracks, but somehow the body slipped past me. I saw it running in the distance. It was already safe." A pause. Shrugs. "The second time was a few months ago. And a surprise. My hunting bodies slipped into an arroyo, and they found a body sunning itself. Just a few strides away from them. But it slipped away, too. It was like trying to catch a ghost."

"How did it look?"

"Gray fur, like the ground. Otherwise, normal. For all I know, it belonged to a human who'd gone wild."

"What about artifacts?"

"Oh, sure. Plenty of them." She winked and warned him, "By the rules, you have to turn in every artifact. A chip of stone, a funny-looking turd." One of her hunting bodies came close, putting a spearhead up to his face. "How does it look?"

Like a razor, he noted. Expert work.

"Better than I could manage," she confessed.

Were bits of metal found in the desert?

"Aluminum, mostly. Which is a tough material to work with. It implies a fair amount of industry, somewhere—"

"And bones? Do you find bones?"

"Once," she said, "I found an entire mind. A big ball of white bones. With oxidized bits of rings and wires nearby, I should add. And in this air, oxidation takes a damned long time."

"Just a mind?" he asked.

"No bodies, if that's what you mean. But then again, scavengers may have carried them away."

Cornell whispered, "A mind," and shook every head.

"Bigger than ours, by the way. Maybe double our size."

He found himself watching the desert, feeling alert. Comfortably paranoid. An enormous world was hiding from him, and so far people had barely explored even this sliver of it.

"Back to your question: How do they live?" Porsche exhaled, tufts of dust rising for dramatic effect. "This is guesswork, so don't write any textbooks. But I think the typical local has a *huge* home range. It would take miles and miles of desert to feed one of us for a long time. And I wouldn't think you'd want to wander like we're doing now. No, it would be better to keep your mind hidden and safe, then hunt a small area bare before moving again. That's how I'd do it, if I was stuck here. Save my energies. Measure my risks."

Cornell thought about the thousand-year-old trees, now dead.

"You've got to wonder what they think," she mentioned. "All these strangers arriving from nowhere. Meaning us. Not the right color, and crazy. They can watch us from a distance, and we busily impoverish their land in order to feed ourselves."

"I'd be angry," Cornell confessed.

"No doubt."

Then he was thinking how anger might not be universal. Perhaps it was too much of a human tendency. His own tendency. The natives might vote for caution, retreating to new country. Anger is a spendthrift emotion, he'd learned lately. It had a way of wasting everything precious.

"If we packed up and left today," Porsche commented, "you'd see traces of us for a thousand years. There'd be a patch of desert with nothing growing, and New Reno might last ten thousand years. Like a little Babylon."

"Why do you do this?" he asked. "If it's so damaging—"

"First, because I'm hopeful. Something's out there. When we get close to the Breaks, you'll feel it."

He swallowed with dry mouths, nodding.

"And besides," she said, "what's ten thousand years to a planet? It's nothing." She looked at him and everywhere else, laughing, every face grinning. "We're just a few people, and we're not so important. You're not, and nobody else is either." A pause, then she added, "And isn't that the best news possible? I mean, think if there was a person who truly mattered, who was absolutely essential, wouldn't that make for one splendidly awful mess?"

* * *

They camped that first night among dunes. The sunset was long, the broad western sky shot full of nameless shades of red. There weren't as many stars tonight, he mentioned; and Porsche said that the day's dusts would settle, letting more starlight through by morning. She helped him make ready for sleep, giving him pointers on how and where to bury his mind, leaving its mouth and nostrils able to breathe. A big round lump wouldn't lose much heat overnight; bodies would. She made him bury five of his bodies in the soft dust, sharing warmth, and the sixth body would sit on top of the mind, exposed and watchful. The rest of him would sleep, one set of eyes able to detect motions and warn him. "Rest," Porsche warned him. "You'll need it." Except he wasn't tired in the right way, unable to relax enough even to pretend sleep.

"Where do the Breaks go?" he wondered aloud.

"Who knows? They're deeper and steeper all the time."

Possibilities occurred to him, no way to test them. The exposed body looked skyward, feeling the mind inhale and exhale every so often. "Where were you when the Change happened?"

"On a basketball court," she answered, her exposed body adding, "Outdoors."

"Where was that?"

"A suburb of Dallas," she said.

"I saw it happen," he confessed. "You?"

"Oh, sure." As if nothing was more unremarkable. "My boyfriend and I had beaten some local kids, three of them, and we were taking a break, sitting off the slab, out from under its lights. I was looking up when it happened. *Pow.*"

Cornell had assumed a special status, but it didn't exist. He breathed with every mouth, then exhaled. The mind's anus made the dust bubble for a moment. He asked, "Were you scared?"

She glanced over at him, then said, "Somewhat."

Except he didn't think so. Somehow he knew she was saying what he expected to hear. And he looked at the dusty stars, remembering how he had felt fear and excitement and an effervescent amazement.

"How'd it happen for you?"

He told the story. At first he used the short form—the one designed for cocktail parties and one-night affairs—but Porsche asked questions, demanding elaborations. She asked about everyone's reactions. He had the impression that she had memorized his files, and she seemed intrigued by his description of Dad holding court over the neighborhood. When he realized he had been talking for more than an hour, his body was becoming chill. "Change bodies every so often," she advised. "Till you get used to our nights."

Our nights.

Then she said, "See? More stars all the time."

It was true. He stared at the radiant sky, one body down and a warm one up to replace it. Would he dream? He'd forgotten to ask if dreams were natural. But his mind drifted into something like sleep, shallower but restful nonetheless. In one dream he saw himself back home, sitting in the street . . . six bodies sitting with legs crossed, their dark faces raised. Each one was tiny, the size of a sewer rat. Yet he didn't feel small or out of place. And while he dreamed, the one body stayed alert, its own little packet of neural tissues immune to such nonsense, eyes gazing through the clear inner lids, its head turning and turning with an imbecile's devotion to duty.

They reached the living greasewood on the fourth day. Full-grown trees filled a little basin, stout trunks spaced as if planted by hand. Every grove had that even spacing. The trees were sharing the scarce water, cooperating according to ancient rules. The leaves were scarce and shiny and always small, glittering like blue gems. Nuts hung in little bunches, protected by leathery husks. Porsche showed him how to pound the husks open. Both of them ate their fill. "We think rock rats spread them," she said. "Ages ago, this might have been a rat's cache." She chewed on the sweet nut meat, an empty mouth saying, "Don't eat past full. You haven't died until you've had a case of High Desert runs."

Cutting down the trees was dull work, slow and tough. The bark was like Kevlar, the wood beneath more like concrete.

Cornell learned how to make teams with his bodies, pairs trading swings with sharp stone-headed axes. Porsche wanted three of his trees down by dusk; she managed four by herself, then helped him until it was dark. They ate more nuts, slept and woke early. Cornell was stiff in every body, arms screaming with each swing; but at least the persistent thirst had given up on him and left.

They felled several more trees, and he paced them out, realizing that most Christmas trees would stand taller. Porsche showed him how to strip away the stout limbs, tying them into bundles, and how to use the bark to make ropelike strips of every length.

Dragging the trees seemed impossible. Crazy. But Porsche said, "Don't worry, you're tougher than you look. Stronger, too."

Maybe so.

"We'll leave tomorrow," she promised. "And go like hell."

He smiled. There was still some afternoon left, and he had nothing to do. He decided to sleep in the partial shade, keeping two bodies awake. He woke to an odd sound. A voice. "Pass," he heard. "She shoots." Then, "Porsche takes the ball." Then, "Rebound, Porsche."

She was playing basketball with herself. Three-on-three, or some mutation of that game. A crude backboard was lashed high on a likely trunk, with a hoop made from bark. The ball was a big empty greasewood husk carried with a dribbling motion. Cornell approached, stopped and watched, then applauded until she said:

"Challenge me?"

"Pardon?"

"I'm world champion. Want to play me?"

Five-on-five. They would rotate in the rested bodies as needed. The game was fun, fast-paced and enhanced by effortless teamwork. Cornell amazed himself with perfect no-look passes and blind shots, his bodies knowing where the hoop was even if only one of them could see it. And he didn't do too badly. They played until it was dark, until it was 121 to

59. Porsche had only doubled his score, which he considered a minor victory. Then, with her best spearhead, she etched the final score into one of the day's stumps. They wrote their names, in English. Cornell asked, "If the natives were literate, would we know their script?" She thought it was a good question, and she didn't offer any guess. Cornell watched her breathing, watched her exhalations lift up tufts of dust, not once thinking about falling in love with her. What he was thinking was that he wished Porsche could have been his neighbor when he was a boy, and a friend. Something about the woman was utterly intoxicating. He'd had too many lovers in his life, and he wasn't in any hurry. Friendship was perfect. And besides, what else could they offer each other?

Friendship or frustration.

Those were the two choices, for now.

**MOST OF THE REST OF HIS SHIFT WAS SPENT DRAGGING DOWNED** trees to the Breaks, two at a time and with Porsche's help, then returning for the next pair. Three bodies could manage a thick trunk, polishing it smooth and slick, but when he was careless—which was often—it could take all twelve of their bodies to pry it out of a hole. To her credit, Porsche let him lead just the same. She wanted him to learn fast, and Cornell appreciated his devoted teacher. She showed him how to read the terrain and where to find landmarks, and she cried out and hugged his bodies when he found the honey-ant nest on his own, without prompting. They had a little midday party; he cut off the heads before eating the sweet swollen abdomens. Then they moved again, again with him leading, and he read the dust wrong, wandering into a little basin where his legs and the trunk sank into a talclike powder.

Porsche sounded like every coach ever born, disappointment mixed with a needling anger. She wouldn't help him. Not this time. His bodies waded out of the dust, then he set to work trying to free the trunk. Tall white dust devils formed on the desert ahead, marching and collapsing and re-forming again. Cornell rigged longer harnesses, and with all six bodies grunting, he managed to pull the trunk partway free. A second try, and a harness broke. A third, then a knot failed. While he was sprawled on the ground, gulping at the useless air, Porsche said:

"Tell me about your parents."

It was the perfect moment. Too tired to work, he had to respond. "You read my files. What do you know about them?"

Porsche recounted bits and pieces. Dad chasing saucers; Cornell and their neighbor helping; Mom gone for a long time. "It's one of the more unique upbringings. I've been intrigued since I met you."

"Have you been?"

"What happened between you and your father?" she pressed.

And he surprised himself, starting to explain it. The story bubbled out of him under pressure, old angers coming with it. Cornell lifted some of his hands and watched them shake, curling them into strange fists and giving the soft ground a few good blows.

He told her about their mammoth fight and how he'd driven off in a rage. His mother had never been abducted. Of course not. The central premise of his childhood had been a thorough and ridiculous lie.

"Did you go back home?" she asked.

"Eventually. For stretches." Sometimes he lived with the Underhills, sometimes with the Petes. "When I graduated from high school, I left for good. For college. Entirely on my own."

"What kind of woman was your mother?"

He didn't know. Mrs. Pete's stories were so different from Pete's and Dad's. He scarcely had a clue. "But really, I don't think about her. She's a habit that I've tried to break, if you want to know the truth."

"Why did she leave?"

"She was sick of my father," he replied.

Staring at him with those bright dark eyes, she made Cornell nervous. She made him too aware of himself. Something about her gaze was worldly and suspicious of everything he told her.

"What about your family?" he asked. "Go on. Show me an ordinary upbringing."

Which it was. Porsche had two brothers, which made sense—strong and tall brothers, handsome and competitive—and loving parents who seemed to come out of a sitcom, too happy to be real. It was the perfect family, and Cornell said so. And Porsche said, "We aren't. We've had troubles, too." Except she had nothing worse to offer than her father's cancer—in remission now, thank goodness—which made Cornell ask:

"How in hell did you get hired? The agency wants people with no close families."

"I aced their tests?" She said it as a question, then added, "Besides, they weren't as particular when I joined up. It was easier to get in."

"Before there were casualties."

A circumspect nod, nothing more.

"Do you tell your family about this job? Do they know what their daughter does with her life?"

"Our jobs are secret," she said. "You know that."

Except he wasn't sure. Those weren't human faces in front of him, and they certainly lacked human eyes, but something in the expressions made him wonder if Porsche was lying to him. He imagined the Neal family gathered around the dining room table, listening to her incredible tales of High Desert and her bizarre other life—

"Enough rest," she told him. "Try to get your tree free, okay?"

—and he said, "Sure." His hands picked up the harnesses again, and he pulled again as part of him was thinking: Nonetheless, you're lying to me. I know. I've been lied to by the best, and I've got a feel for these things.

The Breaks began as bare rock and a nameless dip in the ground.

It was a day and a half from the grove when Porsche had them turn downstream. The dip became a shallow, broad gully that someone had marked with stones. 15SW, he read. There was a master map somewhere, she claimed. This was the fifteenth arroyo in the southwest quadrant. From here, she explained, it didn't matter if they kept track of directions. "Just follow the invisible water downhill, and we'll get there."

The gully was deeper than it looked, filled partway with drifted dust. When did it rain? Cornell wondered aloud. "Not in our memory," Porsche admitted. Was anyone working on the meteorology? "Science gets the short stick," she warned him. "You should know it by now."

The world tilted, their gully becoming a deep stony cut spilling into a snow-white chute. The air filled with a succession of solid thuds as Porsche showed him how to let the steep parts take the trees for him. As Cornell prepared to lower his mind down the same chute, she warned him, "It's your head. Don't treat it like a lump of stone."

He was careful, probably overly careful. So with the next chute, after letting the tree lead the way, he got sloppy, hands only half-holding the braided harnesses and his bare feet sliding. It was just a few yards of smooth rock—earth-scale—but one body slipped and fell hard, cutting the legs out from under another one. And his mind slid faster, twisting and clipping a boulder, all of him going numb. It was like a blow to the head, and he was in agony. Blood-warm tar swallowed him, black and bottomless, and his bodies kicked and pulled, trying to reach the surface—

—and then he was awake again, whole again. Porsche was standing over his limp bodies, conspicuously saying nothing. Like any good coach, she knew when a lesson was obvious enough even for a fool to learn from it.

They found other people at dusk. Their arroyo had fed into a larger one, broad and dry save for a weak spring seeping cool water. Algae or something akin grew on the dampened rocks. Someone had hammered out a shallow pool where the moisture could collect. It was the first standing water he had seen in months, it seemed. His thirst felt genuine, bodies kneeling and drinking, and Porsche told him, "Fill their mouths and spit into your mind's mouth. First. That's done first."

It seemed natural when he tried it, as proper as the salad fork being set outside the dinner fork.

Below the spring was a sloppy campground, and he

counted half a dozen people. Three of them were upbound. Homeward bound. They acted happy in a cautious way, thinking of the desert to come. The others were permanently stationed here, in charge of whatever supplies came to them. They were officious little bureaucrats, one woman making notes about the fresh nuts and lumber. "Put them at the edge," she told them. Edge? Cornell followed his partner's lead, around a mild bend, and found himself at the brink of an enormous cliff. In some long-ago age, an entire river had shot down this arroyo, tumbling into the canyon below. The canyon was rough and barren, half-hidden by shadow. Some kind of wooden ramp had been fixed to their wall. The narrow thing looked slippery and worn, greasewood boards bound together with bark ropes and braided fur. It was a great and crude and clumsy structure, and it seemed wondrously brave, if something inanimate could be brave. . . .

"They'll take it down for us," Porsche explained.

"How far down?" He couldn't see any end to the ramp, losing it in the shadow. "Miles down?"

"Remember our scale. We're tiny."

He could be six foot two, and this place would feel enormous. "The ramp reaches the bottom?"

"Eventually."

"Then what?"

"Another trail, down and down." She nodded, equally impressed with the vista. "I've heard there's a second hanging road, then more canyons."

The western sky was orange flame centered on the burnished sun.

"So what's at the bottom?"

"Who knows?"

"But there's something we can feel, right?"

One body shrugged, then another. "Sometimes, yes."

"What kind of something?"

"Think how you can feel other people. The ones nearby."

Like now. He knew the telltale sensation, as if he was in tune with the energies holding each person together.

"It's similar," said Porsche. "But staggering. A million times more powerful, at least."

"You've felt it?"

"A few times." Eyes closed their outer lids, then opened again. "Not now. I can't now."

"But what's it feel like? Why's it worth all this hard work?"

"Sometimes," she said, "it seems to feel us. And call to us. 'Come here,' it whispers. In a roar."

But not tonight, thought Cornell, gazing into the open air and reddening sun, the brightest stars winking into view . . . and he could feel nothing but a few feeble souls. . . .

They started back to the greasewood, and Porsche—again picking an out-of-the-blue moment—asked him, "Do you believe in the Architects?" Then she answered her own question. "I don't. Not as one godlike species, I don't."

"No?"

"Do you think about them much, Novak?"

It was a jolly challenge and a way of teasing. He thought how being with another person was like visiting another world; both had their rules, their personalities, and you adapted every day.

"Never," he reported. "I never think about Architects."

She didn't seem to hear him. "We imagine them as some kind of first intelligence. First in the universe; first in our galaxy. They rebuilt everything, and we hope that we can find them somewhere."

"Is that unreasonable?"

"But what if? What if life's common? What if intelligence is easy? We've seen a handful of worlds so far, and they have smart beetles and fish and so on. It just seems that good minds are cheap. Nature seems to evolve all kinds of them. See what I mean?"

He nodded. "I guess."

"But now suppose technology converges. Like water always runs downhill, let's say that science and machinery move in the same inevitable direction."

Mixing fact with fancy, she sounded like someone else he knew.

"When we first met," he remarked, "you called the universe one big suburb—"

"Exactly." One of her bodies adjusted its harness; the rest smiled and nodded. "Think of houses. Think of homes. By definition, they've got certain common features. Walls, a roof. Some sense of property, or at least personal space. That's what a home is."

He said, "The universe. As tract housing."

"A magnificent kind." A hunting body waved its spear. "Imagine millions of worlds spawning intelligence. Each house gets too full, too small, and that's why they rebuilt their surroundings. The earth is a natural world caught up in the remodeling. Or maybe it's something built from scratch, from spare dust, then tied up with everything else through the quantum intrusions. . . ."

Cornell listened, quietly absorbing her images.

"Suburbia gets such a bad reputation. Boring and stark, and so on." Hands gestured; mouths whistled little abuses. "I don't agree. Sure, all the houses look the same when they're built. Tidy and boring. But come back in fifty years, and what's happened? People have planted every kind of tree, built every sort of fence. One house has cheap plastic siding, and its neighbor is the original wood. And still another is burned down, replaced by something modern and wonderfully out of place."

"Maybe so."

"No, I don't believe in Architects. I believe in building codes." She had a long laugh, then said, "It's the perfect system."

"What is?"

"The intrusions." She glanced at him. "You've mentioned neighbors? The Petes? What if every time you stepped onto the Petes' yard, you were transformed into a member of their family."

"I sort of was, actually."

"Just like we come here, becoming this other species. But we're the only things that can cross the fence. We can't take anything home with us. Most of us can't visit for long. That makes invasions hard to manage. And even if we could stay here indefinitely, we just turn native. A couple of generations, and we'd blend into the general population, seamlessly and forever."

"You sound like my father," Cornell said. "The way you talk about big picture stuff—"

"Your dad sounds like an interesting man."

There was a reliable tightness around his chests. Then he made himself laugh, remarking, "You're not just a dumb jock, are you?"

She stopped. All of her stopped, gazing at him, her mind making the grit beneath it creak. Then she said, "Deserts are good places for contemplation."

He gave a little nod.

"Try it sometime," she suggested.

But all she had were words. A bunch of words strung along some pretty, unproven ideas. The universe as a crowded real estate development; each world as a home with its own special tenants. Cornell didn't believe it, but he didn't deny the possibility, either. And sometimes during those next days, at unexpected moments, he found himself gazing at the empty desert, imagining houses and chain-link fences and boys climbing over the fences, their shapes and complexions changing from yard to yard to yard.

They brought the last of the downed trees into the Breaks, then came upon a man heading for New Reno. The man said, "We found something new." His whistles bounced off the stone walls, excitement mixed with exhaustion. "There's a forest. And it's not a greasewood forest."

"Down in the canyons?" Porsche asked.

He had five bodies, one visibly pregnant and another injured, an arm wrapped in a stiff blackish bandage. "In the canyons, yeah. Real trees, and water." *Water* was a sound rather like dripping water. "Trees like skyscrapers, thick air and these batlike things flying."

The man wanted to keep moving. His vacation was due, and sleep had become difficult. But before he left, Cornell asked about Jordick. "Black fur. A new recruit. Have you seen him?"

"No, sorry. I never met him."

There was more news when they reached the dried waterfall. The man in charge—someone new, his mind's fur brushed smooth and glossy—said they didn't need any more wood or nuts. There was plenty in the new valley, and people were needed to help there. New orders, he said. "Logan wants everyone to join the main effort."

A woman overheard him. She had three tiny bodies, none of them visibly pregnant. With a cutting voice, she said, "Let Logan do the work himself, as far as I'm concerned."

There was a silence, electric and sudden.

Then the man said, "These are orders. We don't have a choice."

But the woman ran up to Cornell, grabbing his bodies as if to hold him there. "Those trees are full of monsters. Monsters with bodies like shrews, and when they bite you, your body goes rigid with poison. But it's not dead. It doesn't die." Fear sparked from face to face. "The monster drags you away and kills you when it wants."

"But we're killing them, too," the man interrupted. "More and more."

"And we're moving deeper," she continued. "We aren't meant to live in that country."

"How do you know?"

"Everyone knows. Have you been below?"

He tried to say, "Of course—"

And she snapped, "You haven't been. Admit it."

Porsche motioned Cornell away from the others. He was imagining himself dying in pieces, consumed by enormous shrews; then Porsche was saying, "No more point in cutting down the greasewoods, is there?"

"What will you do? Go off shift?"

"Not yet, no." She looked at him, and there was something in her faces, a longing strained through alien genetics and fatigue. He felt a desperate fear that something would happen to her. Something was going to go terribly wrong, and what then?

She was saying, "You're due to go on vacation, aren't

you?" And then, "The thing is, I know a lot of the people down there. I can help them hunt, making things safer."

He didn't care about nameless people. He'd been with Porsche, without break, for longer than he'd been with almost anyone in his life. The idea of leaving her was a shock, cold and sudden.

Porsche grasped his hands, her callused palms warm and their fur warmer. "I was thinking . . . we could schedule our vacations to overlap. You take yours now, then we take the next one together. We'll get a room in Samoa, then turn vegetable for a few weeks. What do you think?"

"Soon," he implored.

"Absolutely."

"And take care of yourself."

"Constantly."

He felt like a schoolboy. A neutered, multibodied schoolboy.

"And take care of yourself," she warned him. "New Reno isn't an easy trip on the best days."

"We'll both be careful," he offered.

"And don't stay away too long." A single finger brushed against one face. "All right? Promise me that?"

Cornell left that next morning, five bodies pulling his mind. He passed the three-bodied woman before midday. Then he was up on the desert, moving as fast as possible. Sometimes in sheltered places he found foot tracks and the broad mark made by a dragged mind. He sniffed at the tracks and realized they were Jordick's. "I'll catch him tomorrow," he promised himself. Except the next day brought strong winds blowing around the distant Rumpleds, lifting dust and the abrasive grit, throwing them into his faces. Cornell half-closed his outer lids, squinting as he moved. An instinct began to emerge, ancient and certain. There was a storm coming, and he needed shelter. A burrow. A ridge of hard white stone seemed to glow in the fading sunlight, and he made for it with six bodies pulling, almost running as the storm swept over him.

In the darkness, by touch, he found a cave and climbed inside. Then he went into a deep conserving sleep, immune to the roaring wind, constantly dreaming and remembering none of the dreams when he woke two days later.

The air was bitterly cold. A body slipped from the cave, breathing in sips, looking at a blood-red sun high in a gray sky. A sloppy soft shadow followed it as it explored. The other bodies emerged, pulling the mind into the open. The fur was groomed, then harnesses were lifted; and Cornell moved fast across the hushed landscape, dust falling over him like a fine gray snow.

That next night he camped in the open, eating the last of the nuts and rat meat. He couldn't sleep. He worried about Porsche and wondered about Jordick, then thought about other people, too. Solitude was bringing them out of his memories, the wilderness populated with ghosts: The Petes. The Underhills. Even Dad, for a moment. And then Mom. He pictured his mother, spoke with her; but the old game felt false, contrived. He gave it up and ignored the ghosts. Instead he concentrated on where he was, gray air fading to black and the serene desert that asked nothing of him. There was a freedom in having nothing expected from him. For the moment, Cornell was the perfect solitary creature, and he smiled when he thought of it, then succeeded in thinking nothing whatsoever.

Not far from New Reno, he smelled Jordick again.

He followed the scent, climbing a gradual slope that ended with a sharp dropoff on the windward side. Jordick must not have seen the dropoff. Judging by the occasional track, the man had moved through the storm, and at this spot, half-blinded, his desperate bodies must have stepped out into the air, pulling his mind after them.

The mind was below him, black and dusty and eerily inert. Cornell eased himself down to it and saw where a sharp boulder had shattered bone, killing the mind, blood and dust mixed to form a crude cement. There was a slight, almost sweet odor of decay. Standing nearby were five small black-furred bodies, placid and lost, Jordick's face showing behind their stupid, dead eyes.

He blamed Jordick. The man was impatient and weak, full of flaws . . . then he felt a twinge of personal blame. I could have found him sooner, he thought. I could have done a better job of looking after him. But it was Logan who had brought him here, stealing him from a place more suitable. Cornell stared at the bodies, wondering if they'd eventually wander into New Reno, begging for food. What was the decent thing to do? he wondered. His instincts told him nothing. He had to decide for himself, and he did the best he could.

Three of his bodies picked up the black harnesses, jerking hard and making the dead mind slide. He couldn't take Jordick across the intrusion—he was empty meat now—but at least he could give him a funeral. There wasn't any cemetery on the New Reno maps, but somewhere there had to be ground, official or not, where people buried their dead.

The black bodies watched their mind leave them, and some instinct, some habit, made them follow. Cornell looked back and wondered if he should put them out of their misery. Except, where was their pain? He turned his eyes forward again. After a little while he could feel New Reno. It was that sensation of bodies linked to minds—that's what Jordick had been chasing through the storm, he reasoned—and he moved faster, dragging two minds up the face of a low gray dune, panting hard and in rhythm, making little dust devils whenever he exhaled.

F. SMITH, RELIABLY ROBOTIC AND SITTING IN HER USUAL CHAIR, told him, "You're near the top in most categories." She sounded carefully pleased, gazing at scores derived from a couple of days of psychiatric shamanism. Clasping thick hands in front of her, she read, " . . . few residual reflexes . . . no phantom bodies . . . normal use of all fingers . . . and eating normally, according to room service. . . . "

"Some people don't?"

There was a twinkle, and she confided, "One girl took to eating ants in our yard. Live ants. And we had a man who'd buy mice at a pet store, eating nothing else."

"What happened to them?"

"Oh, they're fine. Now." A pause. "Retired, and they've recovered."

He gave a little nod.

"Any other questions?"

A hard gaze, and he said, "Jordick."

"Oh, we're sorry about him." She sounded more angry than sad, adding, "If he'd been my case, I would have limited his first-time exposure. It's too bad it happened."

"It is."

The bulldog face changed, trying to smile. "You, on the other hand . . . you have a flair for this work. . . . "

Cornell said nothing, knowing better.

"Consider longer shifts," she told him. "If you have the urge, there's extra pay involved. Quite a lot."

"I'll think about it."

"Please. Do." Another pause, then she said, "By the way," as if it was a casual afterthought, "I'm curious. Your account of the mood on High Desert. It's rather sketchy. Could you elaborate a little bit?"

"I spent most of the time with one person—"

"Porsche Neal, yes. I'm glad you made a friend." The face worked to show nothing, to give nothing away. "Actually, I'm more interested in Hank Logan. You mentioned him as being—"

"Brittle," said Cornell. "Tense."

"I'm sure he's tired," she continued, her tone careful and every word slow. "He's got a tremendous amount of responsibility, of course."

Cornell looked at his hands, momentarily surprised to see so many fingers.

"Did you know?" she continued. "Hank was the very first person to visit High Desert. It's his fifth world, which is a record. He's a legend around here, Mr. Novak. An authentic hero, and I can't count the reasons why."

A glance at the window, at the soft blue sky and fat clouds.

"We're all tired, Mr. Novak. On both ends of things."

"May I go?" he asked. "If you don't have any other questions—"

"Home, is it?" She brightened, perhaps believing she'd made an impact; that she had tempered his hard feelings. "I noticed you applied for a full leave. Which is fine. Our business is done, and you're free to go."

He rose, aware of his feet inside their shoes. "Thanks."

And F. Smith said, "I'm sure I don't have to remind you of your pledge to us, do I? To protect our mission here?" A pause and a contrived smile. "Of course I don't. Have a splendid couple of weeks, Mr. Novak. Enjoy."

San Francisco was vast and extraordinarily loud, chaotic and filthy and collapsing in its corners; and Cornell was astonished by the changes that had swept over the city. People had moved from everywhere, tens of millions of them. Strange hairless faces crowded towards him. Ornate buildings stared with great glass eyes. There was a pressure in the air, in each slow thick breath; and he felt a metallic aftertaste inside his wrong-shaped mouth and against his too-fat tongue.

And he was managing better than most people, he told himself. Which probably was the only reason why they let him free in the first place. Suddenly that seemed obvious.

Two weeks and nothing to do but rest, spend money and readapt. Then back to High Desert again. This was too short a vacation, or it was much too long. His opinion depended on his mood, and right now, walking the last few blocks home, Cornell felt ready to rush back the way he had come. Maybe he didn't have residual reflexes, and no, he didn't feel like chewing on bugs. But it didn't take much to imagine himself as six bodies pulling their mind up the sidewalk, brandishing spears as they crossed streets, perhaps killing one of the rolling monsters that kept barking with their shrill voices.

His apartment's gate was locked, apparently undisturbed.

His computer greeted him with the promise of messages, but Cornell said, "Wait. Give me a minute."

The silence had a wounded quality. He walked back and forth in the apartment, studying the little rooms as if for the first time. This place reminded him of his hut in New Reno. It was the gloom, in part. And it was the staleness and maybe the coolness, too. Cool air, cool grimy surfaces. He paused in the bathroom, promising himself to clean it before he left again. That would fill three or four days, wouldn't it? Then he caught sight of his reflection, not knowing the face for an instant, staring and staring and easily picturing himself with big black eyes and thick fingers, a mouth full of needles and a thin tongue. He touched his face, cheeks and forehead, barely hearing the phone as it began to ring.

The computer answered, asking, "How are you today?"

"It's Pete Forrest again," said the voice. "Has he shown up yet?"

"No, Mr. Novak cannot come to the phone now. May I take—"

"Wait." Cornell came out of the bathroom saying, "I'll take it in the living room."

"Sir? Mr. Novak just stepped inside. Hold, please."

Cornell punched on the TV, sat and saw Pete sitting on a big plain chair. Where was he? In a hotel room, he decided. Some cheap adjustable painting was hung over the bed, dialed to a nineteenth-century landscape. Pete grinned and leaned closer, saying, "Finally." Then he laughed with relief. "Wondered if I'd ever catch you at home."

"I'm here," Cornell replied.

"What's been happening?"

"Not much." It was the largest lie of his life. "What are you doing? On the road somewhere?"

"Actually," said Pete, "I'm in town."

San Francisco?

"And I was wondering. How about supper? My treat."

It took a moment to see the obvious. Pete wouldn't come here by himself, and if Mrs. Pete was along, she'd pop into the picture.

"Where's Dad?" Cornell asked, his voice soft. Wary.

Pete gave a little wink.

"What is this? A surprise attack?"

Bless him. The big man didn't deny anything, saying, "A kind of blindside reconciliation, I hope."

Cornell waited for anger, reliable and trusted. But somehow he couldn't summon more than a steady disgust, asking, "Where is he?"

"Next door."

"Does he know?"

"He's not an old fool, son."

And Cornell sat back. "Where? Want to meet somewhere?"

A smile, another wink. "You choose the place."

He named a nearby restaurant.

"Seven o'clock?"

Cornell said, "Fine. Can you find the place?"

That brought a huge smile, a mild laugh, then a quiet, "What do you think?"

"You look tired."

Cornell might have made the same comment, gazing at his father with a mixture of nostalgia and astonishment. The man had aged—he expected it—but what startled him, seeing Dad in person, was the degree and completeness of his decline. The once-handsome face had gone soft, eyes dulled and the teeth, real or implanted, stained by everything that passed over them. The hair that had looked white on TV was quite thin, strips of pink scalp showing through it. The tops of his hands were speckled and ugly, the right hand showing a clean white scar. Was that recent? He didn't remember any scar. And the slight tremor was new. Was it the effect of a medication? Or was it a crippling, slow-acting disease? Cornell realized the man was in his mid-seventies, which wasn't old. Yet here he was, a pitiful and shrunken old fart. . . .

"You look beat," Dad told him. "What are you doing with yourself? Not sleeping much, whatever it is."

"I'm traveling," he replied, glad for the cover story. "I'm busy with my new job—"

"Talk about traveling," the old man interrupted, nodding and laughing. "How far have we come, Pete? A couple, three thousand miles?"

"Something like that."

"Aiming for Oregon, but I guess we got lost." He picked up the menu, frowned at something and put it down again. "And people claim I've got a lousy sense of direction."

Cornell looked at Pete, gauging his impressions. Pete seemed tense more than anything. Had there been trouble on the way? When did Dad figure out their destination? The old man would feel trapped, and rightly so. Maybe the two of them could gang up on Pete, making him the common foe.

"Starting tomorrow," Dad reported, "we're going north, working our way up the coast. What's the town?"

"Eugene." Pete's voice was more inert than patient.

"You must have heard, Cornell. They've got an old-fashioned saucer, from the sound of things."

No, he hadn't. But he rolled his head as if he knew something.

"A little one," Dad continued. "But sneaky. It's like that little saucer we saw . . . where was it, Pete? We were on that gravel road, in the fall, and it was ahead of us—"

"Calumus County," Pete replied.

Dad turned to Cornell. "You remember it. There was a flash of sunshine when it crossed the road."

"I wasn't there, Dad. I was in school."

"You were there." He sat back, the old hands folding together. "In the backseat, like always. And you said the saucer was a bird—"

"I wasn't there."

"You've forgotten." It was an accusation, sharp and then gone. He turned to Pete, saying, "It's a scout ship in Oregon, I think. Automated, or maybe not." He looked at the center of the table, wearing a vague and odd brief grin. "A crew could be inside, inside some kind of folded space. Twisted geometry. I've been studying the mathematics, the possibilities."

As if he could comprehend the simplest equations, Cornell thought. As if he had a fighting chance.

"After Oregon," said Pete, "we keep going north."

"We might try hunting *Giganthropus.*"

Pete said, "Bigfoot."

Cornell said nothing.

"They're being seen again," said Dad.

Cornell felt happily ignorant about saucers and bigfoot.

"What I'm thinking," Dad reported, "is that *they* have a base in the Cascades. Probably inside a volcano." He looked over a shoulder, then remarked, "The service is lousy, isn't it?" A blink, and he almost looked at Cornell. "Anyway, I've got a new theory. I think *they* are making contact with earthlings, but not with people. We've never been more than a passing curiosity for them. Which seems reasonable to me."

Where was the waitress? Cornell wondered. The place was almost empty, and he shared Dad's impatience.

Pete was studying his menu. "How are the scallops?"

"Good. Great."

Dad coughed and said, "Perhaps they're talking to bigfoot. Perhaps they're preparing our cousins for their golden future, and people are just an evolutionary dead end."

Pete and Cornell were trying to ignore him.

"Peaceful herbivores. The yeti, bigfoot . . . that's what they are, after all. The aliens must have recognized their genuine nobility. . . . "

What part bothered Cornell most? Was it the man's loopiness, or was it the way he used his loopiness to insulate himself from criticism?

"Such a conceit," said his father, the face defiant. Proud. "Us believing that *they* would be interested in our vile little species."

Their waitress finally arrived, very young and thoroughly bored with her life. She turned on her Newton and asked, "Ready?" Pete and Cornell took the scallops, but Dad made a slow study of the menu. What did he want? "You've had forever to choose," said the waitress's expression. Finally he picked the bison steak, twice making her promise that it was lean and authentic. Then he remarked:

"Where's our complimentary ice water?"

She rolled her eyes. "It's a quarter a glass."

He acted stunned, gazing at Cornell.

"Dad, we just came out of a drought."

"Do you want water?" the waitress snapped.

With a sense of great sacrifice, the old man said, "Thank you. No."

She threw her Newton into her apron, then left; Dad asked Cornell in a too-loud voice:

"Is some girl keeping you up nights?"

"I told you," said Cornell, his tone icily patient. "I've got a new job, Dad."

"Oh? Do you?"

It was an old man's question, his memory failing; but the eyes had a clear blue light in them.

"Remember? A couple of men came to interview you—"

"I remember." Dad breathed and asked, "Did you get that job?"

"Yes."

"What kind is it?" Then, before Cornell could answer, "Does it pay well?"

And he said, "Pretty well."

"Oh, I'm sure. I believe you." There was a sudden sharp edge to the voice. "Yes, I believe it does pay splendidly."

There was a pause, cold and long, and what worried Cornell most was the way Pete sat with his elbows on the tabletop, his face concerned and alert, his thick hands squeezing each other.

Then Dad said, "Money." A pause, then, "What does treachery cost today? In dollars, I mean."

There was a sensation like falling, that utter loss of control. Cornell managed a deep breath and held it inside his single chest—

—and Dad said, "Since you're helping them, I hope you're at least getting something concrete out of it."

What did he mean?

Pete looked as startled as Cornell felt, asking, "What's this? What are you doing?"

"The government sends agents to my house, asking me every kind of question, and what do you suppose that means?" The shrill words ran together. He stared at Cornell, asking, "What exactly are you doing for them? You told them about my work, my conclusions. No doubt there. A lifetime of experience, and you sold it away—"

"No, I didn't. No, no, no."

"Nathan," said Pete, "this is really strange. Even for you."

"Asking questions, pretending they were interested in you. Oh, I was fooled. For two minutes, I was stupid. But it was me they were after, wasn't it? I'm their prize, aren't I?"

Pete said, "You're worrying me, friend."

Dad shrugged his shoulders, proud of his vision. Proud of his courage. He coughed with vigor, then said, "I know I'm under surveillance. They've watched me for years—"

"Like hell," said Pete. "How many times have we been over this? I've shown you and shown you that nobody's watching you."

"Three times," said Dad, "they've broken into my house."

Pete looked at Cornell, shaking his head. "Once there was a burglary. One time."

"Treachery, treachery."

"Crazy, crazy," Cornell whispered.

The old man didn't seem to hear him, saying, "Oh, but I fooled them. I left them nothing to find but data. My conclusions are what matter, and they're here. In my skull. Which is why they had to milk my son for the answers."

"You are amazing," said Pete, scornfully.

Dad smiled and smiled, happy with himself.

Pete touched Cornell's arm. "I had no idea. This is new to me."

Cornell wasn't simply angry, though his heart pounded and his vision blurred and every muscle screamed to move. It was anger, but it also was panic and a kind of terrified amazement with the man's delusions. Pete was asking, "What's the government need from you?" and Cornell put his hands over his ears, trying to hear nothing.

"I know things," Dad promised.

"What things?"

"Something secret."

Pete drummed on the tabletop, getting the attention of everyone in the place. "Whatever Cornell's involved in," he declared, "it means nothing to you. Isn't that right, son?"

Dad blinked, then blinked again.

And Cornell said, "That's right," with his voice almost calm, barely audible. "They don't give a damn about you, Dad."

A snort, a scornful expression.

Pete said, "See?"

"I know the truth," Dad replied.

"You don't," Cornell snapped. "You're not even close to it."

It was more than he should have said, and for a panicky instant he wondered if this scene had been invented to test him. Maybe he hadn't left the agency's grounds; maybe this was some elaborate virtual world, and he was sitting alone inside another tiny white room. Then a hand pressed on his shoulder. Pete's hand. He had read Cornell's mood and was saying, "Now take it easy, son—"

"You don't know," Cornell shouted. "You don't."

Faces stared at him, but nobody spoke. It was as if everyone in the room were one person, their bodies united by invisible threads.

Dad licked dry lips, satisfied by something.

Cornell pushed away the big warm hand, saying, "Saucers are old news. Out of date. The universe is put together differently, Dad, and even you're not even crazy enough to guess how."

Nobody spoke.

Cornell nearly explained everything. His mouth was open and he had words lined up, ready to emerge. He'd tell them about the intrusions and how people passed through, changing their physical selves; he'd describe where he had been and what he had seen. He didn't care who was eavesdropping. A brigade of black-coated government men could take him away. They would be his proof, his vindication. Dad would have to believe him. But his paranoia didn't stop, and he imagined everyone else in this restaurant being silenced. With warnings; with accidents. Conspiracies perched on conspiracies, the public at large kept ignorant. . . .

His anger stopped, out of energy. He closed his mouth and took a long look at his father, wrinkles and thin tears and one speckled hand pulling through the thin snowy hair. A fucking pitiful old man, and he couldn't stay angry with him. Which made him angry in a new way, hating himself as he turned toward Pete, telling him, "Sorry."

Pete offered a tiny, circumspect nod.

"I tried," Cornell told the room, then he rose with a squeak of the chair. What was Dad thinking? He looked at the face, thinking how people never knew what really was inside another person. Where did he hear that? Long ago, it felt like. He turned and started for the door.

Pete might have spoken, perhaps to Cornell, but the sound merged with the street noise as Cornell walked outside. People were everywhere . . . a small round world filled with stinking human bodies. He heard voices and singing and sometimes laughter, always grating. Then he was running, weaving around bodies and into the street. Cars honked at him and he glared back at the drivers, his face causing several people to gasp aloud. They had seen a madman, they knew; and later, they told friends they were fortunate that the madman hadn't reached through their windshields, killing them with his pale clenched fists.

A week later, he was packing to leave, tired of his vacation and of the tiny apartment. The mail came before he left, one of the letters postmarked from Oregon. He recognized Pete's handwriting on the envelope, big letters full of confidence and a surprising grace. Inside was a note that read:

> I used to think you were my surrogate child, the one Elaine and I never had. But I think we both know who my child is. Anyway, sorry for the scene. Believe me, I was as surprised as you. Which, I suppose, has been the attraction all along. I never know what your father will do. You've got to admit, he keeps things interesting.
>
> I hope things work out for you. And stay out of trouble. And here's our itinerary, in case you want to cross paths sometime soon.
>
> Best wishes. Pete.

The itinerary was on a single sheet of photocopy paper, in Dad's writing, always small and precise. Cornell nearly threw it in the trash. Then he thought of hiding it. "God, who's the paranoid here?" Finally he put it in his pants pocket, and while riding beneath the Bay, no one nearby, he pulled out the paper and unfolded it and studied the dates, some vague thought lurking at the back of his mind.

A secret even to him.

# 10

**This time the desert crossing was relatively easy. Rela**tively swift. Cornell kept the two highest peaks on the Rumpleds in line—Porsche's trick—making the Breaks on the third day, dropping into them and meeting no one until the arroyo and the dry waterfall. There weren't as many people as before. He walked two bodies to the edge, examining the suspended highway. In New Reno, at least three times, authoritative people had ordered him to join the vanguard. "As fast as you can get there, or faster."

A red-furred mind and five bodies were nearby, every eye on him. A sixth body, newborn, was hanging from the mind, elaborate braids supporting its back and head. This wasn't any human baby. Its proportions were too adult, the eyes hard and wary. Chewing on a slice of dried meat, its teeth made a *chump-chump-chump* sound. The face showed a vague smile when Cornell asked, "How long to reach the front?"

No answer.

"Can I make it by dark?"

Two other people were back on a little delta of water-worked sand, broken spears and old sacks scattered around them. They seemed alert, intensely curious.

"Well," said Cornell, "I'll find out for myself." But when he dragged his mind toward the ramp, the red bodies drew spears with fancy obsidian blades. Artifacts? They seemed to be. And a male voice whistled, "To pass, you pay the toll."

"Since when?"

"Since always. You know that."

Cornell glanced at the others. They were anxious but unsurprised. He asked the man, "What kind of toll?"

"What's in those sacks?"

Nothing special. He had a ration of greasewood nuts and the usual dried meats, but wasn't there food below? The tolltaker found a shiny stone mixed with the nuts. A gemstone, or quartz. Cornell's semester of introductory geology was inadequate. And now the red-furred man was asking, "How was your crossing? Was it easy?"

"Yes."

"You were lucky."

Cornell swallowed with one throat, then another. "Maybe," he allowed. "I suppose."

Three fingers squeezed the prize. "So this is your good luck charm?"

He hesitated, then said, "Sure."

And more hands claimed a sack of dried rat meat, several mouths saying, "I knew you were lucky. I could tell." He wiped the charm against his mind and faces, saturating himself with good fortune. Then the faces glared at Cornell, suddenly suspicious. "What? You think I'm unfair?"

Be careful, he thought.

And a black spearhead swished past a nonexistent nose, bodies shouting, "Go away. Go." Even the newborn tried to say those words, sloppily and slowly, chewed meat spilling from its mouth.

Cornell worked fast, positioning his mind as he'd seen others do it, bodies above and holding fast, wearing harnesses and fingers gripping strategic knots. He was nervous, almost jittery. Hands pushed the mind, and it tilted, sliding onto the worn planks. Curling toes slipped, then held. Just one head turned to look back at the tolltaker. If the man tries anything, he told himself, I'll run. I can't fight him here.

But the tolltaker had lost interest in him.

The other people were approaching, one saying, "An easy trip across. I heard him."

"You can see the charm's luck," said the other. "I can smell it."

But the rock was just a rock. Cornell moved faster, one of the old braces creaking under him. This was a bumpy and haphazard highway, and he felt safer here than above.

"Let me touch it," someone shouted.

"Me," said the other.

"Get back," snapped the red-furred man. "Stay away."

"Just a touch," said a woman's whistles.

Then came a thump, curses and a second thump; but Cornell was too low to see them fighting, and after a little while he couldn't hear them over the clean dry sounds of wind.

He camped alone at night, setting his mind into a little basin at the base of a great white cliff. Sometimes, for no clear reason, he would wake and feel the chill air, smelling people nearby and sometimes hearing them squeak and warble as they dreamed. Here the glitter of the stars seemed subdued, the sky squeezed between the cliffs. Once he tasted moisture on a breeze. From below? Every time he woke, Cornell tried to feel the alien presence below, wanting some kind of confirmation that all this effort and sacrifice had a worthy goal, but he felt nothing. Nothing he could point towards and say, "There you are."

The dry canyon had been built by floods that had shattered rocks and thrown boulders into high mounds. There were gravel beds on the flat stretches. Almost nothing grew here. The last of Cornell's greasewood nuts were breakfast. Not long after dawn, he had one body climb to the crest of a tremendous rock pile, and it gazed at the country below. There was a sense of frozen motion, energies suspended but not lost. Cornell's slow progress seemed inconsequential. He had never felt so small, his senses overwhelmed by this stone wilderness. His bare feet made the loose stones *chink* with a dry porcelain sound; his exhalations smelled of fatigue poisons and nuts; the canyon remained oblivious of him, sleeping now, awaiting the next thundering flood.

Strangers were moving upstream. Sometimes they said,

"Hello," in passing. Some gave Cornell odd stares, bodies missing and their minds exhausted by shifts that had run too long.

The canyon bent and narrowed to a chute, very straight and steep; here was a second greasewood highway, wider than the first and better built. The ramp hugged one wall, gray wood fixed to gray rock, and it seemed to dissolve into the rock before reaching the bottom. Someone charged past him, heading down with her bodies trotting after her sliding mind. Eventually she vanished into the grayness. It was dusk when he reached the bottom, the thicker air holding on to the day's heat. He camped, dreamed of food, then woke and continued once again.

A blond mind and bodies came up the mindworn trail, and Cornell asked, "Where's the camp? How far?"

She had three bodies, all of them in the harnesses. And one body was little better than half-grown.

"Two days further," she answered him.

"That far?"

"Maybe a day and a half," she allowed.

"You're heading home?"

Heads nodded. Cornell imagined having just three bodies, having to cross the open desert with nothing else. Yet suddenly, without prompting, she asked, "Do you like venison?"

He blinked, and she added:

"Of course it's not real venison. The animals aren't much bigger than rabbits, frankly." A pause, then her tiniest body said, "I've got plenty. Don't worry."

He took what he could eat now, no more, and she breathed and rested, watching him chew on the dried smoky meat.

"Good?"

He said it was, not quite lying. Then as she began to leave, he thought to say, "Find a shiny rock. Then carry it as if it means something to you."

"Why's that?"

"People above are looking for lucky charms."

And she laughed. Three bodies short and a long journey

home, and she pointed out, "Nobody will believe I'm lucky."

Yet he wished her luck all the same, waving his hands as she turned and moved away.

The sun climbed above the canyon, pale against a strange anemic blue. Cornell thought of Porsche, wondering how she was managing. He thought of asking passersby, but he lacked the courage. What if it was bad news? Or worse, what if it was wrong news? Even good people could be mistaken, and until he saw Porsche—until she spoke to him and touched him—he could believe anything with a perfect innocence.

The air tasted damp, tinged with honest rot. Copper-colored bugs hovered above the sandy ground. Smaller bugs landed on his mind, trying to drink blood. He swatted at them and pushed his pace and was rewarded with another dry waterfall. Bodies on the brink, he looked down on a great white mass of clouds, patches of yellow-green showing through them. *The forest.* He sniffed, smelling vegetation and a rich watery aroma. Hearts raced as he positioned his mind beside the last greasewood ramp, then he eased onto it, feeling himself suspended over nothingness and hearing the wood creak, almost softly, as if to quietly warn him that it felt very, very tired.

Soon Cornell was immersed in clouds, a new chill permeating his flesh. He couldn't see far, couldn't think clearly. Instincts surfaced, telling him this wasn't his country. He should climb back to the desert again, no delays. Cornell was meant for drought and impoverishment; here he was a cactus set in a banana grove.

The ramp and fog-clouds ended together. Cornell found himself on a lush slope above a wide valley—a postcard scene with the wrong shades of green. He had trouble with distances, with proportions. The distant trees would look modest on earth; here they were sequoias, mammoth trunks rising to a tangle of limbs and spruce-colored needles. And closer was a grassy, mossy foliage, yellow stalks with tiny cobalt flowers on their tips and flying bees hovering, alertly chewing at the petals.

The foliage bent as he moved through it, reminding Cornell of prairie grass. And he recalled riding with his father and Pete, looking at the cornfields, wondering how it must have seemed to the first pioneers on that endless pasture.

This was how it felt.

Amazing. Frightening. Delicious.

There was water—a mountain brook that looked as big as a river—and a broad smooth path running parallel to it. Cornell stayed on the path after dark, listening to the water and thinking how it was different than at home. Higher pitched, brittle. Then he smelled smoke and saw a flickering curtain of light. Bodies moved against the curtain. Several people's bodies, he sensed, and he knew Logan's by their silhouettes. Six bodies now, the newborn nearly as tall as its siblings.

"What's your business?" someone snapped. Large bodies stepped in front of Cornell. "What do you want?"

"An assignment," he replied.

Suspicious stares became suspicious smiles, the man turning just one body to shout, "This one wants work."

Logan's bodies turned together. The voice, animated and perpetually tense, came from every mouth. "Well, well. Locke, is it?"

"Novak."

Faces became puzzled, then brightened. "I know you. Cornell? Let's find your schedule." One body dug through a sack full of parchment sheets, pulling out several of them. "Back early? Just in time, Novak. Hungry? We've got meat on spits, if you want. But between you and me, if I shit venison once more . . . " He gave a high-pitched laugh. "Anyway, I suppose you're tired. Yeah, let him pass. He's a solid fellow, a real find!"

What to do? Cornell decided on silence and false respect, nodding submissively. Then he said, "Sir?" and motioned with a single hand. "Do you know where I can find Porsche Neal?"

"Ah! Neal?" Eyes opened, reflecting firelight. Then the inner lids closed, and Logan said, "Alan. Who drowned today?"

Cornell felt himself become rigid, aware of his surroundings and the icy shock moving through him.

"It wasn't Neal," someone said.

And Logan laughed. "Oh, I know *that.*" Hands sorted the parchment sheets. "I'm doing bookkeeping, that's all."

Cornell didn't speak, didn't move.

"Ever do any rock climbing, Novak?"

"No," he lied.

"Too bad." His hands fought with the frayed edges and old tears. "So go help your lady friend, I suppose." A giggle. "She's at the tree—"

*The tree.*

"—and tell her, will you, we need plenty of boards tomorrow. As many as she can squeeze out. Understand?"

"Sure."

Again he shuffled the files, and he pulled one out and squinted, saying, "Oh, him," and folded it once before casually tossing it into the fire.

Alan asked, "Who was that?"

Logan paused—each body perfectly still—then laughed and said, "I'm not sure." And with that he reached into the flames, snatching out the withering, unreadable piece of skin. There was a little rain of ashes, and the hand was burned. But what mattered was that Cornell had seen it happen. One of the subordinates approached him, telling him:

"You've got an assignment. Go."

But Logan said, "No, wait."

Cornell wished he had left, the chance missed.

One mouth sucked at the burned fingers. Another asked, "What are they saying on the other side? You're honest. What's the chatter these days? Tell me."

He remembered F. Smith's misplaced, innocent confidence in Logan. "Nothing," he offered. "I didn't hear much of anything, really."

"But they know we're close, don't they?"

A vague shrug of the shoulders.

Logan took that as a *yes.* "They ask about casualties?"

"No."

Alan said, "Told you. They understand."

Someone else remarked, "If we had better stuff to work with . . . "

"Let *them* come over for a day," groused a third man. "Just let them see what we're up against."

Logan was stuffing his files back into their sack, heads shaking, one mouth saying, "It doesn't matter. The first First Contact, and everything's forgiven." The voice was confident, almost loud, working to build confidence in everyone. Perhaps some of the original Logan was showing—the talented, heroic leader. Yet a second mouth, at the same exact instant, seemed to mutter something else. Something like, "We're fucked." The same person speaking in two simultaneous voices, as if from two minds, his war-weary bodies standing stoop-shouldered against the strong flickering wall of yellow fire.

*The tree,* Cornell learned, was the long trunk of a dead tree. It had uprooted at its base and toppled in the recent past, its sapwood dried by the elements. Porsche's team was camped near it. He woke one of them, and her guarding body pointed the way.

"There's a ramp to the top," she said. "Now good-night."

He climbed the ramp with five bodies, making little noise, and his schoolboy excitement slipped into a schoolboy worry, a sudden lack of confidence causing his legs to slow and his hearts race. He felt like an idiot for investing this much emotion in a platonic relationship, if it even was a relationship. Then he saw her. There was a long white gash in the trunk, and he saw a mind and a pile of sleeping bodies. "Porsche?" he said. Then, "Hello?" Bodies stirred—five of them, he counted—and a single blinking face said:

"What?"

And he said, "I'm back . . . Cornell . . . ?"

"But you're early." A laugh, big and strong. Then she snapped, "What in hell are you doing here now, love?"

That made him pause.

Porsche came at him with every body, knocking his bodies over. Then she was on top of them, saying, "I'm leaving tomorrow. It's all arranged. I was going to hurry and catch you before you came on shift, giving us time together. Know what I mean?''

He laughed with relief.

''Hey, don't enjoy this. I'm not letting you enjoy this.'' She punched him with fists, laughing with him. Then they wrestled on the hard wood, ending up kissing and not enough lips between them to do it well. Too many sharp teeth, and they nipped each other, Cornell saying through the salty blood:

''Sorry.''

''Go to hell.'' She laughed.

''Do you have to leave? Are you as nuts as Logan?''

A pause, a look. Then she said, ''I wish I could stay a while. I do.'' She paused for a long moment, then added, ''We'll talk tomorrow. In the morning.''

Cornell said nothing, staring up at her faces, his smiles unconscious and his hands picking at her fur, combing it and caressing the wrong-shaped rumps and faces, feeling wondrous just to have this moment, this place and her and this strange perfect instant.

That next morning Porsche taught him how to do the work. ''You'll learn fast,'' she promised. ''Provided you brought your brain.'' Her crew supplied lumber to the crews below. This valley ended with its little river pooling, then streaking down a deep curling gorge. A world's worth of granite stood ahead of them, most of it baby-ass smooth and tough to work on. ''We've had losses,'' she warned. ''Bodies fall. Sometimes minds.''

''How did you lose a body?'' he inquired.

''A bite got infected. One of the last predators did it.'' A pause, then she warned him, ''This isn't the desert. Moisture and heat don't do your cuts any good.''

He described Logan from last night. ''Is he always nuts?''

''Most of the time, no. But sometimes he's worse.'' She was concerned but not gloomy. ''Basically, people here are willing and able. You don't cross the desert unless you're motivated, and most of us routinely put in double shifts. You've seen our organization. It's almost nonexistent. But we're excited enough to take risks—reasonable risks—because sometime, somewhere, someone is going to find a real native."

"The one you can feel?"

"Or one that's smaller and closer." A wave of the hands. "Some kind of native has lived in this valley. We've found more artifacts here than on the entire desert."

"But it's gone now?"

"As far as we can tell." A pause. "But this is enough talking. Let's get back to work."

Cornell's new vocation was to make boards using stakes and hammers. They weren't lovely boards, or smooth, and no two resembled each other. But at least the wood was easy to work, breaking along its grain and never varying its personality.

The morning was overcast, clouds thin but constant, and the forest's canopy diminished the sunlight even more. By afternoon, Cornell's job had eased into something steady, gaining a rhythm of its own. The clouds broke apart and let the heat build. He didn't sweat. Excess warmth left when he exhaled. If he were human, he realized, this would feel like a nice day in the mountains. But for his working bodies, it was like being in a sauna.

"It'll get better," Porsche promised. "You'll adapt."

"Hope so."

A careful look, and she said, "I am leaving in the morning."

He had no reply.

"My second-in-charge takes over. A sweet lady, but don't let her fool you."

"Careful on the desert," he told her.

"I don't think I will be," she said sarcastically.

Then finally, with a calm practiced tone, he told her about the dust storm and Jordick, and she said, "I'm sorry. I didn't know about him."

"How will they tell his family? Assuming he has one—"

"An accident. At least that's the usual way." She wiped her

nearest face. "A nice discreet death, and no body left to claim."

Naturally.

Then she said, "No, he's part of why I'm going. I want to meet with our case officers, explain a few things. Make sure they appreciate—"

"Yeah," he interrupted. "And get Logan canned."

"If I can, I will."

"But will they believe you?"

"Yes, and it might not help." A sigh. "Their lives would be simpler if they didn't hear me."

What else? Cornell thought of things to add, to repeat, but then instead put his hands into her hands and said nothing, satisfied to hold on to her, feeling the alien bones.

Porsche left in the morning, five big bodies into the harnesses and one of them showing the first tentative bulge of its pregnancy. "Very matronly," Cornell joked. "Now make them listen, okay?"

"One way or another," she promised.

Cornell went straight to work, focusing on the boards, hands blistering and splinters knifing through his thick skin and his nighttime dreams full of fresh white lumber stacked higher than he could see. Sometimes he would help drag a finished load down the valley. Just as Porsche had promised, there was a wall of pink granite with a gorge through its heart, a pond at the top, and a plunging river that vanished in an instant. People had managed to build a sturdy ramp on the right wall. The new leader, Susan Acts, warned him not to let his bodies get too far ahead of his mind. Whatever their telepathy was, it wasn't able to reach through rock or around too many corners. Bodies lost touch, which was how some accidents began. Lost bodies wandered. Or sometimes a closer mind—not their own—seemed to gain partial control over them. They stepped when they shouldn't, plunging into the river. That's why all of a person had to move into the gorge to work. It was demanding work, bodies climbing, hammering while clinging to wet stone, and people needed every trick possible.

Susan was a sweet-sounding person, yet she had a way of worming people into doing more, doing better. She treated everyone equally, knew names and quirks, and she entertained her crew with horror stories of her life on earth.

She had had two husbands, both of them disasters. The decent one had stepped in front of a drunk driver, and afterward, at twenty-eight, she found a breast tumor. Stress-related, no doubt. Even here, she would, out of habit, examine herself for odd lumps. Bodies and mind. "So far," she would remark, "I'm clean. Safe."

In some fashion, it was the same with everyone in the crew. Cornell heard lists of misery and heartache. Failure and bad fortune. A couple of women spoke openly, almost brazenly, about being sexually abused by their parents. Toxic families; distorted souls. It was almost a game, everyone trying to one-up the others.

Cornell remained silent throughout. He thought about his past and legacy, measuring them against the new standard.

One night, very late, Susan and another woman talked about their fathers. Addicts, both of them. Chaotic and violent and past all forgiveness. By firelight, each tried to pick through her friend's fur, hunting for scars left over from childhood beatings. Scars didn't translate, Cornell recalled. And sure enough, they found none. Except they began to cry, or what passed for crying here, low whistling sobs with their bodies clinging to each other, reassuring voices saying, "The bastards can't get us here." Choking sobs, then, "Here we're safe." Then, "Safe as safe can be."

One day, Logan arrived and spoke to the crew. Work stopped to give him an audience, and his subordinates stood around him like guards. "You're doing a spectacular job. You are. The work's going fast again, and there's plenty of wood. A surplus, really." The man seemed more competent today, save for a slippery vagueness in the eyes. "That's why we need more people in the gorge. More hands, more backs." Then he gave a little laugh, smiling at them.

Nobody responded.

"Volunteers?" said Logan.

Subordinates whispered and pointed, their intention obvious. Then Susan stepped forward with several bodies, arms rising as if to ask the teacher some question.

"Take me," she said.

Maybe she thought Logan wouldn't take her. She was protecting her people, knowing he wouldn't dare take the crew leader.

Except Logan said, "Good, good. Who else?"

Susan appeared stunned, then angry.

"One more person," Logan demanded. "A good six-bodied volunteer."

The woman who had cried with Susan came forward, and Susan sputtered, "Why not someone fresh? Someone new?"

But Logan said, "This one's fine. Perfect."

A subordinate approached, whispering into one of Logan's earholes. The boss seemed momentarily puzzled, then blinked and said, "Right. I know we need one, I know."

A pause.

"Novak! Till your girlfriend comes back, take charge of this crew. All right? All right. Back at it, everyone. All right? All right."

Little changed for Cornell. People knew their jobs, so there wasn't much coaching involved. Discipline dropped in those next days, as did production, but that was because of their missing people. Cornell would pull loads of lumber down to the gorge, and sometimes he met people heading for the desert, three bodies left and the fear obvious. They told him about slick rock and the endless roar of the water. It was brutal terrain. If you were down to three bodies, he learned, you were taken off duty. That was the rule. Building a section of ramp required at least four bodies in perfect sync, which meant three was a ticket home. And there were rumors that some workers—the disgruntled or uninspired ones—were sacrificing bodies, committing partial suicides when they wanted to escape.

But others came to replace them, most of them raw recruits. They reminded him of Jordick, out of their element and fragile. He asked them about Porsche. Had they seen her? Or heard about her? But he wasn't concerned when no one remembered her. Counting travel days and the days spent talking to the agency hierarchy, Cornell calculated exactly when he should allow himself to worry.

He dreamed of Porsche. In one dream she was in his apartment, watching the old TV, six hands picking at her deep brown fur. Suddenly she looked up and gave him six smiles, bright and predatory, and said, "How are you, love? How are you?"

Cornell awoke when she spoke. The voice was real.

Porsche had found him in the dark, sleeping on the tree, and it was a replay of last time, roles reversed. He wrestled her bodies down, and they kissed and fondled each other. Then Porsche listened to his camp news, congratulating him on his promotion. Then he asked about her trip. Was it worthwhile?

"Well," she allowed, "I think I did some good."

Her pregnant body was bloated, and he placed a hand on the bulge, feeling motion.

"They've got it under advisement," she continued. "But who knows? Logan sends home glowing reports, and how can they tell what's real?" She sighed, hands over his hands. "He claims that he's in direct communication with the aliens. There's a city of them on the other side of these mountains—"

"Logan's insane," he interjected.

"Maybe," she agreed.

Cornell was sick of the man and said so.

"Maybe we can coax him home somehow. If the agency can give him tests, maybe he'll stay home."

Cornell shut every eye, saying nothing.

"How are you feeling?"

"Fine."

"No," she told him. "You're not."

He admitted to having dreams and waking early—

"Time for your vacation, love."

He said nothing.

She bent with one body, kissing one mouth; then she said, "Soon as you can, leave. I mean it. Orders from your superior."

He thought for a moment, then asked, "And do what with myself?"

"Sit by the pool, if you want." She caressed his faces, saying, "Do whatever you want. Just take your three weeks, then get back to me." Smiles. "I need you. And not some frazzled quail version of you." Laughter. "One Logan is plenty, love. I can't handle two of you."

The trip to New Reno was endless and uneventful, save for one brief moment. Cornell had worked his way up the highest ramp, almost to the top, then thought of the red-haired man taking tolls. He rested and selected his best spears, then finished the climb. But there was no one waiting. The arroyo was littered with garbage and piles of dried shit, the air closing in on him . . . then suddenly he wasn't alone . . . someone vast and close . . . a sensation like New Reno, but magnified a thousand times. . . .

More.

It was the *something* in the Breaks, and it touched Cornell with a scorching white light. Suddenly he wasn't in the arroyo, but instead found himself standing on a tall stone building overlooking a plaza and a city—a glorious and ancient great city—and he saw a harbor and the sea beyond, and ships on the sea, black against the emerald water.

A hand touched his shoulder.

He turned.

A tall white body was smiling—an expression full of charm and joy—and a thundering voice said:

"Hello friend how are you friend come come come see me . . . !"

Then the *something* was gone, and Cornell was back in the arroyo, alone, each body on its knees, every mouth quietly whistling with the equivalent of a gut-shot moan.

**His car was rented, Brazilian and uncomfortably large.** Driving from the airport was a clumsy experience. Cornell's coordination was iffy; his brain would still try to move a dozen hands at once. But he knew the way, which helped. He didn't have to ask the car's computer for directions; he was driving by habit, following the curling streets and going slowly, watching everything. Since he'd last been here, the houses had turned old and small. Broad lush trees had grown up over empty yards, and once lush trees had been cut down, stumps made into planters or pulled from the ground like corks. It was the same neighborhood, and it was all different. These were the same people, only wearing different names and lives. And that's how it was for every street in the world, he thought. And fifty thousand years ago, it was the same for every cave and skin hut. Sameness and novelty. Sameness and novelty. Humanity was an infinite assortment clinging to changeless themes.

"I'm so profound," he muttered.

"Pardon?" asked the computer. "What did you say, sir?"

Cornell didn't reply. This was the last turn, left onto the rising street, every moment bringing him deeper into his old domain, his private fiefdom. When he was a boy, he had ruled this stretch of concrete and the landmark island in the cul-de-sac. Now the island bobbed into view, and he drove around on the right, slowing almost to a stop. The old juniper bushes had grown big and shaggy, but otherwise it looked the same, down to some kid's carbon-fiber bike resting against the curb. He looked right, the Lynns' house sporting a second story, the old bachelor den revamped and civilized. Then came the Underhills' house, big and quiet. Todd was a dentist, and Lane was various things, according to Pete. And now Cornell looked at the Petes' house, always neat and always surrounded by a trimmed green yard. Cornell's old home looked tiny beside it, shabbier than ever, its white walls darkened with grime. Had it shrunk? Or maybe Dad had whittled off pieces, using them in some bizarre experiment. Standing in the next yard was an old man, scrawny and shirtless and looking ready to fall from sunstroke. For an instant, Cornell saw old Mr. Tucker, right down to the sagging chest and a certain meanness in the ruddy face. But Mr. Tucker became worm food years ago. The illusion evaporated, and Cornell laughed at himself as he pulled into Dad's driveway.

According to the itinerary, Dad and Pete were in the wilds of British Columbia, not due home for another couple of weeks. Sasquatch hunting, of course. Pete hadn't intended to have the itinerary used this way, giving Cornell a way home . . . or had he? The guy was shrewd. Maybe he shouldn't dismiss the possibility.

The scowling neighbor glanced at him, snorted and turned back to his weeding. Dandelions and crabgrass were waging an endless assault from the west, and there was no time for pleasantries.

Cornell walked to the front door. His key, kept all these years in various drawers and boxes, had picked up a layer of rust that felt rough under his fingertips. His stomach tightened. One hand grasped the doorknob; didn't it feel small? But that was memory getting proportions wrong again. Sure. He tried to insert the key, three times he tried, finally thinking to kneel and examine the lock, discovering that it took a modern chip key. This wasn't part of the plan. . . .

Uprooting a long taproot, the old man tossed it into Dad's

yard. The occasional glower helped make his point even more clear.

Fuck you, thought Cornell. He moved around back. The old chain-link gate hung at an angle, hinges squeaking like burglar alarms. But this was his house as much as it was Dad's, by rights. Cupping both hands around his face, he peered into his old bedroom. There was nothing to see but file cabinets and cardboard boxes and head-high stacks of magazines. No bed, and no chest of drawers. It took him a few moments to feel sure it was his room, not some storage shed slapped together after he'd left.

The back door was the same, little glass panes needing to be caulked. He found a stone and paused, looking at the stone in his pale finger-rich hand. Thinking how he could work it into a serviceable stone axe. Then he busted out one of the panes with a crash, reached through and unlocked the bolt. Someone spoke. Someone said, "Wait." He glanced over a shoulder—as if he could look more guilty—and opened the door, smelling sour garbage and odors more ancient, tireless and familiar. Home, he smelled. A stew of wood and plaster and mold and dust; he nearly didn't hear the voice saying, "Too late." A woman's voice. He turned again, discovering Mrs. Pete standing beside the chain-link fence, a single chip key dangling at the end of a string. "I tried to stop you," she said. "You weren't listening."

Of course she had an extra key. He hadn't thought of it, feeling both foolish and relieved. Now he could come and go as he pleased, not leaving the house unlocked.

"Are you here for business?" she asked.

"On vacation."

She looked very white in the sun. Old but vigorous. She was exactly the person he remembered, dropping the key and string into his hand. "Are you staying long?"

"Just a few days."

"Pete called and told me what happened. Your father was in quite a mood, wasn't he?"

Cornell shrugged and left it at that.

"Anyway," she continued, "if you need anything . . . dinner, maybe? . . . come on over and I'll dish something up. I've got a full freezer and no one to cook for."

"Thanks," he said. "Maybe I will."

"I'll take that as a 'yes.' "

Then he heard a noise and looked over his shoulder, the old man now standing in his own backyard, glaring at the two of them while his garden hose made a muddy puddle beside him, its water bright and noisy and utterly forgotten.

Dad had never believed in computers. It was a quirk that Cornell hadn't noticed while growing up; but now, standing inside the computerless house, he tried to remember why Dad had outlawed those machines. He had complained about viruses and loopholes in their security, but thinking back, Cornell wondered if his flustered, easily lost father had tried computers and failed. The old models had been monsters with arcane rules and lousy screens. Maybe before Cornell was born, Nathan Novak tried them and gave up, throwing them in the trash out of frustration.

Everything worthwhile was on paper and tape. Dad kept most of it locked up, probably to frustrate his nameless government pursuers; but Cornell recalled a certain salad bowl in the back of a kitchen cupboard, finding keys and a tattered notebook inside the bowl. The notebook held maps of the house, every cabinet and box labeled, combinations included where they applied.

But he didn't start with files. Instead he dug out the old photo album with the fading family pictures, thinking he could jump-start his memories. More than twenty years had passed, but he recognized every image—knew exactly where an image would sit on the stiff gray paper—yet he wasn't the boy looking at them. New details were obvious. Like the way Mom appeared bored in some of the shots, angry in others. The anger was just in the eyes, or in her hip-cocked stance, Dad beside her and happily holding her, completely unaware. Every shot of Dad was the same. He was a middle-aged man in love. Stupid in love. And Mom looked like a high school girl with an affectionate father. She and Cornell together could have been sister and brother. It was a wonder she stayed with Dad for as long as she had. Then in the next instant, without warning, he realized that he wasn't much younger today than that grinning man with his indifferent cheerleader.

Cornell removed a few photographs, then replaced the album. Then he began in the basement, opening cabinets and finding files arranged by date, sometimes, and sometimes by location. And sometimes by no clear method at all. It was astonishing how many cases he could remember. A salesman in Dover saw a dozen saucers flying in formation; a waitress at a truck stop had been buzzed by a brilliant light; an elderly couple across town had seen a glowing something land smack dab in their geraniums. All were witnesses to oddities, explainable or not. Cornell remembered their nervousness and their curiosity, their willingness to talk and their bouts of silence, thoughtful or worried. They were the most ordinary people he could imagine, some bright but none remarkable. Yet something remarkable might have happened to them, causing them to reflect. If they had seen an alien spacecraft, then what else in their lives could be as thrilling or important? One witness, according to Dad's handwritten transcript, had wished aloud that she hadn't been so scared, or she would have approached the ship, seen more, and perhaps even met its pilots face-to-face. When would she get a second chance?

Cornell moved to the files about the black glass disks, having an agenda but unable to put it in concrete terms. He studied the clear crisp photographs of disks in parks and horse pastures, farm fields and woodlands. He found the disk they'd visited on the Change Day, complete with Dad's summary of the farmer's testimony. There was a surety of detail that wasn't true—the farmer hadn't claimed there was a light, for instance—but the records had their own existence, their own muscular life. At the end, Dad wrote there were signs of heat, perhaps in excess of several thousand degrees. He hypothesized how a tiny black hole might have created it, the disk to serve as a marker. Which struck Cornell as being an inelegant, overblown way to make bad glass, and probably physically impossible, too.

Buried in the file, neatly wrapped in wax paper and arranged in order, were the photographs Pete and Dad had taken in the cornfield. Cornell saw himself and the farm boy at the center of the disk. He felt pity for his twelve-year-old self, and empathy, and when he touched the face a surge of electricity ran up his arm. He wept for a little while, for no real reason, then quit as suddenly, wiping his eyes dry with his shirt. Then he replaced everything but one picture of him, adding it to the ones of Mom.

What time was it? After dark, which meant after eight o'-clock. An entire day had evaporated, and he had too much left to do. Standing in the basement, feet apart, he fixed his eyes on his father's long workbench, a million concerns flowing through his mind.

Mrs. Pete heated up leftovers in the sonic oven, then sat opposite him at the kitchen table, in her house, lights bright and the whole place feeling clean. Everything had a shine, even her, and she watched him eat, finally risking the question:

"So why are you here?"

"Got in the mood, I guess." A noncommittal shrug. "Some time off, and I knew nobody was home—"

"Pete's sick about that dinner," she interrupted, sympathetic eyes watching him. "He hoped he could get you two talking."

"How'd he like the scallops?"

"Pete? He didn't mention them."

Both laughed softly, without energy. Then Cornell asked, "How is my father lately? In a general way."

"Honestly," she told him, "he's odder than ever."

That was obvious.

"Except when Pete says so, you know it's true." She shook her head sympathetically, a finger teasing the mole on her cheek. "In fact, they've had arguments. A few good long ones, and you know how hard it is to make Pete angry."

"The old man's paranoid."

"More and more," she agreed. "And those two government men didn't help, I'm afraid."

"Sorry about that."

"Why? How could you know?" She waited for a moment, gathering her thoughts or letting the drama build. "Or maybe he hasn't changed. Not really. Everyone has weird ideas. Maybe in your father's case, he's just become more obvious about them."

"Obvious," he echoed.

"He watches us. Watches everyone."

"But he left you a key," Cornell observed. "Does he trust you?"

"It's Pete's copy," she replied. "Pete gave it to me, in case of emergencies."

"I got in without one."

"Anyone can," she agreed.

Cornell was done eating. He looked at the last cold bites of casserole, thinking how greasewood nuts would be the perfect dessert.

"Pete worked on your father for an age, convincing him to go on this trek of theirs. It's their last one, a final taste of youth and all that."

"Chasing saucers and bigfoot."

"They're still children." She laughed.

He stood, and Mrs. Pete asked if he wanted a comfortable bed. "The guest room has everything but the guest."

"No, I'll be fine." He thought of the old sofa, recoiled and decided to try the living room floor. After a few passes with the vacuum. "I might keep some odd hours anyway."

She walked him outside. It was a warm night, earthshine masked by the thin clouds and haze. Kids were up late and playing in the street, riding bikes in weaving paths, always shouting.

Cornell asked, "Whose are they?"

Mostly the Lynns', she said. Although one boy was from down the street, and another was a stranger. There were too many children now, and they grew up too fast.

Cornell was amazed by the kids' energy.

"If Pete calls, do I mention you?"

"Maybe not. Not yet."

"Sure."

There was something binding in being coconspirators. Binding and pleasant, too.

"Good luck," she told him. "With whatever it is."

He thanked her for dinner, then walked down to the street on his way home, moving slowly, studying an impromptu race of bikes. The kids passed him, once and again and again, sweeping past and with such noise, going nowhere with a ceaseless, giddy joy.

Cornell didn't sleep. Instead he went into the files about the Change. Dad had kept every clipping and purchased tapes of the news coverage. He had also interviewed the neighbors. Cornell had forgotten the interviews. Using his sudden credibility, Dad had asked everyone what they were doing and how they had reacted. With surprise? Fear? Awe? And he'd done followups on most of them, the last entries from three years ago. "Underhill thinks it was God's will," he had written with scorn. "Which is why he's such a drab man. That's God's will, too."

Cornell collapsed after four in the morning, then woke at seven and was working by ten after. He existed on coffee and nerves, moving backward in time, searching out every account of humanoid pilots. Cornell was five when Dad interviewed a truck driver who had claimed to have been abducted, the story almost laughable from the start. The man talked about being stripped and examined, the details clinical and rather painful. Wrote Dad: "It seems unlikely that star travelers would employ such methods. Proctology must have advanced by now." Then he concluded: "An hallucination, perhaps brought on by a blow to the limbic system."

Cornell ate lunch—barley chips and microwaved stew—then pored over the oldest files. They were thinner, less thorough. A younger, less patient man had done them. But Cornell found part of what he wanted, a file including photographs of burned grass and samples of soil and ash, the stink of diesel fuel long gone. Mom stood in the foreground of one photograph, hands on hips and eyes fixed on the camera. She was so pretty, small but never frail, her dark hair worn in a ponytail and the face tanned and those eyes never young. He had never seen such coldly certain eyes. Except on another planet, he realized. Mom had High Desert eyes, made for hardship and solitude: He read everything in that file, rereading every mention of her and her long-dead father.

"A clear alcoholic," Dad had decided. "I dislike him. I don't trust him. If he told me it was day, I'd look for the sun before believing him." And about Mom: "She suffers. I feel sorry for this girl and wish I could help her. She's alone on this ranch. I suspect abuse. Today, helping me collect samples, she remarked, 'I think it'd be wonderful to be taken to some beautiful alien world.' I've been telling her about the real aliens, and she listens. She does seem to believe me."

Later, in summation, Dad wrote, "An obvious fake. I only hope the man never sees a real spacecraft, because I won't believe him."

And on the same page, with a different pen:

"I'm in love. In love, and I've never been so scared."

Mrs. Pete had a full dinner for both of them, Cornell exhausted and happy to be thinking about ordinary things. There was gossipy talk about the neighbors. Fun talk. The Lynns had had troubles, Mrs. Lynn running around with young men. And Mrs. Underhill had become Mrs. Pete's best friend, which was a big surprise to both women. "I told her you were here. Go over and say hello sometime." The Talbots down the street had been robbed twice in two months, which had everyone scared. The local curmudgeon was Old Man Fraizer—Dad was a teddy bear next to him—but she suspected he wouldn't live here much longer. "Bitter old farts don't last. Have you noticed that?"

Cornell looked out back. Houses once new and modern had gone shabby, becoming more interesting. Swing sets and elevated playhouses were painted candy colors. Looking between two houses, he remembered being able to see farm fields. But not anymore. Houses covered the world right up to the horizon, then came the dusk-shrouded glow of the distant Pacific.

"Does it bother you?" he asked. "Living alone like this?"

Mrs. Pete shrugged and said, "But I'm not." Then a wise smile, and she added, "Thirty-five years in this house, how could I be alone?"

That next day, in chaotic fashion, Cornell studied the records of the glass disks, using Dad's maps of the state and region, the continent and the world as a whole. He read every analysis of the glass, particularly those done in professional labs, and nothing was particularly odd or interesting. Glass was glass. Heat had turned local materials into disks, some shallow and a few several feet thick. There wasn't any apparent pattern to their appearance, either. They were as likely to have formed in India as they were in the States. In California as much as here.

"But they mean something," Dad kept writing. "I know they do. They've got to have some clear and certain purpose."

"Some things don't," Cornell whispered to himself. "Sometimes, Dad, they just don't."

"How is your new job?" Mrs. Pete asked the question while dishing up dessert. Apple pie, frozen yogurt. Very American. "I hope it's going well, whatever it is."

"It's all right." He shut his eyes, feeling the alien's presence again. With his mind's eye, he stood above the ancient city, marveling without being certain it was real. A hallucination brought on by fatigue? By wishful thinking, perhaps? Then he said, "No, it's ordinary enough. Some stress, but a lot of boredom, too."

She nodded and watched him, almost smiling.

Yogurt melted against his tongue, cinnamon in the French vanilla.

"I keep forgetting," she said, "what exactly do you do?"

Cornell blinked, then said, "It's a secret." No cover story, but no confessions, either. "I can't talk about it. Sorry."

"A secret," she repeated. Then a sly, knowing smile, and she noted, "That's right up your family line, isn't it?"

His old bedroom was full of newer files and an assortment of recent, oddball periodicals. The last trace of Cornell was the map of Mars, still tacked to the wall but hidden behind cabinets and stacked boxes. Of all places, here he most felt like the intruder. The periodicals were cheap and clumsy, practically screaming *oddball* as he glanced through them. There were articles about bigfoot and the Change, religious visions and strange disappearances. Dad never used to approve of low-rent researchers, particularly if they were called Madam Madam or the Astral King. His stance was one of professional disgust, asserting a pecking order in the oddball community. He was saying, in effect, "I'm not like the weird ones. I'm a different creature entirely."

One magazine opened itself, the binding cracked from use, and Cornell saw highlights and cryptic notes in the margins. The title—"They Walk Among Us!!!"—shouted at him. Yet the tone of the piece was sober, even stilted. The author's vague biography implied that he was someone inside the U.S. Census Department. The bulk of the article concerned discrepancies in the last several censuses: too many people versus too few births. Something like a million extra citizens, he read, and where did they come from? What did they want? There was a hyperbolic epilogue, obviously written by someone else, and every inflammatory possibility was explored. Invasion was a central theme. And in the margins, Dad had written, "Too simple . . . one million seems unlikely . . . but what, pray tell, if????"

There was a journal inside a locked cabinet, buried in the front and dogeared by use. It was older than the magazine, its first entry from the Change Day three-plus years ago. Dad had written:

"Something obvious occurred to me this evening.

"Frankly, I've never held much credence to the idea that aliens move among us, disguised as mortal humans. Yet during the cul-de-sac's annual get-together, something obvious and ripe struck me. I gave out a little moan, in astonishment. Pete had to ask if I was all right, the poor man. The poor sweet simple man. All these years, and I hadn't once considered one blatant possibility.

"It would be easy for *them*. Cosmetic surgery married with *their* superior minds. Why not?!! Couldn't they move among us, if they wished? Indeed, they could occupy any position in our society. If so, I'm absolutely certain that I'm of interest to them. That's why I'm beginning this new study. As an enlightened citizen on this otherwise backward world, I'm sure their operatives are close, studying me with relish.

"I am my own bait!!!!!!"

"So," Cornell asked, "do you still do the Change Day picnics?"

Mrs. Pete nodded. "Always. Of course."

"How are they?"

"The same."

"What's that mean?"

"The adults drink too much. Except this adult." A laugh. "The kids stay up too late, and usually there's a fight. And your father brings out his telescope after dark—"

"Still?"

"It's a tradition."

"But how's he act?"

"Distant, most of the time." A long, thoughtful pause. Then she added, "We look at the earth, and he's busy watching us."

"The neighbors?"

"Me," she said. "Particularly me."

The rest of the journal was filled with broad speculations about aliens and their motives, none of them taken as the final conclusion. In the same drawer were files about the neighbors. The Petes. The Underhills. Even the people behind the cul-de-sac, men and women and children named and photographed over the last few years. Dad had done a thorough, embarrassing job of it, recording behaviors with a zoologist's eye, using a parabolic sound mike to eavesdrop on private moments. Cornell listened to a couple of tapes, in trimmed doses. Fights and sex were interspersed with banality. A lot of them involved Mrs. Pete, and it made no sense. She came across on the tapes as being absolutely ordinary, worried about her gardens and her teaching job and her husband's weight. What was the obvious thing that Dad had seen? And how did it involve this ordinary woman?

In the back of the drawer was a worn spiral notebook, its cardboard cover patched with strapping tape. Inside was a list of names, some familiar and some famous.

*Elaine Forrest* was written at the top of the first page, in bold red letters.

*Lane Underhill* was second.

And *C.* was third. Just C. Which had to mean Cornell, he realized, although it took him several moments to comprehend what everyone here shared in common. "Oh, God . . . of course . . . !"

"Remember when we saw the Change?"

Mrs. Pete looked at him, laughed and said, "Am I that old already?"

He didn't mean it to sound that way.

"You were sitting," she said. "I was walking."

He shut his eyes, and she added:

"I remember it perfectly. All of it."

There were celebrities on the list. There were ordinary people and high-ranking politicians, and everyone's name was accompanied with a specific coded number. Their files were inside a different drawer, everyone belonging to that honored club that had seen the Change. Astronomers had their names in green, not red. Because they watched the sky for a living? Because they were expected to see it? In the first journal, in an entry dated two years ago, Dad wrote, "It stands to reason that the aliens would have had foreknowledge of the Change. And wouldn't they want to watch it? Which is how I can identify all of them!"

In C's file he read: "He was with Elaine. I've gone over his testimony a million times, and I'm sure he is wrong. He looked skyward because she did. He was mimicking her, nothing more."

Yet later, in ominous oversized lettering: "What if C isn't human? He could be an agent of theirs. Perhaps my real son was abducted years ago. Shortly before the Change? It would explain much . . . !"

Cornell took a slight breath and held it, beginning to tremble.

Another note: "I guess I'm glad I drove him away, if he is some kind of alien creature."

And when he read those words, in that instant, he imagined Dad sitting before him. "You didn't drive me away," he whispered to the phantom. "It was my fault, more than not. More than not. Alien or not, it's my own goddamn fault, Dad. . . . "

"Pete called."

Cornell was sitting on the curb, the earth particularly bright tonight. He blinked and turned to Mrs. Pete. She had come outside to walk, or maybe she'd seen him here, then donned shorts and the headphones to have an excuse. "They're coming home soon," she told him.

"What's soon?"

"In a couple days." A pause. "They didn't quite find bigfoot, but they saw some pretty country. You know Pete. Always looking at the bright side."

Cornell made a quick mental tally. What else did he want to accomplish here? In two days' time—?

"In the mood for some late dinner?"

He shook his head. "No, thanks."

She began to walk, not fast, once around the island and stopping, saying, "You'd better tell him you were here. It's going to make him crazier if he doesn't know who it was."

"I'll leave him a note. A letter."

"Why not stay and talk to him yourself?"

"Because I need to get back to work." That was somewhat true. He felt normal, no residual sense of other bodies, no desire to bury his brain in the backyard. Beside, he needed to know about Porsche . . . to be reassured that she was surviving. . . .

"Leave a letter, then," Mrs. Pete told him.

"I will."

"Tell him I looked after you."

"No," he cautioned, "I don't think that would work. He'd get the wrong message."

And bless her, she seemed to understand. A quick nod, a smile. Then she was walking again, almost fast this time, Cornell able to hear the buzz of her headphones whenever she came past him.

There was an old file cabinet in the basement, one that he'd noticed but that no key fit. It was heavy steel with old-fashioned locks, and for a long while he assumed it was empty. A relic meant for overflow, perhaps. But no, that next morning he managed to give it a shove and hear something shift inside. He stepped back, standing next to Dad's workbench while trying to predict his father's mind. Where would Dad hide a key? Somewhere convenient, probably up high. Metal shelves stood against the concrete foundation, a sloppy mess of cans and tools before him; what made him pause was an old paint can, its label faded to near-white and nothing in it. Cornell grabbed the can without stretching, shook it and felt nothing inside but dark air. Odd, odd, odd.

The lid came off with just his fingernails. The key was tucked inside a velcro envelope stuck to a velcro patch glued to the long-dried enamel paint. The key fit the old lock, freeing both drawers, and they rolled open by themselves, with smooth, well-greased motions. Neither was full. The top drawer had several manila envelopes filled with photographs of Mom—hundreds, at least—and they were different from those in the family album. More intimate, maybe. But why hidden? Maybe after she left, Dad had hidden them, out of easy reach, diminishing her place in the house.

The lower drawer had another envelope. More photos? But then he saw the old videos behind them, no labels besides a series of Roman numerals from I to V. Old, but not a trace of dust. An old-style TV and VCR were at the far end of the basement. Dad and Pete used to watch their videos of landing sites and whatnot on that TV. The VCR took tape III without complaint, Cornell noticing how his hands shook as he punched the *On* buttons and grasped the VCR's remote control. The screen filled with snow, and he hit *Fast Forward* while stepping back. The machine hummed, snow dissolving. He recognized the bed and bedroom at a glance, people moving in jerky, too-quick motions, and he recognized Dad's face, and Mom's, the pale body over the tanned one. It was all very clumsy and staged, even at high-speed, and he watched the rapid copulation, almost immune to what he was seeing, feeling a gray detachment and then a staggering indifference, and he was shaking everywhere, and he gave out a weak long moan, finally hitting the *Stop* button.

The photographs in the last envelope were handworn images of his mother, in lingerie and naked, posing and smiling and something in that smile lingering with him. A beautiful woman, no doubt. But sometimes, in the harsher light, there was something severe and cold about her beautiful face and how those big dark eyes stared up at him, unblinking and unnaturally calm, sharper than any obsidian point.

Cornell replaced the photographs and tapes, trying to put everything back as he had found it. That's when he noticed the smaller envelope at the back of the drawer, not hidden but something about it anonymous and intentionally unnoticeable. He picked it up, turning it over. The address and Dad's name were written in a woman's artful cursive, no return address and the postmark smudged. The letter inside had torn along the folds, tape repairing the damage more than once. "Nathan," it began, "how are you? It's been quite a year, hasn't it?"

Cornell breathed, looking at the date. In the upper corner

was June 15. And the year after the Change. He breathed again, then started to read all over again.

"Nathan, how are you? It's been quite a year, hasn't it? You were right about the aliens. They've certainly shown themselves. I'm sure it's been very exciting for you, and gratifying, and I hope you're doing well.

"I can't say the same, I'm sorry. And I know it's awful to write you out of the blue, without warning. I'm sorry, sorry sorry sorry for all the pain and worry I must have caused you. Leaving like I did was wrong, but I was a child. I was a silly young girl, and I'm sure you understand that. Trying to raise Corny, and always knowing that I'd never be a real mother. You're the wonderful parent, I'm certain. And I'm sorry, sorry for writing like this, at such a time. But I need help!!! I'm desperate, nowhere to turn, and if you have any feelings left for me, then *please* help me now!!!!"

She wanted money, he read. "A loan," she called it. "I know you're not a rich man, and you need your money for your important work. But this is an emergency, a terrible one, and who else can I ask?" She wanted twenty thousand dollars, unless he could manage more . . . and Cornell thought how Dad's mood had soured during that summer. "I need the money sent at once!!!" Instructions followed, including a post office box in another city. Then a final note:

"Don't try to find me, please please. It wouldn't do anyone any good. I am trusting you. I know you still love me, and you can forgive me. Do this for me. For Corny. And kiss Corny for me. Tell him that I do love him, that mothers always love their children.

"Your little girl,

"Pam."

He walked into the bright sunshine, suitcase in hand, blinking and blinking and finally wiping at his eyes with his free hand. He wasn't crying anymore; wiping was a habit. What was left to do? He'd written Dad a long rambling letter, telling him that he'd come home just to be home for a while. He mentioned his job and hinted at danger, then thanked him

"**Novak, is it? Get your asses over here.**"

He knew the voice, the bodies. It was one of Logan's minions, back from the Breaks and coming for him. Cornell was pulling equipment from a storage hut. Someone had stolen his best spearhead and a rawhide sack—*bastard*—and he wasn't in a mood to stop and chat, thank you.

"Got a chore for you, Novak."

Cornell said nothing, feeling a sinking sensation.

"See those two? Take them. You've got desert experience, right? Steer north. Someone saw someone up in the Rumpleds, and it sounds like a native. You're going to check it out—"

"What?" he whistled.

"You're going on a hunt." The man snorted, laughed. "Never been on one? Well, here's the deal. A cash bonus if you make contact, a fat bonus if you bring it back here. Mind and bodies both, and alive."

"I'm supposed to catch it?"

"If it's real." Faces blinked and turned incredulous. "Hell, talk to it and that's something. That's a first. Tell it, I don't know . . . that we've got food down here. That we want to be friends, and it's welcome to visit. We're neighbors and nice as anything." A pause, then he added, "Whatever you think might work. Understand?"

for being a fine father, probably better than eith
had guessed. . . .

What else?

Find a specialist, he thought. Give him or her the
including photocopies of the letter, and explai
wanted a modern day Sam Spade to take up his cha
any cost.

"You're leaving?"

Mrs. Pete walked up to him, and he said, "In a n

It was a brilliant day, but a little cool. A whiff of au
in the air. Kids played in the street, a mutt dog chasi
them, then another, then back to the first one agai

"Good to see you," she offered.

"Thanks for having me. Thanks for everything."
second letter, just finished and sealed in a white
He removed it from his back pocket and said, "Do
this. Don't."

She looked sober and calm. "What is it?"

"In case," he whispered. "Hide it and give it to
in case."

He didn't mean to sound so ominous.

Mrs. Pete put the envelope out of sight, under
swallowed and said, "Please be careful, Cornell. Wil

He didn't answer. Exhausted and frazzled, he fo
self looking at the round concrete island in the n
that white, white concrete ring. And he asked hims
*does it mean?* Of course it meant nothing—no me
tended; no information hidden in the bushes or soil
an instant he felt like a stranger, an alien, gazing
round island and wondering what was its purpose.

Like a giant green eye, he was thinking . . . perm
gazing up at the wondrous bright sky. . . .

Cornell thought of the empty cage outside New Reno, one of his bodies glancing in that direction. The broad barren street was empty, save for the two recruits, bodies huddled around their minds. He had never seen this town so still, so empty—

"What about the Breaks?"

"What about them?"

"I'm expected there," Cornell reported. "I was cutting lumber—"

"Lumberjacks we've got," the man informed him. "We need someone with an ounce of experience and six strong bodies, which is you." A brief pause, then he added, "What are you waiting for? Kisses? Get those kids equipped, rationed and out of here. And bring something back for our scientists to play with, will you? They're getting bored."

The "kids" were named Harold and Jennifer. Harold was reddish gray, a forty-year-old one-time advertising executive; the girl was mouse-colored and claimed to be in her twenties. She'd been a store clerk and factory worker, and she seemed fascinated by Harold's past career. Did he make much money? Did he travel much? No? "But still," she insisted, "it sounds wonderful. Why did you quit?"

Harold never quite explained why.

Both of them watched the surrounding desert, fondled themselves, and generally looked lost. New Reno was behind them, out of sight. They were scared and excited, not quite believing any of it. Cornell thought of ignoring his orders, abandoning them. Or he could take them into the Breaks instead of the Rumpleds. Why not? Because he didn't want to face Logan's wrath. And because he was responsible for these people, like it or not. He decided to take them on a little tour of the Rumpleds, then bring them home again. Safe and grateful.

"What kind of car did you drive?" Jennifer asked Harold.

"Mercedes."

"Oh, God. I'd love having one of those."

Harold nodded with every head. "It was nice, I suppose."

"I'm going to buy a house first, then a car. I'm going to put in all the hours I can here, and I'll make a ton."

"If we survive," Harold whistled softly.

Cornell tried to reassure him, and he tried teaching them some of Porsche's tricks. But they weren't good students, the woman prattling on about her goals and poor Harold too cowed by his circumstances to concentrate. Eventually Cornell was talking only to Porsche, in his mind, apologizing for not arriving on schedule. He told her about his vacation, about what he'd learned and how he had hired the specialist to hunt for his mother. And the imaginary Porsche asked, "Why do you want to find her?"

He couldn't say. Curiosity, maybe. Maybe because children are supposed to find lost parents.

"When do we get our vacation together, love?"

He tried to imagine them on a tropical beach, and he realized he couldn't quite remember how Porsche looked on the earth. He kept seeing her as so many big brown bodies, black eyes sheathed in golden inner lids. Lovely eyelids, he thought. And those little pinhole ears . . . God, he was crazy! He'd have to tell her—his affections fixed to a multibodied alien—and Porsche would love it, probably laughing herself sick.

Cornell didn't believe in this alien. Hadn't the Rumpleds been searched? Flat desert bled into eroded hills, greasewood stands cut to stumps. They didn't have much food with them; New Reno was being fed from the Breaks now, only there had been interruptions. Glitches in the young system. Cornell tried to teach his people how to hunt, but Harold didn't pick up scents very well, and Jennifer lacked patience. It was Cornell who found a big nest of honey-ants, and his bodies were the ones that were bit and stung while excavating the sweet goo. Harold refused to eat raw bugs, which was fine. Looking at the high dry peaks, Cornell sensed that he could use all the fat he could lay in now.

They had a crude map that led them to a set of high valleys, and they searched the area for most of a week, bodies climbing and sniffing and finding nothing but some rock shards that resembled aborted tools. There were no tracks, no signs of foraging. There was barely anything to hunt, and at night the thin air turned brutally cold.

"Maybe we should climb higher," Jennifer remarked, faces staring at the dome of stars. "Has anyone ever gone way up in these mountains?"

Cornell couldn't say one way or another.

"I don't think we should," Harold argued. "This is too high already, and besides, it looks treacherous."

But Jennifer's impatience won over any caution. She teased Harold, telling him, "You're an old woman, aren't you?"

With a cowering dip of heads, Harold said, "We should be reasonable. That's all I mean."

There weren't any natives, but their food stocks were running low. Maybe the higher valleys had better hunting. "What we're going to do," Cornell told his audience, "is travel light. We'll drag our minds a little farther, then leave them—"

"Just leave them?" Harold moaned.

"Each of us will leave a couple of bodies behind, as guards," he promised. "The rest spread out and hunt. Not too far above, because bodies can lose touch with the mind. But you'll sense when that's happening. Don't worry."

"Sounds good," Jennifer decided.

Harold dipped his heads, glowering at the ground.

One of them would make it, one wouldn't. Cornell could see their prospects; smell them. He felt sorry for Harold and whatever had dropped him out of respectable life. Getting him through his first shift was the goal now, probably the only one worth pursuing. Then Cornell would have a chat with his case officer, or maybe with F. Smith. Whatever it took.

Harold went to sleep in a sheltered hole. Jennifer winked at her teacher, asking, "What's possible?"

From her tone, he knew what she meant.

"What can we do with these bodies?"

Cornell thought of Porsche naked on a vast bed, her human body covered with a thick brown pelt—

—and Jennifer said, "Penny for your thoughts."

His faces lifted, mouths saying, "Nothing."

She unconsciously scratched at one of her crotches and looked back out over the desert. "What's it going to look like in the future? In a hundred years, say?"

"How will what look?"

"New Reno," she said, trying to be patient with him. "What are we going to do with it?"

It wasn't something he expected from a one-time clerk. "I'm not sure we'll last another year, honestly." He mentioned the lousy hunting and the countless other worlds waiting for brave souls. "If we don't find intelligent, technological critters soon, they'll pull us."

"Think so?" She sounded doubtful. "There's food in the Breaks, isn't there? And water. We could farm. We could find metals and build up industries." She had given this considerable thought. It was a game to her, but a fun one. "We could build a train, maybe. It'd take people back and forth between New Reno and the Breaks."

A train on the desert, sure. Electrically powered; O-gauge; minds strapped on flatcars while their bodies rode in the coaches, dressed in comfortable and brightly colored clothes.

"Tourists would pay to come here. It could be like the real Reno," she assured him, "with gambling and big hotels."

He was amused and disgusted in equal measures.

But all he said was, "We've got to sleep now. Okay?"

"Think about it," she advised him.

"I will." And he fell into a deep hard sleep, his dreams full of fancy hotels and furred lovers and a clean endless desert under a purple sky.

True to plan, they fanned out through a series of higher valleys, each using four of their bodies. The girl was caught up in the adventure; Harold worked hard to do nothing dangerous. Cornell took the middle valleys, ending up on a high exposed ridge, a steady wind screaming in his ears. There was a bowl-shaped valley below him, a little grove of greasewood tucked into the low ground. They were stunted and scattered, but otherwise healthy. When he saw nuts hanging in bunches, he knew people hadn't been there. One body crept forward, almost stepping on a pile of shiny black scat; he stopped, stared for a moment, then retreated back to the ridge.

"What do you see?" Jennifer would ask periodically. One of her guarding bodies would whisper the question, as if a native might hear anything louder. "Have you found anything?"

"No. Nothing."

"I haven't either."

"Keeping trying," he coached, positioning his four bodies out of the desiccating winds. This was more drudgery than adventure. A native would need an enormous range in these mountains. It was poor, cold country, and it would have to roam enormous distances, towing its mind to the rare oasis. But that scat had been fresh. Fresh enough to stink, he realized, and it hadn't smelled quite the same as human scat. Humans had subtle differences, perhaps because of diet. Or maybe there were little imperfections in their translations, a slight alienness always clinging to them.

He watched the valley and the desert below. In the afternoon, dust clouds formed, moved with the wind and then collapsed again. Aborted storms, he guessed. Could people last here? Were there humans who had gone native, as rumored? Maybe a few; maybe someday they would have children. But would the children retain their human qualities? And would that be a good thing?

He'd have to ask Porsche what she thought, soon as he saw her again.

Soon.

Then there was a motion. Sudden; minuscule. Moving slowly, Cornell turned just one head. A solitary body was walking below him at a modest, casual pace. Where had it come from? It was whiter than the ground. Was it mindless? A body lost by someone careless, or dead? But then a second body emerged from the valley's wall, and a third came after it.

It was not human, he knew, without any doubt.

Cornell stared, sensing that the alien's mind was tucked in a tiny hole. He couldn't feel the connections between bodies and mind—he was too far away, and the creature was too small—but he knew that a camouflaged burrow would be the perfect home.

As the three bodies made for the greasewood, he watched them, admiring the details. They moved efficiently, wasting nothing, every calorie spent to gather as many calories as possible. Ripe nuts were harvested, slung over their shoulders and brought home. Whenever possible, they walked where the dust was blown from bare stone, leaving no tracks. The creature was shepherding its energies. Maybe it would remain here until the food was gone; maybe it had a regular cyclical pattern that it followed. Like the greasewood itself, it might be extremely old, extremely tough. . . .

What should he do? Cornell went through the motions of deciding, but he knew the answer. There was no guilt, no nagging sense of duty. Once the bodies returned, vanishing into an apparent stone wall, he crept off the ridge and moved elsewhere.

"Have you seen anything?" Jennifer whispered.

"Nothing."

"No?"

"Nada," he said. "Zip."

One more day hunting the natives, it was decided. Cornell made the decision. Jennifer was disappointed but compliant, admitting to him, "I'm feeling odd. Just like they warned us."

"I haven't felt right yet," Harold complained. "Not for a minute."

"How about you?" she asked Cornell.

He was fine. Perfect. And he was happy being able to say so.

Later that night, while Harold slept, Cornell decided to take his turn at speculating. "What if it happens the other way?"

"What if what happens?"

"Aliens come through the intrusions, visiting the earth . . . how would they look, do you suppose?"

She considered the prospect. "Like us, I guess."

"It depends where they enter," Cornell argued. "In the ocean, they might end up being whales or dolphins. Up in the Himalayas, they could become yetis, instead. What's important is accepting that they can cross to the earth—"

"But so what?" asked Jennifer.

"You were right before." If not in quite the way she had meant it. "We come here, and naturally we're going to remake our home world. Within our limits. But why shouldn't *they* be the same? Except that aliens might be more advanced technologically. Of course some of them would be."

She nodded with one head. "I suppose. . . . "

"What is the universe?" He paused, then answered his own question. "It's an enormous set of tiny geometric compartments, packed close together, and linked wherever life touches compatible life. Each compartment's history is different, and every lifeform is unique."

"Okay," she whispered.

"Think of the earth," he told her. "What's likely for the future? More people every day, less room for the masses. Sure, we can fly the short hop to Mars. There are places that are nice and dead, ready for colonies. But for how long? A thousand years? A million?"

Jennifer said nothing, watching the stars.

"But there are other ways to make room," he said.

Her hands fidgeted, and she said, "What do you mean?"

"Look at us now." His voice was sharp, excited. "We're adapted to scarce food, water and air. Maximum intelligence; minimal volume. Maybe this is the way every intelligent world moves. Miniaturization. Not with biology, necessarily. But it could be done with computers and microscopic machines, people shrinking themselves. Where ten people felt crowded, a thousand people could live in comfort. Or a million. Laser-interfaced minds smaller than dust, and our world has an enormous amount of room left over."

She tilted her heads, shaking them as if to clear her ears.

"Suppose it happens, at least sometimes." He was breathing fast, kicking up clouds of dust when he exhaled. "Aliens could visit the earth, becoming sort of human . . . and they could build industries on the sly, fancy machines and flying craft. It might take a few generations. Maybe it happened a million years ago. Who knows? But the point is, they could miniaturize themselves, vanishing from our view. There could be a million New Renos, and we'd never see them."

"They'd build sin cities on the earth?"

No, he didn't mean it literally. He just meant . . . well, he wasn't sure where he had been heading. He said nothing, trying to think. Then the one-time clerk told him, "You need to sleep, I think."

She was tired of speculations, eager for tomorrow's hunt.

"I'll bed down in a minute," Cornell promised; then he didn't move for hours, staring at the sky and the dark world below, his bodies losing heat until they shivered, and Cornell still lost in thought. Still struggling to make sense of it all.

They searched other valleys in the morning, and somewhere Jennifer became lost, her bodies wandering down a towering ridge and ending up above the little bowl-shaped valley with its greasewood grove. "Did you know it was here?" she asked.

Cornell waited an instant too long, then said, "Sure."

Her guarding bodies stared at his bodies, judging him. He hoped she would grow bored and move on, but no, she was hungry. She climbed down and found fresh scat and tracks. "Small tracks," she whispered, excitement mixed with a sudden caution. "I can see where they lead. Come up here, will you?"

Cornell was trapped, no excuse ready. He was angry with the alien for being careless, for letting itself be discovered twice—

"Should we go?" Harold asked Cornell.

Jennifer glared at him. He was a liar, she knew, or an incompetent. Suddenly her two bodies squatted and began drawing in the soft dust, making a map of the valley. Inventing a plan. "We come in from three sides, at once and straight on. Okay?"

It wasn't a plan, it was a charge.

"Don't we have another choice?" asked Harold.

"Don't you want the big bonus?" she asked. "Because if you don't, I'll do it alone."

And Cornell said, "We move close and talk to it. Reason with it." He tried to sound self-assured. "This isn't a war."

Jennifer's bodies stood and said, "Straight at it."

In review.

Twelve bodies; three groups. Cornell took the south flank, passing through the stunted forest with spears held high. He could just smell the native, and he was almost on top of it. A secretive creature, he knew. All of them were solitary, intensely private . . . and not at all human, he reminded himself. *True aliens.*

Jennifer's bodies found a hole covered with a gray door made from skin.

"Slow down," Cornell warned her. "Take it easy."

But she was too excited, probably thinking of the bonus. The first trap, hidden where the dusts had pooled, was triggered by a foot. It made a solid *whap,* wooden spikes driving into her thighs. The body crumbled without a sound, but the pain made her guarding bodies shiver, fur standing erect. Another body, pausing to help the injured one, stepped into a different trap. Smaller spikes pierced its foot, driving straight through the tiny bones.

Now she screamed, with every mouth.

The alien burst from its hole, three bodies with spears. Fancy stone heads glittered in the sunshine. A whistling voice, shrill and clear and *wrong,* shouted, "Leave me leave me leave me."

Jennifer's healthy bodies pressed closer.

Cornell shouted, "Wait!"

He had watched the creature's careful stepping, and he should have guessed there were traps. . . .

"You prick," Jennifer yelled. A curse without any translation.

The alien saw everyone, eyes tracking the mismatched bodies. Surprise didn't resemble human surprise, but the voice had an unmistakable terror. "Strangers," it whistled. "Insane strangers, I smelled you . . . demons demons demons!"

Cornell was past the crippled bodies, staying on the rocky ground.

"Kill your pieces, I will. I cut kill eat shit your pieces!"

Cornell tried to speak, tried to say anything to defuse this mess. But Jennifer was stabbing at the closest body, clumsily and repeatedly, the alien slapping her spears aside. Then it stabbed, just once, neat and swift and one body falling dead in an instant, its heart punctured by a long razored blade.

"Oh, my," cried Harold.

Jennifer had one healthy body left in the fight. "Will you fucking help me? Come help me!"

Nine bodies against three. No amount of skill could save the creature, and the battle couldn't be defused. Adrenaline, or whatever its equivalent, put them in a skirmish line, and it was a war. Harold tossed a spear—a clumsy, desperate toss—and it caught an arm, slicing to the bone. The alien responded by charging, its two healthy bodies screaming and thrusting. To scare them; to drive them away. Cornell stepped back and jabbed, and jabbed, and clipped a chest, a face. And the little white bodies fell, a thin spatter of bright red blood everywhere. Harold and Jennifer—the one-time executive and clerk—pinned the bodies and cut them apart, faces grim and enthralled.

Where was the third body?

Cornell approached the hole, the rat skin stretched and cured to resemble the gray stone. "Surrender," he shouted. Was that a native concept? "We'll take care of you . . . we don't want to hurt—"

A sound, a whistle. A combination of prayer and curse, he sensed; then came a solid rumbling noise. The door lifted with a burst of wind, Cornell feeling it against his faces. Another trap? For whom? Then came dust and the smell of blood. The body must have kicked away the burrow's supports, the ceiling collapsing. Cornell didn't know what he was thinking, too stunned, too tired, squinting until the dust cloud had blown away and his companions were standing over the corpses, Jennifer's wounded bodies writhing in misery. Doomed now, he sensed.

"What happened?" asked Harold. "What did it do?"

Behind the skin door were stones, dry and still; Jennifer jabbed at them, shouting, "Serves you right. Serves you right. We would have fed you and kept you happy, you bastard!"

This was wrong, Cornell knew. All wrong.

"Fed and happy," she screamed. "Fat and happy. Safe and happy, and you deserve this, you fuck!"

"DISAPPOINTING," SAID F. SMITH. A SHAKE OF THE GRAY HEAD, A tightening of the jaw. "It should have been handled differently, of course."

Cornell sat across from her. The same office, the same window and sunshine and great green lawn. He had come straight from the intrusion, as ordered, wanting to get through his debriefings as quickly as possible. Was he in trouble? Who would they blame?

"Differently," she repeated, plainly waiting for him to speak.

"Jennifer shouldn't have charged the burrow," he argued. "I told her, more than once—"

"Yes, she did test as impulsive and aggressive." An agreeable nod. A tense smile. "I'm sure you did your best. And we'll let the girl recover in New Reno, produce new bodies before her next assignment."

The girl should be sent home, he thought to himself.

"More and more, the HD natives seem antisocial. Death is always preferable to being with another of their species." A shake of the head, then she said, "I can't give details. But let's just say this wasn't the first incident. Our first example."

"They've killed themselves before?"

She seemed to nod once.

"If I'd been told—"

"And you should have been," she admitted. "There's no reason to send people out ignorant."

Yet F. Smith volunteered no other lessons now.

Instead she asked for a blow-by-blow account of the mission, taking notes and going back over certain issues. How did the recruits perform? What were the conditions in New Reno? How about his own health? She seemed pleased that he hadn't lost any bodies, or even suffered an important injury. "You're doing splendidly." She nodded with authority. "Mentally as well. Wonderfully well."

"Can I pick my assignment?"

A quick smile, almost wise. "Where would you like to work?"

"In the Breaks. With Porsche."

"Ms. Neal, yes. An amazing woman, that one." Sitting back, she gave the sky a long intense stare. "Actually, I should warn you. It's all discussion at the higher levels now, but there's a fair chance that in the not too distant future . . . well, we might scale back our work on High Desert. At least temporarily."

"Why?"

"You know our goals," she said. "Our central hope is to find a technological species and learn from it, then bring that knowledge home. For the betterment of humankind—"

"But why quit now?" he asked.

"What do we have so far? A species geared for a solitary existence, simple technologies and a tiny population. People report a larger presence, I know. Perhaps you've felt it now and again."

Cornell gave a noncommittal shrug.

"But our project heads are becoming impatient. Casualty rates are too high, and morale is poor. Should we keep pressing, using resources and volunteers on something increasingly unlikely . . . ?"

"What if there's something there?" he asked.

"But what? We have a species with no sense of society, no capacity for cooperation. Can such a creature build better computers? What do you believe, Mr. Novak?"

He rose to his feet, saying nothing, aware of the smallness of the office and wishing he could leave now.

"There is another factor, too." She watched him pace, then said, "A tangential factor, and new."

He paused and looked at her.

"It happened a few days ago. Without warning."

Cornell felt a sudden quiet dread, not breathing, standing with his arms limp at his sides, waiting.

"All at once," she told him. Then she gave an odd quizzical grin, tilting her head—

"What happened?"

—and enjoying herself, saying, "The moon changed."

The moon? What did she mean?

"Changed. Everted, just like the earth did." The grin got larger, teeth catching sunshine. "It turned inside out, in an instant. And what's more, *we think we know why.*"

He wasn't Sam Spade; he was every bookkeeper ever born.

"No, it wasn't too difficult. Not really." The bland face smiled, for an instant, spidery hands massaging the air between them. He was an African American, though race seemed inconsequential. His looks and voice seemed designed to be forgotten. The man made a living without ever leaving his vast office, using computers to pry into other computers, charging fortunes for his experience and sheer zest. "I found her in a couple of hours, which is about normal in this kind of case—"

"She's alive?"

"Oh, yes." The man smiled in no particular direction. "She did a fair job of obscuring her past, and there are gaps in the records. She must have had facial surgery during one ten-month gap, and she changed her hair color—"

"You found her," Cornell interrupted. "You actually did?"

Soft brown eyes closed, then opened. "Sure."

"You have an address?"

"And much more." A pause. "All in all, she seems like a fascinating person."

It was like the business about the moon's Change; Cornell sat without moving, delaying his response. It was as if he was rationing his energies, waiting for a block of free time to become excited.

"I've got quite a lot of material," said the man. "If you need help to interpret anything, don't hesitate to ask me."

A thick manila envelope was handed to Cornell. He untied its tab and opened the flap, glancing at the contents. He noticed newspaper clippings, credit reports and official documents. *New Zealand,* he read; and the detective mentioned:

"Her current address, phone and E-mail numbers are on top."

On a square of vanilla-colored paper, yes.

"Any questions?"

The address put her a day's drive to the east, which was a surprise. Somehow New Zealand seemed more appropriate. The other side of the world, and all that.

The man sighed and said, "She's lovely. I couldn't help but notice."

"Is she still?"

"And remarkable," he added, almost whispering.

Cornell closed the envelope's flap, deciding to wait. His hands were shaking as he rewrapped the tab, and he was aware of his own breathing and the big rubbery heart inside his chest. Setting the envelope on his lap, he said, "I was wondering."

"Yes?"

Cornell looked at him for a long moment, then asked, "Could you do a second job for me?"

"Certainly."

"I mean now. In the next few days." He waited for a moment, then said, "I'm going back to work, and you can't reach me after that."

The face was composed, just a hint of curiosity betrayed in the narrowed eyes. "I have several clients now. I won't be able to start for a few weeks." He paused, then said, "Corporate clients. Very involved work."

"What if I pay double?"

A shake of the head. "Sorry."

"Thought so." Cornell made a show of resignation, then added, "Even if I'm right, you wouldn't find anything."

A blink, a knowing expression.

"It's just that I have a crazy idea." He had always had it, or it had come to him two minutes ago. He couldn't be sure which was true, and he explained nothing, simply saying, "If I'm wrong, I'm nuts. And if I'm right, you wouldn't find enough clues anyway."

"Are you baiting me, Mr. Novak?"

"Never." A big grin.

The man sat back in his squeaky old chair. "Tell me what you need. Maybe I can find an extra hour somewhere."

Cornell fed him slivers of the story, leaving out the strangest and most dangerous elements. He mentioned suspicions without drawing definite lines. And when he paused, he saw a thin smile blossoming, eyes turning distant, and that smooth unmemorable voice was saying:

"Family histories take less than an hour."

"Think so?"

A shake of the head. "I'll eat my supper here. I'll do the work tonight, all right?"

"I'd appreciate it."

"And I'll call you," the detective promised.

Where will I be? Cornell wondered. Driving, probably. He could reach Mom's by tonight, if he drove fast enough. "Shall I call you? At least tell you where I am?"

"No, I can track you down," the man boasted. Then he asked, "Are you planning to see her?"

Why not?

The detective sighed, then said, "Do me one favor. Read the files first, will you?"

Cornell picked up the envelope, promising himself to wait. Somehow patience seemed essential. Years of ignorance, of guesses and fantasies, and suddenly that ignorance seemed valuable in its own right. Read the records, he knew, and his mother would be reduced to exactly who she was—

"Read everything," he heard. "Before. Please."

"I will."

"And I'll call you this evening." The bland face gave the mildest grin. "Are you feeling all right, Mr. Novak?"

"Sure," he lied.

"You look tired." And now curiosity showed itself, the man leaning forward and asking, "Exactly what do you do for a living?"

"Don't you know?"

He leaned back, a little bruised.

"Porsche," said Cornell. "Neal. She used to play pro basketball, and she's from Texas."

"I remember, Mr. Novak. I'll have what you need tonight." The thinnest of smiles. "Or the work is free. How's that?"

It was late, almost ten o'clock, when Cornell checked into the motel and got his overnight bag upstairs, lights coming on for him and the fancy room computer already knowing his name, speaking with a woman's soothing voice, asking if he would like a drink or anything from the late-night kitchen.

"No, thanks. Nothing."

"Then good-night, sir. And sleep well."

Except he didn't feel like sleep. Hours of driving hadn't fatigued him in the slightest. Traffic and reading maps had just made him more awake, more alert, and he sat on the edge of his bed with the wall-sized TV set on CNN. It was another special about the moon, about its Change. They were showing shots from several vantage points; United Europe and Japan had their own high-tech telescopes, as did the CEA. It was the new Russian operation that had gone on-line just a few days ago. Above it, in what should have been a starry night sky, was the moon's own gray craters and jumbled gray highlands. Luna had been turned inside out, all right. The same as the Earth, right down to the lower albedo when seen from a distance. The short horizon was the same, but without an atmosphere it felt as if he was standing on a dusty hillside, stuck at the bottom of a tremendous spherical cavern.

Explanations. Experts were arranged in a horseshoe, sitting up straight while cameras panned over their exhausted faces. As a body, they had workable, reasonable explanations to offer tonight.

Cornell remembered what F. Smith had told him, not two days ago. It was the new Russian telescopes that had caused this Change. There was almost no doubt. "Both times," she had claimed, "people had asked the sky to deliver so much information. So much data. So many photons and gamma rays and neutrinos, and the system has its limits."

He had listened intently, too stunned to ask questions.

"Limits," she had repeated. Then she'd explained how a world, presumably any world, had limits defined by its size. The moon, being smaller, was easier to Change than the earth. What had been a great mystery was answered, finally and decisively, and it wasn't the flashy answer that everyone had expected, either.

"Our Change didn't happen because people were ready for the aliens." It was a scientist talking on the TV, but it could have been F. Smith. They had the same wry smiles, the same steely gazes. "It didn't happen because we became smart enough to understand the event, and there's no god-like species waving its limbs to remake the sky. It's just a matter of machinery. The mechanisms involved. On both worlds, we built enough telescopes to suck in more information than the sky could supply. And that's what causes a Change. And the Change seems irreversible. We've already shut down the lunar observatories, but the switch has been turned."

Cornell turned down the sound, then unpacked tomorrow's clothes and his bathroom items, finding the manila envelope at the bottom of the bag. All day he had ignored it. Now he let himself sit back against the firm pillows, opening the flap and promising himself that he would only recheck the address. Just that. But then his fingers removed everything, and he breathed and looked up at the giant screen, at the soundless experts, then breathed and looked down, eyes focusing on the paper beneath the address.

And the paper beneath it.

And so on.

* * *

"I hope I didn't wake you," said the detective. It was after one o'clock, and Cornell replied:

"No, I'm awake."

Audio only. The sheepish voice told him, "I'm sorry to take so long. I got an early jump on it, but . . . well, I'm having trouble. There is something, I just can't tell. . . ."

"How soon?"

The man said, "Tomorrow, maybe. No, I'm sure. I'll get you something definitive by tomorrow."

"Thanks." Cornell picked up the documents and newspaper clippings, tax forms and assorted profiles. "For everything, thank you."

"My pleasure."

A long pause.

Then the detective asked, "Did you read the material?"

"Twice."

A pause, then, "Well?"

"Well, what?"

"Are you going to see her?"

"Sure." He flipped to the back pages. "Will she be home?"

"Most likely."

"How do you know?"

"By studying her phone records, her electricity use." With a calm professional pride, he explained, "Occupied homes have signatures. Power surges, that sort of thing."

Cornell said, "Clever."

"She's an interesting woman, all right." The voice sounded impressed and wary, in equal measures. "I've seen her kind before. Tough and resourceful."

"Yeah."

"Smart."

"That's my mom."

The man nearly added another word. Dangerous? Remorseless? Or did he want to say *beautiful?* But he caught himself, perhaps deciding to drop the subject. Instead he said, "Well, have a good day tomorrow. Good luck."

"And to you," Cornell managed.

"Call me," said the detective. "Afterward, all right?"

But Cornell didn't hear him, turning back to the newspaper clipping from Auckland, New Zealand. The headline read: *American Woman Denies Charges, Pleads Innocent.* And beside the words was a grainy photograph of a woman who might have been his mother. The hair was too fair, the nose had been doctored, and her breasts looked augmented. But he knew the eyes, dark and unchanged. Cornell took a breath and held it, then heard the distant tone and realized that the phone line was disconnected, an electric hum filling the room, filling the universe.

There was a tall gate and a taller fence, trees and more trees, and nothing resembling an address visible from the road. This was the most exclusive house in an exclusive neighborhood, at least several acres of forest between him and the house. The gate was closed and locked. No guards, but there was undoubtedly some kind of security service, sensors and private police. Cornell parked on the street—a winding potholed affair with next to no traffic—and he climbed the gate, dropping to the crushed rock of the driveway and walking for several hundred yards, feeling nervous and tired after three hours of bad sleep, yet alert, too. The moment was squeezing his adrenal glands dry, and frazzled neurons were marshaling their energies, sparking faster now as he came around the last long bend.

It wasn't a mansion. At least Cornell had expected something larger, more splendid and older. Instead it seemed almost too new, built from modern woods cultured in giant tanks—glossy and dark, almost plastic in appearance—and from stone chiseled from underneath these very hills. Two stories tall; no trees around the house itself; a faintly Spanish design bathed in a sudden zone of bright sunshine. A three-car garage on the right, doors down . . . and an ornate marble fountain where a winged woman poured an endless stream of water into a basin, goldfish huddling in the scarce shadows.

Cornell mounted the stone stairs, telling himself that he'd

ring the bell and talk to the house computer, explaining himself. Somehow he didn't expect to find his mother. She wouldn't be home, today of all days, or she would refuse to open the door. Then a carload of security men would come, red lights whirring, and he'd be carted off to the city jail. He could see it that clearly. He went as far as imagining himself handcuffed, helpless, catching a glimpse of a curtain parting, someone looking down at him on the sly.

That's what he expected. What he wanted. What would be easiest.

But he didn't even make the front door, or the bell. Suddenly the door opened of its own volition—he couldn't see anyone, at least—and he paused on the top step for an instant. When he saw the face, small and pretty, he seemed to know it. How did he know it? He felt stupid, forgetting where he was and who this was . . . the strange woman saying, "Yes?" with a mixture of emotions. There was suspicion and caution and a courage. Women who lived alone rarely opened their doors to strange men, and she didn't seem to even suspect who he was. "What is it? Why are you here?" A glance at the empty driveway, then she growled, "You're trespassing."

That temper. He'd heard about it for years, had tasted it in himself, and hearing it in her voice was a signal. The switch. Suddenly he knew where he was and who this was; he was outside himself, watching the scene with amusement and astonishment. Mom stood at her door, ready to slam it shut if he took another step forward—he knew it by her stance, by her expressive face—and suddenly he heard his own voice saying:

"You're my mother."

With such calmness. He hadn't believed he could ever sound so calm. Then he added, "I found you," and he was like a little boy winning the game. "I found you." As if she should hug him and give him chocolate for winning it. As if that's what the rules said.

Later, replaying everything in his mind, Cornell remembered the blooming surprise in his mother's face and how surprise made her features taut and more youthful. She wobbled, just for an instant, and she seemed ready to shut the door in panic. But she didn't. She squeezed at the fancy brass handle, and Cornell opened his wallet, showing her photographs of the two of them, then saying, "You look well. You do."

She nodded, then with a breathless little voice said, "Corny?"

"Yes."

And she said, "My, my." She swallowed and took a step backward, collecting her wits. He felt sorry for her, which he hadn't expected. She seemed deceptively ordinary, saying, "My, my," with a stronger voice. Then she said, "Come inside, if you want." Another glance at the driveway. "How did you get here?"

He told her.

And she said, "Come in," once more.

The house, he realized, was the antithesis of Dad's house. There was space and a rigorous cleanliness, a sense of order that had started at the gate and culminated here in the entranceway. Cornell felt cleaner just for standing in this air. He smelled wildflowers. He saw a large staircase and dark wood—cultured walnut, probably—and a ceiling two full stories overhead. Mom said, "Here," and led him into a spacious living room, polished stone giving way to deep white carpeting. Everything was perfect, like the homes in decorating magazines. Giant couches; tasteful chairs; fancy knickknacks set on ornate built-in shelves. Comfortable old money had done this work. New money would have brought splashes of color and inspired mistakes. And she let him step closer, asking him, "How are you, Corny?"

He didn't know. He had never felt less sure of his state of mind. But he managed to say, "Fine," and she offered him a drink. What would he like? "Water?" It came out as a question, but she didn't notice. She vanished into some distant kitchen, leaving him to wander about the room, exploring its details. A huge TV was in a corner, a soap opera playing with the sound muted; there were *National Geographics* in a stack, their bindings never bent; a stylized camel had been cut from obsidian and set on the glass-topped coffee table; well-cleaned fireplace tools, brassy and bright, rested beside an only slightly blackened fireplace.

"Your water," his mother announced. Then, "Corny."

Water for two, perfect cubes of ice glittering inside tall glasses. He sipped and knew it wasn't tapwater. She offered him a seat, gracious and flustered and smiling without pause. In her mid-fifties, yet she looked forty. Clean taut cheeks and minimal crow's-feet. Not athletic, but fit. With a very unfashionable load of melanin in her skin. Her love of the sun hadn't aged her, had it? Blond hair was cut in a simple, elegant style. A girl's style. Only her voice had an old roughness, just a hint of it, and those white, white teeth had to be fancy caps.

"How's your water?"

"Fine." He nodded and looked at the melting cubes.

"Well," she offered, "isn't this something?"

He could hear the ice, little fissures opening along lines of weakness. Then he looked up and said, "Dad's doing okay."

She blinked.

She said, "Well," and then, "Good."

Then she said, "You do rather look like him."

That was funny. He didn't tell her how everyone else thought the opposite, that he was her child. Instead he told her, "Nobody knows that I've come here."

"Okay," she said.

"Except the guy that tracked you down for me."

Nothing. The face showed nothing, not even in the clear unblinking eyes. Cornell realized she had recovered her balance, probably in the kitchen, and from here on it would be harder to catch her off guard. She was sitting opposite him, crossing her legs. Dark trousers with red highlights; white socks and no shoes; a light short-sleeved blouse. The air-conditioning was pushing the temperature below 70, but her only concession to the chill was a lacy white pillow held in her lap, eyes glancing over at the TV, then back at him.

"You know," she began, "I've thought about finding you. But it's difficult, after so long."

"It is tough," he agreed.

She became more confident, saying, "You can blame me for running." A quick pause, then she added, "Don't be patient with me."

A smile. Cornell saw the intoxicating smile, feeling its pull. It was as if she was trying to cast a spell on him, against his will, bringing him into her state of mind.

"I don't know what you remember," she mentioned, eyes joining the smile. "You were so little. It was so long ago."

"It must have been tough," he conceded. "Living with Dad, I mean."

"Tough." A sigh. "Yes, it was."

He watched her.

"Sometimes." Then she took a dramatic sip of her fancy spring water, adding, "I was too young, which is my fault. I was a child pretending to be your mother."

He nodded, saying nothing.

"And your father's all right?"

On the brink of insanity, but he didn't mention it. Instead he said, "He went with Pete on a long trip, just recently—"

"Still chasing little green men?"

He didn't bristle with the question's tone. "Yeah. Always."

"And Pete helps?"

"Always has."

She seemed a little shocked, just for an instant. Then, "How is Pete? Still married to Elaine?"

"And still next door, too."

"Really?" She hadn't expected that answer. "Huh," she said. Then, "Well, that's nice."

Cornell sipped his water, nodding.

"And what about you, Corny? Are you married?"

"Never."

She studied him, always careful.

Then he said, "I work for the government. The CEA? On a top secret project in California." He said it point-blank, no hesitations. "We go through these things called quantum intrusions, into alien worlds."

Mom kept her face still, her eyes half-closing and then coming open again. Then came a thin, forced smile, nothing else to offer.

And he said, "I'm an alien, when I go through. I've got several bodies and a brain that I drag across the desert." A pause, then he said, "And I've got a girlfriend. . . . "

"Good," she offered, her voice cracking. "That's nice."

"Porsche Neal? The basketball player?"

She couldn't respond. The eyes became huge, and he could see her asking herself why had she let a madman into her house. What possessed her?

Cornell laughed mildly, sitting back in the deep cushions of the sofa. "No, I'm teasing. I made all of that up." Then he laughed louder, telling her, "I do odd work, but not with aliens. Sad to say."

Mom was relieved.

She breathed and began to laugh herself, probably too much, then she mentioned, "You almost sounded like your father, for a moment."

"I guess I did," Cornell said. "Sorry about that."

They changed topics.

At one point, in a carefully off-handed way, she asked, "How did you find me?"

Cornell rose, putting his glass on a cork coaster, then strolling to the back of the room, looking out on a long green yard, bigger than a football field and sprinkled with little gardens of robot-tended flowers and neat hedges, at least half a dozen bird feeders suspended on fine wires. Glass doors opened on a large stone patio, but he left them closed. He stared outside, Mom approaching him. He could barely hear her in the heavy carpeting, then the roughened voice was saying, "I have a different name. It's Pam Voos."

That wasn't the first change, either.

She told him, "After I left you, I had some very bad experiences."

He turned and said, "Really?"

As if he knew nothing. As if her life was a perfect mystery to him.

"Mistakes." She nearly whispered the word, then added, "After your dad, I stayed with one fellow . . . a mistake . . . anyway, after him I traveled, really just wandered. . . . "

"Where?"

She blinked, then swallowed. "Places." Then she smiled, as if realizing how inadequate that word was. "I started around the world, trying to find myself—"

Cornell knew her route, his detective having pieced it together from a thousand clues. South America, then Africa, and always supporting herself by obscure means. Then she ended up in Auckland, not long before the Change.

"—and I found a lovely man. In a different country." She nodded, naming no place. "You know who he reminded me of? Your father. He was sweet and thoughtful, and he made me miss you two. It was all I could do not to go home to you."

Cornell believed her. He knew better—knew the truth—yet the woman had a way of making everything plausible.

"But I made too many mistakes with your father, and you, and I had too much guilt." A deep sigh. "I married that other man. We weren't married very long. He had an accident." She shivered, showing him an aging woman still grieving for her dead husband. "A tragic accident."

No mention of a police inquiry. No hint of her careful letter to Dad, mailed by an intermediary in the States. She had needed the best possible defense attorney, and it paid off in the end. The dead man's grown children had contested the will, but between her attorney and her own resilience they hadn't had any chance. Afterward there was a final identity change, thorough and done so that anonymity could be regained, her bank accounts left healthy. Fiscally fat by any definition.

"I'm sorry," Cornell offered.

She shrugged her shoulders sadly, making certain that he felt sorry for her. What decent man wouldn't?

Then he turned and said, "You've got a lovely place."

"Oh," she said, "I like it."

"A beautiful home," he assured her.

Now she was wondering what he wanted; something in his tone made her wary. He saw it in her eyes, her stance. Was she calculating what she could afford to give him? Because Cornell might be one of those sons who appear from nowhere, demanding payment for past offenses. . . .

"You've done well for yourself," he assured her, looking through the glass doors, watching cardinals and finches and sparrows and sometimes raucous bluejays. Those bird feeders were cosmopolitan worlds unto themselves, the inhabitants aggressive and quick, nothing able to rest near them. He could hear the birds' chatter through the glass. He could hear his mother's breathing, quiet and steady and only a little fast.

"Where were you?" he asked. "When the Change happened?"

She was relieved by the question, ordinary and reliable. A question she'd answered countless times. "A long ways from here," she said, then gave a soft laugh. "Indoors, actually."

"Watching television?"

She nodded.

"Was that before you got married?" he asked quietly. "Or afterwards?"

She said, "Before," and paused. "Just a few weeks before, frankly—"

Which he knew. He had gone over the dates last night. "A lot of marriages got started right after the Change." He looked at her hair, at the impossible golden shine of it. "In our neighborhood, too."

She watched his eyes.

She admitted, "The Change might have been part of it," and turned to look outdoors, her face not quite smiling at the memory of those times.

Cornell stood beside her, not close, watching the birds and noticing how the feeders were built to resemble tiny wooden houses. Maybe the earth was someone's elaborate bird feeder, he was thinking. Maybe High Desert and the rest of them were world-sized baubles hanging in God's green yard.

A pretty and horrible thought, wasn't it?

"I'm sorry," he offered. "About your husband, I mean."

"At least we had a few months together." A pause. "I've always taken consolation in that."

"I wish I could stay," he said. "I wish I could."

She didn't turn, still watching her birds. And she didn't make any sound.

Then he said, "But I can't. I've got to get back on duty."

"To that other world," she kidded.

Laughing, he said, "Right." He said, "Anyway," and waited for her to turn to him, to focus on him. Then he said, "It is dangerous work, Mom." Nothing. Her face didn't respond, not even with suspicion. "That's part of the reason I found you now. It's because . . . well, because I'm not all that close to Dad anymore. And the job comes with an insurance policy. I named you as my beneficiary. I hope that's all right."

She didn't speak, her mouth not quite open.

"Is it all right?"

"Whatever you think is best," she whispered.

Cornell felt ashamed of himself, for an instant. Black-hearted and cruel. Then he looked outdoors and said, "For half a million dollars, in case I die. . . . "

"Oh." The word came from her belly, very soft and sudden.

And he lied, saying, "It's just that I need concrete proof of who you are." His voice sounded full of puzzled frustrations. "The policy is intended for my next-of-kin, you see—"

"Proof? Like genetic tests?"

"Nothing that elaborate, no." He moved his hands in the air. He gave a little laugh. "Just something physical. Something I can take to the right people and say, 'Here, she had this. . . .' "

"Like what?" Her face was becoming simpler, easier to read.

"Like a photograph?" he offered.

It sounded silly. Contrived and silly. Yet she believed him, still hearing, "Half a million dollars," while she told him, "Oh, sure. Let me see where."

"Maybe of the two of us? I'll show it to them, then mail it back again. In a week or two."

Mom turned, hands finding each other and squeezing.

"Do you have a photograph?"

"Yes." She started to walk, not fast, back toward the front door and Cornell behind her, wondering if she would surprise him. But he didn't think so. The woman looked her age, legs mounting the carpeted staircase, her entire body tired and too willing to hold on to the banister with one hand, old-woman style. She said something, something too soft for him to hear, and he asked:

"What?"

She didn't seem to hear him, pausing at the top of the stairs, hands wringing each other. Then her feet found a direction, and she went down a long hallway, saying, "I just remodeled." Adding, "That's the problem." Then she told him, "I still haven't put my pictures up. They're still all boxed away."

"That's fine," he lied.

She hoped so. Her face and posture said that much, glancing back at him with a ragged wishfulness. Then ahead. They pressed ahead, turning into a small bedroom converted into an office. There was a massive desk with a built-in computer. In the closets were an assortment of big boxes. Where to begin? "It's been a while," she muttered. Then, "But not that long."

She pulled one box into the open, removed the lid and began sifting through a mass of papers. Receipts and more receipts, and she paused and said, "A different one."

"Do you need help?"

"No," she said. Then, "Thank you, darling."

Two more boxes, both wrong, and she acted miffed with herself, a little cranky at the edges.

"Maybe you're not my mother," he said. As if joking, only he gave the words a barbed edge.

She rose and said, "I know. Wait!"

They went down the hall, into the master bedroom, vast and quiet with a king-sized bed and excessively feminine features. Too many pinks, too much lace trim. A skylight made the place radiant. He blinked, and she opened a hidden door and exposed a substantial wall safe. A combination, plus her thumbprints, made it open. *Thunk.*

There weren't any portraits of friends and family on the walls. Not even one of her poor deceased husband. And the room looked as if it hadn't been remodeled in ages, which wasn't much of a surprise. Again he felt sorry for her, in a fashion, wondering how someone could live for more than half a century and have nobody worth framing, nobody to watch over them while they slept.

There were metal boxes inside the safe. She said, "Here," with confidence, digging one box out of the back. "This is it." A laugh. "When you get old, darling, your memory plays games with you."

He said nothing.

She opened the box, finding it half-filled with mementos. Staring up at her through waxed paper was a thick-faced man, a millionare, his bald scalp glowing in the New Zealand sunlight. She paused for an instant, and Cornell spoke. Maybe under that picture was a picture of Cornell as a boy, but he didn't care anymore, wanting instead to ask:

"Did you kill him, or didn't you?"

The woman almost kept her composure. Almost, bless her. Then her hands pulled back, and Cornell noticed how they'd speckled with age, and how they shook, her nerves frayed, almost useless.

"Because someone murdered him," he persisted. "The case is still on the books as unsolved, isn't it?"

She swallowed, blinked and swallowed, then looked up at him with a cutting gaze, saying, "You know."

Just those two words.

"Parts of it," he allowed. "I know he was rich. That he met a mysterious American woman and divorced his wife to marry her. And that he was clubbed to death one night. A prowler struck him from behind, and he wasn't found for hours, and the new wife was tried—"

"—and exonerated," she snapped.

"And his last will and testament was contested."

"Cornell," she said, "what do you want?"

He made a show of being open-minded. "I don't know what you did, if anything. And even if you murdered him, what's that prove? He could have been a cruel son-of-a-bitch. Maybe he treated you the same way your father treated you."

A pause. No response but that dark icy gaze.

"I don't know," he confessed. "Last night, going through the records, I kept thinking I could figure you out. One way or another, I would. You'd think with all that data, you'd be able to get to the heart of a person. Don't you?"

She said nothing.

"You killed him, or you didn't. You loved my father, or you didn't. You're a treacherous bitch, or you're misunderstood and blameless." He shrugged, then said, "I keep looking for something definite. . . . "

"Well," she said, putting aside the metal box, "have you come to any conclusions? Corny?"

He looked out a window, watching the fierce little birds feeding on the raw grain. After a minute, he said, "All I wanted was for you to have just one picture of me. For whatever that's worth."

Now she was crying, tears bright on that overly perfect face. She was angry, probably close to hitting him. With the box? Her fists? Or maybe she kept a bat under her pink bed—

—and Cornell said, "I don't think I've ever seen a better looking prison. Because that's what all this is. I think so."

"Get out of here!" she exploded.

He felt calm, no trace of temper now. Walking out into the hallway without a backward glance, he was halfway down the stairs when something shattered above him. A window, maybe. Something hard, like a metal box, had been thrown through one of those big windows, maybe.

Then he was jogging, nice and easy, through the front door and down the rocked drive. He was calculating how long it would take him to get back to High Desert. But first he needed to call the detective, on the off chance that he had found something of consequence. He should use a pay phone, just to keep people from listening. And now Cornell was running, almost sprinting, the tall gate straight ahead of him, his shoes making dry porcelain sounds on the dry white expanse of raked gravel.

# FIRST CONTACT

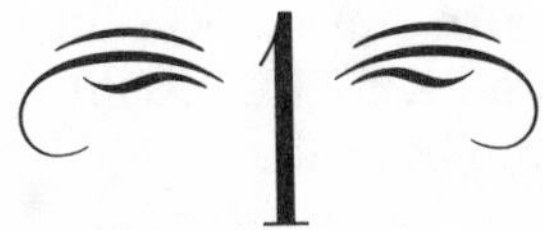

**Clouds had blown in from the south, piled on top of one** another and lifted high enough that Cornell began tasting them in the desert. The arroyos were full of fog. Mists against the faces brought an instinctive fear, and he wondered what the chances were of a meaningful rain. How bad could it be? He reached the first ramp at dusk, barely able to see through the blowing fog, and for the first time in his life he felt dangerously claustrophobic, deciding against a nighttime descent of the ramp. Better to rest, he told himself. Better to let the clouds blow away and disperse, then get a first-light start. It was best to be rested and ready.

Except he slept badly, awakened in the night by a dream or hallucination, or by the alien *something.* His guarding body stared out at the clouds, a city emerging from blackness, ethereal and brilliant, floating in the air before him and illuminated by colored lights beyond number. It was the electric sensation of peace that woke Cornell, every body jumping to its feet. He saw stone buildings with crystal windows and wide stone avenues stretching on for miles; the avenues were filled with bodies, a tall white body approaching him, smiling at him like before, and touching each of his faces in turn while a thunderous voice said:

"Come see me."

Said:

"You are almost here."

Then:

"Hurry."

Then it was dark again, the city and its emissary evaporating in an instant, and Cornell couldn't decide what had happened. A dream, or a message? Or perhaps both things at once, in equal measure. And it was all he could do not to leave then, at that instant, risking his life to follow a voice that might have come from himself.

The clouds seemed thicker in the morning, the sun like a wafer cut from rusted metal. Cornell went down the ramp, feeling his way, several stretches creaking badly, begging for repairs. Then he was in the dry canyon, charging down the path, and a man burst from the fog, upbound and shouting, "You don't want to. Turn around. It's a miserable mess down there!"

"What's happened?"

"There's no order. None. People steal food, steal equipment, particularly if you're alone—"

"There's not enough food?" Cornell interrupted.

"Stealing's easier, that's all." He was a big-bodied person, but only four bodies were healthy. The fifth one was wounded, infections leaving it useless, lying on the mind and shivering without pause. The mouths pleaded, telling him, "Turn around. Come with me."

"No."

Outer lids blinked, and the man asked, "Are you crazy?"

"Do you know Porsche?" He used a single mouth, almost whispering. "Have you seen her?"

"No."

"You know Porsche Neal?"

"She's at the bottom somewhere, I don't know . . . you can't get there, friend." A dismissive swipe of the hands, then he said, "Save yourself. Nobody'll care."

Something struck Cornell. It hit the top of one head, like a hammerblow, and he thought: *Rain.* Bodies leaned against their harnesses, and he slipped past the hysterical man. A last backward glance, and he saw the man's mind and shivering body vanish into the fog and rain. Then he pressed the pace, carried by panic. The rain stopped and started again, stopped and started. Finally there was no break in it, after nightfall, and he didn't sleep or even rest, feeling his way in the blackness.

By first light he was in the forest, almost to the gorge.

Saturated branches dripped rainwater, making dark rich mud. The speed and force of the drops were astonishing, like buckets of water hurled by giants, and suddenly Cornell could see how it was to be very small in even the mildest summer shower.

Except this wasn't a little storm.

Two worlds of instinct were telling him it wasn't going to pass or dissolve. It hadn't even begun yet, in truth, and his tired legs wrestled with the mud and his sleepless mind.

"Novak?"

He recognized Susan, his one-time boss, and his first words were, "Where is she?"

"In the gorge." They were beside the pool at the gorge's mouth, rain beating at the water. "We gave up on you, Novak. What happened?"

He told about his hunt, in brief.

"Did you have trouble getting here?"

"Not much." Twice he had heard people up ahead, and he'd moved off the path as a precaution.

"You can't take chances," she agreed.

"It's that bad?"

"It's falling apart, the whole operation is. Too many recruits too fast. Too long to get here, and people staying past schedule. Good ones lose their judgment, and the iffy ones go mad."

"Logan?"

"He's a mess," she snapped, "last I heard."

"Does Porsche need help . . . ?"

"Absolutely. Go," Susan said. "She's asking for you, I hope you know."

Again he took up his harnesses, hands numbed by the chill rain.

"But it's not a jog," she warned him. "We've gotten through the gorge, at last, but this little river . . . well, you'll see. Go on. And here, take some of this."

Half-dried meat in wet skins. "Thanks."

"I'll try and get my crew working today," she promised. "But I don't know." Hands over eyes, she looked straight overhead. "It's got everyone spooked, this weather does."

Cornell moved into the gorge, four bodies dragging his mind and the other two scouting ahead, slipping around the first bend and seeing an enormous chute with the river white and loud and the sky shrunk to a remote gray band. There was as much river mist as there was rain, clinging and tasting like rock. He was amazed by the ramp—how it fit into the crevices; how people had used tiny ledges and balancing tricks when there were no crevices—and there were long stretches where he felt as if he was walking in air, suspended miles above a straight white thread of river while the ramp tilted forward, Cornell using every body to inch his mind down the steepest, slippery grades.

Once the chute closed in tight, so close he reached out and touched the opposite wall, ancient stone cool as porcelain and nearly as smooth. Then the world opened up with the next turn, a great gray pool below him, and waterfalls, and something white on the rocky shoreline. A mind, he realized. It had been shattered by the fall, elements and rot having scoured the bones clean.

He felt the world breathing, winds gusting back and forth, and his bodies would curl their toes around the damp white boards to hold tight. Sometimes Cornell played a game, wondering which of these boards he had made. In the cramped places his claustrophobia would return, the dim light and the patient weight of the stone making it worse. He would forget to breathe. Then he would pause and make himself take in the thick humid air, shaking his limbs to bring back their strength; and sometimes he would shout, strong sharp whistles echoing once, then swallowed by the roaring waters.

He came upon a person. A woman. Her mind was set on a rock ledge broad enough for several people, just two of her bodies watching him. "How much farther?" he asked.

She didn't answer, scarcely moving.

"Am I almost there?"

"Almost," she muttered, then she wouldn't say another word.

But later, he found a second stranger, a man; and the man said, "Oh, it's another day's travel. Hard travel." He was camped on a smaller ledge, five waif-like bodies pretending to patch the nearby ramp. "No, no. Stay!"

"Can't."

"Help me here. Don't leave!"

Cornell started past him, and two bodies picked up spears, threatening him. Clumsy, muddled voices said:

"I order you. Stop now and help."

Cornell grabbed one of his unarmed bodies, holding it over the ramp's edge, saying, "Now step back. Want me to toss him?"

The man retreated, making a show of dropping the spears.

"Good."

"I'll be nice," the captured body said. "Just please don't leave!"

He kept moving, around another bend and down, the ramp dropping to the river and Cornell close enough to taste the river water with each breath. The sound of it made his ears hurt, made his muscles sore. It was gnawing at the tough old rock, and he laughed, saying, "Give it up. You can't carve through this stuff." Though it had, obviously. "Give it up." He couldn't even hear himself anymore. "Quit!" And then he would let a body stop, putting its tongue against the granite, tasting the mountain for a moment. If only he could steal just a fleck of its strength. . . .

The chute made a sudden right turn. Following an old fault line? A flaw in the world? And the river fell away, milky water diminishing to a thin cold murmur. The ramp danced with the smooth wall. In places, the whole show was held up with nothing. With wedges in tiny cracks, if that. He imagined dozens of tiny bodies clinging to the wall, laboring to drive home struts and set down these boards, lashing them in place and getting how far in a day? Losing how many bodies to accidents? All because of some alien presence, beatific and persuasive and vast; but if that wasn't a worthwhile goal, what was?

The chute straightened; the river plunged downwards.

Then it was gone, ending abruptly, and Cornell found himself peering out into an expanse of roaring air, thinking for an instant that it was the same river, but knowing it was too loud, too much. Winds gusted, fat raindrops soaking his bodies and the mind, splattering on the granite and flowing towards the noise. He could feel the roar as much as he heard it, feeling it cut through the air and even through the stone. Carefully, one motion at a time, he eased his bodies to the edge of the ramp, peering through the endless rain and the weak sunshine. There was a river, an honest full and titanic river, all of the world's water pouring through a gorge perhaps a full mile across. What he had been following was a trickle, a thin runnel of sweat. And suddenly, without warning, a great flash of light came with thunder, the ramp shaking and Cornell's bodies leaping backward, clinging to each other and to the inadequate little chunks of soaked-through lumber.

He made himself move, dropping fast and sometimes finding himself on long rock ledges. It became night, dark as a closet. Lightning gave him snapshots of his surroundings. A great canyon; the fierce rain; the ramp lost against the face of stone. He was drenched, bodies and mind burning fat to warm themselves. Suddenly the rain quit. No, it was just excluded. The next bolt of lightning made a violent orange glow on his left; he saw the long wedge of rock overhead, acting as a roof. Thousands of years ago the river had run here, at his feet, undercutting its bank where the canyon managed a slight turn.

Cornell rested, ate and breathed in little gasps. The air was thick, almost too rich, his blood unaccustomed to so much oxygen. Then he moved again, feeling tired enough to sleep with his bodies standing—a dangerous fatigue—five bodies towing the mind and the sixth one in the lead, using a spear to feel its way. He was tired and sloppy. The stone spearhead touched wood, touched wood, then touched nothing but air. Yet he stepped again, a careless long step into nothingness; and the body was falling, tumbling out of control, Cornell thinking: This is how it feels, losing one. . . .

There was lightning, a series of hard blue bolts, and he saw where the ramp ended in front of him. It wasn't a gap; there was nothing. He screamed out of despair, nobody here to find, Porsche and the others swept away by the floods, and he knew that he hadn't the strength or the will to turn around and climb all the way back to California.

His falling body struck water, cushioned by its tiny size and the heavy air. Still conscious, it submerged and swallowed river water and grit, coughed and vomited, then surfaced again. It was being swept downstream. Cornell could feel the distance growing, and he remembered hearing how drowning was a peaceful death. He tried to let the body relax, accepting fate; yet its tiny mind refused, panic making it kick, managing a kind of frantic dogpaddle until it was completely out of his reach—

—and Cornell tried to weep, bodies curled up on the soaked rampway with the mind. Only he didn't have the energy or the concentration to cry, or even feel the single hand that began to caress one of his faces, a familiar voice saying:

"Look at you."

Porsche. One of her bodies was kneeling with him, a rope tied around its waist and the next bolt of lightning showing the rope plugged into the canyon wall high above, like an umbilical cord. Which seemed reasonable. In his fatigue, after everything, an umbilical to the world was no more incredible than anything else.

"You're just in time," she was saying. Shouting. Over the storm sounds, she told him, "We're just about to pick up and go home." A flash of blue-green light, and her face was smiling at him.

He coughed and blurted, "I was looking for you."

Then the rain increased, like a wave breaking over them, and she was tying her umbilical to his mind's harnesses, saying, "Up. We've got to get up and in, love. Up and in."

The cave was a fortunate bit of geology, cut deep and large enough to keep a dozen people—minds and several dozen bodies—dry and almost comfortable. They used ropes and simple pulleys to bring Cornell up to them. He knew some of them. He saw Logan and a pair of his minions in the back, doing something that looked remarkably like cowering. And sure enough, Logan sounded changed. Transformed. "Novak?" he whispered, faces twisted in despair. "Are you part of this mutiny, Novak?"

What did he mean?

"We've changed leaders," said one woman. "Porsche's in charge."

"And we're leaving," said someone else. "With first light, we're starting for home."

Porsche nodded, watching Cornell. Then a single body held him close, speaking into an earhole. "How was the ramp? Still in one piece?"

When he had come down, yes.

Worry and silence. Then she told him, "Eat and sleep, love. Whatever happens, happens."

He wasn't thinking of the ramp or the storm. Nothing as small as that. He stared at her nearest faces, as if for the first time; and perhaps she sensed his mood, trying to tickle him—to distract him—while saying:

"I'm glad you made it. I thought you'd died somewhere, or forgotten about me."

"Never," he promised.

"Rest," said several bodies. She was speaking to everyone, telling them, "We've got a tough day tomorrow, so rest. All you can."

Cornell glanced back at Logan again. A muted flash of lightning made the black eyes look red and scared, and he thought of mice huddling in a corner, ineffectual and terrorized.

*Good.*

He slept hard and dreamed constantly, remembering none of the dreams when he woke. Then he ate from the communal stocks, every piece of meat frosted with a colorless sweet fuzz of mold. Porsche and another person had gone upstream at dawn, he learned. Bodies and minds. Logan remained at the back of the cave, and Cornell counted his bodies. Four of them. Eight hands clinging to each other.

Walking bodies to the cave's mouth, Cornell peered out into the ceaseless rain, then downward. Sunlight was dissolving into the airborne water, the occasional flash of lightning lending depth and distance. The river looked even larger in daylight, and it wasn't an illusion. "It's higher," one woman warned him. "I'm keeping track. See that cleft down there? It was high and dry at dawn."

And now it was nearly submerged, he realized. There was something hypnotic about gazing into that torrent. He blinked and stepped back, asking, "When's Porsche coming back?"

"Soon," people promised.

He returned to his mind and began grooming it, needing something to do. Combing fingers worked at snarls in the fur. He inspected his harnesses and the rotting sacks, very little in them now; then someone approached, saying, "I know you."

Cornell said, "What?"

"You're Novak, aren't you? When did you get here?"

He stared at Logan, saying nothing.

"Get help," Logan whispered. Then he swallowed as if his throats ached, and he promised, "I'll make you my assistant. Bump up your pay. Anything if you help me with these mutineers."

"Don't listen to him," said one of his one-time assistants. Alan? "He's a fucked up loon."

Logan might or might not have heard that assessment. But with conviction he said, "I can trust you, son. I know I can."

Alan slapped that face with an open hand, with force. The blow made the body reel, eyes blinking and a pained voice coming from the other bodies. "See what I mean? A mutiny!"

"Son-of-a-bitch," Alan growled.

Then someone yelled, "Porsche's back."

Too soon, Cornell learned. He helped haul her parts up into the cave, and her first body looked at everyone with sorrow and a smoldering anger. "The gorge is flooded," she confessed. "The ramp's washed away."

People cursed. Some turned on Logan and his men, threatening them with spears. Then Porsche was saying, "No more." She put her body between them, warning her people, "I'm not leading a mob."

Silence, and tension.

Logan gave a sob, then squeaked, "I'm feeling better. . . ."

Cornell felt pity for the shit, and anger that he couldn't blame him for everything.

Alan asked Porsche, "What do we do now? Wait for help?"

She said, "We aren't waiting for anything."

There was strength in the voice. That single body dominated the others, glaring at them while her mouth sucked at the thick damp air, and she said, "Stay and we starve. Climb, and we'll have to navigate the gorge. Which I don't want to try." A pause, then she said, "We need to find a new way home."

"How?" asked Cornell. And others.

"We keep building the ramp," she announced. "Starting now."

"With what?" people demanded.

And she told them, "We'll dismantle what's above, piecemeal, and keep extending the ramp downstream." She knelt, one thick finger drawing her scheme in the foot-packed mud. "Eventually we'll reach a side canyon, then head upstream. We'll take our road with us." A pause. "About a thousand canyons have to lead to the desert. We only need one to get home."

There wasn't time to be with Porsche, much less talk to her. But there was a union, a sense of clear concerted purpose that kept Cornell focused and hopeful. He was part of the salvage team, his five bodies traveling with several dozen more, their minds taken only partway and left protected under a crude lean-to. His bodies made it to the narrow gorge, finding an enormous sideways fountain roaring out of it. Mud was in the water, gray desert soils mixed with rain. The high arroyos had to be flooding. Was this a million-year rain? What if New Reno had been drowned? Then he told himself to stop it. Worry took energy, and he didn't have calories to spare.

The rain worsened in the afternoon, driven against the canyon wall and flowing over them. They had to untie ropes never meant to be untied, or cut them and save as much as possible. Then the wood and useful ropes had to be carried down, each body bent under its load. There wasn't time to cut the struts out of the canyon wall. "We'll build with what we've got," Porsche warned them. "Not to last. Just to get us from A to B."

A sketchy, rickety array of struts and crossbeams followed the canyon's next bend. It was astonishing to see the little bodies climbing in space, holding on to cracks and sand-sized knobs, ignoring the criminal weather while working, almost never falling. Cornell was delivering boards when one body slipped, and he watched it tumbling, a thin rope of hair drawing taut—*tunk*—and the body dangling for a moment, bruised but breathing, the wet knot slipping, then breaking, and the victim lost against the roaring waters.

"We need more faster," Porsche told him. Her faces were focused, two minutes left in the game and her team down by seven. "Set up a chain of bodies, okay? You're in charge. Someone dismantles, and someone hands the stuff along."

He almost told her that he was glad to have her here, but instead he just said, "Okay."

"And I'll send word when you can stop. Everyone gets a few hours of sleep, or we'll end up like Logan."

At least the rain slackened at night, sometimes no worse than a miserable drizzle. Cornell was in the middle of the human chain, bodies carrying boards over the same stretch of ramp. He recognized where he stepped by its feel. And sometimes, in the dark, there was nothing but the feel of the place, the clouds locked over the stars and every sound muffled by the river.

He got to sleep, as promised. Bodies curled around the base of his mind, inside the lean-to, and it took him forever to wake up again. Someone handed him a last share of meat, now moldy to the gristle. His team went to work on the dry stretch of ramp beneath the rock overhang. Two more bodies fell to their deaths. Alan tried to prove his new loyalties, climbing out too far to retrieve a loose strut, grabbing it and giving it a push. The strut took the bodies down with it. It was a stupid, brave act, leaving him with three bodies. But now the salvage team seemed to trust him more, and Alan was pleased with himself.

By evening, they were out from the overhang, and everyone's mind was moved lower, onto the new ramp. Cornell let one of his bodies walk ahead, round a long bend, nothing to see but the stone walls and the river and the clouds masking whatever vistas were above him. A sudden despair came over him. He was exhausted, hungry and feeling ill in ways he didn't know. It was a general ache and troubled breathing, and his thoughts came in graceless bursts between long thoughtless stretches.

One of Porsche's bodies climbed up to him. She watched him, touched him. A single black finger started on his forehead and moved down over his nostril slits, his mouth and his chin. Then she was smiling; maybe she had been smiling from the first. The other hand pointed along the steep sketch of the ramp, and she asked, "Do you see it?"

He did. A single tree and perhaps some low brush were wedged together on a narrow shelf. The shelf was above the river, not very far above, and the ramp's aim seemed to be that shelf. "We're going there?"

"And make a new base camp," she promised. "Fresh wood, and food. Maybe we can fish from there. We can certainly rest."

Rest was an addictive word, deceptively simple, exploding against his sleepless mind and his muscles.

"Then we'll zigzag up," she added. "To the top."

She could be describing a walk to the moon, as preposterous as it sounded. The canyon wall had to be a mile high, probably higher. But he was too tired to doubt, much less argue; never in his life had he wanted to believe in someone so much.

Back to work.

The rain lashed at them. Cornell took a load of boards from the man above, and that man's body turned and stepped badly, into the air and gone without sound, without fuss. Then it seemed to take the man forever to realize what had happened, a second body walking down as if hunting for the missing one. Peering over the edge, it sniffed at the air.

"Go rest," Cornell advised. "I'll cover for you."

By the next morning, they'd dismantled the last of the old ramp; their steep, treacherous ramp was within throwing distance of its target. Porsche met Cornell at the midway point, with one body, telling him, "Great news." Her voice was flat and tired. "It looks like a giant greasewood covered with nuts. I've got a body down there now, trying to cut to the meat. . . ."

Cornell couldn't walk his bodies far from their mind anymore. It was a symptom of fatigue, not too different from being too stiff and sore to touch the top of your own head.

"One last push," she told him.

He said, "We need to talk."

The eyes closed, opened. Then she said, "Soon."

"Soon," he echoed.

A weak smile, and a wink. "Do something for me?" The body breathed, words forming in the belly. "Get Logan. He's supposed to be waiting in the cave."

"You think he'll come with me?"

"Give him the chance. Use your discretion."

He looked past the body, watching tiny dark figures work on the last stretch of the ramp, pounding with worn stone hammers. He couldn't hear them and could barely see them—motions puny against the greater motions of wind and rain and the river—but as he stood watching, one of Porsche's arms began to swing for no reason.

"What are you hammering?" he asked.

And she looked at the arm, astonished and then amused. And she broke into a soft dead little laugh.

Logan was waiting in the cave, huddling behind rancid skins.

"Are you here to rescue me?" he asked Cornell with a bright, sloppy voice. "Are you with the rescue team?"

It made everything simpler. "Yeah, that's me."

"Don't listen to the others." Logan's eyes were huge, sleepless and somehow dead in appearance. "They've stolen my authority. Even my best people are poisoned."

Cornell stopped, watching Logan's bodies shuffle forward. "Do you recognize me?"

Logan squinted. "Should I?" Faces tried a different angle. "No, I'm sorry. I don't know you."

Cornell waited.

"Have we met?" The voice was icy calm, utterly reasonable. "Are you high up in the agency?"

"Very high."

"Oh, good. I'm glad you've come. You have to see these things for yourself." A pause. A collective shake of the heads. "They've all turned on me."

"We know." Cornell thought for a moment, then said, "That's why we've replaced them. It's all new people now."

"Wonderful!"

Cornell grabbed Logan's mind and dragged it to the cave's mouth, then began fixing its harnesses to the ropes and pulleys. Logan's bodies stood about passively, one and then others leaning out over the edge.

"We don't have far to go," said the madman.

Ignore him, thought Cornell. He concentrated on his knots.

"It's a golden city, the one at the river's mouth. I'm eager to get there. I wish I was there now."

What else did he need to do?

"Can you see the city?" asked Logan.

"Not now, no."

"Have you?"

"A couple times, yes." Cornell paused, then asked, "Can you see it right now?"

"Clearly."

Could he? Or was he suffering a hallucination?

"It loves us."

"What does?"

"The City." Logan's faces smiled without smiling, eyes wrong and every needly tooth showing. Then the expressions changed, and he asked, "What did you do with them?"

"With whom?"

"The mutineers." A quick pause, then he asked, "Are you keeping watch over them?"

"Absolutely."

"Particularly that bitch Neal. Watch her!"

"Think so?"

The man giggled suddenly, with force. Then he said, "Just take care of her. Like you did with that one woman—"

"Which woman?"

"That Mayfly. Remember? She went off to CNN during her off shift, slipped her tail and spilled everything—"

"I remember." Cornell felt very cold, completely awake now.

"You sure fucked her over, didn't you? Not that it's hard. Crazy aliens and worlds and new bodies . . . but that business with those medical files, giving her a mental history. That was a sweet way of handling it."

Cornell pushed the mind into the open air and rain, Logan's bodies showing only a vague interest.

"Neal is dangerous," Logan muttered.

Cornell said nothing, holding the ropes as the mind dangled in space.

"Maybe you should do what you did to that one jerk."

"Which jerk?"

"Mine. From HD. I'm sorry, I can't remember names just now." He shook his heads. "Threatening to go to the U.N. and report us. Thought he could slip past Security with proof . . . but you stopped him first, didn't you?"

"We did," Cornell replied.

A laugh, almost soft. "Where do we find these unbalanced types?"

"Was that jerk unbalanced?"

A thin, piercing whistle, and Logan said, "You are when you jump from a big fucking building, you are."

"Did he jump?"

"Did he jump?" Another giggle. "You tell me."

Cornell waited, then made one mouth ask, "What about Novak?"

"Who?"

"Cornell Novak. Is he much of a risk?"

That brought an enormous laugh, hands swiping at the air. "With his father? That shit even steps toward the media, and we'll make him look like the craziest fucked up shit ever born!"

Cornell was aware of his hearts beating, synchronized, and the feel of ropes in his hands. He thought how he could release the ropes, the mind falling and probably punching its way through the ramp, spinning blind into the maelstrom—

"Porsche the Bitch," said Logan. Scornfully. "A gold-plated cunt, and a natural. Not fair, is it?"

Cornell began lowering the mind, hands over hands, using excessive caution because he wasn't a murderer. This man was in his care, and ill, and he wouldn't let any harm come to him.

"Know what we should do?" asked the madman. "Ship

that cunt through the worst intrusions. The ones nobody ever comes back from."

"How many are there? Like that?"

"You know how many. Most." He watched his own hands close into fists, then open again. "Maybe we should ship every sick shit and danger into those intrusions. Empty our jails? Empty our world?"

Cornell said nothing.

"We could pour Chinese babies into the intrusions. Think about it!"

The mind touched the ramp, wet boards creaking.

Logan peered down, faces quizzical. "Whose mind is that? Do I know him?"

"Does he look familiar?"

Eyes blinked and blinked, the question already forgotten.

Then Logan gave a start and said, "Look! The ramp goes down all the way, doesn't it?"

"To the river," Cornell promised.

And the dead eyes turned to him, trying to focus on him. "That's going to be far enough."

"Far enough? Why?"

"The City will find us there," Logan assured him.

Cornell stood motionless, trying to think.

"The City loves us," Logan told him.

"But why does it love us?"

Faces turned together, as if hearing the same distant sound. Then the mouths were smiling, showing teeth, and an odd slow voice said, "Because it knows we're such good people. . . . "

THE RIVER WAS DAYS OLD AND THOROUGHLY AMORAL, CHARGING down the arroyo and the canyons, gaining speed and depth as it uprooted forests and gnawed at the canyon walls. It collected trophies—tree trunks and stones and drowned bodies—and the bodies would bloat, bobbing to the surface, legs stiff and extended with a strange deathly vigor. Cornell would watch the bodies sliding past, small against the churning gray-black waters, and he felt compassion mixed with cold amusement and a genuine sense of relief. They weren't his bodies. But sometimes, for brief moments, the dead eyes seemed to gaze up at him, outraged yet confident, and Cornell could hear ghosts whispering:

"Very soon, you. Very soon, you."

They had rested on the rock shelf for more than a day, sleeping for most of that time and eating the sweet fatty nuts while awake. Cornell felt new bulk on his bodies, his strength returning. He seemed to adapt to the thick air and dampness. People began to feel good enough to complain among themselves, a couple of near-fights brought on by a collective rage. Logan was cursed openly, without pause or effect. The one-time leader just stared off into random directions, intent on something, and he muttered to himself, the words incomprehensible.

The river kept rising, but maybe it wouldn't reach them.

Maybe. The old tree must have weathered these floods, Porsche argued. But just in case, she told them to pick limbs where they could lash their minds, putting themselves a little closer to the sky.

She made plans for good weather. One of Cornell's bodies found one of hers sitting at the shelf's edge, using a stick to draw the canyon wall and an enormous ramp zigzagging to the top. She was deciding on angles and likely distances. "Guesses, guesses," she said, offering a smile. Nobody else was in earshot. She put down her stick, and the smile dissolved into a sudden little bitterness, and she said, "All right, I give up. What's happened to you? Why not just tell me?"

"What? Tell you what?"

"Ever since you've come back," she began, "you've been strange. If I didn't know that pretty face, I'd say it wasn't you."

She touched him, cool hard fingers across his mouth.

And he said, "I found my mother."

Her outer lids closed tight. "Tell me."

Cornell didn't think he wanted to tell it, but once started, the story had its own life, its own rhythm. He told about the man he had hired, about the biography that was compiled, and the actual meeting, including his ugly trick about the insurance money. He began to quietly cry, tears impossible but the rest of it the same. He shuddered, aching within. He had a sudden premonition of death, not wanting to die now. Not here. Looking at those crude diagrams on the ground, he knew it would take months for them to manage such a ramp—if they ever could—and his body shivered, holding itself while saying:

"It's funny. Funny-strange. I've been angry at my father forever, and because he lied about Mom. And now all I want is to believe that lie again. I might do anything to convince myself—"

"But you can't," Porsche said, her voice sharp. Certain.

He breathed and nodded, and he smiled with resignation.

"And that's not the problem," she continued. "Not the problem I mean. That comes when you look at me, love."

They weren't lovers. He resented her little endearment, then realized he wasn't being fair. Porsche deserved fairness. Trying for it, he talked about going home, going back through his father's extensive records about black glass disks . . . and how Dad had invested half of his life into trying to understand them, striving to give the disks some clear meaning, glorious and perfect.

Porsche listened, waited. Scarcely breathed.

"Anyway," he said, "I had an idea. Or maybe I adapted an old idea that comes in all kinds of flavors."

"What idea?"

"The disks are markers." He swallowed. "Their meaning is simply to say, *Here. This spot. Here.*"

She said nothing.

"But for whom?" He swallowed again. "Did you know there's a disk on the agency's grounds? It appeared when it was a weapons lab, and it's in line with the other intrusions. I checked. There's a big building around it now, and it's under guard. But nobody seems to use it, which makes me wonder if our bosses tried their fancy equipment on it, and they failed."

"Failed?" she said with a quiet voice.

"How many intrusions are there? I mean on the earth. Millions? Billions?"

A vague shrug of the shoulders, then she asked, "Why?"

"At New Reno, we mark the intrusion with flags and stones." He waited for a moment, then added, "Glass makes a good, long-lasting signpost."

She bent lower and gave him a little smile.

"If the agency's equipment worked on the disks, then we would be sent around the country to the ripe ones. But you see, the worlds we're visiting have old-fashioned skies and no great technologies. High Desert and the rest are backwoods places. Intelligence is new, or it's at a dead end."

"Perhaps," she allowed.

"Moving through a disk might take a different set of keys."

"Maybe so."

"I'm guessing, I know." He offered an embarrassed shrug.

"But I can make assumptions from what I do know. For instance, there were a lot of strange lights seen before the Change. Yet not anymore. You told me that we're trespassing in other people's yards, but what if *they* came to visit us? Like kids exploring an unfinished house?"

She picked up her stick, using just her fingertips, eyes focused on Cornell. "What else?"

"The lights were some kind of general evacuation. Hidden bases were being torn down, moved out. Humans were going to become aware soon. At least more aware. Maybe they didn't want confrontations, or maybe . . . I don't know . . . maybe leaving is the mannerly thing to do."

"What about the disks?"

He looked past her, across the river, trying to choose his words, saying just what he needed to say.

"The disks are markers, you claimed." She set the stick aside, then asked, "Why leave markers when you leave the earth? If you wished to avoid confrontations, why show the way?"

He could think of reasons, and he could stop the conversation now, giving whatever explanation would suit the sketchy data.

But he didn't. Instead he asked, "What happens to us if we stay here? By accident, or by choice. Suppose we reproduce and leave descendants, and a thousand years from now High Desert everts its sky and discovers the intrusions. Who is picked for the first missions? Our distant descendants would have inherited some of our talents. They would go. And maybe on a second world, by accident or choice, they would stay and mix our same talents into the genetic pool." A pause. "Can you accept that, Porsche?"

She said, "Maybe."

"Now imagine millions of years, thousands of worlds, and a kind of natural selection." A wave of one hand. "Imagine the earth over the last million years. Creatures come to visit through our intrusions, and the human species gets the occasional useful gene. Genes that translate through and make us ready for our own Change. The genes that make me talented enough for the agency to hire me—"

"And me," she interrupted.

Cornell gave a very slight nod of the head. "My mother and my father gave me double doses of whatever this talent is. Like it or not, I was born to trespass."

"And not just you," she whispered.

Then he said, "No," and waited for her eyes to look at him. "With you, I think, there's more. I don't think you've ever needed a vacation day. I think you'd be comfortable as a fish or a Mayfly or any other creature that could be wrapped around your intellect."

Her eyes shone like obsidian, and she held her breath, mouth closed and hands at her sides.

Now Cornell touched her, at last. Fingers on the face. And he told her, "There are thirty-two disks in northern Texas," before asking, "Which one is yours?"

"None of them."

For a slippery instant, he was terrified that he was completely wrong.

Then she said, "It's in New Mexico, up in the Gila wilderness." Her hand rose and grabbed his hand, squeezing as she said, "Besides a few backpackers and hunters, nobody's found it yet. Which is fine by me, love. Which is perfect."

Now it was Cornell's turn to listen, the stories incredible and reasonable, and after a while, almost routine. Porsche's family came from an everted world, and the glass disks marked the proper intrusions. They were permanent gateways, sophisticated and much tougher than the crude intrusions that the agency used. "Which are more like knotholes in the fence than gates," she claimed. Several thousand families were scattered over North America, assimilated by almost every measure. The products of eons of selection, they had their own society, their own tried and true means of keeping in touch with each other. "I don't even know where most of my family began," she admitted, whispering it, looking about to make sure they were alone. "My mother's mother is first generation. She lived on a cold planet with ammonia seas and a weak red sun, and its sky everted when she was a little girl. A strange man saw something in her and brought her parents gifts, honoring them and her." A pause. "Did I mention? Her species were giants, and they live in floating seaweed forests. Very lovely, really."

"You've been there?"

"Once. Just once." A wistful smile.

"What do I call you?" he asked.

"Why not Porsche? That's my name."

He squinted, watching a single tree trunk racing past, worn slick by the abrasive waters. "What's your species' name?"

*"Homo sapiens."*

He must have looked surprised.

"We become whatever species we become. A perfect translation." She sighed, then asked, "If we took some all-encompassing name, how could we assimilate, love?"

He saw her point and grinned.

Then she said, "Tell me. What gave you the idea?"

Her talent, and his father's paranoia, too. "You were watching the sky, knowing it would Change. And my dad guessed that someone with special knowledge wouldn't be able to resist the chance to watch."

"A clever man," she admitted. "But there has to be more, right?"

He told about the detective who examined her past. "He found one, and it seemed real enough. Your parents have a history, two family trees and so on. Tax forms on file. References to past addresses. Your mother even got a speeding ticket in the eighties, according to someone's records."

"What's the problem, then?"

"Holes. Oddities. Tendencies." He thought he heard motion, turned and saw no one. He made sure before he said, "Your mother is supposed to be an orphan, her foster parents long dead. Your father, bless him, pulled himself out of an old coal town that had the good grace to die and blow away in the intervening years. Both have reasonable records, but a lot of past employers have dissolved. No comprehensive records left." A pause, then he explained, "The records got a lot clearer eight months before the Change. That was the telltale clue."

"What does your detective think?"

"That your folks are in one damned good witness protection program." Cornell grinned and asked, "Are you proud of me?"

"Very proud."

"I figured it out for myself, didn't I?"

Porsche turned her head, hearing something now.

A low voice? He rose and saw nothing, then kneeled and asked, "But why join the agency? If you can go wherever you want—"

"Why be human at all?" she asked point-blank. "We go from world to world because we're good at it. Because we're curious and rootless. We aren't a species, Cornell, so much as we're a collection of ideas, of common assumptions—"

"You're here because you are curious?"

"Aren't you?"

Of course. He was enormously curious about their fate.

"I let myself be found," she admitted. "*We* wanted someone on the inside, which is only reasonable."

He said, "Sure."

"There's something else," she began to say. "Something obvious about the disks, if you think about it—"

—and she paused, turning as something approached. Four stout bodies were walking toward them, the faces intense, the eyes fixed on them. No, on something else.

Logan made a sound, brief and soft. Wrong.

A chill moved through Cornell, and he recognized the sensation. Porsche was already on her feet, looking out over the river. He saw a low gray body moving against the current, and some part of him stupidly wondered why a downed tree would head upriver. But it was far off, almost hugging the canyon's opposite wall, which made it an enormous tree—

—and Logan's bodies said, "Stay. Where you are."

Except it wasn't his voice, and the eyes had a sudden sparkle to them. It was someone else saying, "How many are you? And why are you together this way?"

The tree was some kind of powerful boat.

Porsche said, "Oh, shit."

Logan's bodies lifted their hands, gazing at them while saying, "All the way from the top of the world, you are. And together."

A long pause, then it said:

"No, from someplace even farther. You are."

Cornell took a step backwards.

Said the alien, "Strange strange, you are. All of you."

**The alien boat disappeared upriver, then made the long** turn and came back hugging the near shoreline. What could they do? Cornell asked Porsche, and she glanced up at the canyon wall, as if wondering whether they could climb to escape. Ten seconds left in the game; they were twelve points down. Other people had seen the boat, bodies moving to the shelf's edge, fear and curiosity showing on the faces. There was a hum of engines, low and steady, and a whiff of something chemical—alcohol?—carried on the breeze. A gunlike projection stood on the bow. A huge body, perhaps a foot tall, waited beside the gun. A small, scared voice asked, "Should we fight?"

"No," said Porsche. "No, don't."

There was a dull explosion, smoke from the gun and an impact beneath them. Cornell guessed it was a warning shot, then saw the line leading back to the boat and a harpoon driven into the rock. A mooring line, sure. The engines throbbed, and he watched the boat maneuver, its stern swinging out into the current and downstream as the engine noise rose to a higher pitch. A second *boom.* A third. Scrambling bodies of every size, every shade, tied off the lines. The boat was longer than the shelf, a bright aluminum hull and a wooden superstructure with a streamlined profile and what looked like a pilot turning a wheel inside a crystal-walled bridge. The pilot was blind. By accident or design, its eyes had been carved from their sockets.

"Who are you?" asked Logan's bodies, again with the odd cadence.

Porsche asked, "Where's Logan?"

"Who are you?"

"What did you do with our companion?"

*"Who are you?"*

In a soft, angry voice, she said, "Humans."

"Humans," the bodies repeated, the single whistle liquid and brief, tinged with an amused scorn.

Some kind of gangway was unfolding, tall strong bodies climbing out on it before it reached the shelf. They wore belts and slippers and odd partial gloves, each one carrying some kind of firearm, too stubby to be rifles and too intricate to be primitive. Their eyes were a new color, tropical blue and small. They showed every sharp tooth, and each one aimed at a different *human* body.

Porsche stepped toward the soldiers, extending her empty hands.

In an instant, Cornell was terrified.

"We are a long way from home," she said, standing her ground. "We are lost. We need help. Can you help us?"

Cornell felt a presence, thick and close. Familiar.

One voice said, "I have sensed you coming, all you tiny ones . . . together, coming . . . "

"And we felt you too," Porsche admitted.

The air around them felt electric, alive. It was as if they were being caressed by invisible hands, meat and minds probed with an intensity that left the fur on their bodies standing on end.

Cornell swallowed, then made himself ask, "Who are you?"

*"The City!"*

Every mouth spoke. Shouted. It sounded outraged that its identity was in doubt.

*"I am the City!"*

Soldiers moved across the shelf. Blue eyes gazed up at the ramp, its remnants clinging to the canyon wall.

"You are clever people," the City assured them.

A pause.

Then it added, "You are stupid people."

Cornell did nothing, feeling another electrical surge.

"More stupid than clever," was the verdict. Yet in the voice, from some of the mouths, came a grudging, baffled admiration.

The soldiers found the human minds, grabbing harnesses and jerking them into motion. An instinct was triggered, or maybe he panicked. Either way, Alan let out a scream and charged, spears raised and useless. A single soldier selected his mind, one shot fired. Cornell felt the blast against his faces. A slug pierced bone and brain, and Alan was dead, his bodies pressing their attack for a moment, then slowing, faces a little lost before a repossession took place. Along with Logan's bodies, they said, "Climb on board and behave, you will. Now."

Porsche said, "We have to," with angry resignation.

A thousand points down; no time on the clock.

"Leave your sharp sticks, humans."

At once, they obeyed.

Walking up the gangplank, Cornell had a thought, and he remarked to Porsche, "This is ironic."

She said, "How?"

"Here I am," he said with a soft, scared voice, "abducted. By an alien and against my will."

She managed a soft half-laugh, saying, "You'll have to tell your father, soon as you get home."

The City left two minds on the shelf, the dead one and Logan's spent one. The rest of the minds were stowed on the deck, in the open, while the bodies were herded into a deep hold, a fishy smell in the air and a nameless grease coating every surface.

"It wants us," Porsche offered, her voice calm but tired. Calm and sad. "We've made it curious, I think."

There was a powerful surge of the engines, an acceleration and little navigational motions. The only light fell through a single grate, and sometimes bodies walked over the grate.

One pair of bodies knelt. They were Logan's, already carrying guns. No need for training; no litmus test of trust. Those were the City's eyes peering down on them, and there was a kind of curiosity in the expressions. Cornell hoped so. There were worse things to hang your fate on.

They waited, nobody wanting to talk. Cornell thought of a hundred questions he would ask Porsche—about her family, life and goals—but it was too late. The boat's progress was marked by the presence of the City, invisible but obvious, threads of power coursing through the leaden air, every moment taking them deeper into the organism.

Cornell napped, then woke.

Porsche whispered, "Sleep well?"

It was night, utterly black in the hold. He felt a momentary panic, then managed to say, "We're close."

"It feels close, doesn't it?"

Hearts beat faster. He took deep breaths, making himself sick on the rich oxygen. Porsche's bodies were curled up beside his own; he knew them by feel and the strong touch of their hands. What was going to happen? Nothing worthwhile, he knew. Most likely death. He waited to feel misery, grief and regrets. Cornell even put one of his mouths next to an ear, ready to apologize to Porsche for every shred of bad luck. But all he felt was a kind of sturdy joy, a closeness and a sense of peace. "Is the City doing it?" he whispered.

"Doing what?"

Or was it his joy?

Around him bodies stirred, someone crying out in a dream.

"What are you thinking?" Porsche asked.

He said nothing.

Then with a soft, almost soundless voice, she said, "We have a belief, some of us do. A faith."

*We.* She meant her nameless, speciesless people.

Mouth to his earhole, she said, "Death frees the soul, and it falls through the worlds until it finds another home."

"Yeah?"

"Some of us even use our marker disks as dying sites for

the old and ill. We hope our honored dead end up in the better worlds we left behind."

The idea intrigued Cornell, and he nearly asked about what she had said, about something that was obvious about the disks. But before he could open any mouth, there was a loud *crump* and the engines quit. Their boat was drifting. Everyone was suddenly awake, alert. A hatch opened, light falling over them, starshine mixed with something nearer and brighter. Then the City spoke from the grate and the hatch, telling them, "Humans, come here. Now."

The river was broad and smooth, flowing the last few feet to the ocean. Cornell smelled salt and smoke and their own filthy bodies. He and Porsche huddled together on the bow with the others, superfluous guards surrounding them. Where could they run? The shoreline was a mass of buildings lit from within, and it was a city only in appearance. Only in a snapshot sense. So quiet . . . an unnerving silence imposed by the uniting *self* . . . and over the sound of lapping water, someone whispered, "What do we do?"

To Porsche. She wanted Porsche's best guess.

It was Cornell who said, "Look fearless." A pause, then he added, "We're representing a powerful world. We should act like it."

Porsche nodded, saying, "Why not?"

A smaller boat approached, the gangway lowered to it. Their minds were loaded first, stacked two-deep while coal smoke belched from the boat's little smokestack. Then their bodies were ushered down to join the minds, and they started for shore, another blind pilot at the helm, undistracted by its own eyes while dozens of others gazed in all directions.

The buildings were enormous on any scale.

Cornell saw the sameness in them—variations of the same taste, the same ideal—and there was a palpable sense of great age. Not centuries, not millennia. More like geological time. Everything was built of stone, cold and tired, cracked by the eons. The City's onboard bodies threw lines to bodies on the closest dock—big bodies with bulging backs and arms—and every mouth said, "Humans, pull yourselves to *me.*"

Cornell went to his mind, hands trembling with excitement and relief. At this moment, he was alive. Functioning. He wrestled the mind up onto the dock, following Porsche, all of their bodies wearing the harnesses and scarcely breathing, empty hands hanging at their sides.

The street was wide and eerily clean. Its stone face smelled of soaps, absolutely free of dirt. Here was the ultimate totalitarian state. The buildings on both sides of them were full of a weighty yellow light that poured from the windows, coloring every surface, every face. Cornell saw no rooms inside, just vast spaces and supporting pillars, countless bodies gazing at this most peculiar parade: freeborn souls moving among perfect slaves.

They didn't need to ask for directions. They could feel the City's center straight ahead, the powerful sense of union sickening. Unwavering. Real cities had street-level shops and people chattering, fighting and repeating old jokes, invisible honored lines marking property. But this place was the antithesis of every city and everything interesting. Cornell had to smile nervously, feeling a mild pity for the beast. It was like some enormous anal bachelor, isolated and unhappy, filling its days making everything clean, perfect and bland.

Cornell remembered his own advice: "Look fearless."

Dragging his mind up a long slope, he managed a sturdy, calm gaze. If not fearless, at least he was in control of his emotions. And he made a show of smiling at the various bodies standing to the side, allowing the City to see his alien expression, trying his damnedest to unnerve the creature the littlest bit.

A different kind of building stood on the high ground, not as tall and with rounded faces in contrast to the pragmatic cubic structures behind him. Cornell thought of a covered sports arena. And he knew in a dream-certain way that here was the reason people had taken risks and done questionable deeds; here was something alien and intelligent, superior in its fashion, and this was a historic moment for his species, his world.

A vast doorway swung inward with a rattling of metal gears and chains. A sudden wind blew at their backs, helping to push them inside, harsh arc lights above and the windy air blending with heavier stuff. A rich fecal stink made them cough. Porsche was still ahead, pausing now. Cornell pulled up beside her and saw a single enormous room, the floor made of footworn stones, descending toward a living mind.

Voices said, "Closer."

Cornell saw traces of older buildings, smaller and dismantled, where nothing remained but tough stone buttresses worn slick by countless hands and feet. The voice came from thousands of bodies, all speaking while toiling beside their single mind. Otherwise, the great building was silent. Cornell's mind was a watch battery; this mind was a fusion reactor. It was that kind of contrast, vivid and demoralizing in the same instant.

"Closer, closer. Closer."

Yet Cornell tried for a courageous walk. Eyes up, he studied how the City cared for its soul. A latticework of aluminum surrounded it. Attending bodies seemed to endlessly groom the pale white fur. Others brought meat and bright fruits carried to the mouth with pneumatic lifts, the mouth opening, the throat large enough to swallow whole cattle. Then the mind exhaled, vapor and spit rising in a fountain. Elaborate blowers came to life, and a portion of the domed roof opened, stale air replaced with the outside air. The mind took a deep breath in response, holding it, and the roof closed again, sealing with a harsh *crunch.*

"It's another species." Porsche was talking, her voice diluted by the spaces around them. "It must pirate bodies, somehow. Takes them and uses them as it needs."

Logan's bodies approached, three-fingered hands curled around the gun stocks and the barrels pointed at the floor. "Humans," they said, "from where do you come?"

Someone said, "The earth."

"Another world," said another.

"We mean no harm," begged a third.

"I am grateful," said the City. "You look like mighty fighters."

A long silence.

Then each of Logan's bodies touched the prisoners, free hands groping faces and crotches and ankles. "Once before, ages ago, I met creatures such as you. Small. Desert-built. But not right. Minds that didn't feel proper to me, like yours feel wrong."

"Let us go," said Porsche. Not with force, but with a reasoned tone. "We want to go home again. Please."

"The other strangers threatened me," said the City, apparently amused. "I thought they were creative liars. They spoke of another world, single bodies with the mind carried everywhere with them. I assumed they were liars and insane, too, since only warped souls can live in groups."

A long, tense pause.

Then the City asked, "Are you from their world?"

"Describe it," said Porsche.

The City resurrected ancient memories, describing creatures that sounded like elaborate praying mantises and a tiny weak sun. To those strangers, this world was fiercely hot and quite bizarre. Water was a mineral on their world. On their home, people lived for ten thousand revolutions around the distant sun, and the thought of an early death had terrified them.

"What did you do with them?" Porsche asked.

"I took their bodies. I ate their minds."

Cornell felt a weakness, a certain resignation. He had a clear premonition about the future, hopeless and brief—

—then Porsche amazed him, saying, "As you should have done. You were being true to your nature, weren't you?"

Cornell was amazed, and perhaps the City, too. Logan's faces didn't blink, but some kind of reaction showed deep in the eyes, in the quality of the golden light shining on them.

Then Porsche was saying, "No, we come from a warm world. It's more like yours, and there are many millions of us."

The faces tilted, if only slightly.

"On the earth," she said, "we have cities larger than yours. We have too many people and terrible long fights. Like you, we have a killing nature. Like you, we need to follow it."

"Human, what are you telling me?"

It was pure bluster, Porsche saying, "We are a vanguard. We've been sent crawling into a hole, seeing what there is to see. If we never come home, others will come here seeking vengeance. Do you understand vengeance?"

"I understand everything." A pride shone in the voice.

She smiled, glanced at Cornell and said, "It understands everything."

"I heard," he whispered.

"It knows how to travel between worlds." She kept smiling, bringing others into her bluster. "It knows how to fly. It knows how to make rain. It can build stars inside tiny bombs and lay to waste whole cities."

People nodded.

"You know everything," she told the City.

The creature seemed puzzled, wary. There was a lost quality in every eye.

"Follow your nature," Porsche advised. "Kill our minds, then take our little bodies."

Nothing. No change in the expressions, even when the mind exhaled again. The roof opened, giant blowers kicked on, and again the air smelled of the sea.

"I know what you are thinking," she told it. "You're wondering if I am lying to you, threatening you with nothing behind my words."

The faces stared at them, saying nothing.

"Lying," she admitted, "could be our nature."

The City said, "You are very strange. I know that much."

"What is your nature, City? I mean your essential nature. What do you treasure before and above all things?" Then she answered her own question, saying, "Life. First and last and always, you love to breathe and eat, make shit and live."

The bodies before them straightened their backs.

"Let us leave," she advised. "At worst, you are out a few

little bodies meant for thin dry air. At best, we will go home and tell of your kindness and your strengths, and none of us will ever come to bother you again."

No response.

"But you understand everything. People working together, like us, what can we accomplish? What could a thousand million of us, given anger, do to you inside this little stone house of yours?"

Silence.

"What are you going to do?" asked Porsche.

The City made simple sounds with various mouths, then lapsed back into silence. Empty hands lifted, then fell, and Logan's faces gave a little jerk to one side.

"What will you do, City?"

And all of the bodies, Logan's and the thousand of others, attempted a human-style smile, needlelike teeth framed by thin lips and a single voice saying:

"I know."

With finality.

"I know what I will do, I know."

The mind ate and breathed, and breathed, its inhalations becoming regular and expected, every process as regular as a heartbeat. Cornell decided that everything would be fine, and he let himself feel relief as the roof opened between breaths, when it wasn't expected. Above should be stars, diluted by lights and the thick air but stars nonetheless. Yet he saw something oval and black, something blotting out the sky. It was as large as the City's mind, or larger.

"An airship," whispered Porsche.

A blimp, not much of a leap for this technology.

"Tell your species that I want to be respected." The City spoke as cords were lowered through the opened roof. "Tell them what you've seen here, what a powerful presence I am. Tell them."

Porsche allowed herself to wink at Cornell. "We will tell them."

The cords were tied to their harnesses, and someone tried

to grab the nearest cord, ready to ride into the sky. But her body was pulled away, forced to its knees. Then the City said, "I select. A single body for each mind, and I keep the rest of you."

Nobody spoke; nobody moved.

Then the City made its selections, keeping the strongest, healthiest bodies for itself. One of Cornell's had a festering wound on its left hand, and it was lashed to his mind like an infant. He looked at Porsche, and she returned his gaze, nothing to say. Then came the pulse of engines, the whirring of propellers, and they were lifted without warning, with a smooth strong tug of the cords, off the stone floor and through the open roof as the City exhaled once again.

A heavy mist fell against one of Cornell's faces.

Untying himself partway, he looked down at the City, marveling at its brilliance and scope once more. The orderliness; the unity; the stark perfection of trust. He remembered being a boy and thinking of the aliens in just these terms. When he was twelve, this was the future. And in one sense, it was his future. Four of his bodies remained below. Already he could feel the threads between his mind and them diminishing. The City was stealing their eyes and hands for itself. Parts of him would exist on in this Utopia, the poor things, and he thought to wish them luck just as the threads were severed.

How far would the blimp carry them? he wondered. And could they drag their minds all the way to New Reno?

"Novak," shouted Porsche. "Hey, Novak."

He turned his one head, squinting with just two eyes. In the starry gloom, he saw Porsche's body untied and clinging to her mind with hands and toes, doing something . . . something, and he couldn't quite decide what she was doing . . . asking, "What—?" and then knowing the answer.

He joined her.

It was a childish and useless gesture, and it seemed perfect, Cornell untying his body and turning around, rump in the air and the City far below, too large to miss.

Too vast to anger, he hoped.

Laughing aloud. Looking ahead. The great mass of the

Breaks rough and black, and the airship still climbing, fighting for altitude, tiny bodies standing at its lighted windows, watching so that some blind pilot would know exactly where to steer.

# CUL-DE-SAC

*"We sail within a vast sphere, ever drifting in uncertainty, driven from end to end."*
*—Pascal*

THIS TIME IT WAS F. SMITH, BUT IN A DIFFERENT OFFICE, LARGER and set higher in the building, and the office's occupant was with her, a cheerless round-faced fellow with the deep full voice of a disc jockey. Porsche was there, too, sitting beside Cornell, not quite close enough to touch. This was Cornell's fourth interview today, and the easiest. F. Smith began by saying, "I'm thankful both of you made it," and then she smiled in a brittle, sad fashion. "Only two lost in your party. That's amazing, particularly when you consider what you've been through. . . ."

They had been carried to a place high in the Breaks, then lowered and left to fend for themselves. One body per person meant slow going, bodies joining together to help the minds over the roughest ground. But the rains had saturated the desert, reaching as far as the Rumpleds. Ancient salt pans became lakes. Hidden spores and seeds had burst into life. Queer little creatures grew and bred and died again in the temporary lakes, and they kept Cornell and the others alive in the week-plus it took to reach New Reno.

It was a time of wealth and irony. More than a hundred people had died in the floods, and New Reno was being abandoned. High Desert was being closed down for good.

"We just want to make certain a few points," F. Smith cautioned. "While they're fresh in your memories."

Porsche said, "Of course."

Cornell remained silent.

"This organism you met . . . that you conversed with—"

"The City," said the round-faced man, in case anyone had forgotten.

"Yes." She paused, her head lowered. "Did you see any technology that you'd categorize as advanced? In human terms, I mean." She looked at Cornell until he shook his head, then watched Porsche until she did the same. Then she asked, "In your best judgment, could this creature, the City, pose any threat to the earth or humanity?"

This was a new question. Cornell was a little startled.

"We're just getting your general impressions," explained the disc jockey voice. "No need to worry."

"The City is too large to move," Cornell responded. "It can't reach the intrusion, and if it could, there's no analogous organism on the earth. Is there?"

The man rolled his eyes. "Guess not."

But he already knew that.

"What about the desert dwellers? Could they come here eventually?"

Cornell almost spoke, almost saying, "It's harder work crossing into an everted world." Porsche had told him so. And he had no business knowing it, pausing and looking foolish with his mouth hanging open.

"I can't see how they'd invent the technologies," Porsche offered.

The man gave a satisfied nod.

Then F. Smith admitted, "We're taking precautions just the same."

"What precautions?" asked Cornell.

"New Reno is going to be leveled. What the rains started, we'll finish. Buildings dismantled. Trash buried. Nothing left around the intrusion." She looked older today, particularly in the eyes. "Another rain or two, and nobody could tell we were there."

Somehow that made Cornell sad, if only for a moment. Then he was wondering about the men and women who might have gone native—assuming they existed—and how they could prosper on the wet desert. Make babies, even. An entirely new kind of High Desert citizen, and what if they rebuilt New Reno for themselves?

What happens in the next thousand years?

"Anyway," said the nameless man, "we're pleased you made it. Sorry about the casualties, but pleased for you."

Cornell watched Porsche tilt her head, the rich brown hair spilling over a shoulder.

"We're glad to be here," she offered. "And we're glad to have had the opportunity to take part, too."

The man smiled, the expression calculated to lull his audience into trusting him.

"Imagine," he told them, "you're two of the first humans to ever meet with an alien intelligence."

Two faces grinned, struggling not to laugh.

Walking in the hallway, heading to their respective rooms, Porsche asked if he wanted to come visit. It was night, almost late, and for the next ten hours they were free of their interrogators. It was much like their first evening together, Porsche standing at Cornell's door; only now she was making the invitation, offering her room.

"Sorry," said Cornell. "I'm tired."

She looked straight at him.

"I need sleep," he said with a calm, certain voice.

One of Porsche's big hands grabbed him at the elbow. She lifted his hand to her mouth, saying, "Fine," as she put his index finger into her mouth, sucking on it for an instant and then getting a devilish look. He felt teeth, sharp enamel grabbing him behind his knuckle, and now Porsche started to back away, towing him after her, keeping the pressure on his poor wet finger and Cornell alternating between pained complaints and laughter.

Her door wasn't far, thank God.

She released him when they were inside, lights turning on for them. "Subdued lighting, please," she said, and the computer left only a corner lamp and the bathroom lit up. The room was a mirror image of Cornell's room, its furnishings reversed and reliably institutional. What he noticed at first glance were the touches, those signs that showed she had lived here, off and on, for years. There were decorations and wall hangings that couldn't belong to anyone else. A top-quality photograph of a Siberian tiger was hung over the drawers. It stared at Cornell, sitting unconcerned in the snow; and she told him, "Back in a minute, love," while closing the bathroom door, making the room even darker.

Cornell was happy and expectant, and worried. Just a little worried. He stood in front of the tiger, giving himself a light touch, his penis familiar but not. Natural, but not. All this time and longing, and what was he doing? Checking his pipes like a plumber, fearing some kind of cataclysmic failure.

Faces smiled up at him, one familiar and the rest with a familial resemblance. The photograph was taken on a summery day, the light not quite right and the mood effortlessly happy. He picked it up by the frame, thinking Porsche looked five years younger and five pounds lighter. It was a strong handsome collection of human beings. It was the kind of family that everyone admired, and the families living next door would envy. Shamelessly, thoroughly envy.

The bathroom door opened, water running.

Cornell set the photograph back on the chest of drawers, not looking over his shoulder. Barefoot motions, the creak of a mattress. But he stared at the tiger instead, saying, "I had a picture of a leopard on my wall." His throat was dry, his voice slow. "When I was a kid, I mean. Some coincidence, huh?"

"Funny," she said.

She said, "Come here, Novak. Will you?"

He turned, seeing a nude woman sprawled out on the bedspread. Sprawled was the perfect word, and his breathing stopped, his diaphragm made of concrete. An enormous weakness spread from his toes, and he moved sluggishly, with a shuffling gait.

"Get naked," she suggested. "If you'd like."

He managed to pull off his clothes.

She said, "Nice," and gave a big contented smile.

Then Cornell saw the spot above her pubic hair, noticeable because it was the only flaw in otherwise perfect skin. What was it? He found himself curious, climbing onto the bed and bowing his head, Porsche saying, "My, my. Aren't you the forward fellow?"

It was a tattoo, he realized. A tattooed heart.

And not the valentine variety, either. It had arteries and veins, the whole thing big as a thumbnail and glowing in the weak light. Practically shining up at him.

"Say, love," Porsche whispered.

"Yeah?"

"If you're going to be down there long," she mentioned. "I mean, if you wouldn't mind . . . "

"Just a few more questions," said F. Smith. Again.

It was late morning, early afternoon. Cornell wasn't sure about the hour, sleeplessness doing peculiar things to time. They were back in the upstairs office, the nameless man joined by two other nameless people. A man and woman. Glancing out the long window, Cornell saw nothing but the soft blue sky and its harmless clouds, then the flash of a silver plane climbing and streaking east.

"About Hank Logan," said F. Smith. Then she paused, obviously pained by the subject. "You saw him last where?"

She meant his mind, and Cornell told them again.

Nods, sober and steely. Then she asked, "How was he during those last days? What do you remember?"

Porsche didn't quite look at Cornell, and he kept his gaze fixed on the old woman, telling her, "He was crazy. That's the only reason she took over for him."

A defensive tone, more than he intended.

And yesterday's nameless man said, "We know. We accept that. We're sure it was for the best." A diplomatic tone, a careful smile. "In fact, we're thankful for your help, Miss Neal."

F. Smith sat up straighter, her face unreadable.

"We're just a little concerned," the man continued. "Some survivors of your group . . . a few . . . mentioned that

Hank made some silly statements, provocative and false.'' A pause, then more of the careful smile. ''Delusions of a major sort, if you know what I mean.''

Cornell said, ''What kinds?''

The new woman warned, ''Some things shouldn't be dignified by being repeated.''

A shrug of the shoulders, then Porsche said, ''Hank and I weren't talking much. Delusions or not.''

The new woman turned. ''What about you, Mr. Novak?''

''Once,'' he began. Then he paused, as if to carefully frame his answer. ''Once he talked about the City. I think he was in contact with it long ago, or it was with him. I can't tell you how.''

The audience watched him, weighing every word.

''I didn't like Logan,'' Cornell admitted, ''but then I didn't know him in his prime, did I?''

''No, you didn't,'' said F. Smith.

A long pause, and some shared glances between the interrogators. Then yesterday's nameless man was saying, ''Of course we appreciate your help, and I know it's early, but if you wish to be reassigned . . . on the strength of your records and talents . . . we'd love to have you.''

Yet nobody looked very pleased with anything.

Porsche said, ''I can't answer for Cornell, but I'd like to wait a while. I could use time off, if you don't mind.''

That brought a round of nods and patient smiles.

''Same here,'' said Cornell.

Then the nameless man made a show of looking at F. Smith, coughing into his fist once before saying, ''What do you think? Are we done here?'' A little laugh, as if this was nothing but routine. ''We let our friends go?''

Cornell showed them a hopeful, timid face.

''Go,'' said the man. ''We'll be in touch.''

Such mild words, but why did they sound like a threat?

IT WAS THEIR SECOND NIGHT OFF THE AGENCY GROUNDS, IN A Holiday Inn near Salt Lake City, when word came that a charter jet belonging to Tangent Incorp. had crashed in the Pacific Ocean. More than a hundred and eighty people had been onboard, all employees of the corporation and all feared lost. Spokesperson Farrah Smith, visibly upset, told the cameras and the world that it was a tragedy. These people, many of them friends of hers, were returning from a Samoan holiday. No effort was being spared in the search for survivors. Then the woman allowed herself a shudder and a faraway glance; and Porsche remarked:

"It's probably been a contingency plan forever. A plane crash over open water, sure."

"What about next time?" Cornell asked no one in particular. "A cruise liner goes down?"

Porsche glanced at him, measuring his expression.

He didn't feel like saying more. Not now. The news moved on to taxes and Congress, and Cornell ran his fingers along the woman's spine, down the length of her bare back, quietly humming. Not here, he was thinking, culturing a useful paranoia. *Wait.*

"Anyway," said Porsche, rolling onto her back and offering a cynical smile. "Eventually nobody's going to want to work for them. If Tangent planes keep dropping out of the sky . . ."

*Wait.*

"What's on your mind, love?"

*Wait.*

Several times during the day, in public places and while driving their rental car, Cornell described their route through the Rockies. He went as far as highlighting highways on the car's internal maps. Then he took a different road, some nameless winding thing that was paved for the first hundred yards, if that. Porsche knew they were off course, but she didn't complain. They spoke purposefully about little things, his paranoia contagious. It was lovely wild country, wasn't it? And high. Cornell parked at a scenic lookout, and they climbed on foot, reaching a long ridge that let them look down on the road, nobody trailing them in obvious ways.

Porsche looked at him, her face almost amused.

"Reminds me of the Rumpleds." He motioned and started down into a bowl where a turquoise mountain lake lay. Legs ached. Breathing was work. "Wish I had flow-through lungs," he allowed, sitting on a sunny rock.

She sat opposite him, saying nothing.

"What can you do?" He stared at her, then rephrased the question. "Are there rules about what you can and cannot do?"

"Do how? Make yourself clear, Novak."

She knew what Logan had told him in the cave. They had talked about it while crossing the desert that last time, and he didn't have to mention it now. "I've decided what to do," he told her. "Risks or not, I've got to try it."

She said nothing, looking across the lake.

"It's not supposed to be this way," said Cornell. "All the years with my father claiming aliens would lead us to a utopia, and I guess I can't stop believing him."

"So what are you planning?"

He glanced at the high blue sky. "Exposure."

"By yourself?"

"That's why I'm asking what you and your people can do for me." He was breathing hard, and not entirely with the altitude. "If you can't help, you can't. I'll find others."

She flipped a stone into the water.

"If we can't see each other, we won't. But I've got to do this, Porsche."

"*We* can't do anything intrusive," she told him.

He felt weak and a little dizzy.

"But *I* am free to do what I want, with restrictions." She waited for him to look at her, then explained, "I won't expose my family or the others. Don't ask me to. I might help with a few tricks, but we didn't come here with an arsenal or any godlike technologies."

He managed a quick nod. "Fine."

She flipped another stone, then said, "Hope you weren't hoping for more."

Maybe he had been, but not seriously. It would be lovely if she could wave an arm, dispelling ignorance and cruelty in that one motion. But then again, it would be nice if a lot of things came true.

"Any ideas where to begin?" she asked.

He mentioned a few possibilities, then paused, remembering a moment from the other world. "When we were down by the river? When I got you to admit who you are—?"

"What is it?"

"You started to tell me something about the disks. 'Something obvious,' you claimed, then the City arrived."

A broad serene smile. "Figure it out?"

"No."

She told him.

Porsche waited for him to stop laughing, then with a grave tone, she asked, "What if Logan was telling the truth? What if they hurt and kill people in order to keep everything secret?"

"For that matter," he responded, "what if it's worse? I doubt if Logan was privy to every dark closet."

"Exactly. What if?"

They had considerable work to do, and for a little while longer they talked about it, sketching out their plans. Then they made love, managing despite the rocks and the chill mountain air; and in the middle of it, some part of Cornell was thinking:

I don't know how many times we've done it. I don't have a count.

Now they were established lovers, in his mind.

They dressed and returned to the car, over the ridge and down again and Porsche noticing a cloud of white dust rising from the road below them, as if someone was driving fast. Except no car was visible, just the dust. They waited for a few minutes, to be sure, and Cornell picked out a likely shard and gave it a few expert hits with a harder shard, his five-fingered hands making a crude and effective little hand axe.

Morning, cool and tasting of autumn, and he drove a different rental car up the hill and around the concrete island, parking in front of the Petes' house. "What do you think?" he asked.

Porsche peered over the tops of her sunglasses. "It's bigger than I guessed. Quite a lot."

"That's not it. Mine's that one."

"The shoebox? That one?" She snorted and said, "God, I thought I was getting involved with money here."

"Who told you that?"

She opened her door. "Your lawn needs a trim. Did you know?"

"You take charge of that." Cornell was excited and nervous with a dose of happiness mixed into the mess. He climbed out onto the pavement and heard a door opening. Pete was standing on his porch, hands on his hips. Porsche surprised everyone, striking straight across Pete's yard, saying, "I know you. Hello there!"

Cornell followed.

"He's told me a lot about you, Mr. Forrest."

Pete was grinning. "Porsche Neal? Why do I know that name?"

Mrs. Pete emerged from the house, slow and suspicious.

"Mrs. Forrest," Porsche called her.

Pete kept saying, "I know you. How do I know you?"

They seemed like old, befuddled people.

Then Mrs. Pete brightened, asking, "Are you with Cornell?"

A wink, and Porsche said, "Scary, huh?"

Everyone laughed, maybe with too much pleasure. Cornell turned and noticed a window shade dropping in one of Dad's windows, and he felt a pang in his guts. This was it. A few moments later, the old man emerged, wearing old trousers and a stained shirt, his bare feet as pale as cottage cheese. He blinked in the sunshine, as if he hadn't been outdoors in days. Shuffling through the shaggy grass, he came partway and stopped, more baffled than anything. He seemed to doubt his senses, twice rubbing his eyes with bony fists. Cornell walked up to him, stopping a couple of yards short, and he was aware of the silence as he said, "Have a minute? I want to talk."

The words were easy, calm and studied and easy.

Dad said, "Yeah?"

"Not out here," said Cornell.

A backward glance at the little house.

"Not in there, either. Just to be on the safe side."

Two paranoids; the perfect match. Dad seemed to understand, and Cornell went to the Petes, asking, "Can we use your place?"

Mrs. Pete started to say, "It's a mess."

Pete cut her off, telling him, "Go on."

Dad had trouble with the porch stairs, shaking out of nervousness. No telling what he was imagining now. His traitorous son had returned, and who was the strange woman? And why was she saying, "Hello, sir," to him? "How are you this morning, sir?"

Dad couldn't say. He paused at the top of the stairs, considering the question with a slow thoroughness, then whispering, "Puzzled." It was the perfect word. "Puzzled."

Porsche glanced at Cornell, then said to the Petes, "Show me your garden. I love gardens."

"Do you?" Mrs. Pete asked with great hope.

A knowing look from Pete, for an instant, then he was herding the others into the backyard.

"Let's go inside, Dad."

It was going to be easy. Cornell had a feeling, intense and sudden, this being one of those moments when the world seemed to make total sense. He knew how he would start, having practiced it a thousand times in his head, and he could guess the questions Dad would ask. Of course the old man would believe him. That was a given. Who else in this world, told this incredible, impossible business, would even give Cornell the possibility of being right?

The Petes and Porsche were out of sight. Cornell was in the big living room, feet apart, Dad watching him with a growing alarm.

Finally he asked, "What is it, son?"

"I've got a story to tell you." Just as he'd practiced saying it. Right down to the steady dry voice. "It's the most incredible thing you've ever heard . . . "

And then he wasn't talking, his voice gone.

It was as if a vise had closed on his throat, and for an instant he believed there was a vise. The agency, or whoever, was focusing a weapon on him, destroying his voice and breath as his body began to tremble, a weakness spreading through him.

I'm dying, he thought. They're killing me.

"Cornell? Are you all right?"

He had to sit, collapsing into Pete's big chair. What was this? He found himself crying. He had been crying for some time, apparently. Unaware of it. And he shivered and mopped his eyes with both hands, Dad sitting opposite him, asking, "What's this story, son?"

Something nobody would believe, Cornell remembered.

But he talked about something else. He talked while weeping, a wet clumsy voice saying, "I'm sorry . . . all my fault, I'm sorry . . . !"

"Sorry?" said Dad, the worn face bright with tears. "What do you mean, sorry?"

And now both of them were crying, flooding the room and the house, tears becoming rivers and floods filling up the round world.

**Somehow Cornell got them lost near the end.**

Which seemed appropriate.

He stopped by the side of the road, and Porsche said with sarcasm, "It's even smaller than your dad's house." She was looking at a birdhouse set in the middle of a marsh. "How many bedrooms?"

He ignored the prattle, unfolding their instructions and rereading them. The voice on the phone had warned him that the road signs had been stolen or knocked down over the years, the county's budget crunch leaving them that way. That's why the instructions included landmarks like feedlots and a threesome of windmills. I probably went right instead of left, Cornell decided. Or left instead of right. Which one? And when?

"This isn't it," Dad remarked.

Porsche smiled, saying, "I know. I'm just teasing."

The old man snorted and told them, "It's up over there."

That he was lost badly enough that he would look at his father's vague gesture meant something. It meant he was desperate, almost ready to relinquish the wheel.

"Up on that hill. See the trees?"

"You think so, Dad?"

"That's where we want to be." No hint of doubt, which was worrisome. A sharp grin, and he added, "Who's been here the most times? Huh?"

Cornell decided to turn around and try the last intersection again. On the premise that passengers never paid as much attention to the landscape as did the driver, he said, "I know what I did. We're almost there."

"Almost there," Porsche chimed.

"I bet," Dad groaned.

Faster. He drove faster on the graveled road, crops on both sides and everything turning color after the first hard frost. But today was warm, even as the sun dropped, and the warm smell of the country came in through the vents. Cornell knew the smell and found it evoking half-memories that made him smile at nothing, his passengers busy talking among themselves.

Porsche was more than patient with Dad. She was the perfect audience, asking questions and listening to every word, eager to hear about adventures in chasing the unknown. Dad kept rattling on about the sasquatch trip. The current tale hinged on some suspicious fecal matter found in the Cascades, now encased in plastic and stored in the deep freeze at home. When they could talk freely, Dad would propose that the sasquatch was alien, a visitor from an intrusion whose soul was put inside an extinct ape's body. "Wouldn't that make sense?" he would ask his audience.

"Maybe so," Porsche would allow. "Maybe so."

Dad didn't know about her. Not yet. They'd decided to wait for a better time to tell him the rest of the story, although neither of them doubted he could handle the truth.

Not for an instant.

They reached the intersection, and Dad broke from his story to say, "Now left. Left."

Which made Cornell certain that it was right.

But he went left to prove a point, saying, "It's on your shoulders from here."

"Then left again," the old man sang out.

"We're lost," Cornell told Porsche with pleasure. "Just wait. We're going to end up in Death Valley before we're done."

"Nathan's been here before," Porsche cautioned.

"I've been here, too."

"Left," said Dad eventually. "Left."

They were climbing out of the river bottom, and suddenly Cornell knew this was the place. The country looked different, and it didn't. The house was waiting at the top of the bluffs, still hidden in a dense block of trees. Dad said, "Right," and Cornell told him, "I know," and Porsche laughed, sitting sideways on the front seat and poking at him with a big bare toe.

There were no dogs to escort them this time.

The house itself looked remarkably unchanged, less white and more worn but still intact. A solid roof; a good foundation. The owner lived down the road, in a new home, but the old one hadn't been empty for more than a year. "You'll have to catch some mice," Cornell had been warned. "And some raccoons have been living in the crawlspace. But it's weather tight and ready, complete with furnishings."

The owner was waiting for them, and they were late. He gave his watch an obvious glance, showing them that he wasn't completely pleased.

Cornell recognized him. A plain weathered face; the good jeans and clean shirt. The man looked more like his father than his boyhood self, didn't he?

"How's it going?" the farmer asked. "Find your way?"

"He got lost," Dad said, pointing at Cornell in case of confusion. "But I knew the way."

"You did," Porsche agreed.

"I sure did!"

While Porsche and Dad went through the big old house, opening windows and claiming bedrooms, Cornell mentioned that someone else was coming soon. "A computer expert, of sorts." He glanced at the wires leading to the telephone pole. Aboveground, old-fashioned. Probably wire, which meant they'd have to be replaced. "He's a colleague of ours."

A dog was waiting in the truck. "Come here," the farmer snapped. With a fluid motion, the dog leapt from the cab.

"Sit." She sat beside him, watching her master with a look bordering on worship.

"Looks like a German shepherd," Cornell mentioned.

"Is, in part."

"What else?"

"Wolf, in part. Plus some extra genes. She's smart as hell, and obedient, too."

"I remember that German shepherd you used to have—"

"Her great-great-grandfather. Something like that." The man moved his seed cap forward on his head, eyeing his new tenant. "You know, you've never told me just why you want this place."

"I know."

The man licked his lips, then asked, "Is it about the disk?"

"The disk's still there?" The intrusion was, regardless.

"Sure, it's there. Dad never got up the juice to rip it out, and I don't think the soil underneath is worth the trouble." A pause. "So it's not about the disk? Is that what you're saying?"

Cornell was thinking about the computer expert. The detective. He had been a logical choice. They needed someone who could get in and out of classified files, no one the wiser. Presented with the chance to expose the CEA, the detective had grinned for a very long moment, then said, "I might be able to help you. I might."

The farmer gave up waiting. "Guess I don't need to know."

"This place is about perfect," said Cornell.

The farmer scratched the dog's head, the big tail beating on the ground. "I remember when you came here. You and your dad and that other guy . . . I remember thinking it was neat, you getting to do what you were doing." He had a big laugh, shaking his head and saying, "I was jealous and said so. Told my old man so. Which got me paddled, I think for the last time ever."

Both of them laughed. The dog kept wagging its tail.

Then Cornell mentioned, "You may see strangers. Ordinary looking, except they won't belong here."

An odd grin. "Who?"

"Feds." Cornell owed that much to the farmer. "Not the FBI, but similar. Sort of."

"If I see them, I'll tell you."

"Thanks."

A look at the house, then the farmer said, "Let's go home."

He was talking to the dog, who turned and jumped a perfect arc back into the cramped cab.

Another tip of the seed cap, and he mentioned, "She's pregnant. Want a couple pups?"

Cornell blinked.

"They make great watchdogs, if you want them."

"How much?"

"Nothing." A big shrug. "If it keeps the neighborhood safe, why do I need a price?"

It was Dad's idea to heat up the casserole and take it behind the house, eating dinner in the open. He carried the folding chairs. Porsche managed the food and plates. Cornell was left in charge of what looked like a toolbox. Some weeks before, passing through Texas, they had dropped by her parents' house and gotten the box as a gift.

The field was planted with sunflowers, tall and brown with their black and yellow heads drooping toward the ground. Porsche walked straight for the glass disk, reaching it first. Dusk was falling into evening. The earth was above them, barely obscured by dust and faraway city lights. A perfect evening, Cornell thought, setting the box on the glass, then touching the glass with his fingers, his palms. The day's heat made it comfortably warm. The earth's reflection was distorted by the slumping spots and diminished by a layer of dust. After a moment, Cornell looked up at Porsche until she gave him a knowing smile, and she turned and asked Dad, "Could we sit over here? Please?"

Dad had unfolded the chairs and put them in the middle of the disk. "Over where?" he asked amiably.

"Here is fine. Just not there."

Cornell flipped the latch and opened the box, trying to remember what was what. The big hammer. The little screwdriver. And the battered scrap of pine, crazy as that seemed.

"Why not in the center?" Dad asked.

Three scrupulously ordinary objects. Even if someone suspected a hidden purpose, no human tests would be able to find their delicate mechanisms or their power sources.

"What are you doing, son?"

Cornell put the hammer on the glass, sliding it with his foot until he felt a slight surge of electricity. The screwdriver went to the right of the hammer. The pine scrap was set on both of them, making a little bridge, and he saw a green glow that told him he had done it right.

"What's he doing, Porsche?"

"We've got something else to tell you," she replied, touching Dad on the shoulder. "Maybe you should sit down. With me?"

"Tell me what?" said Dad.

"If things go badly," said Porsche, "we have an escape route. We have a means of getting out of their reach, which is why we picked this place. Are you following me, Nathan?"

Three more objects would open the intrusion. A bent nail; a second screwdriver; and the tool box itself. Cornell had sworn that he wouldn't use them outside of an emergency.

"Hey," Dad shouted. "Look at the sky!"

It was changing. This intrusion was awake and interacting with every other friendly intrusion, making them glow, the effect visible only for the three of them and only while they stood on the disk. But it was a wondrous effect just the same, thousands of intrusions shining like stars against the softer blues and whites of the earth. With the right tools, a person could look at an everted world at a glance, seeing just where to find gateways to other worlds considered safe—

"Nathan?" said Porsche, "May I tell something about myself?"

—and Cornell looked down again, ignoring the sky.

# ABOUT THE AUTHOR

Gold Award winner of the first Writers of the Future contest, Robert Reed is the critically acclaimed author of five previous novels: *The Remarkables, Down the Bright Way, Black Milk, The Hormone Jungle,* and *The Leeshore.* Also a writer of short fiction, Reed's "Utility Man" was a finalist for the 1990 Hugo Award. He has been published in *Isaac Asimov's Science Fiction Magazine* and *The Magazine of Fantasy and Science Fiction.* He currently resides in Lincoln, Nebraska, where his interests include the sciences, such as ecology and biology, as well as running and cycling.